FIVE HIGH[...]
AUTHORS[...]
FIVE BREATH[...]
OF LOVE

MARY BALOGH has won many awards, including the *Romantic Times* Award for Best New Regency Writer and the Reviewer's Choice Award for Best Regency Author. She is also a four-time winner of the Waldenbook Award for Bestselling Regency. She lives in Kipling, Saskatchewan, Canada. Her most recent books are *A Precious Jewel* (Signet) and the historical romance *Deceived* (Onyx).

MELINDA McRAE, author of *The Highland Lord* (Signet), holds a master's degree in European history and takes great delight in researching obscure details of the Regency period. She lives in Seattle, Washington, with her husband and daughter.

ANITA MILLS won the *Romantic Times* Award for Best New Regency author in 1987. She lives in Kansas City, Missouri, and is the author of *Autumn Rain* (Onyx).

MARY JO PUTNEY is the author of many best-selling books, including *Veils of Silk* (Onyx) and *Thunder and Roses* (Topaz). She has won four writing prizes, and was the winner of the 1988 *Romantic Times* Award for Best New Regency Author. She lives in Baltimore, Maryland.

MAURA SEGER, the critically acclaimed author of numerous contemporary and historical romances, has over 5 million books in print in 13 languages. She lives with her husband and two children in Connecticut.

Rakes and Rogues

Mary Balogh

❧

Melinda McRae

❧

Anita Mills

❧

Mary Jo Putney

❧

Maura Seger

A SIGNET BOOK

SIGNET
Published by the Penguin Group
Penguin Books USA Inc., 375 Hudson Street,
New York, New York 10014, U.S.A.
Penguin Books Ltd, 27 Wrights Lane,
London W8 5TZ, England
Penguin Books Australia Ltd, Ringwood,
Victoria, Australia
Penguin Books Canada Ltd, 10 Alcorn Avenue,
Toronto, Ontario, Canada M4V 3B2
Penguin Books (N.Z.) Ltd, 182–190 Wairau Road,
Auckland 10, New Zealand

Penguin Books Ltd, Registered Offices:
Harmondsworth, Middlesex, England

First published by Signet,
an imprint of New American Library,
a division of Penguin Books USA Inc.

First Printing, June, 1993
10   9   8   7   6   5   4   3   2   1

Contents

Hide-and-Seek

by

Melinda McRae

1

George Farron Chevening Atwell, the sixth Viscount Belmont, stood upon the top step of his house in Chelsea, frowning at the green-painted door before him. The sleeping child in his arms grew heavier with each moment, but without a free hand he saw no way of lifting the large brass knocker to announce his presence. A perplexing dilemma.

He glanced down at the diminutive daughter he held in his arms. Finding carriage travel to her liking, she had slept nearly the entire journey, her tiny form slumped in trusting security against his side. A fond smile flitted over his face.

If only he could get her into the house. . . .

His problem was solved when a delivery boy came bounding down the street. "You there," the viscount called. "A half-crown if you knock upon this door for me."

The boy's eyes lit with the thought of such a munificent reward and he raced up the steps, applying his efforts to the knocker with unbridled enthusiasm. The door swung inward and the viscount immediately stepped past the surprised footman. "Give the lad a half-crown," Belmont commanded, as he ascended the stairs to the first-floor drawing room. Another footman scurried before him to open the door.

Belmont's face broke into a grin of relief when he found Miss Waldron and the younger children in the large, airy room at the front of the house. Henry and Freddie looked to be absorbed in building some sort of tower out of wooden blocks, while Lucilla and Suzanne applied themselves to their samplers.

He caught the governess's eye as she looked up from her own sewing. "I've brought you another one, Miss Waldron," he said with an apologetic smile. "I hope you do not mind." His expression relaxed when he saw her calm acceptance.

"Why are you holding her?" eight-year-old Lucilla demanded. "Is she sick?"

"She is very tired," the viscount replied, but as he said the words, the tiny girl in his arms began to stir. Everyone in the room turned to look at this newest member of the household.

The small girl took one sleepy look at the five unfamiliar faces and shyly buried her own in her father's coat.

"Now, now," chided the viscount gently as he shifted her weight in his arms, "there is nothing to be afraid of. These are the brothers and sisters I told you about. See, that is Lucilla and Suzanne, by the fire. Henry is that stout fellow over there and I see we even have little Freddie visiting from the nursery today."

"Arthur napping," Freddie greeted his father with a wide smile.

"As he should be," Belmont replied. He had not objected to adding his brother's new son, Arthur, to the Chelsea nursery.

"What's her name?" Suzanne demanded, staring at the new arrival with avid curiosity.

"Arabella," the viscount replied. He crossed the room and set the girl upon the sofa. "And this lady," he smiled at the tall, dark-haired woman who stepped to his side, "is Miss Waldron, who will take care of you."

"Hello, Arabella," said Miss Waldron, kneeling down before her. "I am so glad you are coming to live with us. We were just getting ready to have our midmorning tea. Would you like to join us?"

"Oh, yes, do," shouted Henry. "We're to have some of cook's macaroons and they are the bestest."

"Best," Miss Waldron corrected smoothly as she stood.

Arabella looked about with widely rounded eyes and her thumb found its way into her mouth.

Belmont drew Miss Waldron aside. "She is only four and a trifle shy," the viscount explained in a whisper. "The family she was placed with"—he shuddered at the remembrance—"was more interested in the remuneration than in her care."

"Poor thing," Miss Waldron said. "However did you find her?"

The viscount's face darkened. "Her mother decided that she had contributed to her upkeep long enough and it was now my turn." He shook his head in anger. "I would be tempted to strangle the woman, but it is not worth the effort. Suffice it to say she shall never see her daughter again."

"They rarely do," Miss Waldron murmured.

The viscount darted her a chastening look. "Do not be too condemning of them, Miss Waldron. Some stay away by choice, to be sure, but others would be here if they could."

Miss Waldron colored faintly at the gentle rebuke and turned her attention to her charges. "Now, who would like to sit next to your new sister first?" she asked, smiling again at the instantaneous clamor that arose.

The viscount gave Arabella a reassuring look and watched the other children approach with eager interest.

It never ceased to amaze him, these offspring of his. Despite the fact he had sired them all, they were as unalike as could be. Stephen and Samuel, who must still be with their tutor, looked the most like himself, but Belmont also saw traces of his own characteristics in Lucilla's jade-green eyes, Henry's long, thin nose, and Suzanne's and Freddie's sandy-colored hair. Arabella, he had already decided, looked decidedly like her mother, but there was still a hint of the Belmont expression about the mouth and chin. An independent observer would no doubt think the children a motley collection, but the similarities were quite apparent to his doting father's eye.

Despite their odd assortment of mothers, and the brand of illegitimacy placed upon them by society, they were a cheerful and lively brood. Already Stephen was showing a sharp talent for study. He would be well-suited to several positions when he grew older. And they were all remarkably free of the pretensions and arrogance that usually marked the children of aristocracy. Belmont idly wondered whether banishing the legalities of marriage for a generation or more might do more good for the nobility than all their years of privilege.

His eyes lit with approval when three older boys entered the room, having at last been released from their morning studies. The boys' faces broke into smiles when they saw him.

"Papa," exclaimed Samuel. At eight, he was the youngest of three. "Guess how many Latin verbs we learned today?"

"How many?'"

"None!" he shouted. "We've been working on Greek all morning!"

Belmont grinned and playfully ruffled the boy's hair.

The tallest lad, with a solemn face, bowed before him. "Good day, my lord."

"Good day to you, Master Geoffrey. I have brought a new addition to the household." He nodded toward the settee, where Lucilla and Suzanne had won the honor of sitting next to Arabella. "I hope your mama will not be displeased with me."

"Another girl?" the scholar, Stephen, demanded. "We've too many of them already."

"Hush," said the viscount, "or we will not get the soldiers out today."

That threat quieted them and soon everyone was seated around the tea table, waiting in well-trained politeness while the biscuit plate was passed around.

Belmont watched appreciatively as Miss Waldron poured. As he had done a thousand times before, he once again thanked providence for bringing her to his notice. Society had smiled knowingly when he had hired such an attractive governess, but it was not her countenance he admired, but her skill with the children. It took a special lady to take on such a mixed brood as his and to work for a man of his reputation.

But as a "fallen woman," with an out-of-wedlock son of her own, Miss Juliet Waldron could not afford to be choosy about the positions she sought. And he knew, with a self-satisfied smugness, that she was quite lucky to have found this one. In return for taking care of all his children, she was paid a handsome salary, and her son, Geoffrey, received an education that would enable him to find an advantageous position when he grew older.

As he listened to her gently, but firmly, correct the children's manners, Belmont found it difficult to envision Miss Waldron succumbing to the depth of passion that would have left her with a child. Her seducer must have been extraordinarily persuasive. She was pretty, in an unexceptional manner, but her sober gray dresses and dignified lace caps spoke of a reserve he found off-putting. Belmont liked his women to have passion. And passion was the one thing he was quite certain Miss Waldron lacked, despite her youthful fall from grace.

All in all, however, it was a good thing that she held little allure for him. She was worth far more to him as a governess than a lover. He suspected Miss Waldron would not have uttered a word of complaint about Arabella's arrival, even if she felt it. But Belmont was confident she had not. Miss Waldron seemed to have the uncanny talent for remaining singularly unperturbed no matter what transpired. How he envied her serene composure.

Belmont cringed inwardly at the memory of her first few weeks in the household, when the boys had tormented her without mercy. But she had taken their large frogs and slithery snakes in her stride, and once his sons found she could not be routed, they accepted her with eager enthusiasm. The girls had adored her from the first moment.

In short, Belmont could not imagine how he had ever managed before she came to them. He could only pray that she stayed. He would do everything in his power to keep her happy.

Following tea, Belmont lured the older boys away from their amiable tutor and led a rousing battle between their massed armies of tin soldiers. Once again, the boys fought the dastardly French at Waterloo, a particular favorite of theirs since their uncle's last visit, when he had regaled them with exaggerated tales of his role in the famous battle. Miss Waldron read to the younger children in the drawing room, and the house was enveloped in a warm cloak of cozy domesticity. So much so that Belmont lost all track of time.

Not until he heard a vaguely familiar voice in the corridor did he recall the passage of the hours. With a guilty start, he glanced at the mantel clock, which pronounced the afternoon far advanced. And what was worse, after listening more carefully, he was able to put a name with the voice.

Sybil. He forgot that today was the day she came to see Lucilla and Henry. Putting a finger to his lips, he motioned for the boys to be quiet. As soon as she was busy with her two children, he could make his escape. Thank God he had directed the groom to put his carriage in the mews. Belmont had learned from sorry experience that a personal encounter with Sybil held untold dangers.

Once he successfully fled the house without being intercepted and set the carriage toward home, Belmont uttered a hasty prayer of thanksgiving. While he admired Sybil's apparent devotion to her two secret children, he sometimes thought it was an interest developed more to impress him than out of any maternal desire on her part. Despite the fact their affair had ended years ago, by mutual decision, he always had the feeling, when they met by chance, that she had often regretted her choice.

Belmont followed one strict code—if he once parted from a woman, he never returned to her. It kept his life uncomplicated. And there were always enough interested and interesting women that he never suffered from the lack of one. After all, was it not said that variety was the very spice of life? It was a credo he embraced with heartfelt enthusiasm. Had not that lovely new dancer at the Opera House caught his eye for that very reason? Her fiery Latin looks—the dark hair and eyes and golden, olive-toned skin—had instantly appealed to him. The contrast in appearance between her and the pale, blond creature he currently patronized was exciting. The one remaining question in his mind was how they would compare in bed, and he would find the answer to that tonight. If he timed things well, he could pay an early visit to Chloe and be at the Opera House with ample time to watch a bit of the dancing before he treated Maria to an intimate late supper.

It might prove to be an illuminating experience.

When Juliet Waldron had seen the last of her charges tucked into bed for the evening, she took the double-branched candle holder and went to examine the last unoccupied room in the house. The former master bedroom was far too large for a young child and so had remained empty. But the addition of dear, sweet Arabella to the household necessitated a slight re-arrangement of things.

Juliet recalled Lord Belmont's boyishly apologetic smile when he brought Arabella to her. However could he have thought she would object to such an adorable child? Juliet would never grow tired of caring for his children. Would never grow tired of doing anything he asked of her. It was the only way she could demonstrate her love for him.

She should not have allowed herself to fall in love with Belmont. It was an exceedingly foolish action for a governess. But over the months, as she grew to know him, she could not help but tumble top-over-tails. She saw beyond the licentious rake to a man who was as well-educated as the tutor he employed, enjoyed reading novels nearly as much as she, was devoted to his children, and a kind and generous employer.

Still, there was more that drew her to him. He spoke to the part of her which remained hidden, the part of her she struggled to control. The passionate nature that had led her to her fall those many years ago. Until she met Belmont, Juliet felt certain she had successfully buried all her dreams and wishes. But in his presence, she once again was forced to acknowledge her true nature. There was something elemental in Belmont that spoke to her across the gulf of employer and employee, spoke to her as a man did to a woman. Yet because there was no hope for her love, she need not fear him. Despite society's suspicions, Belmont would no more dally with his governess than with his kitchen maid.

Entering the darkened chamber, Juliet set her candle down upon the dressing table. It was a beautiful room, decorated in delicate pinks and fragile greens. A very feminine room—perfect for three young girls. They need not know that it had been the abode of several of the viscount's former mistresses, until he purchased another house to entertain his inamorata of the moment and gave this one over to his growing family. What, after all, did a mistress need with seven bedrooms, a nursery, a walled garden, and close proximity to several parks?

Only the mirrored dressing table and a large wardrobe stood in the room, all other furniture having been removed—probably to the other house. Juliet was glad the bed was no longer there. Even without its physical presence, the thought of it dominated her mind. She did not want to guess how many pleasurable hours Belmont had spent in this room—or with how many different women he had spent them. Had the viscount brought his married lovers here as well, or had this house been for the exclusive use of his paid companions? Had any of the children been conceived in this room? One? Two?

Juliet found herself wondering more and more these days about such things, even though she firmly told herself it was none of her concern. The viscount had been quite blunt about his proclivities when he had hired her last spring. Where, after all, had those six—no, seven, now—children come from? Fruit of his loins. The tangible evidence of at least a brief moment of passion and pleasure. That Belmont was adept at pleasure she had no doubt.

Juliet shook her head at the turn her thoughts were taking. If she did not regain control over herself, she was going to make some imprudent revelation in front of her employer one day. And that would ruin everything. For Geoffrey's sake, she had to firmly rein in her emotions. It was pointless to yearn after the impossible.

Better to see what needed to be done before the girls could move into this room. Juliet pulled open the wardrobe door, then gasped in surprise at what lay within. With a shaking hand, she reached out and stroked the rich, shimmering fabric of the dress that hung there. Had this exquisite gown been left behind deliberately or by accident?

Unable to resist the temptation, Juliet reached in and drew out the gown. To her admittedly inexperienced eye, it looked very much like the dress a mistress would wear. The bodice was minuscule, the fabric soft and draping, and even the dim light of the candles caused the silvery-white material to sparkle and glisten. It looked like a dress meant for a night of enchantment—and love.

Juliet held up the dress against her, darting a quick

glance toward the mirror. She burst out laughing at the sight of her reflection. It was not at all the type of dress for a governess. Prim lace caps did not suit it in the least.

Setting the gown carefully down on the bed, she looked again in the wardrobe, but found nothing more inside. Satisfied that the girls' clothing would easily fit within, she closed the door.

She should show the dress to Lord Belmont when he arrived tomorrow. Perhaps he would wish to return it to the lady to whom it belonged. Or perhaps he had another whom it would suit as well. After folding the gown over her arm, Juliet picked up her candle and went down the corridor to her room. She lay the dazzling gown carefully upon the chair, and began to tidy the chamber.

The dress would not be so easily ignored, however. Juliet's gaze kept straying to it. It was not the sort of dress that a governess needed. It was not at all the sort of dress a governess should want. Or have.

Slamming shut the lid of her dressing case with a loud snap, Juliet turned around. Perhaps if she tried on the dress, she would get this strange obsession out of her system. Once she saw the absurdity of such a fanciful costume on her form, she would be able to forget the entire matter.

Quickly slipping out of her plain gray silk, Juliet reverently donned the spellbinding garment. It did not fit perfectly, being a trifle short and designed for a more well-endowed figure. But looking in her pier glass, she did not think she made a terribly frightening picture. With sudden determination, she untied the ribbon of her cap, drew it off, and flung it onto the bed. With unsteady hands she removed the pins from her thick hair, allowing the chestnut tresses to fall down in jumbled curls upon her shoulders. Juliet looked in the mirror again and sucked in her breath at the sight.

She no longer looked like a governess. She looked like an elegant, worldly lady of the *ton*. Juliet knew full well she was not beautiful; her face was too square and her mouth too full for fashion's tastes. But in this dress she felt attractive. Alluring. Enticing. A woman who could command the attention of any man. One special man.

She would never have the opportunity, of course. A governess had no chance to wear a dress such as this. No one would ever see her in the gown. *He* would never see her.

With a sad smile, Juliet reached behind her and unfastened the dress. It was a foolish dream. Belmont would recognize the dress instantly if he saw it, and would be horrified to find his employee masquerading as a lady. Even if, once upon a time, she had been one. Juliet would die of mortification if he knew she had even tried on the dress.

She quickly removed the garment and lay it across the chair again. Enough time spent on foolish fantasies. Tomorrow, she would give the gown to Belmont and he could do with it as he wished.

Sinking down into the other chair, Juliet picked up the *Morning Chronicle*. Arabella would need a head-to-toe wardrobe, and Juliet recalled that one of the drapers was offering a significant reduction on some fabrics. But while scanning the commercial notices, her eyes were caught by a large announcement:

Masked Ball, Opera House, Wednesday next. 1 G. Tickets and costume rentals at Fenton's Masquerade and Music Warehouse, No. 78 Strand or Melward's Masquerade Warehouse, 2 Brook St., Hanover Sq.

A public masked ball, she mused. Where lords and ladies mingled with all manner of people. No one was refused admittance if one had the wherewithal to purchase a ticket. Juliet would be only one more mysterious lady amidst the throng of merrymakers. No one would recognize her. No one would ever know.

She flung down the paper. How could she even think of doing such a thing? It was madness, sheer madness. It could cost her this job, Geoffrey's future, her security, everything. All for one rash, impetuous gesture.

Besides, it was highly unlikely that Belmont would even be there. He was probably promised to an elegant rout that evening, or had a scheduled meeting with his latest mistress. It was far too great a risk for her to take on the slight chance he would be there.

But what if she come somehow make certain he attended? Entice him with a message that he would not be able to resist? Pique his curiosity so that he could not stay away?

She buried her face in her hands. She dare not think of such a thing. It was all the fault of that horrid dress. It caused her common sense to flee and filled her head with frivolous nonsense. She should toss it in the fire now, before its seductive spell pulled her deeper into folly.

But what if her plan worked? What if she could bring him there, for a time? They could have one evening together. One evening spent in light conversation and delicate flirtation, two strangers who would never see each other again. What other chance would she ever have to spend a night with *him*?

She would be completely safe at a masked ball. With her skill with needle and thread, she could transform the dress into a costume he would not identify. And surely, who would ever recognize the plain Miss Waldron in such an elegant gown? She could even add to the disguise by cloaking herself in a domino, rented from the masquerade warehouse. Add a clever mask that hid her face and Belmont would never guess that she was the mysterious woman. He would not suspect that his steady, dependable, uninspiring Miss Waldron lived in a world of fantasy and imagination centering around him.

One night would surely be enough to still her distressing longings. She would have lived out her dream. Then she could be content with her present situation, and would not wish for what could not be. Juliet had learned long ago that dreams only lasted for a short while; they were not the substance one built a life upon. No harm would come from this one evening, and then she would be able to tuck away her feelings and her longings for many a year, until she was too old to think such things anymore.

Perhaps then she would be safe from herself.

Belmont sat in his favorite chair, savoring a glass of particularly fine claret. The rich liquid felt like smooth velvet inside his throat. He made a mental note to order another case of this vintage from the wine merchant.

He looked up with curious expectancy when his butler entered the study. Smithers knew not to disturb him unless it was important.

"This package was left for you, my lord."

Belmont reached out and took the small, wrapped parcel. There was no indication of the sender, only his name, in an elegant copperplate script, showed on the paper. "Who brought this?"

"The footman said a young lad rapped on the door, handed it to him, then ran off before a word could be said." The butler coughed hesitantly. "Should you like me to take care of it for you, my lord?"

Belmont shook his head. The strange manner of its delivery intrigued him. "Go along, I will deal with it." He waved his hand in dismissal.

Once the butler was gone, Belmont sat for a few moments, turning the small package over in his hands. It was wrapped in quite ordinary paper, tied with ordinary string. Plain, inexpensive items available to nearly anyone. There was no clue there. At last, curiosity got the better of him. He took the silver-chased penknife from the top drawer of the mahogany desk and carefully slit the strings. Folding back the paper, he looked down at the small box inside. There was no identifying mark upon the lid.

Cautiously, he lifted the lid, revealing a skillfully fashioned flower of red silk, nestled against a green baize background. A faint scent of roses wafted to his nose.

How very odd, he thought.

Belmont then noticed the scrap of paper tucked inside the lid. He drew out the folded sheet and scanned its message.

My Lord Belmont,
Should you be interested in meeting one who has admired you from afar, attend the masked ball at the Opera House Wednesday next. If you wear this symbol of acceptance upon your costume, I shall know you are interested in a meeting. I will find you.

He set the paper down upon his deck. Curious. Very curious.

Belmont was accustomed to any number of women laying out lures before him. Indeed, he had grown weary of the whole process. He much preferred to make the approach himself. Something was lost when he knew the woman was too interested. The possibility of failure—however slight—made victory all the more sweet.

But this note appealed to him. It obviously came from someone who was reluctant to make her self known—else why would she choose such a secretive method of communicating with him, or pick a masked ball to make her approach? If she wore a clever costume, he would have no idea of her identity.

He found it a rather diverting idea. His secret "admirer" could be almost any lady of his acquaintance. Married or single? Married, no doubt, which explained the secrecy. He deliberately avoided cuckolding his closest intimates, but beyond that he had no compunction against bedding a woman who belonged to another. He had done it often, usually with great pleasure.

Was this perhaps the lady of a friend, whom he had chosen not to approach? It would make the situation more awkward. But the anonymity of the setting meant he might never know the identity of the letter writer. And what he did not know for a certainty could not be bothersome.

His pulse quickened. He thought of the fete he was attending this evening. Would his mysterious admirer be there, secretly watching him? The very idea generated an edge of anticipation that he had not felt in some time. He would look quite carefully at all the likely prospects tonight. Most particularly at any lady wearing red roses.

There was no question that he would attend the masque. As a rule, he rarely attended the public ones, preferring more select company. Yet he remembered how he had enjoyed a particularly satisfying encounter at a masque at Willis' Rooms two years ago. The cyprians had been out in full force that night, and he fondly recalled the fair charmer he had brought to bed. A most delectable evening. He hoped that this one would be equally satisfying.

Although this woman was not a cyprian. He was quite certain of that, else there would be no need to conduct the matter in such secrecy. No, his correspondent was a lady, in every sense of the word. One who was not averse to a little variety in her life. He would be most amenable to accommodating her wishes. Most amenable.

His life had been missing some indefinable something for a long time. Even that evening with Maria had not been as exciting as he had hoped.

It was not that he was growing tired of women— Belmont thought he'd have to be dead and in the grave for a great many days before that urge finally faded. But he had noticed that his encounters were becoming less satisfying. As if he wanted more, but could not find it. Yet he had no idea what it was he wanted.

Perhaps it was mystery. If that was the case, this invitation was a godsend. He was to attend the masquerade, wearing the red rose, and wait for a lady to seek him out. It was the most nonsensical thing he had done in a great while. For that reason alone, it appealed to him.

His life was becoming too settled, too ordinary. Perhaps it was age. At six-and-thirty, he was not yet ancient, but he was no longer in his first youth, either. The years had a way of adding up before one realized it. Forty was not far away.

Forty. It had an awesome ring. Firm middle-age. The time when a man began to look back over his life and take stock of things.

He would not cringe from an objective analysis. His only true regret—his only remaining regret—was that he did not have a legal heir. He was proud of all his children, but the fact remained that society and the law labeled them bastards. Stephen would never become the seventh Viscount Belmont.

But to have a heir, he needed a wife. And Belmont had never been able to bring himself to take such an irrevocable step. It was one of the main reasons he dallied only with the married ladies of his class. One might find oneself staring down the barrel of a pistol in the wet, predawn grass, but one would not be forced to confront an error in judgment every day of his life.

For he actually wanted more from marriage than an heir. He wanted companionship. A woman whose conversation could extend beyond fashion and *ton* gossip. A woman who could discuss parliamentary politics and literary themes with equal ease—in and out of bed. The few women he knew who fit that mold were already married.

Most important, he needed a woman who would be a willing mother to his children—all his children. It would take an exceptional lady to undertake such a duty. It was not unheard of—he knew more than one household where an understanding wife had welcomed "orphans" into the home. Yet how many women would be so generous?

What he needed, he realized, was someone like Miss Waldron. She was of good breeding, bright, well-read, full of conversation, and adored his children. She had nearly every qualification he desired.

Except passion. And he would remain forever unwed rather than give up that one critical requirement. Without reciprocal passion, marriage would be an earthly hell. Until he found a woman who met his strict criteria, he would take his pleasure whenever and wherever it was offered, and not worry after more. In time, perhaps he would find a woman who would suit.

2

Belmont strove to contain his excitement when the carriage pulled up before the gaslit exterior of the Opera House. He had been in a heightened state of anticipation for days, awaiting this evening, and now it was upon him. He stepped down from the carriage, carefully adjusting the red flower that was securely fastened to his long green domino. He wore no mask—there was no need to hide his presence here. He did not want to make himself *too* difficult to recognize.

Was his mysterious lady already inside? It was half past eleven; he had timed his arrival to appear neither too eager nor too indifferent. He would allow her to wonder about him for a little while, but not to the extent that she would grow discouraged. There was still ample time for her to seek him out before supper.

Would she approach him immediately, or keep him in suspense for a time? The very thought of seeing her at last caused his blood to stir. In anticipation of this evening, he had deliberately forborne from patronizing his latest inamorata for the last two evenings. His appetite was keen and his senses at a fever pitch.

It would be a night to remember above all nights; he was certain of it. His steps were light as he mounted the stairs to the theater.

The lobby was only thinly occupied, and it took no more than a cursory glance to assure him that no one of interest stood there. Belmont continued on into the theater, carefully eyeing each and every female he saw.

He felt oddly exposed—and defenseless. She might be watching him now, marking his progress across the floor. What was she thinking? Did she experience a deep sense of relief as she saw him, knowing that her ploy had succeeded?

Where was she?

A hand tugged at his arm and Belmont turned eagerly. He peered intently at the gaudily clad figure who stood beside him.

"Looking for a partner, love?"

Belmont grimaced. Was this the mystery? A light skirt looking for a new patron? He smiled with a cynical twist to his lips and shook his head; the woman melted away into the crowd. He looked about the room again.

Bright splashes of color dotted the chamber, looking to Belmont like a bevy of exotic birds trapped amidst the sparrows and wrens of the less fanciful costumes. Belmont grinned in male admiration as a young lady, dressed in the sheerest of fabrics, laughed at her escort's sally. A most inventive costume.

Slowly, he maneuvered his way through the throng until he reached the far wall. No one else spoke to him, or tried to catch his attention. Leaning against the wall, he crossed his arms over his chest, a slight frown upon his face.

He did not want to believe that the lady who had sent the red rose was a mere cyprian. He wanted her to be more than that. Yet only a cyprian had approached him this night. Were all his fanciful hopes to be dashed?

Belmont inspected the revelers. There were many lone women among the crowd, most actively seeking new customers. He thought he recognized a dark-haired lady dressed as a Spanish *senorita*. Perhaps he would avail himself of her for the night if his mysterious lady did not approach soon. He did not intend to tarry here much longer.

Perhaps he would even leave alone; he did not think he was in the mood for company. As his gaze traveled from one costumed figure to another, he grew more discouraged by the moment. His disappointment was palpable. It had been a jest, after all.

He caught a glimpse of a woman garbed in white, standing on the opposite side of the room. His glance slid past her, but then his eyes were drawn back. There was something about the way she stood, the tension evidenced in the manner with which she twisted her gloved fingers together, that caught his attention. She looked this way and that, as if searching for someone. A caped reveler spoke to her, but she dismissed him with a quick shake of her head.

Belmont watched her most carefully. Could she be the lady who had sent the rose? He took a step forward, away from the shadow of the wall.

She noticed him then. Despite the distance separating them, Belmont saw the signs of recognition in her stance. He watched as she first took a halting step toward him, then stopped. He held his breath and restrained his impulse to rush to her side. This was her adventure, her plan. Let her approach him in her own way.

But please let it be soon.

She now moved toward him with clear purpose, deftly avoiding those who were in her way with unwavering determination. She ignored the importuning approaches of more than one man as she crossed the floor. Belmont's anticipation built.

His eyes narrowed in perusal as she drew closer. She was dressed all in white, a flowing domino concealing her figure with maddening effectiveness. All he could

tell for certain was her height, which looked to be pleas-
ingly tall. A flowered white toque upon her head was
cunningly constructed to serve as a mask as well, effec-
tively hiding the top part of her face from his view.
She had gone to a great deal of trouble to disguise her
identity. A slow smile spread over his face and his pulse
quickened. It must be her.

" 'Tis a shame to hide such a magnificent domino in
the shadows," she said as she stepped in front of him.
"Such a striking costume should be in full display."

"Amidst all this colorful plumage, I fear my plain
garb would be overcome," Belmont replied, eyeing her
with curiosity. What would she say? How would she
reveal her interest?

"Ah, but there are so few men sporting red roses
this evening," she countered, with a smile. "Surely that
would draw the attention of many."

"Then perhaps I should remove it," he said, reaching
up to do just that.

The woman laid a staying hand on his wrist. "May-
haps you wish to keep it there," she said. "It is a signal,
I think?"

"There is someone here who would recognize it as
such," he began. "But she has been strangely negligent
in seeking me out. I fear the entire matter is a hoax."

"Perhaps it is only that you delayed your arrival to
the point that she despaired."

"That would be unfortunate, as I particularly wished
to meet her." Belmont's lips curved into a seductive
smile as he grew more certain that this was the lady he
sought—and the one who sought him. He reached out
and touched one of the white roses decorating her
toque. "How interesting that we both should be wearing roses tonight. Yet mine is red while yours are
white."

"But do not the red and white together signify unity?" the lady asked. "Could it perhaps be a sign that we are to be together?"

"If I come with you, how am I to know if I am disappointing another?" he asked.

She drew out a single, red rose that had been concealed in the folds of her cloak. "It seems as if I carry a red rose with me as well, Lord Belmont. Is it coincidence, do you think?"

Belmont expelled a long breath. He took the flower from her and fastened it to the front of her domino. The bright splash of red gleamed against the shimmering white fabric. The meeting had been accomplished. What was to come next?

He nodded toward the stage and held out his arm. "Would you care to dance, my lady of the roses?"

Belmont drew her close to his side as they threaded their way through the crowd toward the dancers on the stage. Despite the heavily perfumed air, he caught a clear whiff of her scent. Rose, of course. For some reason, it seemed vaguely familiar.

Darting a swift glance at the woman beside him, Belmont realized that his mysterious lady had disguised herself well—he had no inkling of her identity. She knew him, certainly. Did he already know her? Lady Dauntry, perhaps? No, this woman was taller. And he did not think that Lady Dauntry, who blushed so becomingly in his presence, would have the nerve to seek him out in such a bold manner.

Who was she?

Juliet accepted Belmont's escort silently, not trusting herself to speak again. Now that she had succeeded in her aim, she felt strangely tongue-tied and awkward.

She had not thought beyond the moment of finding him—what would the remainder of the evening bring?

As they took their places in the set, she could not help but smile at the sight of the mismatched group. A Harlequin danced with Diana, a sailor partnered a lady in a flame-red domino, while Marie Antoinette linked arms with a Cavalier. She and Belmont were conspicuous in the simplicity of their costumes.

Growing more confident at the success of her disguise, Juliet avidly scrutinized Belmont with a boldness she dare not employ at the house in Chelsea. Tonight was different. She was free from the constraints of society, her position, her responsibilities. Free from her role as the efficient Miss Waldron. A frisson of excitement raced up her spine. Tonight was a night to be savored, minute by minute. Tonight, she would think only of Belmont.

At the conclusion of the dance, he took her gently by the arm. "I feel the need of some refreshment," he said, as he led her toward the room where the wines and edibles were laid out upon the tables. "The air in here in quite warm, do you not think?"

"Indeed," Juliet replied, striving to keep her voice deliberately low and husky. She claimed the glass of wine he handed her, and raised it toward him in salute.

Belmont placed her hand on his arm again and they strolled among the crowd.

"I have not been to a masque in years," he said, nodding a greeting to a passing friend. "I had forgotten how entertaining they can be. I thank you for drawing me here."

"Everyone enjoys the opportunity of pretending to be someone else, for a time," Juliet said. She glanced at him with a teasing smile. "Except you, perhaps."

"I am quite content with who I am," Belmont replied, then grinned widely. "I did not wish to make it *too* difficult for you to find me."

"I think I would have known you no matter the costume," Juliet replied.

"Indeed?"

She nodded. "Your green eyes are quite distinctive, my lord. Even a mask could not have hidden their color."

"Yet from across the room, they would not be easily recognized."

"There are other things, as well," Juliet said, with a mysterious air. "The way you walk, and stand. That particular look of amusement about your mouth as you watch your fellow man."

Belmont looked at her closely, puzzled by her astute observations. Who was this woman? She evidently knew him well. Was she an old lover, hoping to entice him back? His eyes narrowed in speculation. Caroline? No, surely not. Caroline had always pronounced white an insipid color. She would not wear it now no matter the reason. This woman had merely been watching him carefully. This sign of her attentiveness flattered him.

"Why are you here?" he asked.

She smiled. "To see you. What brings you here, my lord?"

"Your note intrigued me."

Juliet uttered a low laugh. "I said that I knew you well, did I not? I thought such an invitation would arouse your curiosity."

"I am flattered."

"You flatter easily, Lord Belmont."

He touched a finger to her cheek, drawing it slowly downward toward her chin. "Do I?"

Juliet looked at him for a long moment, unable to tear her gaze away from those seductive green eyes. At last, she turned away. Despite her costume, despite her mask, she feared he would see the truth in her eyes.

"Why must we meet like this?" he asked. "Or are you fond of masquerades and games?"

"We cannot meet openly."

"You fear what society will say?"

Juliet darted him a sidelong glance. "I have long disregarded what society thinks."

Belmont laughed. "I find, my fair lady, that you and I are of like mind."

"Oh no," Juliet protested, shaking her head. She touched her fingers to her mask. "You are far bolder than I. Despite my brave words, you see how I have protected myself."

"Yet it was boldness indeed to conceive the manner of our meeting," he said, his eyes sparkling. "But I have never objected to boldness in a woman."

Juliet blushed. If only he knew how truly bold she was! But if she could convince him that she was somehow part of his world, he would never suspect. "You daily flout convention with your attention to your children."

Belmont stiffened. "You do not think it proper for a man to look after his offspring?"

"Oh, on the contrary, I find it a highly admirable quality. It is a rare man who is willing to stand up to his obligations in such a case."

"It is no obligation, but a privilege," Belmont said. His face lit with fatherly pride. "They are an adorable lot." He smiled and took her arm in his. "But I do not think either of us came here tonight to discuss my children." He turned their steps toward the stage. "They will play a waltz soon," he said. "I should like to dance that with you."

Juliet hesitated. "I fear I do not know how to waltz,

my lord." She laughed lightly to cover her apprehension. He would think her very odd indeed to be ignorant of such a popular dance. But governesses had little opportunity to practice a waltz.

"Then I shall have to teach you." Belmont's eyes gleamed with anticipation as he led her onto the dancing floor.

When the country dance concluded, the first strains of the waltz began and Belmont swept her up in his arms. "Follow my lead," he said, and swung her onto the floor.

Juliet found the steps not too difficult to follow. Yet the sensation of being held so tightly in Belmont's arms caused her feet to falter at times. It was quite apparent why the waltz was labeled a scandalous dance. The weight of his arm about her waist caused a delicious warmth to spread over her body. The feel of his taut, leanly muscled shoulder under her fingers was electrifying.

They swept across the floor in ever dizzying circles. Juliet felt as if she were floating on air, tethered to the ground only by the warm heat of Belmont's touch. He drew her closer until their bodies were pressed together in a manner far more intimate than allowed in society ballrooms. Yet she did not pull away; she enjoyed it far too much.

Juliet almost cried aloud her disappointment when the music stopped. Belmont smiled down at her, his eyes a deeper and richer green than usual. He released her hand, but kept his arm firmly around her waist as he led her to the side of the stage and down the stairs.

Once in the corridor, he headed swiftly toward the steps that led to the gallery and boxes above. At the landing, Belmont hastened down the passage, leading her toward the farthest box. He closed the door behind them and took her in his arms.

"Much better," he murmured as he bent over her face. "Much better." He lowered his lips onto hers.

Juliet found herself wilting under Belmont's skilled attentions. Swaying against him, she again felt the heated warmth of his body. Juliet clung to him as she had during the steps of the waltz, then gasped with surprise when she felt his hand slide beneath her domino and curve around the swell of her breast.

Catching her in mid-gasp, Belmont thrust his tongue possessively into her mouth. She tasted delightfully of warm claret and peppermint. With a skillful move, Belmont freed her breast from the low bodice of her gown and caught the tip between his thumb and forefinger. All the while, his tongue kept up a steady, stroking rhythm.

Juliet felt helpless to draw away. It had been so long, so achingly long, since a man had held her thus. She was acutely aware that it was Belmont who held her so—Belmont whose bold kisses sent waves of longing rushing through her blood.

And it was precisely because it was Belmont that she had to draw away, had to pull back before it was too late. Matters were already going far beyond what she intended.

The door to the box burst open, letting in a shaft of light from the corridor.

"Beggin' yer pardon," slurred a drunken voice, which was followed by a sharp laugh. "I sees this box is already occupied. Unless you be wanting some company."

"No," said Belmont, fixing the interlopers with an icy glare. The tipsy revelers edged away at the menace in his voice.

Juliet shrank back against the far wall. Dear God,

what was she about? In another moment she would have lost all will to resist him and would only have become another of his conquests. No different than all the others. Her damnable nature was leading her down the road of folly again.

"A most untimely interruption," Belmont whispered as he reached for her again.

"I must go," Juliet said as she struggled to bring order to her dishabille.

"My carriage is waiting below," he said, his voice hoarse with desire. "Let me take you home."

"No!" Juliet tried to brush past him toward the door.

He grabbed her wrist. "You cannot go!" he said with barely suppressed agony. "Stay, please. We can go below again if you wish. Only do not leave."

"I must, I must," said Juliet. She frantically felt about her head, sighing in relief when she ascertained that her mask was still firmly in place.

"Then when may I see you again?" Belmont pleaded.

Juliet stared at him. She had never thought to carry on this charade for more than one night. And after what had nearly happened, she knew she dared not see him this way again. "I do not think . . ." she hesitated.

"Name a place," he said.

"We cannot meet again," she replied firmly.

"We will," he said with equal determination, taking hold of her arms. "At another masque, if secrecy is your aim. These things are held often enough."

Juliet nodded eagerly at the suggestion. All she wished to do now was escape to the safety of the house in Chelsea and pray that she would never, ever be discovered.

"Is your carriage waiting?" he asked, half hoping that it was not. With a bit more time, perhaps, he could persuade her to stay. No woman could resist him for long.

"Yes, it is," she said. "And I dare not tarry longer. Stay here, until I am away."

Belmont reluctantly accepted her need for secrecy. She was married, of course. It made sense—her refusal to leave with him, and now her insistence that she must go secretly. Her husband probably thought her at home, or with friends. She did not wish to arouse his suspicions.

"I will wait for you next time," he said. "I shall wear this same domino—you will find me?"

"Yes, yes," she cried, gathering her cloak around her and moving toward the door.

Belmont caught her up in his arms again. "One more kiss, sweet lady. I shall die of longing, else." His mouth covered hers, his lips insistent and demanding as he sought to both punish and reward her for her actions this evening. He was going to die of frustration once she left, and if he could leave her equally discomposed, he would have some measure of comfort.

All too soon, she broke free and fled from the box. Belmont resisted the temptation to follow her. She was clearly worried, and he did not wish to do anything that would prevent her from meeting him again.

Now he must discover the date of the next masquerade.

Juliet did not truly draw a deep breath until she was in her room in the house in Chelsea and the dress and domino were hidden in the depths of her wardrobe. She vainly attempted to drag a brush through her hair, but her trembling hands made it impossible.

She stared at her face in the pier glass. Her lips were red and swollen, her breasts throbbed, and deep inside her an unfulfilled ache screamed for release.

At the last moment, she had held on to the last vestiges of sense and ran. Not because she wanted to, but precisely because she did not want to. She knew she did not have the strength to resist him. In a few more moments, she would have allowed him to take her right there in the Opera House. Would have begged him to do so.

Juliet knew now that her plan had been an even greater folly than she first imagined. However could she think that Belmont would be interested in only light flirtation and a few dances? How could she ever have thought that *she* would be satisfied with such an innocent evening? What a fool she was!

It was quite obvious that time had not dimmed the streak of passion within her; it burned as brightly as ever, even after all these years. It had been the cause of her grief once, and had nearly been so again tonight. The unexpected depths of her love for him frightened her witless.

She had lied to herself, thinking that she could suppress such a deep, instinctive part of her. If it was such an easily suppressed emotion, she would not have raced down the path to ruin those eleven years ago, when she had allowed herself to love and be loved by a man who filled her head with sweet tales and vague promises. Geoffrey had been the only good thing to come of that mistake.

It was a shock to discover that she was still as vulnerable now. At twenty-eight, she was no stronger than she had been at seventeen. Even less so, for Juliet knew at the outset there could not be a successful outcome to a liaison with Belmont. Yet, even knowing that, she had nearly given in to his desires tonight—and hers.

She had foolishly labeled her longings as a mere yearning for the life she had once led, but she now knew that for the lie it was. She wanted Belmont as a lover.

There. She had admitted it. And by doing so, maybe she could keep it from happening.

Tonight, she had pulled back from the brink just in time. She must never, ever allow herself to get so close again. It was imperative, then, that she not see Belmont in any other guise than as governess to his children. It was the only safe thing to do.

Juliet looked again at herself in the mirror, smiling sadly at her reflection. She had successfully submerged her passionate nature for many long years; she could do it again, she was certain. Having Belmont visiting the house almost daily would not make it easy, but she would do it. She had to.

For she feared that if she once allowed her desires to dominate her behavior, she would never be able to contain them again. And that path led only toward future ruin. Even if she could be with Belmont, it would not be for long. He would part with her eventually, and then what was she to do?

If she did not love him, it would not matter. But because she did, Juliet knew that she would not be satisfied with anything less than his love in return. And that, she knew, she would never have. Belmont had never given his heart to any woman.

No, it was better this way. She would give up her foolish dreams and look upon Lord Belmont only as her employer. She must ignore the fact that she wanted him to be so much more. It would be difficult to act normally in his presence again, but act normal she must, or he might suspect.

And that would be the very worst of all. He would be embarrassed to discover that the drab Miss Waldron brightened her day with dreams of him.

The mysterious lady of the red and white roses would never make another appearance at a masked ball.

After all, had she not achieved her goal—an evening with Lord Belmont? In many ways she had received much more than she had bargained for—and far less as well. She would have to remain content with that.

Belmont slammed the door of the theater manager's office and stomped down the stairs. Each and every person he had spoken to today told him the same thing—no more public masques were scheduled for at least a month.

A month! He would go mad in less than a week if he could not see his lady of the roses before then. He had not been able to get her out of his mind. Thoughts of her dominated all his waking moments, and tormented his dreams. He had to see her again. *Would* see her again.

Belmont was not used to denying himself anything, and this new torment was all the more unpleasant for that. Why had he not insisted on a more definite rendezvous? The next masquerade was far too long in the future. There must be some way of finding her before then.

Maybe he should go to Chloe tonight. She would be able to divert his thoughts.

Yet he realized with a stab of surprise that the prospect did not attract him. He did not want to be diverted from his thoughts of the lady in white. It was an unfamiliar sensation, to want one woman to the exclusion of all others. How had this lady developed such a hold over him, that only she would do? He feared he would think of her and no one else until they met again.

Belmont carried his ill-humor all the way to Chelsea, and only the sound of childish laughter that greeted him in the hall banished his blue-devils. He vaulted up the stairs. Thank God for the children.

He was late today and everyone was assembled around the table in the grand drawing room, enjoying their tea.

"Is there room for one more?" Belmont asked as he strode into the room.

"Sit here, Papa," Henry cried. He pushed against his brother. "Move over, Sam."

"I shall sit next to this lady," Belmont insisted, drawing up a chair and sitting next to Lucilla. "She demonstrates proper decorum." He flashed a rueful smile at Miss Waldron.

Juliet quickly averted her eyes. She had not seen him since the masque, carefully avoiding him when he visited the children two days ago. The situation was fully as awkward as she had feared.

She felt as if his eyes were boring into her, seeing through her clothes to the skin he had caressed. She could feel the touch of his heated fingers on her flesh. Despite her high-neck gown, she felt as if she were stripped naked before him. How could she have behaved with such wantonness in his arms?

Perhaps it was as her mother said all those years ago—there was truly something wrong with her. Some strange mark upon her nature that made her unable to rein in her passion as a lady ought. It had been her downfall once, and had nearly proved so again.

"I would say you are not attending, Miss Waldron."

The viscount's voice broke into her thoughts and Juliet colored. "I am sorry, my lord. I fear my wits are elsewhere today. What is it that you desired?"

Just her very utterance of the word brought everything flooding back into Belmont's mind. Desire. He was trapped by it, consumed by it, obsessed by it. With no possibility of assuaging it until he saw the White Lady again. He cleared his throat. "I suggested that since the weather is so welcoming today, the children might wish to go for a walk in the park."

All the young faces turned toward her in silent appeal. Juliet laughed lightly. "Of course you may," she said.

"Hooray," said Sam. "Can we bring the cricket bats? Will you pitch us a few?"

"Certainly." Belmont smiled. "But first we must allow Miss Waldron to finish her tea."

"I will get the bats while we wait," said Sam, slipping out the door.

"I will find the shuttlecocks," Harry said.

"And Bella's hoop," chimed in Lucy. In moments, every child except Geoffrey had fled.

"Go along," said the viscount to Geoffrey. "Everyone else has deserted your mama; I give you permission to do likewise."

Juliet abhorred the silence that fell upon them after her son departed. She hastily set down her teacup. "I should gather up the children's wraps . . ."

"Nonsense," said the viscount. "I am throwing your day into enough turmoil without ruining your tea as well. Sit until you are ready. Those rascals can wait a few moments without coming to any harm."

Juliet feared to reach for her cup again, certain that her hand would tremble noticeably.

"How is Arabella adjusting to her new home?" Belmont asked. "Has she settled in well?"

"Oh, yes," Juliet replied, grateful to have a safe topic of conversation. "Lucy and Suzanne adore her, of course. And she is, in turn, fascinated by your nephew, Arthur. He must be the first baby she has ever seen."

"Arabella was the youngest child at the house," the

viscount explained. "It must be a treat for her to now be numbered among the elders."

"You mean there are other children with that family?"

He nodded his head. "She was the only 'boarder,' " he explained. "But I doubt she was petted and cosseted like the baby of a family should be. Arthur enjoys all the attention?"

A fond smile flitted over her face. "He is the most well-behaved thing. Nurse is constantly singing his praises."

"Most unlike his father," Belmont mused. "I seem to recall Dickie as a holy terror in the nursery."

"Perhaps his mother provided a sobering influence."

The viscount laughed. "Hardly, if I know my brother. She was probably the gaudiest bird-of-paradise in the city. Highly unlikely to be a lady of soothing spirits."

"I only hope he is more cautious when he next arrives home," said Juliet before she could stop herself.

"I had a stern talk with him," the viscount said, amused by Miss Waldron's criticism. "I told him that a man with his limited resources could not afford to have a large family. I believe he understood the message." He smiled at her. "Besides, I cannot afford to do anything that would upset you, Miss Waldron. You are far too valuable a governess."

Juliet ducked her head to hide her blush. If he only know how very unsuitable she was! She stood and headed for the door. "I should see that the children are all bundled properly," she said. "These spring days can be deceptive."

Once in the corridor, she leaned weakly against the wall. However was she going to endure the rest of his visit? Or the next one, and the next one after that? Thank goodness they were going to the park, where he would be running and playing with the boys and she need not converse with him at any great length. How many more visits would it take until she could remain tranquil in his presence?

She was very much afraid she did not want to know the answer to that question.

The boys and the viscount played a rousing game of cricket in the park, while Lucilla and Suzanne inexpertly batted at the shuttlecocks. Juliet attempted to teach Arabella the fine art of hoop rolling on the well-trimmed lawn. All in all, it was a successful expedition to the park. Juliet handed out peppermints to each child as a reward for good behavior.

As they walked back to the house, Belmont fell in step beside Juliet.

"Geoffrey is nearing the age when some decision must be made upon his future. Have you discussed the possibilities with him yet?"

"We did talk about a few things," Juliet admitted. "Enough to ascertain that he is interested in neither a career in the military nor the navy."

The viscount nodded. "If he wishes to continue his schooling, then no choice needs to be made for some time. Is that what you wish?"

"I think so," said Juliet. "I am hopeful he will be able to find a scholarship place at one of the schools."

"There is no need of that," Belmont said. "I told you I would take full responsibility for his education as long as you are in my employ."

"I did not think you anticipated such a lengthy obligation," Juliet said with a short laugh.

"Miss Waldron, it is, quite frankly, such a trifling sum to me that I do not wish you to think twice about the matter. If you continue to object, I will have no other recourse than to add his tuition payments onto your salary."

"You are very generous," Juliet murmured.

"Nonsense," said the viscount. "I am selfishly looking out for my own interests. You are a marvelous influence on the children and I do not wish to lose you."

Nor do I wish to lose this position, Juliet thought. For even if she never dared indulge in such a bold action as her folly at the masque, she could not quite bring herself to leave the viscount's employment. Once her memories of his caresses had faded, she would be content again to see him like this, when he came to visit the children. She had no right to expect anything more of him.

With time, she would be able to put her love back in its hiding place. Perhaps this time her feelings would stay buried forever. Juliet fervently hoped so. Working for Lord Belmont would be an exquisite hell, else.

3

Belmont remained deep in thought as he tooled his curricle back toward Mayfair. Playing with the children had distracted him momentarily, but the instant he shut the door on the Chelsea house, the problem of the White Lady returned to his thoughts. If only he could devise a plan. There must be some way . . . of course! The very thing. He laughed aloud at his cleverness.

He had no need to wait for a public masque to see his White Lady again. He would host a masque of his own and broadly promote the fact. A story about Lord Belmont's latest party would attract the attention of all the fashionable columns in the papers. Every member of the *ton* would be sure to learn of it. He did not doubt for a moment that the White Lady was numbered among that exclusive group. He knew from their meeting at the Opera House that she was a lady. And he would inform his butler that no female need present an invitation at the door. Belmont would make it laughably easy for her to attend.

He would leave the matter of arranging music and food to his competent staff. All could be accomplished in a few days. Time was critical. He did not wish to wait any longer than he had to before seeing the White Lady again. His interest in her was rapidly becoming an obsession, and Belmont knew he would not be comfortable again until he had delved further into his attraction to her mysteries.

By the time he arrived home, he was whistling a jaunty air in anticipation of the upcoming reunion.

His spirits were not quite so high the next morning. The printers insisted they could not possibly prepare the invitations in the time he demanded, so they must be written out by hand. His secretary blanched at the task, and Belmont, taking pity upon him, wondered if he could enlist Miss Waldron's aid. He departed for Chelsea, willing to grant her any manner of reward for her assistance.

"I hate to ask such a personal favor of you," he said, when he stood before her in the drawing room. "I know it is completely outside your normal course of duties. But I would be most grateful . . ."

"I shall be glad to be of help, my lord," Juliet replied.

"Delightful," said Belmont, as he plopped down the boxes of cards and the lists of addresses on the table. He handed her a sample invitation. "This is what I need you to write. Nothing fancy, you will see, merely a simple invitation."

Juliet scanned the lines and the blood rushed to her

head so quickly she feared she would faint. She gripped the edge of the table in her distress.

"Miss Waldron?" Belmont's face mirrored his concern. "Are you feeling all right?"

"Yes," she said, trying to quell her fear. Did he know? He must! He was teasing her, testing her.

Then she shook her head. It was impossible. The situation was as he explained. His secretary could not prepare so many invitations by himself. He needed her help.

But why ever was the viscount hosting a masked ball at his house?

"It looks to be an interesting evening," Juliet said with a deliberately prim expression.

The viscount laughed. "You sound most disapproving, Miss Waldron. As indeed you should. Masked balls can be notoriously improper. I have discovered, however, that I am inordinately fond of them." He grinned audaciously.

Juliet could barely breathe. He expected the lady in the white domino to attend his ball. Had she fooled him so completely that he thought her name was included on the list he had given her? She was almost amused by the thought.

Almost. Yet behind her amusement lurked a deeper foreboding. Belmont wanted to see the lady with the roses, yet Juliet had promised herself she would never don the costume again. But that had been before today, before he planned his own masked ball in the hopes she would attend. Dare she disappoint him?

Dare she disappoint herself?

She must. Because she knew that she was not strong enough to resist him. Here, in Chelsea, she felt safe, armored by the primness with which she surrounded herself. The house and the children were her sanctuary.

If she gave up their protection again, she did not know if she would ever be safe from her own desires. It was far too great a risk to take. Belmont would have to endure his disappointment. As would she.

"Send a footman around to the house when you have finished," Belmont said. "I deeply appreciate your assistance in this matter, Miss Waldron. I will devise an extra-special reward for you as well."

"You are already far too generous," Juliet replied.

"Nonsense," he said with a dismissive wave of his hand. "Do not value yourself too lightly. What would be adequate compensation for your time? An increase in your salary? Or a holiday from your demanding charges? How would you like to visit Bath for a few days, Miss Waldron?"

Bath. Juliet cringed at the very word. Bath had paved the way to her downfall and it was the very last place on earth she ever wanted to see again. "Perhaps in the summer, I would like to spend a few days in the country," she said quietly.

"Good." He nodded. "Let me know when you wish to go and I shall have you whisked off to whatever destination you desire. I am truly in your debt."

As I am in yours, Juliet thought. He would never know how much she wished their situation was different.

She was relieved when Belmont left a few minutes later. This had been their longest time together since the masked ball, and it was very difficult to maintain her composure while in his presence. Even so, she moved to the tall window, watching his carriage roll down the street toward London.

She smiled a little sadly at herself in the glass. If she had not ruined her life all those years ago, she and Belmont would likely never have met. She would no doubt be married and busily raising a family, with little opportunity to know one of London's notorious rakes. Even if she could go back in time and change everything, it would not have altered things between them.

Why could she not remain content with the way things were?

By that evening, Juliet had finished writing Belmont's invitations. She felt a small qualm of apprehension, fearing he might recognize her handwriting from the note she had sent him, but this she easily stilled when the footman arrived to take them for immediate distribution.

Belmont's ball was not scheduled for several days. By the time the date arrived, Juliet reasoned, she would not feel this all-encompassing urge to attend, no matter the danger. The routine of daily life in the house in Chelsea would soon calm her jangled nerves.

She almost wished her duties were more onerous, for she had far too much free time to dwell on her dilemma. Her head told her sternly that she was treading the path of folly, but her heart warred against wisdom.

Would one more night be so harmful? One night where she could surrender to her desires? For she was very certain that Belmont would not let her slip from his fingers so easily again. The only person who could possibly be harmed was herself—and if she chose to be a willing participant, it was her own fault.

Her skin still flamed at the memory of his touch. Juliet could not deny it—she did want him, wanted to feel his hands and lips upon her again. Wanted to feel his body atop hers, gently pressing her down, giving and taking the one gift only a man and woman could share.

She was shameful. And shameless. But her life was ruined already. Nothing she did now would make matters any worse. She had already paid the price for passion's folly at the age of seventeen. Was she not now entitled to grab a mote of happiness for herself?

She had so little chance for happiness. She would never have a husband of her own, nor brothers or sisters for Geoffrey. Was it so wrong to want something for herself, even for only a short time?

And this would be the very last time, she promised herself. She would throw the dress on the fire the moment she returned home so that she would never be tempted again. This one night would have to last her forever.

She fully intended to enjoy herself.

Belmont dressed for his masque with exquisite care. His shirt and cravat were of the snowiest white, his pantaloons and waistcoat of the blackest black. A ring of deep green jade provided the only flash of color. He eschewed a domino tonight. There was no need for the pretense of disguise. He was hosting this masquerade for one reason, and for one reason only—to see the White Lady again. He had no intention of attending his own party. He would wait for her to find him, then he would take her away.

He paced across the floor of his study with barely restrained impatience, waiting for the minutes to crawl by. He was ready far too early, but the anticipation had been throbbing in his veins for so long he could not help himself.

Belmont carefully glanced about the room to make certain all the preparations were complete. Artful arrangements of red and white roses stood upon the mantel and his desk, their fragrance permeating the chamber. He would never again be able to smell the scent of roses without thinking of *her*. Tall, fluted glasses stood upon the small side table next to the couch; the iced champagne would not be brought until the last possible moment. A small, leather-bound volume rested next to the glasses. He smiled, eager to discover her reaction to his gift. He only wished it could be something more—but a gift that spoke of her value to him would occasion comment. Turning toward the door, Belmont patted the key in his waistcoat pocket. Once his lady arrived, they could retreat to this room and not be disturbed.

He did not even consider what he would do if she did not come.

His green eyes blazed with a fierce light. She would not dare stay away. He had felt her acquiescence that night at the Opera House, before she fled. For a moment, she had wanted him as badly as he had wanted her. Tonight, he would use all his considerable skills to bring the matter to a satisfactory conclusion.

He laughed at the thought. Conclusion was certainly the wrong word. Consummation was better. Or commencement. For he hoped tonight would mark the start of a very satisfactory liaison. It had been a long time since he had enjoyed an affair wholeheartedly. With this woman, he knew he could reclaim the thrill and excitement that had been missing in his recent conquests. The White Lady would make everything right again.

She was everything he wanted, and needed. He would convince her tonight that they belonged together. Belmont firmly believed she could bring him the elusive happiness he sought.

Sitting in the bedside chair, Juliet could barely keep her attention upon the story she read to the girls. Tonight was the night of Belmont's masque and she had thought of little else for days. Now the evening was here and it was all she could do to contain her fluttering nerves until the children were safely tucked into bed and she could slip from the house.

She listened impatiently while the girls said their prayers, then kissed each one in turn. At last she was able to dim the lamp and return to her room.

Juliet sat down at her dressing table, staring at her flushed face in the mirror. It was not too late to change her mind, she told herself. She could go to the wardrobe, pull out her night rail, and go to bed herself.

Or she could go to Belmont.

Juliet rose and walked to the wardrobe. Opening the door, she drew out the dress and domino.

Really, she had very little choice in the matter. She could no more stay away tonight that she could deny her love for him. However wrong it may be, she would never be free of him. She only wanted this one chance to be his. Once again, Juliet would follow her foolish heart down the path of folly.

Belmont's spirits sank when he heard the tall clock at the base of the stairs chime twelve. She was not coming. All his effort had gone for naught.

He had a sudden urge to order his butler to throw all the revelers from the house. He did not want them here any longer. Ripping off his constricting cravat, he flung it over his shoulder and ducked back into the drawing room.

Everyone here looked to be enjoying themselves, he thought sourly. It was his party and all except the host were having a grand time. It was sweetly ironic.

Then he smiled wryly. He had discovered a few things about himself in the last week. One was that he did not deal well with thwarted wishes. He was ill-accustomed to such a situation, and did not like it one bit. In the future, he would do well to remember to stay away from mysterious ladies and masked balls. With a paid companion, matters were much more straight-forward. And he controlled them.

He grabbed a tall flute of champagne off a footman's tray and drained the glass in a few gulps. If his lady planned to disappoint him, he may as well devise some other method of amusing himself this evening. Drinking expensive champagne seemed as good a way as any. He took another glass and stepped out into the corridor.

It was fortunate his fingers instinctively curled around the stem, else he would have dropped the glass in his surprise. There, at the head of the stairs, stood a lady dressed all in white. Hardly daring to breathe, Belmont stepped carefully toward her. He had been disappointed by each new arrival this evening and he did not wish to raise his hopes prematurely. He wanted to be certain it was she.

But as he drew closer, he was positive. She was dressed and masked as she had been all those nights ago at the Opera House. Belmont hastened to her side.

"I did not think you were coming," he said bluntly.

Juliet smiled. "It would not do for you to become overconfident, Lord Belmont."

He took her arm and drew her back down the stairs. "I arranged this whole damn affair for you," he grumbled. "The least you could have done was arrive on time."

Her laughter trilled in his ear.

"I was not aware that you held the party in my honor, your lordship. Please forgive me for being so insensitive."

He stopped and turned toward her, his face breaking into an appealing grin. "I do," he said, as he opened a door and pushed her into the room.

The chamber was dimly lit with the soft glow of

candlelight. Juliet noticed a bottle of champagne in an iced cooler on the table, two glasses on either side. And everywhere she looked she saw roses—red and white, in bowls and vases. She breathed deeply, imagining for a moment that she was in a summer garden.

She looked at him with surprise. "You prepared this for me?"

"Yes," he growled. Opening the bottle of champagne, he poured them each a glass.

Juliet sat and gazed absently at the fire screen, taking a small sip of champagne as she tried to still her pounding heart. She had not expected Belmont to be so eager, so intent. It was thrilling and discomposing all at the same time. "I am flattered," Juliet replied, remembering to lower her voice. She must play her part most carefully tonight; there was not a raucous crowd of revelers to distract his attention.

Belmont laughed as he sat beside her. "It is I who am flattered," he said. "Surely, you know that no male dislikes being pursued."

"Ah, but who is pursuing whom?" she teased with newfound boldness.

"Perhaps I should have said a mutual pursuit is the most satisfactory." He reached over to the table and handed her the book he had carefully selected for her. "A mere trifle. I rather thought you might like it."

Juliet examined the elegant, calf-bound volume. "John Donne."

"A favorite of mine." He smiled at the surprised look upon her face. "It appears that you do not know *every-thing* about me, my lady."

He took the book from her and flipped through the pages, stopping at last with a satisfied smile upon his face. "Ah, here is the one I have been thinking upon this past week: 'Twice or thrice had I loved thee, Before

I knew thy face or name, So in a voice, so in a shapeless flame, Angels affect us oft, and worshiped be.' Rather appropriate, I think."

"I am no angel," she replied softly.

"You cannot cavil if I wish to name you such," he said. "An angel in white."

"The truth would disappoint you."

"Nothing about you could disappoint me," he said with a fierceness that surprised him. Belmont took her free hand and slowly drew off her glove, finger by finger. "In my mind, you are perfect." When he had bared her skin, he caressed her palm with his thumb in slow, sensual circles, feeling the tension increase within her at his touch.

Belmont moved his hand up her arm, stroking it with soft caressing motions. "I do love giving gifts," he said, shifting closer. "Or do you already know that about me?"

"I know that I do not know as much as I wish," Juliet whispered.

"Indeed," he said, leaning closer so he could breathe in the soft scent of her. Roses, the flower he would forever associated with her. "I know there are things I wish to learn about you. Let this be an evening of shared discovery."

He eyed her toque and mask with a hopeful expression. "I do not suppose you will remove . . . ?"

"No," said Juliet quickly. "It is best this way."

Her determination to keep her identity a secret only increased the lust that raged within him. The thought was provocative, enthralling, and he felt his body respond to the very idea of making love to this mysterious lady, knowing he might never learn her identity. Would he pass her unaware tomorrow night at a *ton* fete? Sit next to her at a grand banquet and never be the wiser?

But first to come was . . . this evening. His green eyes began to glow with heightened anticipation as his fingers caressed the nape of her shapely neck.

"Then at least remove your domino," he said, reaching to unfasten the garment. His eager fingers fumbled with the clasp, then pushed the robe off her shoulders and down her arms.

His fingers brushed against her skin as he did so and he felt her shiver. Belmont smiled to himself. It was as he thought. His White Lady was full of passion.

Belmont had touched her at the Opera House, but had not seen what he touched. Now, as he pulled off the domino, he drew in his breath at the sight of her smooth skin, the soft swell of her breasts above the low bodice of her gown. She was even more desirable than he had imagined.

Without a word, he took the glass from her and pulled her into his arms. "You cannot know how I have waited to hold you again," he murmured as his lips brushed along the edge of her mask, across her cheek. "You were most unkind to leave me so precipitately at the masque."

He brought his lips down upon hers with possessive determination. His tongue traced the shape of her mouth, seeking, questing, and her lips parted beneath his. His tongue darted between them and he pulled her tight against him.

When she tentatively touched the tip of her tongue to his, he uttered a deep moan of pleasure. His hand found her breasts and she quivered at his light touch. Beneath his skilled fingers, her breasts grew firm, the nipples taut. Desire flooded through him. She was as passionately responsive as he could wish.

Belmont drew back from her lips, trailing kisses down her cheek. He nuzzled at her neck, moving upward to nip and lick the lobe of her tiny ear. The blood pounded in his head and he struggled for breath as if he had just run the length of Piccadilly, but he was in no hurry to finalize his pleasure. He would drag out this exquisite experience for as long as he dared.

With a brief pang of regret, Belmont wished he had arranged their tête-à-tête in his bedroom, where the setting would be more comfortable. But the couch was soft, and the lady willing, and he did not wish to stop for anything. His left hand smoothed down over her hip, drawing her toward him as he leaned back against the cushions. He kissed her with growing passion, his tongue dipping into her mouth in rhythmic motions while he fumbled with the fastenings of her dress.

"So beautiful," he whispered against her ear. "So exquisitely beautiful."

He slipped her dress off her shoulders, and down her arms. His eyes gleamed with appreciation as he took in the sight of the half-naked figure before him. In the light from the candles, her skin took on a golden hue. He softly rubbed a finger against one nipple, watching it harden under his touch. He smiled at her responsiveness. Lowering his head, he drew the soft brown tip into his mouth.

She shuddered as his lips closed over her breast and her hands reached out and clasped convulsively on to his shoulders. With deliberate slowness, Belmont laved first one nipple, then the other, delighted with her response as she arched against him.

When she reached out to pull his coat down over his shoulders, Belmont broke away and completed the process. Her eager hands fumbled with the buttons on his waistcoat and that garment was flung aside as well. Belmont pulled his shirt over his head, then drew her body to his, the feel of her heated skin nearly scorching him. Dear God, she felt so wonderful. It was more than the mystery, more than his curiosity. She seemed made for him, designed for him: her breasts in perfect proportion to his hands, her mouth soft and inviting, her ears tiny and delicate, her shoulders smooth and silky. With a sudden surge of desire he wanted to see her completely naked, lying beneath him, moaning in delight as he pleasured her body.

He heaved himself off the couch, breathing in ragged gasps. She lay back against the cushioned end, watching him through the narrow eye-slits of her mask as he pulled her dress over her hips, down her legs, and flung it onto the floor. He divested himself of his pantaloons in an instant and stretched out atop her, covering her naked body with his own.

His lips and hands touched her everywhere, caressing, stroking, fanning the flames of her desire to a white hot heat. He sucked in his breath as her hands explored his naked flesh, skimming over the rigid muscles of his back.

As he nudged her legs apart, Belmont hovered over her with a feeling akin to hesitation. He had waited for this moment, dreamt of it for days now, and in the deepest recesses of his mind he feared that the reality would never quite match his dreams. It was always that way. But need was too great for him to delay any longer and he slowly eased into her tight, enveloping warmth.

Her heat surrounded him and he plunged deeper, driven by his own frantic desires. She uttered a hoarse gasp and he hesitated, afraid he had hurt her in his haste. But he felt her relax around him and he began to move, slowly but with assurance, knowing she was as eager for this as he. His mouth sought hers, lips eager and hungry as the pace of his thrusts quickened.

She was so exquisite, his mystery lover. Her long,

shapely legs wrapped themselves about him, pulling him toward her as she arched against him with her own demands. Was it possible that this night would live up to all he had imagined? It was his last coherent thought before he focused all his attention on feeling and sensing, giving and taking. He seemed incapable of satiation, hovering on the crest of pleasure for an eternity. She moved with him as if they had shared a lifetime of loving, answering his need with her own. Never had he felt such exquisite pleasure in the arms of a woman. It was mystifying and almost frightening.

As she reached her peak, he listened with delight to her gasps of pleasure, then unleashed himself to tumble over the edge and shudder with his own release. Belmont sank atop her, too stunned to draw breath.

Dear God, he had never felt such pleasure in his life.

He rose briefly, grabbing up the silken white domino to throw over the both of them before he gathered her up in his arms again. He dozed, he thought, for when he looked about the room again the candles had burned lower. She lay breathing softly, asleep, a soft smile of contentment upon her lips.

His hand itched to rip away the mask that still covered the upper portion of her face. But some small vestige of hesitation stayed his hand, the fear that once he knew her identity it would not be the same. He did not want to do anything to ruin this night.

He wanted her again, as strongly as if they had not loved yet. Softly, tenderly, he trailed kisses across her face, dipping his head down to run his tongue along her collarbone. She stirred, then woke. He watched her eyes blink in surprise, then focus on him. A soft "oh" escaped her lips.

For a moment their eyes locked. He saw the surprise in hers fade to recognition, then to an emotion he could not fathom. Wary apprehension, perhaps? He kissed her lingeringly, seeking to reassure her.

Juliet closed her eyes again. She felt the mask over her face; she was still safe. Hesitantly, she stroked her hand down his back and was rewarded with the instant tensing of his body.

It was obvious that Belmont was ready and willing to pleasure her again. She only hoped that he had not found her own inexperience disappointing. She wanted this to be a night he would remember. If not for always, at least for a time.

She would remember it forever. It was a pleasing and sad realization at the same time. Pleasing, because she had never dreamed loving Belmont could be such an overwhelming experience. Sad, because she knew that it could never happen again. Juliet knew now that one night with Belmont would never be enough for her. She would always yearn for what she could not have.

But the night was not yet over. As his hands moved over her, Juliet gave herself up to the sensations he invoked. She tried to touch him as much as he did her, wanting to please him, to give him some of what he had given her. His soft groans of delight were her rewards and she cherished each one of them. She grew bolder, her tongue twining with his as their mouths joined together. Her fingers floated over his sweat-dampened skin, teasing swirling patterns on his flesh.

It was what she had come here for, after all. One brief night of pleasure with Belmont before she turned herself back into stone. She would not deny him anything.

As he brought her own desires to a heightened state, she drew him toward her, arching her body, begging him silently to take her, to again bring the flaming release of their first loving. Then, in less silent ways, she told him of her want and her need. And the result was even more intense and shattering than before.

Belmont raised her hand to his mouth and nibbled at the tips of her fingers. The hour was perilously late, he knew, and at any minute she would have to leave. But he wanted to delay the parting for as long as possible.

He wanted to sweep her up in his arms and carry her to his room, keeping her prisoner there for days, weeks, months. Keeping her until he at last grew sated with her charms. If he ever did.

It was a frightening thought. Simply because he had never thought it before. Always, with his lovers, he was able to keep a wall of reserve between his feelings and his actions. He always held a part of himself back, watching, judging, evaluating himself and them.

This night, he had thought of nothing but her, the pleasure she brought him and the pleasure he brought her. He had even forgotten to think about how much more comfortable this all would have been in the soft bed upstairs rather than on the Sheraton couch in his study.

He looked down at her again, desperately wishing she could stay until he knew every secret she possessed. She had captured his attention in a way that no woman ever had and he wanted to know why. He stared at her half-hidden face, as if trying to see into her thoughts, searching for a clue to her power over him.

"I must go," Juliet said at last, her voice thick with reluctance. But go she must, if she were ever to leave.

"I know," he said, kissing her softly. "You have been here longer than I ever dared hope."

He did not try to restrain her, but got to his feet and gathered up her clothes. He insisted upon dressing her himself, planting soft kisses upon her shoulders and neck as he slowly fastened her back into her gown. Never had he found *dressing* a woman to be such a satisfyingly erotic experience.

Hastily he shrugged on his shirt and buttoned his pantaloons. He stood behind her, his hands gently resting on her shoulders. "When am I to see you again?" he asked.

"I will let you know when it can be arranged," she said.

"Make it soon," he whispered. "This night has made me hungry for more."

Belmont turned her to face him and looked into her eyes. They were brown, he realized. Soft, chocolate-brown. "One thing only," he said, his voice hoarse with his unrelieved passion. "Your name. Tell me your name."

"I cannot."

"Please?"

"If I tell you, there is the danger you will know who I am," Juliet said simply. "And if that should happen, I assure you, you will be quite disappointed."

"I could never be disappointed in you."

"Then let things remain as they are," she said.

"When will we meet again?"

"Soon," she said. "Soon."

"Make it as quick as you can," he said, kissing her. "Already I cannot wait."

Juliet stiffened at his words. She felt the same, only a hundred times more, for she knew that they would never meet like this again. He would find another lady to enjoy. She would have to live on memories of this night for a lifetime.

And it would take a lifetime to forget this night. But she resolved not to rue one minute of it, no matter how painful it became in the days ahead. She had come here tonight with her eyes wide open, and if the experience had been even more extraordinary than she had deemed possible, it had been her deliberate choice. She must accept the future pain it brought as the price she paid for such a night.

Juliet pulled away from his arms and grabbed up her domino. Her fingers trembled as she fastened the clasp. She stood to one side while Belmont unlocked the door, then she slipped past him into the corridor before he could touch her again. A waiting footman opened the front door and she raced down the steps into the early dawn.

Belmont felt empty and hollow after she left. He poured himself another glass of the now warm champagne and sipped it slowly while he stared at the roses upon the mantel.

Instead of feeling satisfaction, he felt strangely unhappy. The evening had been all he could have imagined—and more. His White Lady burned with a passion as deep as his. Their lovemaking had been exquisitely pleasurable. Yet why did he feel this way?

It was only because she was gone, he reasoned. Rarely did he spend the entire night with a lady, but he knew she was one with whom he would like to enjoy innumerable mornings. Ones that followed lengthy nights.

That would be all the more difficult if she was married. Belmont resolved to find out more about her the next time they met. Her name, at least. He could not go on calling her "the White Lady" forever. And by knowing her identity, he would know how easy or difficult it would be to arrange their meetings in the future. He knew a bit more about the habits of the men of the *ton* than most of their ladies did. If her husband was indulging in his own extramarital affairs, it would be all the better for her. And if they must be discreet, he would plan accordingly.

Nothing was going to keep her from him. Of that, he would make certain. Now that he had found such a passionate partner, he would not let her go.

It was only a pity she was married. He could almost imagine proposing marriage to one like her.

The thought brought a flash of shock, followed by a rapid shift of emotions ranging from confusion to fear and back to surprise.

Yet he knew it was true. She *was* a woman he could spend his life with. And suddenly the thought that she belonged to another was more than he could bear. He would not allow anything, *anyone*, to keep them apart. They were meant to be together and he intended to make certain that they would.

4

In the morning, Juliet felt a twinge of guilt when she informed the maid that she was indisposed and would not be able to join the children. But with her emotions in such a tangle, she needed a few hours of rest to restore her composure.

It had been sheer luck she had been able to slip back into the house unnoticed, as late as she had returned. The dress and mask were hidden in a corner of the attic. Later, she would find time to hide them better— or burn them altogether. For she never dare wear them again.

She lay back against the pillows, the aches in her body nothing compared to the ache in her heart. Belmont had been beyond imagination as a lover—skillful in his caresses, tender to the point where she almost believed he cared for her, insistent and demanding as he brought them both to their pleasure. And, oh, the pleasure he brought.

But she valued his tenderness the most. She had seen it often when he dealt with the children and it thrilled her to find he dealt with his lovers in that same caring fashion. As well as saddened her. For she knew that she would not be able to savor that tenderness again. One night would be all she ever had.

Sighing, Juliet began to realize just how difficult it was going to be for her in the future. Belmont's visits would be a constant reminder of the night she had spent in his arms. Juliet feared she would never be able to forget unless she severed the connection between them. But that was too unbearable to contemplate. The pain of never seeing him again outweighed the pain of seeing him, and knowing they could not be together.

Geoffrey must come first. She had recklessly risked his future with this wild escapade, and she must ensure that her ill-considered folly did not cause him further harm. He was already saddled with the brand of illegitimacy; he must not be deprived of Belmont's kindness because of his mother's foolish passions. She would have to keep that firmly in mind whenever she was in Belmont's presence. It might be the one thing that kept her sane.

For several days, Belmont went through his daily routines with ill-concealed impatience. Nothing seemed important except hearing from his new lover. Even visiting with the children did not refresh him as it usually did.

He could not expect to hear from her immediately, of course. After all, it had been over a week between their first two meetings. But he had barely been able to endure that separation—and that was before he discovered just how delectable his mystery lady was. Now, every minute they were apart was an unbearable agony.

There were so many things he wanted to share with her. Did she think of him as often as he thought of her? Did she want him as deeply as he still wanted her? That one night had only sparked his appetite; he wanted her now more than ever.

After three days, when he had heard nothing from her, his temper grew considerably shorter. On the fourth day, he threatened to fire both his secretary and his butler before reining in his anger. The fifth day nearly found him entangled in a duel over the honor of a lady he *ignored* at a ball. By the sixth day, Belmont locked himself in his study and stared glumly at the drooping roses he had not found the strength to remove.

One. Two. Three. Four. He counted the petals that lay upon his desk. Five. Six. Seven. An instant of panic gripped him and he fought against it, but he could not shake his fear.

What if she did not intend to see him again? What if that one night had been all he was to have from her?

It was a thought too frightening to consider.

On the seventh day, he called in Bow Street. He would find her no matter the cost. He must.

The Runners were not optimistic. He had laughably little to go on. A lady dressed in a white domino, with a distinctive mask. Her height he could guess, and her shape. He knew her eyes were brown. Her lips were tender and enticing, her legs long and shapely—but Bow Street did not care about that. They wanted more concrete things, such as where she lived or her name. If he knew that, he would not need their help!

They promised to do what they could, but they were

not the least bit encouraging. If the lady wished to remain unknown, she had done a very good job of making certain she would. Belmont felt a growing sense of despair.

As the days passed and his fears grew, he found himself spending more and more time in Chelsea. The children, not surprisingly, were the only thing that brought him out of his gloom, however temporarily.

He eagerly joined in rousing games of Goose, spinning the teetotum with the enthusiasm of a hardened gamester. He patiently set out alphabet cards for Arabella and listened attentively while Samuel recited his tables of multiplication. He spoke French with Suzanne and Lucilla, and conjugated Latin verbs with Stephen and Geoffrey.

As he watched Miss Waldron go about her duties with calm complacency, he felt a strange urge to confide his fears and hopes to her. He found her serenity comforting and wished he could borrow some of it. She would be shocked at his tale, of course. She had never once voiced open disapproval of his life, but despite her own youthful transgression, he knew she looked askance at his life of pleasure and excess. His obsession with a mysterious lady he had only met twice would not wring any sympathy from her.

The children provided him with momentary comfort, but it was a transitory feeling that faded as soon as he left the house. He demanded daily reports from the Runners, but they had yet uncovered no trace of the mysterious woman in the white domino. No one had seen her entering his house, and no one had seen her leave. On the slight chance that she had come in a hired carriage instead of her own, Belmont insisted that they interview every hackney driver in the metropolis. It would take time and money. He did not begrudge the money. It was the time that was important.

He attended every party to which he received an invitation. But rather than dancing or indulging in flirtation, he prowled the rooms, searching the face of every woman he saw. He had never imagined just how many brown-eyed ladies there were in London.

Some he could easily dismiss, for they were too tall, or too short, or too plump, or too thin. He narrowed down the possibilities as far as he could, then pounced upon the likely suspects with the quickness of a cat upon a mouse. In his wake, he left a train of enraged husbands, women who were either insulted or flattered by his attentions, and inquisitive whisperings among his friends. But for all his efforts, he could not find her anywhere.

Once again, Belmont found himself sitting in his study in the shadowy dawn. He was tired—more than tired, exhausted. He sat with brandy in hand but he barely took notice of his glass, looking instead at the withered brown petals that covered his desk. He grabbed a handful and crumbled them between his fingers.

He was not going to find her. He had feared it for days, but knew it now with a certainty that caused his blood to turn to ice. He also knew that she had never intended to see him again. That one night had been the last—the only—that they would have together.

Why did it matter so much? He could not even begin to count the number of women he had dallied with during his lifetime. Why was this one so different? Why did he feel such an all-consuming need for her?

A need that went beyond sheer physical want. He would be content now to merely see her, talk to her. Anything, only to be with her again.

He slammed his fist down upon his desk. He had spent all his adult life in an endless round of pleasure, but he had harmed no one. Why was he being forced to suffer now? Certainly, he had availed himself of innumerable women's charms, committed adultery, and fathered several illegitimate children. But he had adequately recompensed those who had pleased him, had never bedded a married woman who did not ask him first, and he doted upon his children.

He had been without a woman for a fortnight, but the mere thought of slacking his desires with another lady was an immediate bucket of cold water upon his heated system. He could not imagine experiencing pleasure again unless it was in the White Lady's arms. The thought was frightening to one who put such a great stock in pleasure.

Why had she come to him at all, if she only meant it to be for one time? Was it merely a game? Had she devised the whole event as a marvelous jest, with himself the intended butt? If that was her plan, she had succeeded well.

Still, he could not quite believe she planned the whole episode as a lark. Belmont had been with enough women to know when their pleasure was genuine or feigned, and there had been too much intensity in her response that night for her feelings to be anything but genuine. She had enjoyed herself as much as he.

Then why would she not see him again? He would promise her anything if she returned; he would make no attempts to learn her identity. She could wear a mask in his bed at all times, if that was her wish. But how could he tell her she was safe if he could not find her?

He lifted his glass with a shaky hand and took a long, burning swallow of brandy. Taking a look at the ormolu clock upon the mantel, he shook his head at his folly. Brandy at five in the morning. It was not a good sign. He was falling apart, yet felt helpless to stop the disintegration.

Belmont realized, with a strange feeling that twisted his insides, that he had never felt this way about a woman before. If he did not know better, he would almost say he loved her. But he could not be in love with a woman he had only met twice, whose name he did not know, whose face he had never seen. It was a laughable idea.

But if not love, what was this discomposing sensation that flooded his being whenever he thought of her? It was not mere lust—he was quite familiar with that sensation. No, it went beyond physical wanting. It was deeper, stronger.

Never before had he thought one could experience any feeling stronger than lust. What was it then, this mixture of longing and pain, elation, and despair.

It could not possibly be love.

Yet why else would he spend all his waking hours thinking of her? Why were his dreams filled with tantalizing, elusive glimpses of her? She was the only woman he wanted, the only woman he could imagine wanting.

The only thing he ever wanted that he feared he could never have. And it was his damnable luck to have fallen in love with her.

Too wrapped up in her own misery, Juliet remained unaware of Belmont's pain. Every moment he spent in the house was exquisite torture for her. She was grateful for the extra attention he showered upon the children, for it allowed her to keep out of his presence as much as possible. But he spent so much time in Chelsea that she could not elude him entirely. She strove to keep their contacts brief, and businesslike.

If he noticed that the formerly friendly Miss Waldron treated him with a bit more coolness than before, he did not comment upon it. And she was very careful to make certain that she did not allow her eyes to dwell upon him for more than a brief moment, so he would not see the longing in her gaze.

Each time he came to the house she resolved to approach him and ask for the extra holiday time he had promised her. If she could only get away from him for a while, things would be better. She would use the peace and serenity of the countryside to patch up her tattered resolve and to purge her mind of him.

However, she knew the latter was a hopeless task. As long as she was forced to deal with him, she would never be able to forget him. For Geoffrey's sake, she needed to stay in Belmont's employ. But she was not certain whether she would be able to survive in her position for much longer without growing mad.

Each time she saw him, her longing only increased. He was everything she wanted—and everything she could not have. She had thrown away any chance of happiness at the age of seventeen. That brief lapse from propriety had ruined her chances for marriage and happiness. Dreams were all she would ever have now. Dreams of Belmont. Dreams of the life they could have lived together, the talks they would have, the children they would raise. The nights they would spend in each other's arms. She was filled with a deep need that nearly made her ill with its intensity.

But because she loved him she could not—dare not—let him know.

She had thought she had paid a deep price for her youthful folly already. Now she saw that all that had come before was only a prelude to the pain she experienced now. Then it had been easy to reconcile herself to a life outside the circles of society, a life without a husband and family. She had Geoffrey, after all. But now she knew that she wanted more, wanted a life with a husband who loved her. Wanted Belmont.

And she could never have him.

On a particularly cheerless, wet May morning, Belmont braved the elements and rode his horse toward Chelsea. He was miserable anyway; a thorough wetting would not worsen his temper. There was always the chance that he would be able to forget his troubles for a bit while he romped with the children.

The dreariness of the weather had permeated even the usually cheerful house in Chelsea, for he found the drawing room in turmoil when he entered. Freddie stood on the sofa, jumping up and down. Arabella was flinging her alphabet cards onto the floor with gleeful laughter, while Suzanne chased Lucilla around the room. Belmont looked about for a sign of Miss Waldron and finally spotted her, standing over a sullen-faced Henry who scrubbed at an ugly stain upon the carpet.

Juliet took one look at Belmont and her face brightened with relief. "Thank goodness you are here, my lord. I cannot tell you what a morning this has been."

Belmont turned about and began barking out orders. "Freddie, sit down. Arabella, pick up your cards. Suzanne, stop chasing your sister and take a seat at once."

Juliet looked on in amazement as the children hastened to comply. They had totally ignored her when she had given the same commands.

"Now," continued Belmont, "what do you think you are doing to poor Miss Waldron here? I come into the room and you are acting like a bunch of wild savages. Is this how you have been taught to behave?"

"No," they chorused loudly.

"Do you want Miss Waldron to take a disgust of you and leave today?"

"No," they echoed with even more intensity.

"Good." He glared at them sternly.

Juliet came to his side. "Thank you, my lord. I rather fear we have an excess of high spirits in the house this morning. 'Tis the weather."

"I see." He looked speculatively at the children. "What you need is some rousing entertainment," he said. "A game of some sort."

"Cricket!" cried Harry.

"Goose," shouted Lucilla.

"Houth," lisped Suzanne, whose two front teeth had fallen out the previous week.

The viscount shook his head at each suggestion. "No, those will not do." He thought for a moment. "I have it. Hide-and-seek! You shall hide and Miss Waldron and I will try to find you."

The children dashed out of the room before Juliet could utter a word of protest.

Belmont looked at her with a sheepish grin. "I thought you might appreciate a few moments of peace and quiet," he said.

Juliet sank down upon a chair. "Thank you, my lord."

"This should earn you ten or fifteen minutes, at least," he said. "Shall I ring for tea?"

"No," Juliet said hastily. She stood and walked over to the table where Arabella's alphabet cards lay in a tottering pile. With shaky fingers, she attempted to put them in order.

Belmont came up beside her and took them from her

hands. "I did not intend for you to spend the time at your duties, Miss Waldron. Please, sit. You have earned a rest."

Juliet froze at his nearness, unable to tear her gaze from his face.

A familiar scent assailed his nostrils. Belmont stared at her with a puzzled expression before he glanced quickly about the room. Was he going mad? "Do you smell roses, Miss Waldron?"

She stared back at him. "I am wearing rosewater . . ."

"Ah." Now that he thought about the matter, he realized that Miss Waldron always smelled faintly of roses. It had meant little to him . . . before. "Is something amiss, Miss Waldron?" he asked, disturbed at the way she still stared at him. "Have I perhaps forgotten to shave? Or wash my face?"

Juliet hastily turned away. "Excuse me," she mumbled and raced from the room. Tears filled her eyes and blinded her as she stumbled up the stairs toward her chamber.

It was never going to succeed. It was truly impossible for her to remain in this house any longer. Despite all the opportunities it offered Geoffrey, the hell it created for her was too much to endure.

Why, oh why had she set out upon this course? Why could she not have remained content to admire him from afar? It had been one thing to sneak surreptitious glances at him and wonder what it would be like to be held in his arms, to be kissed and caressed by him. It was quite another to know exactly how it felt. And it was far too painful to know that she could not feel it again.

She would never be able to survive in this situation. She had been a fool to think it was possible. Resigning her post was the only course open to her now. The thought was frightening, for the chances of her finding an equally amenable situation were slim. Not only did the viscount pay her far more than the average governess earned, he also allowed Geoffrey to stay with her, and educated him as well. She could not expect another employer to do the same. She might find someone who was willing to overlook her unfortunate past, but not with Geoffrey there as a constant reminder of it. He would have to go away to school.

The thought of being parted from him brought a deep ache to her heart, but she knew that such separation was inevitable. She could afford a year of tuition, she thought, before she must seek scholarship aid. That would give him the opportunity to start out on a equal footing with the other boys at least.

She would have to ask Belmont to write her a recommendation. Juliet dreaded the questions he would ask, the hurt look he would express when she told him she wished to leave. But it could not be helped. She had no other choice.

Her decisions made, Juliet carefully washed her face and smoothed her hair. The children would become restless if she did not seek them out. She prayed Belmont had remained downstairs. If she found the children quickly, she could take the girls to their lessons while Belmont remained with the boys. Juliet did not think she was ready to speak to him about her resignation yet. She must find the right words to mollify his curiosity.

Hastening down the corridor, Juliet first stepped into the nursery. Arthur squealed with glee when he saw her and demanded that she give him a hug. Of the older children, there was no sign, and when Juliet directed an enquiring look at nurse, the girl shook her head.

She investigated all the bedrooms on the floor, looking in the cupboards and under the beds, but found nary a soul. She was preparing to take the servant's stairs to the first floor when she noticed that the door to the attic was ajar.

Pulling the door open, Juliet tip-toed up the stairs. How clever of the children to hide up here, for it was a place they seldom visited.

The light shone dimly through the dusty window at the end of the room as Juliet scanned the cluttered expanse. She stopped and listened carefully, knowing it would be impossible for the children to remain silent for long. It gave her an unfair advantage, of course, but one she would not hesitate to use.

"They are not here."

She whirled about at the sound of Belmont's voice. He stepped out from behind a trunk, clutching something long and white in his hand. It took an instant before she recognized it, then she froze in dread.

The dress. He had found the dress.

"An interesting garment," Belmont said. "A rather unusual thing to find in an attic. But not nearly as unusual as this."

He held up the toque and mask.

Juliet wished she could sink through the floor and vanish forever. Her cheeks burned hot and she truly wished to die.

"It was you," he murmured in hoarse surprise. "All the time it was you."

He took a step toward her and she fought the urge to retreat.

"Why?" he asked, his face a mirror of his surprise and shock. "Good God, why?"

Juliet bowed her head. "I am sorry," she whispered. "So very sorry." She felt the tears welling up in her eyes. She was not even to be given the opportunity to

escape now. Folly had once again ruined her as surely
as it had all those years ago.

"I can be gone in the morning," she said hastily.
"Nurse can deal with the children until you find someone else and . . ."

"No!" Belmont stared at her. Miss Waldron was the
mysterious lady in white? Prim, proper Miss Waldron
was the lady who had brought his so much ecstasy? "It
cannot be."

"I wish it were not," she moaned.

He had been in agony for nearly a fortnight, wanting
her, needing her, despairing of ever finding her again.
And all along he had seen her almost daily, here at the
house, and never once suspected.

Belmont looked at her closely, examining her eyes,
her lips. Now that he made the effort, he saw it, of
course. How could he have been so blind?

Because he had judged her wrongly from the first,
and that had forever influenced his view of her. He
never suspected Miss Waldron because he had only seen
the outward signs of a decorous governess. An image
that now looked to be strongly at odds with the lady
who hid behind it.

He saw her shift restlessly on her feet.

"May I go downstairs now?" she asked. "The children will be growing anxious."

Belmont glared at her. "Downstairs? Do you think I
am going to let you out of my sight for even a moment,
Miss Wal—damn it, what is your given name?"

"Juliet," she whispered.

"Juliet." His green eyes glittered warmly at the sound
of her name on his lips. "Do you know how hard I
have tried to find you? I have had Bow Street looking
for you this last week."

Juliet stared at him in surprise. "You have?"

Belmont reached out and took her chin in his hand, lifting her face until he could look into her eyes. He saw the glint of tears in them.

"Why? Tell me why you came to me, Juliet."

She drew a deep breath. There was no point in dissembling any longer. He may as well know the entire, miserable truth. "Because I wanted to pretend for one night that you loved me."

A faint smile flickered over his lips. "That was all? You do not ask much."

"How can I? You know what I am, who I am. Why I am."

"I know that you are the most exasperating woman I have ever met," he said softly. He released her chin and stroked the back of his hand against her cheek, brushing away the trace of a tear. "Do you have any idea how I have suffered this last fortnight with the growing fear that I would never see you again?" He laughed. "How very wrong I was."

"Why did you wish to find me?"

Laughing, he took a step toward her and placed his arm around her waist. "Because, my dear Juliet, you have totally disrupted my life. I can barely eat, sleep, or even think. The only thing I can concentrate on is you." He pulled her closer until she was against his chest. "Why would you not come back?" he asked. "I wanted you so much."

Juliet shivered at the intensity of his expression. "I only meant it to be for one night. I knew there could be nothing more between us."

"One night was enough for you?" She shook her head and his smile widened. " 'Twill be an interesting experiment," he said at last. "How many nights shall it take? Five? Ten? A hundred? A lifetime?" He lifted an errant curl and tucked it behind her ear. "A lifetime, I think, Juliet. Do you not agree?"

Juliet's eyes widened with disbelief.

"I cannot promise you more than that," he said. "Although perhaps we shall be pleasantly surprised when we pass on to the other side. But will a lifetime be enough, my dear?" His voice turned soft and silky. "Say it will. Say you will stay with me, now, and not ever leave again."

Society would be shocked, Juliet thought, but her resolve weakened. She could not expect a lifetime, of course. But she would take as much as he would give her, and be grateful.

Belmont's lips covered hers, preventing her reply. He demanded her response, forced it from her, and sighed his satisfaction when she melted against him, wrapping her arms about his neck.

"You were meant to be with me, Juliet," he said fiercely. "Do not deny what is right. We are right together." He kissed her again. "Marry me, Juliet. Marry me so we can spend all our days together."

"You cannot possibly wish to marry me."

"Oh, but I do." He stroked her cheek with his finger. "I love you, Juliet," he whispered. "As foreign as that feeling is to me, it is the only explanation for the hell you have put me through. You owe me some happiness."

"It would cause an enormous scandal."

He grinned. "I expect it shall. All the tattle-baskets who giggled and gossiped about the lovely governess I hired will feel vindicated." His eyes grew soft. "You are not afraid of the talk, are you? I know it will cause some comment at first, but I do not think it will last. By next autumn, everyone will have forgotten you were once my children's governess."

"I . . . I do not know what to say."

"Say yes." His lips brushed against her cheek. "Say yes, Juliet. I warn you, I will not permit you to leave this attic until you agree."

He gave her no chance to answer as he wrapped his arms around her and kissed her with a fierce longing that left them both breathless. "Say yes," he whispered as he ran his tongue across her lips.

"Yes," Juliet said. "Yes, oh yes."

She raised her joyful face to him and kissed him with a fervency that led Belmont to suspect that a lifetime with the same woman would be a satisfying experience. Enormously satisfying.

Mad, Bad, and
Dangerous to Know

by

Mary Jo Putney

He was going to be hanged on Tuesday.

Andrew Kane supposed that he should be contemplating his imminent demise, but the misery of the present left no room to worry about next week. The scorched plains of Texas were dismal at the best of times, and in his present situation, they were a fair approximation of hell.

The horse ahead of him kicked up a swirl of dust and Kane began to cough with parched painfulness. If he didn't get water soon, he wouldn't live long enough to be hanged. No point in asking his escorts for a drink, though. When Kane had done that yesterday, Biff, the more vicious of the two, had knocked him to the ground, sneering that he wasn't gonna to pamper no low-down, murdering son of a bitch.

While Biff underlined his remark with a kick in the ribs, the other of the temporary deputies, Whittles, had chimed in. "Witless," as Kane mentally dubbed him, had waved a tin cup of water and said that mebbe they'd give the prisoner some if he got down on his knees and asked for it real purty.

Kane might have complied if he'd thought it would

do any good, but he knew his guards were just looking for entertainment. After a good belly laugh over his groveling, Witless would have poured the water on the ground just out of reach.

Tiredly, Kane raised his handcuffed wrists and wiped his sweaty forehead with one sleeve. In a couple of hours they would be in Forlorn Hope, the last night's stop before reaching their destination, Prairie City. He supposed that in the interests of keeping him alive for his execution, the sheriff in Prairie City would give him water. It wouldn't do to deprive the crowd that would turn out to see justice visited on the ungodly.

Kane had been to a hanging once, when he had been such a young fool that he'd thought it would be entertaining. The convict had been a skinny little fellow, too light to break his neck when the trap fell away under his feet. The poor devil had swung back and forth for quite a spell, gasping and kicking. Kane hadn't seen the end; he'd been behind the livery stable, spewing his guts out. He never went to a hanging again. And, though he was no saint, he sure as hell hadn't expected to end on the gallows himself.

He ran a dry tongue over his cracked lips. As a boy he'd wanted an exciting life, and he'd gotten it. Maybe he should have wished for a little less excitement.

Elizabeth Holden wearily contemplated the yellow dust that saturated her mourning gown. Black wasn't a very practical color in a dry Texas summer, but with both her husband and her father dead in the last month, she didn't have much choice about what to wear. And heaven knew that black suited her mood. She shifted in her saddle, hoping to find a more comfortable position.

A soft southern voice said, "You feeling poorly, Miz Holden?"

Liza managed a smile for her escort. Since there wasn't anything he could do for what ailed her, there was no point in making him worry. "I'm fine, Mr. Jackson, just a little tired. I'll be glad to reach Forlorn Hope. As I recall, the hotel there is a good one."

Tom Jackson nodded, but his dark eyes were still concerned. "Mebbe I can hire a wagon to take you the rest of the way. Mr. Holden will have my hide if anything happens to you."

Liza felt a chill, as if clutching hands were closing around her. Determinedly she shook off the image, not wanting to think of the dreary future that stretched before her. "Truly, I'm fine. The road is so bad that horseback is easier than a wagon would be."

Mr. Jackson nodded, accepting her decision, but the compassion in his eyes almost reduced her to tears. He'd worked for the Holdens for years and must have a fair idea what her life had been like as bride of the late Billie Holden. Not that he could know the worst; even Billie's parents hadn't known just how difficult their son had been. They hadn't wanted to know.

The rest of the ride was accomplished in silence. The town of Forlorn Hope was better than its name, but not much. Besides the hotel, there were two saloons, a handful of stores, and a couple dozen straggling houses. The town was on the route between Liza's girlhood home in Willow Point and her in-laws' ranch outside Prairie City, but with her father dead and his general store sold, she'd probably never come this way again. No great loss, she thought dully as her companion helped her from her horse.

After he carried her luggage into the hotel and located a clerk to register her, Liza said, "Didn't you mention that a cousin of yours lives here, Mr. Jackson?"

"Yes, ma'am, the blacksmith." He smiled reminiscently. "His wife Molly is the best Alabama cook in Texas."

"Then take the rest of the day off and go see them," Liza suggested. "Spend the night if you like. We came through in such a hurry two weeks ago that you didn't have time for a visit, so you should make up for that now."

Mr. Jackson hesitated, clearly tempted. "I should stay in the hotel bunkhouse so's I'm nearby if you need anything."

"I won't need anything. I'll take a bath, have some food sent up, and go to bed early," she assured him. "Think of the time off as a thank you for all the help you were with my father's funeral and all."

He surveyed her face, then nodded. "If you're sure, Miz Holden. I'll come for you at nine in the morning."

The hot bath was wonderful for Liza's sore muscles. After she'd soaped and soaked, she lay back in the tin tub and studied her body, trying to see if her abdomen was starting to enlarge. But she could detect no change. If anything, she'd lost weight in the last weeks. Hard to imagine that a baby was growing inside her.

Not a baby—her jailer.

Desolation swept through her, but before tears could destroy her fragile composure, she climbed from the tub and briskly toweled herself dry. She must not allow herself to sink into melancholy, for she needed all her strength.

Thinking that she'd read a bit before going to bed, Liza donned her other black dress, which was wrinkled but clean. Then she began brushing out her wheat-blond hair. It was still light outside, so she drifted to the window and gazed absently down into the street. A half dozen people were in sight, none of them in any great hurry.

Her eye was caught by the wreckage of a recently burned building. Thinking back, she recalled that there had been a combined town office and jail on the site before.

She was about to turn away from the window when three dusty riders appeared. Curiously she saw that one of the horses was on a lead, and the black-clad rider on its back was slumped forward as if barely able to stay upright.

When the newcomers were opposite the hotel, the heavyset man in the lead saw the charred ruins of the jail. Scowling ferociously, he halted the group right under Liza's window, so close that she could see his small, piggy eyes. After asking a question of an idler sitting in front of the hotel, Pig-Eyes dismounted and tethered his horse to the hitching rail. Then he went to the led horse, whose rider wore the characteristic black suit, ruffled shirt, and brocade waistcoat of a gambler.

Pig-Eyes grabbed the gambler's arm and jerked him from his saddle. The man in black pitched heavily from his mount, barely managing to catch his saddle horn in time to prevent himself from crashing to the ground. As he regained his balance, Liza saw that his hands were cuffed together. A prisoner. She wondered what he had done.

The third rider, a thin, weasely fellow, dismounted and laid a rough hand on the gambler's arm. In spite of his physical condition, there was defiance in the prisoner's posture as he raised his head and answered back.

The results were explosive. With a snarl of fury, Weasel drew back his fist and slugged the other man in the stomach. As the gambler folded over, he lashed out with one foot at his tormentor, his boot connecting just below the knee. Weasel howled and almost collapsed. When he recovered, he and Pig-Eyes began beating and kicking the prisoner. Even when he fell to the ground, the kicks and blows continued, right under Liza's horrified gaze.

Fury blazed through her, burning away her fatigue and depression. Without waiting to see more, she raced from her room, taking the stairs two at a time, her loose hair flying behind her. When she reached the street, she saw that a half dozen townspeople were watching the beating. Though most wore uncomfortable expressions, no one intervened. It wasn't healthy to come between angry, armed men and their victim.

Liza was too incensed to feel such compunction. Furiously she cried, "Stop that this instant, you brutes!"

From sheer surprise, Pig-Eyes and Weasel obeyed, both of them turning to stare at her. Liza took advantage of the pause to say fiercely, "You should be ashamed of yourselves, beating a man who is bound and helpless."

Weasel shifted uncomfortably, his bravado vanishing in the presence of a lady. "Beggin' your pardon, ma'am, but Andrew Kane ain't helpless. He's quicker'n a snake and twice as mean."

"That doesn't give you the right to beat him to death," Liza retorted. "What kind of men are you, to attack someone who can't defend himself?"

She looked down at the gambler, who lay still in the dusty street, blood flowing from numerous cuts. Under the dirt and bruises he looked young and vulnerable, not mean at all. Not that Liza was much of a judge of character; when she'd met Billie Holden, she had thought he was kind and honest.

A lean man with drooping mustaches and a tin badge on his vest pushed through the small crowd of silent onlookers. "I'm Sheriff Taylor," he barked. "What's going on here?"

Pig-Eyes said, "My name's Biff Burns. Me and my partner Whittles are temporary deputies who are taking this murderer to Prairie City for hanging." He prodded his prisoner with one booted toe. "We was gonna put him in the jail for the night, but I see it's burnt down."

The sheriff scowled. "It was fired by some folks from Rapid City. They want to see their town made county seat, so they burned down our public building."

Uninterested in local politics, Burns said, "Where can we put this son of a bitch tonight?" The weasel hissed something and Burns flushed, then glanced askance at Liza. "Beggin' your pardon, ma'am."

After giving him an icy glance, she knelt by Kane. Burns exclaimed, "Don't get so close, ma'am. He's dangerous."

Ignoring the words, Liza took her handkerchief and began blotting blood from a slash on the man's forehead. Long, dark lashes flickered open to reveal eyes of piercing blue—gambler's eyes, that saw everything and gave away nothing.

For a long moment their gazes held. She saw intelligence, shrewdness, anger, and determination in the blue depths—the qualities of a man used to living on the edge of danger. It was suddenly easy to believe that he was a murderer. Disconcerted, Liza sat back on her heels.

Yet when he spoke, Kane was polite enough. "A pleasure to make your acquaintance, darlin'." He had a crisp accent that she couldn't identify because his voice was a barely audible rasp.

Seeing his cracked lips, Liza asked, "Do you need water?"

Desperate longing flared in his eyes, though he tried to keep his voice steady. "I'd be much obliged."

She glanced up at Burns. "Give me your canteen."

Biff started to protest, then subsided, unwilling to argue with a lady in front of a steadily growing audience. He untied the canteen and handed it to Liza. She opened it and dribbled a few drops into Kane's mouth. His tanned throat moved convulsively as he swallowed. Slowly she poured more, careful not to give him more than he could manage. From the way he drank, she guessed that it had been a long time—too long—since he had been given water. Her anger rose again. He might be a murderer, but even a mad dog didn't deserve such treatment.

The sheriff said, "You can put your prisoner in the hotel storeroom, Burns. It's got a solid door that locks and a window too small for a man to get through. Won't be the first time it held a prisoner. He'll be safe there for the night."

Burns cleared his throat. "We'll put him in as soon as the lady gets out of the way."

Liza glanced up, her gaze going to the sheriff, who seemed reasonable. "This man needs medical attention."

Sheriff Taylor shook his head. "There's no doctor in Forlorn Hope."

Liza got to her feet and gave Burns a challenging glance. "Then I'll tend him myself."

Outraged, Biff said, "Nothin' wrong with that son of a . . ." Remembering his language, he coughed. "He's not bad hurt, ma'am, and 'sides, in a coupla days it won't matter. A lady shouldn't concern herself with trash like him."

Liza's eyes narrowed. "Sheriff Taylor, the constitution forbids cruel and unusual punishment. Doesn't that mean that even prisoners deserve food, water, and medical treatment?"

The sheriff shrugged. "If the lady wants to play nursemaid, let her. Most gamblers have a soft spot for women, so he probably won't hurt her, though you might want to chain him up, just in case."

Burns and Whittles grabbed Kane by the upper arms and hauled him to his feet. Not wanting to watch, Liza stalked back into the hotel. She didn't understand her need to champion a criminal who probably deserved everything he got, but the impulse was too strong to deny. Perhaps it was because she felt so helpless about her own life. By taking shameless advantage of the reverence westerners had for women, she could do something to help a fellow being.

It was a nice bonus that her good deed would also keep her too busy to think about her own problems, at least for a while.

Liza spent the next half hour collecting what she would need to treat Kane's wounds, plus food and drink since the deputies couldn't be trusted to feed their prisoner. It was almost dark by the time she made her way to the storeroom, which lay behind a larger chamber which was used as a second dining room when the hotel was busy. At the moment, the only occupant was Biff. His chair was tilted back and his booted feet rested on the edge of a table while he idly shuffled cards and looked bored.

When Liza entered, the deputy's expression brightened and the front legs of the chair hit the floor with a bang. The frank admiration in his gaze made her grateful for the fact that she was wearing mourning; even the Biffs of the world would seldom force unwelcome flirtation on a new widow.

She nodded toward an unused lantern sitting on the sideboard. "Will you light that and bring it in, Mr. Burns?" As he hastened to comply, she murmured, "You're very kind."

The deputy opened the door to the storeroom and she stepped inside. It made a good cell, for the only window was high on the wall and too small to be used by anyone but a child. The walls were lined with shelves, and sacks, barrels, and boxes were stacked around the perimeter of the room. The prisoner had been dumped unceremoniously in the middle of the plank floor.

Though Kane had been lying motionless, his eyes flickered open when they entered. Accompanied by a metallic rattle, he pushed his battered body up so that he was sitting against a sack of flour. Liza saw that his right handcuff had been removed from his wrist, then locked to a chain that looped around a supporting post in the corner. Though he had one hand free and the chain was long enough to allow some movement, she disliked seeing a man treated like a dog on a leash.

Wanting to get rid of the deputy and his hungry stare, she said, "You've had a long, hard ride, Mr. Burns." She set her tray on the floor near Kane. "There's no need for you to stay here if you'd rather go to the saloon for a bite of supper."

Biff licked his lips as duty wrestled with desire. "I shouldn't leave you alone with him, ma'am."

She made an impatient gesture. "Your prisoner is in no condition to hurt anyone. And if he does get rambunctious, I'll just move out of reach."

"I'll have to lock you in," Biff warned. "Can't risk letting him break out."

She shrugged. "As you wish. It's going to take time to clean his wounds. You can let me out when you've finished your own dinner."

"That's what I'll do, then," Biff decided. He hung the lantern from a nail so its soft rays illuminated most of the storeroom, then turned and left.

Kane had been watching in silence, but as the key turned in the door, locking them in together, he drawled, "He's right, darlin'—you shouldn't be here. Twelve good men and true have decided that I am mad, bad, and dangerous to know."

Her eyes widened, and not only because of his cool English accent. Who would have thought a murderer would be so well-educated? Well, she had had a decent education, too, reading every book that had come through her father's store. "Don't try to convince me that you're Lord Byron," she said briskly, "because I am certainly not Lady Caroline Lamb."

Startled pleasure lit Kane's tanned face and his tension eased. "If you're not Lady Caroline Lamb, who are you?" He examined her with appreciative interest. "Guardian angels aren't supposed to be so luscious-looking."

She found herself coloring under his scrutiny. Not wanting to use the married name that she had come to hate, she replied, "My name is Liza. You're an Englishman?"

"I was born in England, but I'm an American now. I came here when I was twenty-one."

"Are you a remittance man?"

"Well, my family didn't actually pay me to keep out of sight," he said with a crooked smile, "but they did heave a vast sigh of relief when I decided to see the world after I was sent down from Oxford. That means I was thrown out," he added when he saw that she didn't understand the term. "The professors said that I lacked a proper respect for rules and tradition. They were right."

"Many of your countrymen must feel the same way, because there are plenty of them around." She'd always enjoyed the Britons who stopped by her father's store, and had encouraged them to talk just so she could listen to their lovely accents. Kane himself spoke with a delicious blend of English crispness and American idiom.

After dipping a pad of cotton into the bowl of warm water, she began cleaning the lacerations on Kane's face. Under the cuts, dust, and several days' growth of beard, she discovered that his features were strong-boned and handsome. She guessed that he'd broken his share of female hearts. His intense blue eyes were disturbing at such close range.

He winced when she touched the deepest gash, which started on his forehead and curved down his left temple. Thinking that conversation would distract him from the discomfort, she asked, "What made you decide to stay in this country?"

"When I first reached Denver, I went to a livery stable to rent a horse. The only man in sight was a rough-looking chap sitting on a stump, so I asked him where his master was. He spat a stream of tobacco juice that just missed my foot, then said that the son of a bitch hadn't been born yet." Kane chuckled. "I knew instantly I'd found my spiritual home." His amused glance went to Liza. "Excuse the profanity, but cleaning up the fellow's language would dilute the flavor of the encounter."

Liza smiled, unoffended. She was tolerant of ungenteel language, for her father's customers were frequently profane. She had found it touching when tall, bristly cowhands blushed and apologized with the shyness of little boys. But Kane was another sort of man entirely, one who was completely sure of himself, even now, when he was on the verge of execution.

The thought produced a jolt of disorientation. It was impossible, obscene, that the man beneath her hands would soon be dead. He was too alive, too vividly real.

Distressed, she bowed her head and moistened a pad with whiskey, then patted the cuts she had already cleaned.

Though the alcohol must have stung like blazes, he endured it stoically. When she had finished working on his face, he remarked, "A pity to waste good whiskey on cleaning wounds when I'm going to die anyway."

She chuckled and reached for the china mug. "I should have guessed you might want a drink more than nursing."

"A sign of weakness on my part," he said with self-mockery, "but the last fortnight has been . . . difficult. I wouldn't mind a bit of oblivion."

"I don't think there's enough here for oblivion," she said as she poured whiskey from the small bottle. "Will you settle for relaxation?"

He laughed out loud. Strange. He hadn't expected to laugh again before he died. Nor had he expected to be alone with a beautiful young lady. He feasted his eyes on her, for she was the loveliest sight he had seen in years. The loveliest he was likely to see for the rest of his life.

To his regret, she had pinned up the thick fair hair that had danced loose around her shoulders when she had come charging out of the hotel, but a few wheat-colored tendrils still curled temptingly around her face. And what a face it was—heart-shaped, with delicate features and wondrous gray eyes that regarded the world without flinching. The women were one of the things he liked most about America. The best of them were direct, confident, as strong as a man, not at all like the simpering misses he'd known in England.

After putting the mug into his left hand, Liza turned her attention to his right wrist, the one that was still handcuffed. Her lips pursed when she pushed the cuff up and discovered that the metal had gouged a circle of ugly lacerations. Without comment, she began cleaning the raw flesh. Her light, cool fingers were soothing as she cleaned and bandaged his right wrist, then the equally damaged left one.

He sipped the whiskey slowly, wanting it to last. It hit hard on an empty stomach. He welcomed the harsh burn, for it eased the aches and pains he'd suffered at the hands of the deputies. The whiskey affected him in other ways, too, and when Liza bent forward, he had to fight an impulse to pull out her hair pins.

Yet much as he would have enjoyed releasing the sunstreaked brilliance of her hair, he restrained himself. He daren't alarm her, for he needed her kindness too much. Already he hated the knowledge that soon she would leave.

Indicating the widow's weeds with his forefinger, he said, "You've had a loss?"

She went still. "Two," she said quietly. "Several weeks ago, my husband was killed. Right after we buried him, I received word that my father had also died. I'm returning to my in-laws' ranch from my father's funeral."

"I'm sorry," he said, knowing how inadequate the words were. Needing to know that she would be all right, he continued, "Your husband's family will look out for you?"

"Oh, yes," she said with a trace of bitterness. "Since I have something they want, I'll be very well cared for."

When her hand unconsciously went to her belly, he realized that she must be with child. It was a surprise, and not only because of her slimness, for she didn't have the glow common to expectant mothers. He supposed that the tragedies she had experienced were enough to extinguish joy. "At least you'll have something left of your husband," he said, wanting to offer comfort.

Her face tightened and she almost spoke. Then she gave a faint shake of her head and glanced up. "Are you hungry, Mr. Kane? I brought some food."

Her face was only a foot from his, close enough so that he could admire the creamy texture of her skin and the alluring fullness of her mouth. A wave of desire swept through him, so intense that he had to bite his lip to prevent himself from reacting. In a detached corner of his mind, he knew that what he felt was not simply normal male yearning for a lovely woman, but a desperate desire to bury himself in passion; to obliterate, for a moment, the terror of knowing how little time he had left.

Exercising all of his will, he said steadily, "It's been so long since I ate that I've forgotten what food is, so I reckon that it's time I had some. And if I'm to call you Liza, you must call me Drew." His smile was a little crooked. "Normal manners don't quite seem to fit present circumstances."

"Very well, Drew." Her tray included slices of cold fried chicken and slabs of fresh bread, which made a tasty sandwich. As he ate, he felt strength flowing into his exhausted muscles. He hadn't realized how much hunger was affecting him.

When he finished, Liza said, "Would you like more?"

He shook his head. "That's all I can manage at the moment, but I thank you kindly. Amazing what food can do for one's state of mind. I feel better than I have in days."

As she covered the rest of the food, a gunshot punctuated the night air. Kane frowned as he realized that the noise outside had been steadily increasing. "From the racket, it sounds like every cowhand in fifty miles has come to town to celebrate payday."

Liza jumped when an exuberant bellow sounded right under their window. "I hope Sheriff Taylor can handle them."

"He seemed like a capable man." Kane cocked his head, trying to decipher the conflicting voices. "My guess is that hands from two or three rival spreads are entertaining themselves by trying to rip each other's heads off."

She shivered and glanced at the door. "They wouldn't break into the hotel looking for food or whiskey, would they?"

"Even if they do, we'll be safe here. Besides the key lock, there's a bar for the door. Whoever built this hotel was a cautious soul." He got to his feet and went for the wooden bar leaning in a shadowed corner, only to be pulled up with a painful jerk when he reached the end of the chain. He swore under his breath; in the pleasure of Liza's company, he had forgotten his restraints. "I'm afraid that if you want the extra protection, you'll have to do it yourself."

She retrieved the heavy bar, then dropped it in place with a solid thunk. "This will stop any drunken cowboys who might want to get too friendly."

A burst of shots sounded from the direction of the saloon, followed by the tinkle of breaking glass. The sheriff would have his work cut out for him. Kane frowned. "Since Biff and Witless are acting deputies, Sheriff Taylor will probably enlist them to help him whip that lot into line. Might be hours before you get let out. Sorry."

"No need to apologize." She gracefully seated herself on a sack of flour. "It's not your fault."

"Maybe I'm apologizing because I'm not sorry you're

marooned here," he said in a burst of candor. After
days of having to maintain a stiff upper lip while surrounded by enemies, the need to have one last real,
human conversation was overpowering. "Thanks for
helping a dangerous, unworthy stranger, Liza. It . . .
means a great deal to me."

She tucked her feet under her, carefully covering her
ankles with her skirt. "You don't seem very dangerous.
And I'm not being entirely unselfish. It's . . . been hard
making it through the nights. Distraction is welcome."
Then, speaking quickly, as if she had said too much,
she continued with deliberate lightness, "Are you a
gambler, or do you just dress like one?"

Kane was still standing, for now that he was stronger
he felt restless. Accompanied by a soft clinking of
chain, he began to pace back and forth within the limits
of his tether. "I was a gambler for years, but I'd about
given it up."

"Why did you do that?"

"I wanted something different. Better." He stopped
in front of the small window and gazed out, seeing not
the clear night sky but the long, winding road that had
led him to this impromptu cell. "I come from a long
line of English squires, respectable folk who wanted
nothing more than to work their land, raise another
generation of little Kanes, and be buried in English soil.
If I'd been in line to inherit the estate, I expect I would
have been exactly like all my ancestors. But by custom
the land goes to the oldest son, and I was the younger."

He turned and leaned against the wall, his arms
folded across his chest. "I couldn't have the estate and
didn't have the patience for the church, the army, or
the law, which are the usual choices for younger sons.
So I became a hellion instead. After being sent down
from Oxford, I came to America, which suited me right

down to the ground. For years, I lived in saloons, moved from one town to the next when I got bored, saw the world and lived high. I gambled with some of the best, and won more often than not."

He smiled a little. "Though I always played straight in an honest game, if I sat down with a bunch of crooks, I could cheat as well as any riverboat gambler. It was a point of pride." His smile faded and deep weariness showed. "But after seven or eight years, I'd had enough. Too much time in dark, smoky, noisy saloons, living on black coffee and hard liquor. Too many sore losers who'll pull a gun rather than admit that they played their cards badly. It got downright tedious."

He looked down at his hands and fiddled absently with the metal cuff. "It's ironic. I was the family rebel and black sheep. I traveled thousands of miles to the wild frontier, braving Red Indians and Lord knows what else—my mother says that my letters are a source of shocked fascination to the whole county of Wiltshire. But when my thirtieth birthday showed on the horizon, I learned that at heart, I'm exactly like all my respectable ancestors—what I really wanted was a piece of land to call my own." He fell silent.

Liza waited patiently for him to continue. When he didn't, she asked, "Have you been looking for a spread to buy?"

"I already found one. Bought it with the proceeds of a four-day poker game in Leadville." He smiled wistfully. "It's up in Colorado, in the foothills above Pueblo. A valley with plenty of water, mountains all around—the most beautiful place I'd ever seen. And only a couple of hours from a railhead—I can be in Denver in a day when I feel a need for civilization."

His voice flattened. "At least, I could have if I wanted to. Only lived there for six months—not long enough to get bored." He shrugged indifferently, as if being a condemned man was of no more consequence than a horse with a loose shoe. "I won't be seeing the Lazy K again."

Liza regarded him with wide, compassionate eyes. "You don't look like a murderer to me. Were you falsely convicted?"

He laughed bitterly. "Oh, I killed a man right enough. Everyone in the Gilded Rooster that night agreed that it was self-defense, but the fellow I shot was a rich man's son, so justice didn't have a chance."

Her eyes widened and the blood drained from her face until she was pale as a death mask. "*What was the name of the man you killed?*"

"Holden. Billie Holden." He frowned. "Did you know him?"

Looking ill, she buried her face in shaking hands. "He was my husband," she said dully.

Dear God, this lovely girl couldn't have been that brute's wife, he thought with horror. Instinctively, he retreated as far from her as the chain would allow. He would have given everything he had ever possessed to be somewhere else—any place on earth where he wouldn't be causing Billie Holden's widow more pain. "I'm sorry," he said helplessly. "So damned sorry."

She raised her head and regarded him with wide stark eyes. "How did it happen?"

Hesitantly, he said, "It was quick. Your husband didn't suffer any. Beyond that . . ." Kane shook his head miserably, "You don't need to know more than that, Mrs. Holden."

"Liza. My name is Liza." She got to her feet and approached him, eyes dry and implacable. "And I do need to know. All his father said was that Billie had been gunned down in a saloon called the Gilded

Rooster, but there's more to it than that, isn't there?" When he still hesitated, she said tensely, "I *must* know, Drew."

He released his breath with a sigh. "Very well. I'd come down into Texas to look over some fancy new stock I'd heard about, and was on my way home when it happened. I stopped for the night in Saline. After dinner, I had a friendly game of poker at the Gilded Rooster with a couple of locals.

"I was about to call it a night when there was a row at the bar. A chap who'd had too much to drink— Holden—took a fancy to a girl. Not one of the regular sporting girls, who'd have been happy to accommodate him, but a little Chinese kitchen maid who'd brought out a tray of clean glasses. Mei-Lin couldn't have been more than fourteen or fifteen. Holden—" He broke off. "Are you *sure* you want to hear this? Only a man who was dead drunk and crazy could even think of looking at another female when he had a wife like you waiting at home."

Grimly she said, "Keep talking."

"Holden wouldn't take no for an answer, and he was scaring Mei-Lin half to death. The other men in the saloon didn't like it, but none of them dared interfere," Kane said. "One of the bar girls, Red Sally, tried to break it up. Even though she looked almost as scared as Mei-Lin, she said she'd be happy to go upstairs with such a fine gent. Holden ignored her. Said he'd never had a Chink, so he was going to have this one. He grabbed Mei-Lin by the wrist and started to drag her away.

"When she began crying, I ambled over and suggested that it might be better to choose a lady of experience. Instead of answering, Holden hauled off and slugged me in the stomach. I went down hard, and the next thing I knew, I was staring at the business end of a Colt.

"As I rolled away, Holden put a bullet into the floor where my head had been. I had a derringer in my pocket, so I shot back before he could try again." Kane fingered the scorched hole in his coat where he had fired through the fabric. "If there had been any warning, I'd have tried to wing him rather than shooting to kill, but it all happened so fast . . ." His voice trailed off.

"If it was self-defense, how come you were convicted?"

His glance was sardonic. "You probably know that your husband was visiting his uncle, Matt Sloan, who pretty much owns Saline. Sloan decided that his nephew had to be avenged, so he sent a posse of his hands after me the next day. I was easy to catch, since I thought I'd been cleared and wasn't trying to hide. When they caught up, they took me back to Saline, where Sloan called a court in the bar of the Gilded Rooster. The saloon owner, who was a crony of Sloan's, sat as judge."

Kane's mouth twisted. "No witnesses were called, and whenever I tried to talk myself, I was ruled out of order—with a fist. I was tried, convicted, and condemned in ten minutes. Sloan sent word of what he'd done to Holden's family. Your father-in-law requested that I be sent to Prairie City so the family could have the pleasure of seeing me hang. Biff and Witless are a couple of Sloan's hands who were deputized to take me back. The hanging must have been organized after you'd gone to bury your father. It should be quite an event." His agonized gaze caught hers. "I wish I could change what happened, but I can't. I'm sorry."

She turned away from him and leaned against the wall, wrapping her arms around herself as if she were freezing. After a long, painful silence, she said, "Don't blame yourself. Billie was a walking calamity. If it hadn't been you, sooner or later someone would have had to kill him." She gave a shuddering sigh. "His parents spoiled him rotten all his life. He was always nice as pie to them, and they thought he could do no wrong."

Knowing that it was none of his business, Kane asked, "Why did you marry him?"

She smiled sadly, her mind in the past. "He could be charming, and of course he was handsome as sin. When he came to Willow Point three years ago, he seemed like every girl's dream come true. My father wasn't so sure, but I was so crazy in love that Papa was afraid I'd run off if he didn't let us get married. And he'd heard of the Holden family, so he knew that I'd be marrying a man who could support me.

"But things started going wrong as soon as Billie took me back to Prairie City. His parents were furious that he'd married a nobody—they'd had hopes of matching him up with the daughter of another big rancher. Still, since the deed was done, they had to accept me. They were civil on the surface, but except for his sister Janie, it was like living in an icebox. Worst of all, Billie changed. Sometimes it was like when we were courting, but more often . . ." Her voice trailed off.

"What was he like then?"

Haltingly she said, "About six months after we married . . ." She stopped, her face white, before finishing in a rush of words. "At a church social, Billie saw me laughing with a neighbor. He pulled me away, and as soon as we got home he went crazy. Claimed I'd betrayed him, then he beat me to within an inch of my life."

She bent her head, tears glinting in her eyes. "I was laid up for a long time. There was no one I could talk to. When I tried to tell his mother what happened, she wouldn't listen. Billie had said I'd fallen down the stairs, and that was that."

Kane swore with suppressed violence. "Where was your husband when you were half-dead from what he'd done?"

"Billie was very apologetic," she said in a brittle voice. "Got down on his knees and begged my forgiveness, swore he'd never hurt me again."

"Did he keep his word?" Kane asked cynically, knowing the answer.

"He never got so crazy again, but whenever he drank, he'd knock me around," she said painfully. "He started taking long trips, supposedly doing business for his father. And . . . and he began seeing other women. He didn't try to hide it from me."

If Billie Holden had been present, Kane would have broken the polecat's neck with his bare hands. "Did you consider leaving him?"

"I did, but . . . well, he was my husband, for better and for worse. Sometimes he wasn't so bad, and I kept thinking that if I tried harder, was a better wife, he wouldn't be the way he was."

"No! Don't blame yourself. Any man who'd treat his wife like he treated you is crazy or evil."

She looked down at her fretfully twisting fingers. "I expect you're right. No matter what I did, it didn't make a difference." Silent tears began flowing down her face. "God help me," she whispered, "when I heard he was dead, my first reaction was relief."

Kane had never been able to stand seeing a lady cry. Without conscious thought, he reached out and stroked her bent head as if she were a hurt child. It wouldn't have surprised him if she had jerked away, but she didn't. Instead, she turned into his arms with a muffled sob.

He held her close while she wept as if her heart was breaking. He wondered when she had last been able to cry. Living in a house where she was despised, with a brutal husband who didn't appreciate the treasure he had married—God, it was enough to convince a man there was no justice in the world.

When her sobs began to diminish, he said quietly, "In time the nightmare will be over, Liza. When you leave the Holden ranch, you'll be able to build a new life—to find the love and happiness you deserve."

She made a choked, hysterical sound. "It will never be over." Her hand went to her abdomen. "I'm pregnant. His parents will never let me go, because they want Billie's child. I'll be trapped in that house until I die."

Kane was silent for a long time. Then he sat down against the wall, bringing her with him and arranging her across his lap so that her head was resting against his shoulder. She was soft, so soft. "It's a bad situation, Liza, but not hopeless," he said as he circled her with his arms. "You don't have to go back to the Holdens. There's plenty of ways a hardworking woman can support herself. And when you're ready to marry again, there will be no shortage of decent men who will treat you right."

"I've thought of all of the possibilities," she said bleakly. "I've thought of nothing else. If I didn't go back, or tried to leave with the baby, they'd hunt me down no matter where I went—I'd never have a moment free of worrying when they'd find us. And with his money, sooner or later Mr. Holden *would* find us. He'd never stop until he did."

Kane's arms tightened around her. "You don't have

to stay after your confinement. Though it would be a hard, hard thing to do, you could leave and let the baby be raised by its grandparents. Or would they insist that you stay, too?"

"The Holdens wouldn't mind if I left after the baby is born—in fact, they'd be delighted to see the last of me. But how can I let them raise my child? Billie was probably born with a mean streak, but they made him worse." She swallowed hard. "Though it's a terrible thing to admit, I don't even want this baby. I've had a feeling of doom ever since I found out. What if the child turns out like Billie? Even if I'm there, I might not be able to make a difference. Yet I can't abandon my own child—I *can't*."

"Life is harder for good people," he said sadly, unsurprised at her answer.

Liza closed her eyes, her grief ebbing away. Shouting and occasional gunshots rattled in the distance. She hoped the trouble would last all night, because when the town quieted down, Biff Burns would surely return and she would have to leave.

Strange that in the arms of her husband's killer, she was finding peace. Strange, yet it felt utterly right. She couldn't blame Andrew Kane for what had happened in the Gilded Rooster. He was a decent man who'd helped a terrified girl, and was going to pay for his decency with his life. Thinking about it, she realized that she and Drew were both victims of Billie's craziness. Maybe that was why she felt so much kinship with him.

No, it was more than that. Drew was special. She would have thought so under any circumstances. "Thank you for listening," she murmured. "My problems aren't much compared to yours. Your courage sets a good example for me."

There was a harsh edge to his laughter. "You think I have courage? Believe me, it's as fake as a wooden nickel. Though I've faced death before, it's always been a sudden thing, with no time to think. That's not so hard, but having to sit and wait to die . . ."

He inhaled, then said in a rush of words, "I'm scared, Liza. Not only of death, but of having to die in front of a crowd of strangers. I'm terrified that when they take me to the gallows, I'll break down and bawl like a wounded steer, begging for my life like the yellow-bellied coward I am." His voice broke. When he spoke again, it was with hard self-mockery. "Pretty stupid to worry about whether I'm going to die with a proper British stiff upper lip. But with death the only thing left to me, how I do it seems powerfully important."

She raised her head and studied Drew's face. In the dim golden lamplight, the planes of his face seemed unyielding as granite. She guessed that when the time came, he would not disgrace his solid Wiltshire ancestors; instead, he would face death with composure, perhaps even a dry joke. Yet she understood his fear. Merciful heaven, how she understood it.

On impulse, she leaned forward and touched her lips to his, wanting to convey her sympathy, her gratitude, her belief in his courage. After a startled moment, his arms tightened around her waist and he kissed her back, crushing her against the hard angles of his body.

Liza was not surprised by the sweetness, but she was shaken by the fire that flared between them. Even when she was an adoring bride, she had not felt like this. Her mouth opened under his and her head tilted back as she lost herself in the depths of his kiss.

It ended when he lifted his head, saying hoarsely, "It's . . . it's time to stop, darlin'."

She opened her eyes, disoriented by the hammering

of her own heart. Or perhaps it was his heart she felt, beating in tandem with hers. "I don't want to stop," she whispered, knowing that what she was suggesting should have been unthinkable. Would have been, before tonight, but the last hour had stripped them both down to raw emotion. She knew that he wanted her, for desire was blazoned across his face. If her body would give him solace, she would give it freely.

More than that, she wanted the closeness of being lovers; she wanted a man's touch to obliterate the failure and pain she had too often experienced in her marriage bed. And, ironically, her unwanted pregnancy meant that she could give herself to Drew without fear of consequences.

"Are you sure?" he asked, a hard pulse beating in his jaw. "You've been hurt too much, Liza. I don't want to add to that."

"You won't." She managed a shaky smile. "I'm afraid of what lies ahead, Drew, but maybe I'll be able to face it better if I have something happy to remember." She raised her hands and slipped her fingers into his hair. "Let's forget the world outside this room for as long as we can."

Wordlessly he raised his left hand and began tugging the pins from her hair. One by one, the heavy coils fell around her shoulders. "You are so beautiful." He buried his hands in the tangled, silken mass. "As beautiful as life itself." Leaning forward, he pressed his lips to her throat through the shimmering strands.

She inhaled sharply, startled at the sensations that flared through her as Drew's firm, knowing lips drifted up to her ear, then back to her eager mouth. Slowly, as if they had all the time in the world, he laid her back against the floor, improvising a pillow from two empty burlap sacks.

As he lay down beside her, the chain on his wrist rattled against the planks in an unbearably poignant reminder of what the future held. With sudden desperation she drew him into her arms, tugging up his shirttails so she could touch the warm bare skin of his back. The only thing that mattered was now, this precious, fleeting moment. Though the world would judge her wicked, she could not believe that what they were doing was wrong. Yes, Kane was a stranger, a convict who had killed her husband, but their pain made them kin, and the tenderness between them was balm to her bruised soul.

What followed astonished her. Three years she had been married, and she had thought that she knew all about what a man might do to a woman.

But now, as Drew worshiped her with hands and mouth, she discovered what it was to make love. He kissed every sensitive bit of exposed skin—her throat, her palms, the fragile flesh inside her wrists. And as he did, he whispered how lovely she was, how much joy she was giving him.

She wished that they shared the privacy of a bed, with loose garments that might be pushed aside so that flesh could press against flesh. That wasn't possible, not when Biff might return and start pounding on the door at any moment. Yet even through the sober layers of her clothing, her breasts came to yearning life when he caressed them.

She tensed when he unbuttoned her drawers and tugged them off. In the past, intimacy had often meant pain, and the taut hunger on his face frightened her a little. But to her surprise he did not immediately mount her. Instead, he pleasured her with slow, expert fingers that created embarrassing amounts of heat and moisture. Only when her hips began to move involuntarily did he unfasten his trousers and lift himself over her.

They came together easily. Not only was there not a hint of pain, but she found that his weight and warmth brought the most profound sense of completion she had ever known. Delighted, she experimentally moved against him.

Her action was like a spark to tinder. He groaned and thrust deeper, and suddenly they were fiercely mating, becoming one with sweet, desperate savagery. Her nails curved into the hard, flexing muscles of his back. There were no words, for none were needed. Until, at the end, her body spun out of her control and she cried out with wonder and joy.

As she did, he groaned and drove into her again and again, with a primal rhythm that shattered them both. When he had nothing left to give, he eased forward, surrounding her with his warmth, resting his face in her hair.

When she could speak, she said with awe, "I didn't know it could be like that for a woman."

"You've never . . . ?"

She shook her head, feeling ridiculously shy. "Never."

Selfishly, he was glad. Though he wished her a happy future with all his heart, he hoped that she would not forget the man with whom she had discovered a woman's passion.

He rolled over and sat back against the sack of flour, then lifted her so that she lay across him, one bare leg between his, her skirts rippling about them. "Thank you, Liza, for a gift beyond price," he said softly. "You've put the heart back in me. Whatever happens in the next few days, I think I'll be able to face it like a man."

Her fingers curled into the ruffles at the throat of his

shirt. "I feel the same way. No matter how bad things get in the future, I'll always have tonight to remember," she said tightly. "If only . . ." She stopped, unable to continue.

"Don't say it, sweetheart," he murmured as he stroked her nape with gentle fingers. "Don't even think it. Be glad we're together now. There will be time enough for grief later."

He still didn't quite believe the miracle in his arms. Liza was a lifetime of joy compressed into a handful of minutes. She, who had so little reason to trust, had given herself with brave honesty, and the poignancy of their union was like an arrow in his heart. He wished that he could stop time, with her forever in his embrace.

But that wasn't possible. The din from the riotous cowboys was fading. How much longer would they have? He offered a fervent mental prayer that Biff would do some drinking in the saloon before remembering that he must release the lady from the convict's cell.

Knowledge that time was running out was like a clock ticking in the back of his brain. Reluctantly he said, "Better put your hair up, Liza. Anyone seeing you would have a pretty fair idea of what you've been up to."

Blushing, she sat up and began combing her fingers through her hair in a doomed attempt to straighten it. "I must look like a saloon girl."

Enjoying her less-than-successful efforts to look prim, he said with a faint smile, "Not at all. You look like a woman who had been well loved."

Her blush deepened, but she didn't avert her eyes.

When she began pinning her hair back, he said, "Liza, I've a favor to ask."

"Anything," she said simply.

"It's a pretty big favor. Someone will have to notify my family of my death. I should write myself, but I can't. Saying, 'By the time you get this, I'll be dead . . .' Well, I've tried again and again in my head, and I can't get it right. Cowardice again." After a long pause, he said painfully, "When I bought the Lazy K, I thought that in a year or so, when the place was fixed up the way I wanted, I'd invite my parents for a visit. I wanted them to see that the prodigal son hadn't gone as thoroughly to hell as they had feared. But it looks like their fears weren't misplaced."

"Where should I send the letter?" she asked, wanting to lift the darkness that had settled on his face.

"Sir Geoffrey Kane and Lady Kane, Westlands, Amesbury, Wiltshire, England," he replied.

After repeating it twice, she said, "Your father's a lord?"

"No, just a baronet. Sort of a jumped-up ranch owner, English-style."

She smiled a little at the irreverent description. "Do you want me to tell them the truth?"

"No!" he said harshly. "Tell them that a horse threw me, or that a fever carried me off. Anything but that I was hanged for murder. No point in their suffering more than necessary."

"Do you have any special messages?"

The muscle jumped in his jaw again. "Just . . . just say that I sent them my love."

With a flash of absolute certainty, she knew that his death would break his parents' hearts, for like the prodigal he called himself, surely he was much loved. "I'll do as you wish," she said quietly, not daring to carry the thought any further. "What will happen to the Lazy K?"

"Lord, I don't know." He rubbed his jaw, the whiskers rasping against his palm. "I haven't wanted to think of it." Abruptly he raised his head and stared at her, his gaze sharpening. "I know—I'll leave it to you."

She gasped and dropped the last hairpin. "You can't mean that. We scarcely know each other!"

He gave her a smile of great sweetness. "I'd say that we know each other rather well."

She blushed again. "When you put it like that . . ." She retrieved the hairpin and stabbed it into the coil at the nape of her neck. "But what would I do with a ranch?"

"More than I'll be able to do," he said with bone-dry humor. "Perhaps it will let you escape the Holdens. Change your name and they'll never find you there." He began rummaging through his pockets, eventually producing a somewhat grubby piece of paper and a stub of pencil.

"Good thing there isn't anyone who would challenge this," he remarked as he began writing. "Pencil on the back of a hotel bill isn't exactly correct form for a man's last will and testament." He wrote a few lines, folded the paper, and wrote more, than handed it to her. "The foreman, Lou Wilcox, and his wife, Lily, will help you run the place if you decide to live there. They'll need to be notified of my death, too. I wrote their names and the ranch location on the outside."

She accepted the paper gingerly, as if it were about to explode. She wasn't as sure as he that she would be able to elude her in-laws, but she didn't want to extinguish the light in his face. "I . . . I don't know what to say."

"You don't have to say anything." His brow furrowed. "Do you have any money?"

Confused, she said, "A little from my father, but

Billie didn't leave much of anything. The money all belongs to his father, Big Bill. Do you need some?"

"Not unless I figure out a way to take it with me between now and Tuesday." The chain on his wrist rattled as he pulled off his right boot, then wrenched off the thick heel. Inside were gold coins packed in raw cotton to prevent clinking.

As Liza watched, bemused, he emptied out the money, replaced the heel, then repeated the process with his left boot. "I've always liked to travel with an emergency stake, in case I run into thieves or a bad run of cards," he explained as he scooped the coins up. Offering them to her, he continued, "You can use this better than I."

She stared at the gold as if it were a nest of scorpions. "I hate the idea of benefiting from your death."

"Personally, I'd like to think that someone will benefit. I sure as hell won't," he said. "I understand your scruples, Liza, but if you decide to leave the Holdens' ranch, you'll need running-away money. Matt Sloan's kangaroo court appropriated the rest of my cash, but this should be enough to take you far and fast if you want to escape."

She couldn't refuse a gesture that was clearly important to him. More than that, it was undeniable that the money might prove useful. She accepted most of the coins, but handed some back. "You may need this for bribes or food or something."

As he pocketed the gold, she added in a low voice, "Thank you, Drew. Your generosity may give me a future."

"I hope so." He gave her a light kiss. "I truly hope so."

He reclined against the flour sack again and drew her

down so that she was sprawled on top of him. She relaxed, content to be in his arms.

As she half-dozed, her soft weight a delicious burden, he wondered how much longer would they have.

Not long. Not nearly long enough.

Soon after the night fell ominously silent, he heard heavy footsteps approaching the storeroom. Liza inhaled sharply, then scrambled to her feet, separating them with harsh finality. Cheeks burning, she scooped up the crumpled drawers which she hadn't gotten around to putting on, and jammed them in a pocket. "How do I look?" she hissed as she smoothed down her skirts.

Kane rose more slowly, buttoning his trousers as he did. "Every inch a lady," he assured her, knowing it was what she wanted to hear. Brushing her cheek with the back of his knuckles, he added softly, "Also every inch a woman."

The key turned in the lock and Biff attempted to open the door, only to be blocked by the bar. "Open up!" he bellowed. "Are you all right, ma'am?"

"She's fine, Burns," Kane called. "Safer in here than out there, by the sound of it."

He and Liza stared at each other. The end had come, and there was too much to say to even attempt words. Fiercely, she threw her arms around his neck and gave him a bruising kiss. As he crushed her pliant body to his, he wondered despairingly how he could let her go.

Somehow he managed to do it. When his arms dropped, she stepped away, eyes bright with unshed tears as she whispered, "You will always be in my heart."

Biff roared. "Kane, if you don't open this door, I'll blow it off!"

Turning, Liza bowed her head and pressed her hands

to her temples for a moment. Then she straightened and stepped forward to lift the bar. Kane retreated to the back wall, then slouched on the floor as if he had been peacefully dozing.

Accompanied by a haze of whiskey fumes, Biff entered the storeroom, his suspicious gaze going to his prisoner. "Sorry to leave you with this trash for so long, ma'am, but there was trouble and the sheriff needed me and Whittles. Did Kane bother you?"

"Not in the least," she said stiffly. "It was a most uneventful interval."

Kane made a sound that might have been a laugh that was hastily turned into a cough. Then he drawled, "Make it quick, Biff. A condemned man shouldn't have to have his sleep disturbed by a face like yours."

The deputy scowled and took a step forward, then stopped, remembering that a lady was present. Liza guessed that Drew had deliberately insulted Biff to draw attention away from her. Trying to look casual, she stooped and lifted the tray she had brought, her brain and heart numb. Already the interlude with Drew seemed incredible, dreamlike—but the warmth in his eyes was as true as anything she'd ever seen.

Biff shifted his befuddled gaze to her, and his expression changed. With heavy gallantry that made her nervous, he said, "Lot of purty ladies in the saloon, but none as purty as you, ma'am. Real fine hair." His hand moved vaguely, as if he was considering stroking it.

Kane's voice sliced across the room. "Biff, if you touch the little lady, or upset her in any way whatsoever, I'll find a way to kill you before we reach Prairie City. I swear it."

Biff jerked, sobered by the icy menace in the prisoner's voice. "Didn't do anything," he mumbled. "Come on, ma'am, time you was away from that no-good varmint."

Liza's gaze went to Kane once more. Silently she mouthed, "I love you."

A muscle in his rigid jaw twitched. It was the last thing she saw before she turned and walked away.

Liza had thought her feelings would be too turbulent to permit sleep, but to her surprise, as soon as she went to bed she fell into a profound slumber. The next morning she awoke clear-eyed and refreshed after the best rest she'd had in years.

Her sense of well-being vanished when she remembered the events of the night before. She supposed that she should despise herself for her immorality, but she didn't; guilt didn't have a chance compared to her searing grief at Andrew Kane's fate.

She washed and dressed mechanically, her mind going round and round, torn between memories of Drew and the sick knowledge that he was doomed. Deciding that she felt well enough to face food, she was about to go downstairs for breakfast when she heard the soft jingle of bridles. She went to the window and saw that the skinny deputy, Whittles, had brought around the three horses and Biff was leading the prisoner out of the building.

The night appeared to have helped Drew as much as Liza. No longer worn down by thirst and exhaustion, he walked tall, looking like a lord among peasants in spite of his handcuffs. As she looked down, hoping for a glimpse of his face, she remembered how he had been deprived of water during the long ride.

She would not allow it to happen again. Seizing her own canteen, which she had refilled the evening before, she dashed downstairs, across the lobby, and into the street. All three men were mounted and the party was on the verge of leaving, but she defiantly walked in front of Whittle's horse and handed the canteen to Drew. "It will be a hot day, Mr. Kane. I believe that you need one of these."

He inclined his head. "So I do. Thank you kindly, darlin'." Though his tone was negligent, his gaze was a caress.

Under her breath, so that only Drew could hear, she said, "*Vaya con Dios*." She had often used the words, but never had she known anyone who so much needed to go with God.

Unable to bear the expression in his blue eyes, Liza turned and channeled all her anger at the situation into a furious scowl at Biff. "I trust that your journey to Prairie City will be entirely uneventful, Mr. Burns, and that your prisoner will arrive in the same condition he is now."

Even as the deputy stumblingly reassured her, she turned and went back inside. As the door closed behind her, her stomach turned sickeningly. She barely made it back to her room before she was violently ill in the chamber pot.

She lay down, hoping that her nausea would pass quickly. Inevitably, her thoughts returned to Drew's impending execution. No honest judge or jury would have condemned a man who had killed in self-defense, but Holden money and influence were going to hang an innocent man, and there wasn't a thing Liza could do about it. Even if she got down on her knees to her father-in-law and pleaded for justice, it wouldn't help. Big Bill Holden was not a reasonable man at the best of times, and his grief and rage demanded that someone pay for the death of his son.

The problem was that Drew had not been tried by

an honest judge. Federal judges were few and far between, so makeshift courts like the one Matt Sloan convened in the Gilded Rooster were common. Generally such courts did a decent job of determining guilt, but because of Matt Sloan, that hadn't happened in the case of Andrew Kane. If a federal judge was notified, maybe he could overrule what was clearly a miscarriage of justice. The trick would be to find a judge and persuade him to intervene soon enough to make a difference.

Liza caught her breath as she realized that Prairie City was in the same judicial district as Willow Point and Saline—and she was acquainted with the judge. Albert Barker had sometimes stopped by her father's store, and even held court there once or twice. At first she'd been surprised at Judge Barker's mild appearance, for he had a fearsome reputation for upholding the law. Then she'd looked into his implacable gray eyes, and believed everything she'd ever heard about him.

And Barker wasn't just a hanging judge; he believed it was his job to free the innocent as well as to punish the guilty. If he could be reached in time and persuaded to intervene, he might be able to save Drew. A new trial, with witnesses and an honest judge, would surely acquit him. But how could she reach Judge Barker, who spent most of his time traveling and could be anywhere in his far-flung district?

Ignoring her nausea, Liza got up and wrote a letter to Judge Barker, reminding him of their past acquaintance, then relating what Drew had told her of the circumstances of Billie's shooting. After expressing a pious wish that the tragedy of her husband's death not be compounded by hanging an innocent man, she had named the two women whom Drew had mentioned. Perhaps Mei-Lin and Red Sally would have the courage to testify to what happened, even if none of the men who had been present would.

She sealed the letter and addressed it to the judge and had just scrawled URGENT across the envelope when Tom Jackson knocked. Now came the hard part.

She admitted Tom, who had a wide smile on his face. "Morning, Miz Holden. Hope you had a good night's rest. It was purely good to see my cousin Jacob and his family."

He was crossing the room to pick up her baggage when she said bluntly, "How do you feel about innocent men being hanged?"

His expression went blank and he regarded her warily. "Ma'am?"

"Something bad's going to happen, Mr. Jackson. I don't know if it can be stopped, but I want to try, and I can't do it alone." She wiped her damp palms on her skirt. "You may want to refuse, because Mr. Holden won't like what I have in mind one bit, and if he finds out, it could cost you your job." Then she outlined what she had learned from Andrew Kane. Tom simply listened, his head bowed and expression inscrutable.

When she was done, he said, "You believe this Mr. Kane was telling the truth when he said it was self-defense?"

"I believed him." Her mouth twisted. "You know how Billie could be."

"I surely do. Sometimes I used to wonder how you stood . . ." Tom cut off his sentence.

She smiled humorlessly. "Sometimes I wondered that myself." Falling silent, she waited for his decision.

Tom gazed at his battered hat, turning it around and around in his hands. After carefully pushing out a dent in the crown, he said softly, "My brother was lynched ten years ago in Alabama because someone thought he was an uppity nigger." Raising his head, he looked Liza in the eye, his face set. "So to answer your question, no, I don't hold with hanging innocent men. What do you want me to do?"

"I've written a letter to Judge Barker," she said eagerly. "Do you think you could find out where he is now and take it to him? It will have to be done quickly—the hanging will be Tuesday in Prairie City."

Tom frowned. "I can't leave you alone."

"I'll be fine," she said. "I can stay right here in the hotel."

"Wouldn't be right," he said firmly. "Mr. Holden would have my hide for neglecting you, and rightly so."

Her eyes narrowed. "If I have to, I'll go after the judge myself."

"You can't do that, not in your condition," he said, scandalized. "Don't think I haven't noticed how tired you get riding, even slow as we've been going." He rubbed his chin, considering. "Mebbe my cousin's oldest boy, Jimmy, could go. He's smart, and a good rider."

"Then let's go ask him." Liza tied her bonnet and prepared to go downstairs. "Oh, before we leave, I'll need to stop at the general store and pick up a new canteen. I gave mine away."

Tom gave her a quizzical look that made Liza wonder if he guessed that her interest in Andrew Kane was more than an abstract desire for justice, but he said nothing. As they went outside and headed toward Tom's cousin's blacksmith shop, she gave thanks that she had confided in him.

Jacob Washington proved to be a giant of a man with a booming laugh and massive blacksmith muscles. His wife Molly laughed with equal ease, dispensing food and hugs to her active brood. Jimmy, the oldest, was a tall, slim youth of about eighteen, with steady eyes and a shy smile.

After Tom introduced Liza and said that she had something serious to discuss, she was invited into the family kitchen and the smaller children were chased away. Then, while Molly plied her with fresh cornbread and scalding coffee, Liza went through her story again. The question of whether or not Jimmy would go was never even raised. The youth simply looked at his father and asked, "Has anyone passing through mentioned where Judge Barker is holding court now?"

Jacob rubbed his chin. "East of here, I think. Least he was a couple of weeks ago."

Molly frowned. "He'll have moved on by now, probably to the north. He usually goes that way."

After a discussion of the judge's possible whereabouts, Jimmy glanced at Liza. "I'll be on my way within the hour, ma'am."

She closed her eyes for a moment, so overcome with relief that she was almost dizzy. It was still a long shot that the execution could be stopped, but at least something was being done. She rose and handed the letter to Jimmy, then reached into her pocket and brought out Drew's gold. "You'll need this."

For the first time, Jacob scowled. "We don't accept money for trying to save a man's life."

"Of course not," she said quietly. "This isn't for your help—it's for Jimmy's expenses. There's no telling what he might run into along the way."

After a moment's hesitation, Jacob nodded and Jimmy accepted the handful of coins.

"God bless you, Jimmy," Liza said unevenly, "and be careful traveling."

"I will be, ma'am," he said. "And if Judge Barker can be found in time, I'll find him."

She prayed that he was right. After bidding the Washingtons farewell, she and Tom started back to the hotel. The excitement that came with action faded as they walked the length of Forlorn Hope's dusty main street. She had done everything in her power. Now she could do nothing but wait and see if it was enough.

It would be the easier to wrestle a cougar bare-handed.

The last leg of Kane's ride was blessedly uneventful. The fury of a virtuous woman had subdued Biff and Witless; not only did the deputies let Kane keep Liza's canteen, but they gave him some of their food. Still, it was a relief to reach their destination. Kane thought it doubtful that the deputies' improved behavior would have lasted through another day.

The Prairie City sheriff, Bart Simms, proved to be an acquaintance of Kane's. They had met in El Paso a couple of years back, played some poker, shared a few bottles of whiskey, and told each other tall tales. Since then, Simms had grown a drooping, lugubrious mustache and acquired a tin star on his chest. In Kane's jaundiced opinion, the result was not an improvement.

Simms' shaggy brows rose when Kane was brought into the jail, but he said nothing, simply locked the prisoner in the cell in the back room. The two deputies left, with a cheerful promise to Kane that they'd stick around to see him on the gallows.

When they were alone, the sheriff asked, "Did you do it?"

With equal terseness, Kane said, "Self-defense."

Simms chewed his tobacco for a time. At length, he asked, "Then why're you here?"

"Because Billie Holden's uncle owned Saline, and his father owns Prairie City."

The sheriff shot a wad of tobacco juice into a spittoon. "A pity. Billie was a no-good skunk."

"I couldn't agree more." Kane regarded Simms narrowly, wondering if the sheriff's sympathy might extend to being careless enough that a prisoner might escape.

Accurately guessing Kane's thoughts, Simms said, "Sorry about this, but the law's the law."

"The law is an ass."

"Sometimes it is," the sheriff allowed. "But it's my job, and I aim to do it right." He withdrew to the front office.

Kane was unsurprised that the sheriff didn't recognize the quote; Simms wasn't the sort to spend his spare time reading Dickens. Wearily, Kane stretched out on the narrow, lumpy bunk, his hands folded beneath his head.

One of the cracks in the ceiling reminded him of the way Liza's hair fell. Actually, just about everything reminded him of her. With a faint smile, he set about recalling the time they had spent together, from the moment she had roared out of the hotel to stop the deputies from beating him to death, to the heartstopping expression in her gray eyes when they parted.

He couldn't think of a better way to spend the last four days of his life.

The Prairie City jail stayed boring but peaceful until the next morning. Then the door to the back room was thrown open with a force that crashed it into the wall. A heavy-set man stepped through, growling, "So this is the son of a bitch who shot my son."

Jerked out of his daydreams of Liza, it took Kane a moment to react. Big Bill Holden was broad as a barn, with a furious gleam in his small eyes and the face of a man who assumed that getting his own way was divine law. Kane felt a pang for Liza, who had lived under this man's roof for three years, and maybe would be trapped there indefinitely.

The thought made him angry. Instead of standing, Kane stayed sprawled on the bunk, as relaxed as if he were fishing on a riverbank. "So I am," he said in his most infuriating tone. "The little bastard deserved it. You should have taught him not to bully defenseless women. Better yet, you should have told him that if he was going to try to kill a man for no good reason, he should pick someone who wouldn't shoot back."

"You'll pay for that!" Holden roared with a rage that made Kane flinch involuntarily. A good thing that steel bars separated them.

As Holden reached for the Colt holstered on his hip, Kane said cordially, "Go ahead and shoot. The good citizens of Prairie City will be deprived of their show, but I'll be spared three more days of jail food. With luck, you might even be convicted of murdering an unarmed man."

After a precarious pause, Big Bill's hand dropped away from the revolver. Breathing heavily, he said, "I can't wait to see you swing."

"I'm afraid you'll have to, but when the happy moment arrives, I shall try to live up to your expectations. In the meantime"—Kane pulled his black hat from under the bunk and lazily set it over his face—"leave me the bloody hell alone."

After more snarling and threats, Big Bill stormed out. Kane exhaled slowly and laced his fingers over his midriff. He wasn't sure whether he was glad or sorry that Holden hadn't gunned him down on the spot. It would have been a quick death—better than hanging. But it was against nature to want to die, even though his prospects of survival were nonexistent.

So far, he wasn't doing badly at showing coolness in the face of death. He rather thought that the Kanes in the portrait gallery at Westlands would approve.

By the time she reached the Holden ranch, Liza was so tired that she scarcely had the energy to be depressed. At least there would be a clean, quiet bed waiting for her.

After Tom Jackson helped her from her horse, she climbed the wide steps of what Big Bill boasted was the largest mansion between St. Louis and Denver. Perhaps it was; certainly it was the gaudiest. Once inside, she removed her dusty bonnet and rubbed her aching temples. Strange to think that when she married Billie, she'd been excited at the prospect of living in such a fine place.

Alerted by the housekeeper, Adelaide Holden came to greet her daughter-in-law. A beauty in her youth, she was still handsome; Big Bill would never have married a plain woman. "It's about time you got back." Adelaide's assessing gaze swept over Liza. "Have you been taking care of yourself?"

Liza was unsurprised that there were no questions or sympathy about her father's death. "Yes, ma'am. We rode very slowly. Mr. Jackson was most considerate."

"You need some tea as a restorative," Adelaide announced.

"Most of all, I need sleep," Liza said wearily. "If you'll excuse me . . ."

Adelaide raised her hand. "Very well, but before you go, I want to tell you the good news. Billie's murderer has been caught and convicted. Mr. Holden has arranged for the revolting creature to be hanged here on Tuesday."

Unable to conceal her bitterness, Liza said, "Is another death really good news? It won't bring Billie back."

"My son's death must be paid for," Adelaide said grimly. "The Bible says an eye for an eye."

Liza's face tightened. "I hope you don't expect me to watch."

"Of course not," Adelaide said, shocked. "It might mark the baby."

Her status as brood mare firmly established, Liza excused herself and went to the bedroom she had shared with her husband. Yet, in spite of her exhaustion, she halted on the threshold, her stomach twisting. She had vaguely assumed that Mrs. Holden would have packed away Billie's possessions, but everything was still in place, as if he might return any minute. It was just like Adelaide to leave the place as a shrine to her dead son.

Sadly, Liza leaned against the door frame, thinking of the charming young man who had courted her. The charm had been only a small part of Billie, but it had been real, and so had her love. Where had it all gone? Perhaps if she had tried harder. . . .

Quite clearly, she heard Drew's voice in her head: *Don't blame yourself. Any man who'd treat his wife like he treated you is crazy or evil.*

His words were like a splash of cold water on the embers of her guilt. Her back straightened and she turned away. There was no point in brooding. She'd rather think Billie had been crazy, not evil. But in either case, it wasn't her fault. Moreover, she wasn't going to sleep in this room.

With a wintry smile, she headed down the corridor to the guest room. No doubt Adelaide would be happy that the shrine wouldn't be sullied by Liza's unworthy presence.

*   *   *

Dawn slowly lightened the cell. Kane tried to ignore it, preferring to remain in the dream, where a soft, loving female nestled in his arms. Wheat-colored hair, unflinching gray eyes, delicious curves. He'd have enjoyed taking off Liza's garments one by one and discovering exactly what was underneath. He'd have liked waking up in his own bed at the Lazy K with her beside him. He'd have loved sitting by a fire with her while the bitter wind whistled off the mountains and snow piled up around the ranch house.

With a sigh, he pushed the blanket back and sat up, running his fingers through his hair. There were a hell of a lot of things he'd have liked to do that he was never going to get to. He'd always assumed that someday he'd settle down and marry, have a family. Why hadn't he done that already? Because he had never met a girl like Liza—who could be both friend and mistress—until it was too late.

He felt a piercing sorrow. With youthful arrogance he'd always assumed that eventually he'd get around to everything he wanted to do. But today, time had run out.

He drew on his boots with an odd feeling of unreality. At heart, he couldn't quite believe that he wouldn't live to see sundown. He felt too alive, too healthy.

It took only an instant for a man to die.

He looked at his hands, glad to see that they were steady. He hoped that would still be true at noon, when he was taken to the gallows.

Sheriff Simms ambled in. "Anything special you'd like for your last meal?"

Kane raised a sardonic brow. "So condemned men really do get their last request."

"If possible. What's your choice?"

"A woman?"

Amusement gleamed in the sheriff's hazel eyes. "In Prairie City, last requests only cover food, boy. The good ladies of the town wouldn't hold with such goings-on in the jail."

Kane shrugged, not having expected any other answer. It didn't matter, since Liza was the only woman he would have wanted. But it wouldn't do to waste a last request. He pondered. Unaccountably his mind leaped back to a hunt breakfast in Wiltshire. "Kippers," he announced. "I want kippers."

Simms blinked. "What the blue hell are kippers?"

"Herring that's been salted and smoked," he explained. "Delicious."

"Mebbe I can find some salted cod," the sheriff said doubtfully.

"Do your best." Kane lay back on his bunk again. "Just make sure there's a bottle of whiskey on the side."

He stared dry-eyed at the ceiling after Simms left. Three more hours.

Fighting a feeling of unwellness, Liza swung her feet from the bed. As she stood, a cramp deep in her abdomen caused her to double over with pain. It passed quickly, leaving her shaky. Probably the pain was because she was so upset. She'd been hoping to hear of a miracle, but the day of Drew's execution had arrived and nothing had changed. Jimmy must not have been successful. *Ah, Drew, I did my best. I'm sorry—so sorry.*

After breakfast, Big Bill and Adelaide set off for town, identical expressions of ugly satisfaction on their faces. Liza was left alone with Janie, her sixteen-year-old sister-in-law. Since Janie had always been overlooked in favor of her brother, the two young women had become allies and friends.

The morning passed with agonizing slowness as they

sat in the parlor and sewed, making desultory conversation that never touched on the subject that dominated their thoughts.

As noon approached, Janie set her sewing aside and got restlessly to her feet. "I'm glad you didn't want to see the hanging, Liza," she confided. "Gave me an excuse not to go. I don't care if that fellow Kane did kill Billie, I couldn't have stood watching a man die."

Liza stared sightlessly at her embroidery. "On my way back from Willow Point, I heard it said that Kane killed Billie in self-defense."

Janie turned and stared at her, distressed. The girl had her mother's good looks, but a far sweeter nature. "Merciful heaven, that's dreadful if it's true." Her voice quavered. "And Billie being Billie, it could be true, couldn't it?"

"It certainly could." As Liza stuck her needle into the fabric, a sick dizziness engulfed her and the point stabbed into her finger. Confused, she watched her blood stain the white linen with crimson. There seemed to be too much blood.

Janie said sharply, "Liza, are you all right?"

She raised her head and tried to say yes, but she couldn't make her voice work.

The mantel clock began striking with deep, melancholy tones. High noon. At this very moment, Andrew Kane was dying in agony. As the last hollow boom died away, she closed her eyes and shuddered. It was over. Drew was dead.

Knowing that she should lie down, she tried to stand, but her legs wouldn't obey her. She pitched to the floor, a vicious pain clenching her abdomen.

Janie's voice came from a great distance, screaming for the housekeeper. As Liza slid through the pain into darkness, she thought with anguish, *Vaya con Dios*,

Drew—I hope you died the kind of death you wanted. And may God have mercy on your soul.

Simms hadn't found any salted cod, so Kane's last meal was a large steak, pan-fried, with lots of gravy and a mountain of potatoes and onions on the side. Tasted a damned sight better than kippers would have. The bottle of whiskey provided had been aged for at least a month—prime sipping whiskey by local standards. Nonetheless, Drew had only had a couple of shots. While the thought of drinking himself into a stupor had a certain appeal, it seemed foolish to obliterate his last minutes of life. Besides, if he was drunk, he'd be a lot more likely to lose control and disgrace himself.

The noise outside indicated that quite a crowd had gathered. There was even a brass band playing—badly. Drew concentrated on picking out the wrong notes, preferring that to thinking the unthinkable.

All too soon Simms and a deputy with a shotgun entered the back room. The sheriff slid the key into the lock. "It's time."

Drew stood and put on his hat, tilting it forward a little, as if he were going into a poker game with unknown opponents and wanted to look nonchalant. Then he walked out of the cell and stood still while Simms tied his hands behind his back. Gruffly the sheriff said, "Sorry."

"You're just doing your job."

A phalanx of deputies fell in around him as he stepped outside into the fierce noonday sun. Several hundred people had gathered for the show, and their shouts struck him like a bullwhip. As his escorts forced a path through the crowd, Drew studied individual faces. Some were avid, some curious, one or two sympathetic.

Then he saw Big Bill Holden. He and Matt Sloan were standing right in front of the gallows with a well-dressed virago between them. Mrs. Holden, no doubt, and one of the few women present.

Drew inclined his head at her with mocking courtliness just to see the outrage spring into her eyes. But as he climbed the steps to the gallows, he told himself that that was not well-done. Though the woman might be a virago, she had just lost her son, and her pain was as real as anybody's. He hoped she'd be kind to Liza and Liza's child.

The crude planks of the platform creaked under his footsteps, and the death that he hadn't quite believed in became horribly real. Fear pulsed through him, making his heart hammer and his breathing turn rough. Before fear could blaze into panic, he summoned up Liza's image—her quiet courage, her clear gray eyes that made a man feel so much a man.

He swallowed hard. He was damned well not going to die in a way that would make her ashamed of what she had given him.

The crowd was so loud that the hangman had to shout. "Any last words, Kane?"

He had to swallow again before he could reply. "Too much noise to be heard. I'm not going to die with a hoarse throat."

The hangman removed Kane's hat, then dropped the noose around his neck. The rope scratched as the noose was tightened until the knot was snug beneath his left ear. How long now? Less than a minute. Good-bye, Liza. If there's any justice, maybe we'll meet again, when there's more time.

He took a deep breath, trying to take his mind as far away as possible. Thank God his parents need never know how he died.

As the hangman prepared to release the trapdoor, the noise increased still further, with an ugly edge of excitement. Then a rifle fired, cutting through the din like a wire through butter.

In the startled silence that followed, a ferocious voice bellowed, "Hold it right there! This man's not for hanging!"

A babble of excitement rose, and a murmured name that sounded like Parker. Not daring to hope, Kane stared at the eddy in the crowd that was a man fighting his way toward the gallows.

When the newcomer reached the steps, he took them two at a time. He was a short, broad fellow dressed as soberly as a preacher, but he had an air of authority that didn't need the rifle he carried in one hand. Turning to face the crowd, he raised his arms and the noise died down.

"I'm Judge Barker," he boomed in a voice that could quiet the rowdiest courtroom, "and evidence has come to my attention that this man was not properly tried— that he killed Billie Holden in self-defense. I'm here to see that he goes back to Saline and gets a fair trial."

"No!" Furiously Big Bill forced his way to the steps and bounded onto the platform. "Kane's a murderer and the bastard's going to hang right now!"

Unintimidated even though he was half a head shorter, the judge retorted, "I'm the law in these parts, you son of a bitch, and I'm not going to see an innocent man hanged."

Big Bill's hand hovered near his Colt. Then Sheriff Simms climbed onto the platform. "I wouldn't do that, Mr. Holden," he drawled. "The law's the law. If Kane's guilty, justice will be done in Saline." He glanced at Drew, and one eye closed in a slow wink.

Holden's bravado crumbled into confusion. The

judge took advantage of the lull to loosen the noose around Kane's neck, then flip it over his head. "Time to make tracks, young man."

Stunned though he was by events, Kane knew enough to follow Barker off the platform and into the crowd. By sheer force of personality, the judge cleared a path as they moved away. A few disappointed citizens looked inclined to finish what had been started, but no one had the nerve to go against the judge. No one until they came across Biff Burns on the edge of the crowd.

With a growl, Biff grabbed at his former prisoner. His balance hampered by his bound hands, Kane almost fell as he twisted away from the other man's grip. "Biff," he snapped, "I've got just one thing to say to you."

"Yeah?" Biff sneered as he tried again. "What's that?"

Kane pivoted on his left heel and swung his right foot in a ferocious kick that landed where a man would least want it. As Biff shrieked and doubled over, Kane said coolly, "Next time you take someone to jail, show some decent manners."

The judge grabbed his arm and hustled him along. "Now that you've had your fun, boy, get your tail moving."

Two minutes later they reached the livery stable. A slim black youth waited in front with three horses, one of them Drew's. With a flashing smile, he said, "Looks like the judge was in time, Mr. Kane."

"Only just." Barker pulled a razor-edged Bowie knife from a sheath under his coat. "Kane, do you have enough faith in your innocence to give me your word of honor not to try to escape between here and Saline?"

"I do," he said promptly.

"You'd better keep it. Try to run away and I'll slice you into coyote bait myself." The judge circled behind

Drew and started sawing at his bonds. It didn't take long to cut through the rope and give Drew the use of his arms again. He rolled his tight shoulders, then swung onto his horse.

Barker did likewise. "Now, gentlemen, we'll be on our way before Holden forgets that he's a law-abiding man."

They wheeled their horses and galloped out of town. After several fast miles, the judge pulled his horse back to a trot. "That should do it."

Still not quite believing that he'd escaped, Drew said, "Don't think I'm not grateful, Judge Barker, but how the devil did you happen to show up at such a propitious moment?"

"You have a young lady to thank for that. Billie Holden's widow had Jimmy here bring me a letter. I figured if the dead man's widow thought you might be innocent, the situation was deserving of my attention."

My God, Liza had done it, Kane thought, amazed. Not only had she given him the happiest hours he'd ever known, but she'd saved his life. Oh, Liza, sweet Liza, will I be able to save you from your captivity? He thought of her sharing a house with Big Bill Holden and the virago, and scowled. When he was cleared of the murder charge, he'd look into that. If she wanted to run away, he'd see that she made her escape safely.

Touching his heels to his horse, he said, "Onward to Saline, gentlemen. The sooner we get this over with, the better."

Liza remembered mercifully few of her nightmares. She knew that Janie was sometimes with her, and other shadowy forms, but when she finally returned to full consciousness, Adelaide was the woman sitting by the bed.

Her voice a thread, Liza asked, "The man who killed Billie—they hanged him?"

Adelaide swallowed hard, a strange expression on her face, then said stiffly, "Yes."

Liza closed her eyes and tears spilled from under her lids. "I . . . I lost the baby, didn't I?"

"You did," Adelaide said, not trying to conceal her bitterness. "But the doctor said *you* would be fine, and there was no reason why you couldn't have children in the future."

"I'm sorry," Liza whispered. She felt empty, too hollow even to grieve.

"So am I." Adelaide stood and gazed at her with hooded eyes. "He should have married a woman who was stronger."

Once again, it was all Liza's fault. Her voice choked, she said, "As soon as I'm able, I'll leave the ranch."

"As Billie's widow, you're entitled to live here as long as you want."

Adelaide would always do her duty, no matter how little she liked it. "You're very generous," Liza said wearily, "but I think it would be best for everyone if I left."

"Yes, it would."

As her mother-in-law turned to leave, Liza said, "You've had two great losses, and I truly grieve for you. But don't forget that you have another child, and she needs you."

Adelaide stopped short. Then, after a half dozen heartbeats, she gave an infinitesimal nod.

Alone again, Liz turned her face into the pillow and let the tears come. She had the freedom she had craved, but at such a price! It was the freedom of absolute aloneness. Oh, Drew, if only you could be here for five minutes, to hold me in your arms and tell me that someday things would be better than they are now.

She couldn't have him, but she could go to the home that he had loved. There, perhaps, she could find a measure of peace.

Liza probably should have rested longer after her miscarriage, but the atmosphere at the Holden ranch was unbearable. Neither a wife nor mother, she had no place there, so she left as soon as her strength started to come back. Apart from Adelaide's token offer of a home, no one tried to prevent her from leaving, though Janie shed heartfelt tears.

Just before departing, Liza said a quick good-bye to Tom Jackson. Neither of them referred to the attempt to save Andrew Kane; she couldn't have borne it.

The only possessions she took away from her marriage to a rich man's son were the fine mare that had been Billie's present to her their first Christmas, and as much clothing as would fit into her saddlebags. Dressed like a man, Elizabeth Baird Holden, unsuitable wife, failed brood mare, unfortunate reminder, vanished from the Triple H ranch as if she had never set foot there.

In spite of her fatigue and the emptiness inside her, Liza's bleakness began to lift as she rode north. Though she still wasn't sure she could accept Drew's legacy of the ranch, she looked forward to seeing his home. There she would write the letter to his parents that she had been delaying.

Mentally she had tried again and again to compose the letter, and the task was proving as hard for her as it had been for Drew. How should she start? *Dear Sir Geoffrey and Lady Kane, your son is dead. He was a gambler and maybe a bit of a rogue, and the kindest man I ever met. He left a ranch that he loved. It should go to you, but since you probably won't come to Colorado, maybe I'll keep it myself and try to run it as he would have liked.*

With a sigh, she put the project aside. She'd worry about it when she got to Colorado.

Even though Liza had been pretty sure that her fast, grain-fed mare could outrun trouble, she fortunately didn't have to prove it. She took the long ride in easy stages, and by the time she reached Pueblo, she was almost her old self, at least physically. An inquiry at the general store gave her directions to the Lazy K, and she headed up into the hills.

When she reached the top of the last ridge and gazed down into the valley, she saw that Drew had told the truth: it really was the most beautiful place on God's earth, with spectacular mountains above and greenery marking the path of a swift creek. So this was the place that had changed Drew from a ramblin', gamblin' man to a landowner like his stuffy ancestors. She smiled. Maybe some of those ancestral Kanes were less respectable than they had appeared in their portraits. She'd like to think so.

She rode into the valley slowly, feeling as if she was completing a pilgrimage. The long, low ranch house was built of stone, so it would be cool in the summer and stand firm against the winds of winter. As she approached it, she saw a stocky middle-aged man coming from a smaller building to the left. Guessing that it was the foreman, Lou Wilcox, she squared her shoulders and prepared to deliver the bad news.

Kane's second trial at the Gilded Rooster lasted considerably longer than the first. Led by Red Sally and the halting, accented words of Mei-Lin, the parade of witnesses attesting to his innocence was a long one.

Cynically, Kane ascribed the testimony of the men to the fact that Matt Sloan was still out of town. The women, he guessed, would have testified at the first trial if they'd been allowed to.

After the last witness had spoken, Judge Barker banged his gavel on the bar. "A clear case of self-defense. Mr. Kane, you are acquitted of all charges."

Kane checked the coins in his pocket, calculating how much he'd need to get back to Colorado. A good thing Liza had suggested he keep some of the money. Taking out what he could spare, he slapped the gold coins on the bar. "Ladies and gentlemen, in honor of the fact that justice has been served, the drinks are on me until this runs out."

A cheer went up. The saloon owner, the very man who had presided over the first trial, shrugged and started setting out bottles and glasses. Business was business.

Drew picked up a bottle and two glasses and made his way to the judge. "Thanks again, Judge Barker. You're a credit to the federal judiciary." He poured two drinks and handed one over.

Being off duty, Barker beamed and accepted the whiskey. "A pleasure, my boy. I never could stand Matt Sloan or Big Bill Holden—the bastards think they're above the law." He raised the glass and drained it in one swallow. "And I got a bonus out of your case. That Jimmy's a clever lad. He's going to be my clerk and read law with me."

"Excellent." Drew emptied his glass, then set it on the bar. "Give him my best wishes. Now I'm going home."

The judge peered over his spectacles. "I suggest that if you're riding north, you give Prairie City a wide berth."

Drew nodded, accepting the wisdom of the advice. He'd have to wait until he got back to the Lazy K before trying to find out how Liza was. He'd send someone to make discreet inquiries, since showing his own face in Prairie City would be distinctly unhealthy, and not just for him. It wouldn't do for Liza to be seen communicating with him, and the last thing he wanted was to cause her trouble.

As he collected his horse at the livery stable and turned its head north, he gave serious thought to the question of what it would be like to raise Billie Holden's child. Liza would be the mother, so the kid couldn't be all bad. Likely Kane and Liza would have children, too. He hoped so; his close brush with death made him want a family as he never had before.

Such thoughts helped the long miles pass more quickly.

Summer was almost over and fall was on its way. The nights were cold at this elevation, and as Liza lay sleepless, she could hear the dry rustle of the first fallen leaves.

She'd been at the Lazy K for a week, long enough to fall in love with it. Even though she had never seen Drew here, his books and clothes and occasionally whimsical possessions created a vivid sense of his personality. And his bed—it was all too easy to imagine him in his bed. That's why she was having trouble sleeping. Strange how a man whom she had known for such a short time could have imprinted her soul so thoroughly. She wondered whether the tragic circumstances of his death meant that he would become a ghost and haunt the living. If so, his ghost would be welcome here any time.

Since she couldn't explain the exact nature of their

relationship, she had told Lou and Lily Wilcox that she and Drew had been planning to marry, and that was why he'd left her the ranch. They had never questioned her story. As soon as he had seen the crude will on the back of the hotel bill, Lou said that he'd recognize that fancy English handwriting anywhere.

As Drew had promised, Lou and Lily did everything they could to help her learn about the ranch. The Lazy K was a well-run spread, larger and more prosperous than she had expected. His parents would have been impressed if they had ever visited.

Liza's eyes began to sting, and she blinked rapidly. With a sigh, she swung her feet from the bed to the bright Indian rug that warmed the floor. She couldn't put it off any longer—she really must write Drew's parents, and she might as well do it now since she was already in a weepy mood.

It was too chilly to sit up in her shift, so she donned a robe of Drew's. It was black velvet with flamboyant scarlet and gold trim, exactly what she would have expected a successful gambler to wear. Though she suspected that it was not entirely wise to take such pleasure in wearing his clothing, she loved the feel of the robe, and the faint, masculine scent that was uniquely his.

Sadly she slipped on a pair of warm wool socks, then padded into the study to write the most difficult letter of her life.

A smart man would have spent the night in Pueblo, but then, a smart man would have stayed in England and become a solicitor. Taking advantage of the full moon, Kane pushed on through the night. He was too close to home to be satisfied with anything less, even though he was aching with fatigue from the hard riding he'd done.

It was well past midnight when he reached the Lazy K. He took his horse into the stables quietly, not wanting to wake anyone. Greetings could wait until morning. After bedding his horse down for the night, he crossed the yard to the house, drinking in the familiar scene. The moonlit mountains and valley were even more beautiful than he remembered.

The front door was unlocked, which didn't surprise him, but a faint glow of lamplight did. Since the Wilcoxes had their own house, his place should be empty.

Curiously he followed the light to the study. Then he stopped in astonishment in the doorway, wondering if his imagination was betraying him because he had thought of Liza so often. But he'd never thought of putting her in his own black velvet robe, which fit her slim frame like socks would a rooster.

His shock was nothing compared to hers. She had been frowning over a letter, her face deliciously intent, but she glanced up when he came to the door. With a horrified gasp, she dropped her pen, black ink spraying across the paper. Her face went dead white.

They stared at each other for what seemed like forever. In his dreams, Drew had assumed that if—when—they met again, they would go straight into each other's arms. Instead, he was painfully aware that in many ways they were strangers. With a crooked smile, he said, "I know that I've been wearing the same clothes for a month, but surely I don't look that frightening."

Disbelieving, she got up and walked toward him, the hem of his robe trailing across the carpet. "Drew," she whispered, "is it really you? Not a ghost?"

He began to laugh, and as soon as she came within his reach he caught her in his arms and pulled her close. "What do you think?"

She began shaking. "M-Mrs. Holden said that you had been hanged."

With a happy sigh, Drew leaned against the door frame and rested his chin on her head. She felt even better than he remembered, probably because she was wearing a lot less clothing. "The lady should have known better. She had a front-row view when Judge Barker stomped up and said that he was going to take me back to Saline for a new trial."

Liza's head shot up, her gray eyes wide. "Then it worked—Jimmy Washington found the judge in time?"

"That he did, though he and the judge cut it pretty close." Drew made a rueful face. "Even two minutes longer and it would have been too late. Scared me out of five years' growth."

Liza's brows drew together as she thought back. "Mrs. Holden looked odd when I asked her if the execution had taken place. She must have assumed that I wanted Billie's killer dead, and since I was ill, she told me what she thought I wanted to hear. Probably the one and only time she tried to be considerate to me. And Tom Jackson must have thought that I knew what had really happened." She gave a choked giggle. "I was sitting here trying to write the letter to your parents that you asked me to send. Lucky I was so slow."

"I'm glad to hear that," he said wholeheartedly. "But you say you were ill?" With a frown, he put his hands on her shoulders and studied her critically. "You do look a bit peaked. What happened?"

Her gaze dropped to the limp ruffles of his shirt. "I— I lost the baby."

He wrapped his arms around her again and began rocking her gently. "Oh, Liza, sweetheart. You lost so much, so quickly. That must have hurt dreadfully even though you were unhappy about the prospect of having to stay with the Holdens."

She began to cry, his sympathy causing all of her sorrows of the last weeks to pour out uncontrollably. Only when her tears began to subside did she realize the strangeness of the situation. Breaking away from his embrace, she said shyly, "It must look odd to you, me acting as if I own the place."

He smiled and took off his hat, then skimmed it onto a chair with a flick of his wrist. "Well, you thought you did. And that robe looks better on you than it ever did on me."

Self-consciously she drew the velvet panels together, because the shift she wore underneath was very thin. "I'll get out of your way tomorrow."

He straightened, his humor dropping away. "Why would you do a silly thing like that? Where would you go? It would make a lot more sense for you to stay here." His voice softened. "I'd like it if you did. Time I married and settled down and became respectable."

Her mouth dropped open. "How can you talk about marriage? We hardly know each other. My husband has been dead only a few weeks."

"And I killed him," Drew said flatly. "Is that an impassable obstacle?"

"I'm not blaming you for that," she said in a frantic bid for sense. "But there's plenty of other reasons not to marry."

"Such as?" He studied her face, his expression sardonic. "I think I understand. It was one thing to have a quick tumble when we were strangers in the night, both feeling desperate and lonesome, but that doesn't mean I'm good husband material. Mad, bad, and dangerous to know. A lady smart as you could certainly do better."

"You've got it backward!" she said, outraged. "You're a rich, handsome man with a ranch and a fancy pedigree. What would you want with a penniless widow whom you've only known for a few hours?" She blushed furiously. "A woman who behaved in a manner that must have given you an extremely low opinion of her morals."

His tension eased and he smiled, with devastating effect. "The way you behaved gave me an extremely *high* opinion of you. You're brave, lovely, and kind, and you saved my life." He reached out and began playing with her hair. "You're a dangerous woman, Liza. Not only have you got me roped and tied, but I can't wait to be branded."

She shivered as he stroked the lobe of her ear. "You don't have to marry me because you're grateful for what I did, or because you feel guilty about shooting Billie."

"Neither guilt nor gratitude come into it." With his dark tousled hair and rogue's charm, he looked like every mother's nightmare, and every girl's dream. "What did you tell Lou and Lily when you turned up here?"

"The truth, except that"—she hesitated—"well, I said that you and I were engaged to be married and that was why you left me the ranch. It was the simplest explanation."

"Splendid!" he said enthusiastically. "That means if you try to run away, I can sue you for breach of promise."

She glared at him. "This is not a joke. Just because we—we helped each other when we were at the end of our tethers doesn't mean there should be anything more between us."

His fingers skimmed down her throat, warm and sensual. "Is that all that was between us, Liza—a little shared misery?"

Why did his delicious English accent have to make her bones feel like butter? Her pulse was pounding and she was having trouble thinking. "It . . . it meant a lot more to me."

"It was more than just a night to me, too," he said pensively. "I think I would have fallen in love with you under any circumstances, but since we had so little time, it happened in an instant. To me, it felt as if we skipped right over the usual courtship and went directly heart to heart."

His hand curved behind her neck and a gentle pressure urged her closer. "You and I have both suffered some terrible things in the last few weeks. You lost a husband, a father, a child. I killed a man, which I'd never had to do before, and almost lost my life." He tilted her chin up. "The only good thing that happened was our meeting. Don't we have an obligation to take that seed of goodness and help it grow into something that's even better?" He bent his head, and his lips met hers.

His kiss was everything she remembered, and more, a promise of both passion and protection. She leaned into his embrace, loving the feel of his warm, muscular body. "Oh, Drew, I'm not very good at being noble. If you aren't careful, you'll be stuck with me for life."

He gave a gusty sigh of satisfaction. "Now there's a life sentence I can live with." Circling her shoulders with one arm, he turned her and guided her down the hall toward the bedroom. "If necessary, we can continue this discussion in the morning, but at the moment, I would dearly like to go to bed." He cocked a mischievous eye at her. "Preferably with you."

When she halted in midstride, he said hastily, "Just

to sleep. I imagine that after what happened, you're not ready for anything more." His voice became intense. "But, Lord, I'd like so much to spend the night with you in my arms, and wake up and find you there."

In a flash of pure knowing, the last of Liza's doubts vanished. Maybe they had started their relationship in the middle, rather than the beginning, but that didn't make this any less right.

"I'd like that, too." She slipped her arms around his neck. "Did I mention that I love you?"

For a suspended moment, there was silence. Then he said quietly, "The feeling is entirely mutual."

This time she started the kissing, losing track of time and place in a rush of joyous emotion. Vaguely she became aware that they were wrapped around each other like squash vines, her back was flat against the wall of the corridor, and the velvet robe had fallen around their feet.

Lifting his head, he said hoarsely, "We're not making much progress toward that bedroom."

She laughed and started unbuttoning his dilapidated shirt. "I'm feeling fit as a fiddle. We could see how it would go. Of course, if you're too tired. . . ." Her voice trailed off provocatively.

"Not that tired." He swooped her up in his arms and carried her, laughing, to the bedroom where he deposited her gently on the bed. Then he bent over her, his arms braced on either side of her head. "A good thing you didn't manage that letter to my parents. Now when I write, it will be good news instead of bad." He kissed the tip of her nose. "Won't it?"

She slid her arms around his neck and pulled him down beside her. "The best, my dangerous man. The very best."

The Wrong Door

by

Mary Balogh

Without a doubt it was the most stupid thing he had ever done. He had spent the last ten years of his life being daring, rash, even unwise. But this was plain stupid. And the outcome was that he was in grave danger of having acquired a leg-shackle for himself.

He had always intended never to take on a leg-shackle despite the fact that he already had a viscount's title and would one day acquire that of a marquess, if he outlived an elderly and infirm uncle, and it was expected of him to marry and produce an heir. Now he would no longer have to worry about disappointing those expectations. He was in more than danger. He was on his way to the altar as surely as if the offer had been made and accepted already.

Alistair Scott, Viscount Lyndon, had been invited to the seaside home of his friend, Colin Willett, for the occasion of the eightieth birthday of Colin's grandmother. Elmdon Hall was within a day's ride of Brighton and the viscount had pictured himself and Colin riding there frequently, it being summer and the fashionable time to be in Brighton. He had not fully realized until it was too late that it was a full-fledged house party to which he had been invited and that he would be obliged to stay at Elmdon to participate in the celebrations. The house was filled to the rafters with family members and family friends.

It was not at all the viscount's type of entertainment. There were altogether too many sweet young things obviously on the lookout for a husband, some of them with a certain air of desperation since the Season in London was over and they were still unattached. Viscount Lyndon was not interested in sweet young things since he could not bed them and had discovered no other pleasurable use for women in his thirty years.

It was to avoid one persistent miss, who distinctly reminded the viscount of a horse, that he attached himself to Lady Plumtree, a widow, during an afternoon ride on the first full day at Elmdon. And then led her in to dinner. And took her as a partner at cards during the evening. And made an assignation with her for that night. It was a very stupid thing to do. Although he had a passing acquaintance with the lady from town and although it was clear that she understood the rules of the game of dalliance and would provide a delightful diversion during what promised to be a rather dull week in the country, nevertheless it was not the sort of party at which one indulged in *affaires de coeur*.

If everything had proceeded smoothly, of course, the chances were that he would never have felt a pang of guilt over the tastelessness of his behavior. Or over its stupidity. But things did not proceed smoothly. The third door on the left of the inner corridor of the east wing, Lady Plumtree had told him, dark eyes peering up at him through long lashes as she issued the invitation. He would be there, he told her, hooded blue eyes gazing back into hers.

But later that night, walking unfamiliar corridors without a candle or the help of moonlight through windows, it was not quite clear which was the inner corridor and which was the outer. And did the doors on the left include the small door, clearly belonging to some sort of cupboard, that was a mere few inches from the beginning of the corridor? He did not feel these doubts at the time, of course, or perhaps he would have been saved from disaster. It was only later that he realized how carelessly stupid he had been.

How disastrously stupid.

Lady Plumtree was small and slender, quiet and elegant. She was, in fact, the picture of respectability to anyone who did not know that she liked to collect lovers as other ladies collected fans or jewels. One would not expect her to behave like any vulgar courtesan. The viscount merely smiled, then, when he stepped inside her room and closed the door soundlessly behind him to find that she was lying quietly in bed, pretending to sleep. Novelty was always welcome to someone with appetites as jaded as his.

"Laura?" he said, his voice low.

No answer. He smiled again as he drew his shirt clear of his pantaloons and off over his head. He pulled off his pantaloons and stockings and stood naked close to the bed, looking down at her slight form, curled invitingly beneath the covers. Her blond hair was spread about her on the pillow. Not that he could see either her form or the color of her hair with any clarity. Although the curtains at the window were drawn back, it was a very dark night.

He drew back the covers slowly and almost chuckled. She was wearing a nightgown, a very virginal one, covering her from neck to ankles by the look of it. And she still pretended to sleep. She was not a particularly good actress, though. Her breathing was too quiet to be convincing. But there was something very alluring about the appearance of innocence she had chosen to portray and about the stillness of her body. The woman knew how to entice. He lay down beside her carefully and drew the covers back up over them.

He raised himself on one elbow and looked down at her. She was lying on her side facing him, her hair covering the part of her face that was not buried in the pillow. He wished he could see her more clearly. With one finger he lifted aside a heavy lock of hair, lowered his head, and touched his lips to her cheek. Warm and soft. He breathed in the smell of soap. Clever. It was more enticing than perfume.

"Mmm," she said with studied drowsiness, bringing back his smile, and she turned her head sufficiently that he could move his mouth to hers.

He touched it first with his tongue, running it lightly along her upper lip before letting his parted lips rest against hers. Warm and soft again, betraying her wakefulness by parting very slightly to mold themselves to his.

"Lyndon," she said, a mere breath of sound against his mouth.

Firm breasts, small waist, nicely rounded buttocks—there was something surprisingly erotic about letting his hand roam over them, a layer of soft, warm cotton between his hand and them. More erotic than nakedness at this stage of the game. The woman was an expert.

Perhaps too expert. He was almost painfully aroused. He liked a great deal of foreplay. He liked lengthy play inside his women's bodies too, but he always felt cheated of some pleasure if circumstances forced him to an early mount. He liked his women hot and panting and pleading before penetration. This woman was trying to cheat him, even if she did not realize it.

He began to undo the buttons at the front of her nightgown, waiting for her to raise her arms. She did not do so. Perhaps she intended to carry through the charade to the end. Perhaps she would feign sleep even after he had entered her and while he worked in her. He smiled down at her darkened form and felt his breath quicken. There was something almost unbearably alluring about the thought. He hoped that was her plan.

He slid his hand beneath the nightgown along her shoulder and down over one breast to cup it in his palm. He felt her stiffen slightly as his thumb rubbed against her nipple. He took it between his thumb and forefinger, squeezing lightly, willing her to relax and feign sleep again. He set his mouth to hers once more, opening it with the pressure of his lips, and slid his tongue slowly into her mouth, as deeply as he was able. She swallowed and he moaned.

And then all hell broke loose. He found himself fighting a hellcat, who was twisting and punching and scratching and kicking and biting and panting beneath him on the bed. For one moment—and one moment only—he thought that she had suddenly and quite deliberately changed tactics. And then he realized the truth. Too late. Far too late. She had not screamed and there was perhaps the glimmering of a chance that he would be able to get himself and his garments from the room without her seeing the identity of her attacker. But then even the glimmer was snuffed.

There was a light suddenly before he could break free of the unknown woman who was so fiercely defending her honor. And a loud, shocked, scolding voice. A maid, he realized when rationality began to return and he turned his head sharply. A large, very angry maid, who must have been sleeping in the adjoining dressing room. She was carrying a candle in one hand. "Oh, the devil!" he said with a groan, turning his head back to look down at the woman in the bed, who had stopped struggling. She stared back at him from huge eyes, her face flushed, her auburn hair in wild disarray about her shoulders and over the one exposed breast. She was the prettiest of the sweet young things, he saw. He could not remember her name.

But before his mind could even begin to grapple with the impossibility of saying anything that might ease the situation, the maid was beating him about the head and shoulders with one large fist and he leapt out of bed in sheer self-defense.

The maid shrieked.

The sweet young thing dived beneath the bed covers.

"Oh, Lord," the viscount said, grabbing his pantaloons and dragging them on and then reaching down for his shirt and stockings. "I do beg your pardon, ma'am. Wrong room. I thought it was my own. I must have taken a wrong turn. I am so sorry to have inconvenienced you."

He left the room just as the maid was recovering from the shock of being subjected to the sight of a naked aroused man and was setting down the candle, the better to use both fists. She did not come after him.

He regained his own room with ungainly and unwise haste, though he met no one on the way from the east wing to the west. He hurled his shirt and stockings to the floor of his bedchamber and swore fluently enough to have made even the most seasoned soldier blush.

Stupid, stupid, *stupid*! What did he know of inner or outer corridors? Or of third doors or fourth doors? What did he know of Elmdon Hall that he had thought he could go creeping about it in the dark and find unerringly the widow of easy morals who was panting for his body?

Perhaps what he should have felt first was embarrassment. But Viscount Lyndon was no fool, even if he sometimes behaved with incredible stupidity. He knew immediately that any embarrassment he might feel was as nothing to the consequences of his deed that were facing him. He could not remember who the girl was, though he had been presented to all the other guests on his arrival. He could not remember who her father was. Was she Brindley's sister? Yes, he rather believed she was. But one thing he knew for certain. He was going to be seeking out that father or brother as early in the morning as he was to be found—before the father or brother could find him, in fact. He was going to be making his offer for the girl before the father or brother had a chance to blow out his brains on some field of honor. Or perhaps the man would not even consider him worthy of a field of honor. Maybe he would just organize a company of thugs to horsewhip him and render his face unrecognizable before hurling him off Elmdon property.

Perhaps that would be the better alternative too. He would recover from a thorough drubbing. He would not recover from a leg shackle. Except that honor was at the stake, of course. The girl had been compromised. Quite spectacularly compromised. She must be offered for.

If there was any obscenity or blasphemy that the viscount had missed in his first tirade, he certainly made no such omission with the second.

The rest of the night did not bring him a great deal of sleep.

At first Caroline Astor tried with great earnestness to persuade Letty never to say anything about the night's proceedings. It would be their sworn secret, she said, clutching the blankets to her bosom and feeling rather as if she were trying to lock the stable doors after the horse had bolted. The buttons of her nightgown were still open to the waist. After all, Viscount Lyndon himself was not likely to go about boasting of the episode.

But she flushed at her own words. Would he? He was known, and well known at that, as the most dreadful rake. Perhaps it had been deliberate. Perhaps he made a habit of invading the rooms and the persons of unsuspecting females. Perhaps if Letty had not appeared when she had, he would have ravished her. Caroline, that was, not Letty.

Letty planted her fists on ample hips. "Lord Brindley is to know it for sure, mum," she said. It was pronouncement more than statement. "Right this minute."

Caroline ventured a staying hand from beneath the blankets. "Oh, not tonight, Letty," she said. "He will be remarkably cross if we wake him. And it is quite unlikely that Lord Lyndon will return. Is there a lock on the door?"

"There is not," Letty said. "I shall sleep at the foot of your bed, mum. Let him just try to get past me."

"I am sure he will not," Caroline said.

"First thing in the morning," Letty said. "I shall summon your brother here, mum, and you can tell him or I will. It is all the same to me."

"I shall tell him," Caroline said, licking dry lips. "But it was all a dreadful mistake, Letty. He mistook my room for his. You heard him say so."

"Does he have a wife that he mistook for you?" Letty asked with a theatrical sniff. "I think not, mum. He is a bad one, that. And he was not dressed decent even for his own bed. He was—" Her bosom swelled with the memory of the indecency of the viscount's dress or lack thereof.

"Yes, he was," Caroline said hastily, remembering

the glimpse she had had of magnificent naked maleness before she had dived beneath the covers. And the glimpse of the splendid and terrifyingly large part of his anatomy to which she would blush to put a name even in her thoughts.

Letty strode off to drag her truckle bed in from the dressing room. She set it across the foot of her mistress's bed and lay on it like a large and fierce watchdog. Caroline blew out the candle.

And stared upward into the darkness, knowing that she would not have another wink of sleep that night. She should have been hysterical. She should have been rushing to the comfort of her brother's protective arms. She should have woken the whole house with her screams. She certainly should not have been making excuses for Viscount Lyndon to Letty. Doubtless she would not have done so had she not been very foolishly in love with him since she first set eyes on him months before.

She had turned down two perfectly eligible marriage proposals, much to the puzzlement and chagrin of her brother, because of that stupid infatuation. In love with London's worst rake, indeed! It was about the only foolish thing of which she could accuse herself in three-and-twenty years of living. She had been remarkably sensible all her life. The normal Caroline would have accepted the first of those offers during the Season with pleased satisfaction. She would not have dreamed of love and forever after in the arms of a handsome libertine.

Her heart and her stomach—all her insides—had turned several complete handsprings when she had found out that he was a guest at Great-Aunt Sabrina's birthday party. He was so very gloriously handsome with his tall, slender, well-muscled frame and hand-

some features that happened to include two slumbrous
and very blue eyes. And then there was his hair, dark
and thick and shining, dressed in the latest style.

Any other woman but Caroline, feeling as she did
about him, might have been sighing all over him and
making cow eyes at him as that silly Eugenia had been
doing all day. Caroline had done just the opposite and
behaved as if she had not noticed his existence—just as
she had behaved at every ball and other entertainment
during the Season where both he and she had happened
to be.

After all, there was no point in trying to attract his
interest, was there? Rakes wanted only one thing from
a woman and even that for a very short time. Rakes
did not deal in love and marriage and forever after.
Caroline prided herself on her good sense. She might
secretly sigh over the man, but she knew that he could
only make her desperately unhappy even if he deigned
to show an interest in her. She was going to accept the
very next proposal she received—provided the man was
eligible, of course. And provided he was at least moder-
ately handsome. And amiable.

Caroline turned over onto her side and curled up into
her favorite position for sleep. Could she smell him on
the pillow beside her? What an absurd idea. She could
not remember how he had smelled, and the pillow
smelled like—well, like pillow.

The stupid thing—the really stupid thing—was that
she had thought for some time that she was dreaming.
It had seemed like one of those dreams in which one
knows one is dreaming and is willing oneself not to
wake up. She had known that she was dreaming about
him and she had wanted the dream to continue. She
had liked feeling the weight and heat of his body beside
her in bed and the touch of his hand moving back her

hair so that he could kiss her cheek. She had moved
her head so that he could kiss her lips. Actually, she
might have known then that she was not really dreaming. She had never thought about a tongue being involved in a kiss. But it had been delightful to feel his
moving across her upper lip. And then to feel his hand
moving over her body, lightly exploring.

It was only when he started to open her buttons that
she had realized that she could no longer hold on to the
dream. She was waking up with the greatest reluctance—only to find that she was not after all leaving
the dream behind. Only to find that she had not in fact
been dreaming at all. And then his hand had been inside and touching her breast, bringing a strange aching
sort of pain as he pinched her nipple. And his tongue
had no longer been tracing her lips, but sliding deep
into her mouth.

That was when dreams and reality had finally parted
company and she realized not only that she was not
sleeping, but that she did not know the identity of the
man who was sharing her bed and who seemed intent
on sharing her person too. That was when she had gone
berserk.

And all the time it really had been he. The Viscount
Lyndon. That was how rakes touched women, then,
and how they kissed. And how they looked. Or that
was how he looked, anyway. Oh, mercy, she had had
no idea . . . It must hurt dreadfully, she thought. Or
else be unbearably pleasurable. Or perhaps both.

Her cheeks burned and she tried not to listen to Letty's snores. What would Royston do tomorrow? she
wondered. Whisk her away back home? Challenge the
viscount to a duel? It was clear what had happened, of
course. He had spent the whole day with Lady
Plumtree, understandably since the lady was both beau-

tiful and not all she should be, if gossip had the right of it. And Lady Plumtree was in the room next to Caroline's. He had mistaken the room, all right, but not because he had thought Caroline's room to be his own. He had been going to spend the night with Lady Plumtree. He had been starting to make love to her, Caroline, thinking she was Lady Plumtree.

What would have come next? she wondered and grew even hotter at the imagined next stages of what he had started. How long would it have been before . . .

Caroline sat up sharply and thumped her pillow as if she wished it were Viscount Lyndon's face.

Or Lady Plumtree's perhaps.

Royston Astor, Lord Brindley, was in a bad mood, having quarreled with his wife again that morning. And again over Caroline. There was no one particularly eligible at this party, she had pointed out. They were wasting a whole week, when they could be in Brighton or somewhere else where Caroline could meet someone suitable to marry.

It had been in vain for him to remind Cynthia that family duty dictated that they put in this appearance at Elmdon Hall and that Caroline had met and rejected two quite eligible gentlemen during the past few months. She was three-and-twenty, Cynthia had said with that slow distinctness she always used when trying to make a particularly telling point, and had only just made her come-out. That was not his fault either, he had said, grumbling. First Caroline had not wanted a come-out and Papa had not fought against her wishes. Then Grandpapa died, plunging them all into mourning, and then Papa.

Caroline was not in her dotage after all, he had pointed out. Cynthia had given him a speaking glance as if to say that yes, indeed, she was. To give her her due, Cynthia's preoccupation with marrying Caroline off was motivated more by affection than by the desire to get rid of a superfluous sister-in-law.

Lord Brindley's neckcloth would never tie neatly when he was in a bad mood. He had noticed it before. There was a tap on his dressing room door and he turned to scowl at his valet as if the man were personally responsible for the uncooperative neckcloth. But he had merely come to announce that Viscount Lyndon would be obliged for a few minutes of his time.

Lord Brindley frowned. Lyndon? He had been annoyed, to say the least, to find that that irresponsible ass, Colin, had invited a man like Lyndon to such a respectable gathering. One did not feel that one's women were safe with such a libertine in the house. Cynthia he could protect very well himself. But Caroline? She should have been put in a room next to theirs, he had complained to Cynthia on their arrival. He had at least insisted that his sister's maid sleep in her dressing room at night. One never knew with someone like Lyndon.

"Me?" he said to his valet. "You are sure he said me, Barnes?"

Barnes merely coughed discreetly, and Lord Brindley realized that the viscount was standing behind him, outside the door. What the devil?

"Come inside, Lyndon," he said ungraciously. "I am getting ready for breakfast. Disgusting misty morning, is it not? I was unable to go riding."

Viscount Lyndon stepped inside and succeeded only in making Lord Brindley feel dwarfed. His mood was not improved.

"I am afraid I have a matter of some delicacy to discuss," the viscount said.

Lord Brindley met his eyes in the looking glass and stopped fidgeting with his neckcloth, which was doomed to looking lopsided anyway no matter what he did with it. He raised his eyebrows and turned to face the room.

"I feel constrained to ask for the honor of making a marriage offer to your sister," the viscount said.

The baron snapped his teeth together when he realized that his jaw had been in danger of dropping. "Eh?" he said. "Is this some kind of joke, Lyndon?"

"I wish it were," the viscount said, his initial unease seeming to disappear somewhat now that he had launched into speech. "I can see that she has not said anything to you yet."

"Eh?" Lord Brindley realized that his response was not profound, but really what did one say to such unexpected and strange words?

"I am afraid," the viscount said, one corner of his mouth lifting in a wry smile, "that I compromised Miss Astor last night. Rather badly, I am afraid."

Lord Brindley's hands curled into fists at his sides. To do him justice, he did not at the moment think of the vast difference in size and physique between the other man and himself.

"I mistook her room for, er, someone else's," the viscount explained. "Her virtue is intact," he added hastily, "but not, I am afraid, her honor. I beg leave to set matters right by offering her the protection of my name."

"Your name?" the baron said, injecting a world of irony into the words and using some of his wife's slow distinctness.

"I beg your pardon," the viscount said stiffly. "Is my name sullied and I know nothing of it? I have the name and the position and the means with which to provide for Miss Astor for the rest of her life."

"I would rather see her thrown into a lions' den,"

Lord Brindley said. "You did not take her virtue, you said?"

"No," the viscount said. "She awoke in time to fight me off, and her maid arrived to champion her cause."

Caroline and Lyndon? Lyndon touching Caroline? And thinking to marry her? It was perhaps a good thing that none of Lord Brindley's gloves were in sight. Perhaps he would have slapped one in the viscount's face and been precipitated into a dreadfully scandalous situation with which to celebrate his great-aunt's birthday.

"I will make my offer this morning," the viscount said. "With your permission, Brindley. I cannot think you mean what you just said about lions."

"What you *will* do this morning," Lord Brindley said, his hands opening and closing at his sides, "is pack your belongings, order your carriage around, and take yourself off with whatever plausible excuse for leaving you can contrive in the meanwhile. I will give you one hour, Lyndon, before coming after you with a whip. I trust I make myself understood?"

The viscount pursed his lips. But before either man could say another word, there was a second tap on the door and it opened to reveal a pale Caroline. She glanced at Viscount Lyndon, blanched still further, and stepped inside, closing the door behind her.

"Barnes said you were in here, Royston," she said, looking directly at him and ignoring the viscount just as if he were not even there, "and not to be disturbed. But I could not wait. There is going to be a duel, is there not? It will not do. For one thing the whole matter will be made dreadfully public, and for another, you are expert with neither a sword nor a pistol. He is, so I have heard. I will not have you killed for my sake."

"Caroline—" her brother began, but she held up a firm staying hand.

"It must not happen, Royston," she said, lifting her chin and looking at him with a martial gleam in her eyes, "or I shall reveal the full truth to everyone." There was a flush of color in her cheeks suddenly.

"The full truth?"

"That he was in my room by invitation," she said. "That if he compromised me, then I also compromised myself. A duel would be quite inappropriate, you see. You will withdraw the challenge, will you not?"

The viscount, Lord Brindley saw in one quick glance, was standing looking back at him, his expression utterly blank. If the baron could have throttled his sister at that moment and remained within the law, he would have done so. The minx. The slut. He had thought her sensible despite her strange rejection of two chances of an advantageous match during the Season. And yet she had given in to the damnably improper advances of a rake just like the most brainless of chits. Well, let her take the consequences.

"There will be no duel, Caroline," he said. "Leave us, please. Viscount Lyndon and I have certain matters to discuss."

She looked at him a little uncertainly, then seemed about to slide her eyes in the direction of the viscount, changed her mind, turned, and left the room. The viscount had stood still and quiet throughout her visit.

"Well," Lord Brindley said briskly, "we have a marriage contract to discuss, Lyndon. Have a seat. There is no time like the present, I suppose, despite the fact that we may miss breakfast."

Viscount Lyndon took a seat.

If he could do anything he wanted to the girl with utter impunity, Viscount Lyndon decided as he returned to his own room a considerable time later, he

would throttle her. No, she was not a girl. He had seen
that as soon as he had had a good look at her. She was
past girlhood. She was three-and-twenty, according to
her brother. Thank goodness for that, at least. If he
must marry—he winced—then let it at least be to a
woman and not a girl straight from the schoolroom.

He could cheerfully throttle her. He had been so
close to getting himself out of the most damnable mess
he had been in in his life. So close to freedom. His
mind had already been inventing an aged relative at
death's door and a few other fond relatives who had
written to beg his immediate presence at the event. He
had already in his mind been away from a potentially
dull house party and away from a dreaded marriage.

Until she, the sweet young thing, Miss Caroline
Astor, had come along with her noble lie to save her
brother from having a bullet placed between his eyes
or a sword sheathed through his heart. If she had only
known it, it was the exact midpoint between *her* eyes
that he had pictured for one ungallant moment with a
blackened hole through it.

And so here he was, a betrothed man in effect if not
quite yet in reality. The formal offer was still to make,
though the contract had been discussed and agreed
upon. But if the girl—woman—had such an enormous
dowry, the viscount thought, frowning, why the devil
was she still unmarried at the age of three-and-twenty?
And she was admittedly pretty too. What was wrong
with her? Something must be—a pleasant thought to
lie in one's stomach in place of breakfast.

If he made his offer with great care, he thought,
throwing himself down on his bed and staring upward
. . . If he made himself thoroughly disagreeable . . .
But no. Honor was involved. If it were not, he would
not even be making the offer. He grimaced.

She had not even looked at him after that one glance before entering the room. She had not even named him. She had referred to him only as "he." And she had lied through her teeth, not to protect him, but to save her brother's hide. And she had looked thoroughly humorless and belligerent while she was doing so. She had red hair—well, auburn anyway. She was bound to be a bad-tempered shrew. That was all he needed in his life.

A damned attractive shrew, of course. His temperature slid up a degree when he remembered . . . But not attractive enough to make a leg-shackle seem any better than a life sentence. The woman did not live who was that attractive.

Damn!

Perhaps after they were betrothed. The viscount set one arm over his eyes and thought. He could make himself extremely obnoxious if he tried. Gaze admiringly at himself in looking glasses and windows when he ought to be complimenting her on her appearance. Talk incessantly about himself. Boast about some of his conquests. Sneer at anything and everything he found her to be interested in. Within the week he could have her screaming to be released from her promise.

He swung his legs over the side of the bed and ran his fingers through his hair. Gad, but it went against the grain. All his attentions toward women were usually designed to attract, not to repel. However, it would be in a good cause. Good for him and good for her too. If she only knew it, he would be doing her the greatest favor in the world. He would make the world's worst husband. The woman would be miserable within a fortnight of marriage.

He got resolutely to his feet. He had arranged with Brindley to talk with her before luncheon. He was suddenly eager to get the thing over with so that he could proceed to the serious business of freeing both of them again. He wondered if he could charm any of the female servants into serving him a late breakfast. He did not fancy making a marriage proposal on an empty stomach.

Not that he really fancied making one on a full stomach either, of course.

He was going to make her a marriage proposal. And it seemed that everything had been arranged already. The proposal itself and her acceptance of it were to be a mere formality.

It had never struck her. Not through a largely sleepless night—she would have said it was entirely sleepless except that there were memories of bizarre erotic dreams. And not through an anxious early morning. She had visualized public denunciations and duels and horrible embarrassment. She had pictured all kinds of punishments that might be visited upon Viscount Lyndon, almost all of which would undoubtedly harm Royston more than the real culprit. But she had never imagined that anyone would consider marriage between the two of them necessary.

And yes, of course she must listen to the offer, Royston had said in a coldly furious voice when he had finally appeared in her room and dismissed a grimly vigilant Letty. And accept it too. He did not know what had come over her. Did she have no pride in herself or her family name? Did she not know Lyndon's reputation? Did she think any but the most unprincipled rake would have agreed to meet her in her bedchamber at night?

She had been unable to defend herself. After all she was the one who had said the viscount was in her room by her invitation. She had merely muttered something about love and romance and just a very few minutes during which to say a private good night.

"Love," her brother had said with the utmost contempt. "Romance. With someone like Lyndon, Caroline? Well, you will have them for what they are worth for the rest of your lifetime. I wish you happy."

She could have him for the rest of a lifetime. Caroline sighed. She could marry him. She could be his betrothed within the coming hour. Viscount Lyndon, over whom the romantical and foolish side of her nature had sighed from afar for months while the sensible part of herself had assured her that it was as well that she admired only from afar. That it was as well his eyes had never alighted on her.

She was to meet him on the terrace half an hour before noon. She wandered there five minutes early, well knowing that it would have been far better to be five minutes late. She smiled cheerfully at five of her young relatives, who were embarking on a walk to the woods half a mile distant, and expressed her regrets at being unable to go with them.

"I am meeting someone," she said.

"I hope he is tall, dark, and handsome," Irene said with a laugh.

And then he was coming through the double front doors and down the horseshoe steps and along the terrace toward her. Toward *her*. And looking at her. She had never been this close to him before—except last night, of course, and briefly this morning in Royston's dressing room. He had never looked at her. He was indeed very tall and dark. And handsome. And if she was not careful, she was going to be sighing and making cow eyes and be no better at all than Eugenia.

"Good morning, my lord," she said and listened with approval to the coolness of her voice.

"Miss Astor." He inclined his head and extended one arm. "Shall we walk?" He indicated the formal gardens before the house and the lawn that sloped beyond it toward the distant beach. The driveway and the road were behind the house.

She took his arm and glanced along it to a strong, long-fingered, well-manicured hand. The very hand that had come inside her nightgown and fondled her breast. She felt as if she had just been running for a mile uphill but quelled the urge to pant.

"I am afraid," he said, "that I have caused you a great deal of distress, ma'am, both last night and this morning."

The best way to cope with her very schoolgirlish reactions, Caroline decided, was to withdraw into herself, to keep her eyes directed toward the ground before her feet, and to keep her mouth shut as much as possible.

"You must allow me to make some reparation," he said.

They were strolling past brightly colored flowerbeds. All the flowers were blooming in perfect symmetry, she thought and wondered how the gardeners did it.

"It would give me great satisfaction if you would do me the honor of marrying me," he said.

Caroline Scott, Viscountess Lyndon. One day to be a marchioness. Wife to such a splendidly gorgeous man. Mother to his children. The envy of every woman of the *ton*. And the proud owner of their pity too as her husband philandered his way through the rest of their lives. Ah, it was such a dreadful pity. And it was taking a superhuman effort to put common sense before inclination. Perhaps she would wake soon from the bizarre dream that had begun some time the night before.

"I am sorry," he said, bending his head closer to hers

and covering her hand on his arm with his, "you are quite overwhelmed, are you not? I am more sorry than I can say to be the cause of such bewilderment. Would you like some time to consider your answer?"

"No," she said, her voice as calm as it had been before and quite at variance with the beating of her heart, "I do not need any longer, my lord."

"Ah," he said, his tone brisker, "then it is settled. You have made me very happy, ma'am." He raised her hand to his lips.

She spoke with the deepest regret. "I am afraid you have misunderstood, my lord," she said. "My answer is no."

"No?" He stopped walking abruptly in order to stare down at her. Her hand was still clasped in his.

"I will not marry you," she said, "though I thank you for the offer, my lord. It was kind of you."

"Kind?" he said, a new sharpness in his voice. "I believe you are the one who does not understand, Miss Astor. I compromised you last night. I must marry you."

Ah, romance, Caroline thought with an inward sigh. Whenever she had daydreamed about him, he had been gazing at her, eyes alight with admiration and passion. His eyes up close were even more beautiful than she had dreamed of their being, but they were frowning down at her as if she were a particularly nasty slug that had crawled out onto the path after the early morning mist.

"It seems a singularly foolish reason for marrying," she said. "Nothing really happened, after all." She willed herself not to flush, with woeful lack of success.

"Miss Astor," he said, "not only was I alone with you in your bedchamber last night, but I was also naked in your bed with you." Caroline would not have been surprised to see flames dancing to life on her cheeks. "We were seen together by your maid with the result that the story is by now doubtless common knowledge belowstairs. I admitted the truth of what happened to your brother with the result that a considerable number of people abovestairs probably know by now. And you even confessed to having invited me into your bed."

"Into my room," she said. "To say good night."

"Inviting a man into your room at night," he said, "is the same thing as inviting him into your bed, ma'am. And saying good night under such circumstances is the same thing as making love. It seems that your education in such matters is somewhat lacking. We have no choice but to marry, Miss Astor."

"Letty will have said nothing," she said, "and neither will Royston unless he has unburdened his mind to Cynthia. She will not spread the story. The idea that we must marry is ridiculous."

He had released her hand to clasp his hands behind him. He regarded her in silence for a while. She looked up into his face, memorizing its features, in particular the rather heavy-lidded blue eyes. She tried to memorize his height and the breadth of his shoulders. She knew she would dream of last night and this morning for weeks, perhaps months to come. And she knew that a part of her would forever regret that she had not seized the moment and made herself miserable for the rest of her life.

"You know nothing about me. Is that it?" he asked. "Your brother is satisfied that I will be able to keep you in the kind of life to which you are accustomed, Miss Astor. I have estates and a fortune of my own. I am also heir to a marquess's title and fortune. Is it your ignorance of these facts that has made you reluctant?"

"I knew them," she said. "You are not exactly an

unknown figure in London, my lord, and I was there for the Season this spring."

"Were you?" he said, looking her over in a way that confirmed her conviction that he had never knowingly set eyes on her before this week. "Your objection to me is more personal then?"

Her mouth opened and the words came out before she could check them. All she would have to say was that she objected to being forced into marriage because of a mere mistake in identifying a room. But that was not what she said.

"You have a reputation as perhaps the most dreadful rake in England, my lord," she said.

"Do I?" His manner became instantly haughty. He looked twice as handsome if that were possible. "I thought women were supposed to have a soft spot for rakes, Miss Astor. You are not one of them?"

"Not as a husband," she said. "I would be a fool."

"And clearly you are not," he said. "So I am being rejected because I like to bed women and have never made a secret of the fact."

She thought for a moment. Yes, that was it exactly. Alas. "Yes," she said.

"And you would not like to be bedded by me, Miss Astor?"

Yes, she had been right to describe his eyes secretly to herself as slumbrous, Caroline thought. They were exactly that and his voice low and seductive. And then the meaning of his words echoed in her ears.

"No," she said. "When I marry, my lord, I want to know that I am everything to my husband. I want to know that I am the only woman in his life and always will be."

"If you—and your maid—had awoken just a few minutes later last night," he said, "you might have been singing a different tune this morning. The bedding process had barely begun and yet your body was responding with pleasure. There was a great deal more to come. A very great deal."

"Do you mean," she said, beginning to feel indignant, "that I would have been begging for more this morning? Begging even for marriage so that the pleasure could be repeated?"

"I could make you fall hopelessly in love with me in no time at all," he said, reaching out one long finger and carelessly flicking her cheek with it.

"Poppycock!" she said, now so thoroughly angry that she totally forgot that she *was* in love with him already.

"I would wager my fortune on it," he said. "One day is all I would need."

She drew breath audibly. "The assumption being," she said, "that there is everything to fall in love with in you and nothing in me. *I* would fall in love with *you* in the course of a day, but you, of course, would remain quite immune to my charms. You are a conceited, a-a conceited—"

"Ass?" he suggested, raising his eyebrows.

"Fop, sir," she finished with a flourish. She was glad all this had happened. Oh, she was glad. The scales had fallen from her eyes and she could see him at last for what he was—not so much a charming rake as a conceited ass. She wished she had had the courage to say the word aloud.

"Well," he said, "perhaps we should make a formal wager, Miss Astor, since we seem not about to make a formal betrothal after all. Twenty-four hours. At the end of it if I have fallen in love with you I lose my wager of—shall we say fifty pounds? If you have fallen in love with me, you lose yours. If we both win or both lose, then we end up even. Agreed?" He stretched out an imperious right hand toward her.

"Either one of us would be foolish to admit to having fallen," she said, "when it would mean the loss of fifty pounds and the ridicule or pity of the other."

"Ah, but we must trust to each other's honor and honesty," he said. "Do we have an agreement, Miss Astor? It will mean spending the rest of today and tomorrow morning together, of course. As for tonight, we can discuss that later."

"What utter nonsense," she said, staring down at his hand and remembering the strangely pleasurable pain she had felt when two of his fingers had squeezed her nipple. "I have no wish to spend any more time with you, my lord, and as for this wager you suggest, it is stupid. What if one of us does fall in love with the other? What if we both do? Nothing will have changed. It is just stupid."

"In the clubs of London, Miss Astor," he said, "it is considered the mark of the most abject cowardice to refuse a wager. A man can easily lose his honor by doing so."

"I am not a man," she said.

"I had noticed."

Again the seductive voice. She did not look up to observe his eyes. She slapped her hand down onto his.

"This is stupid," she said.

"I take it you are accepting the wager?" he asked.

"Yes," she said as his hand closed about hers. "But it is stupid." She looked up to find him grinning down at her. His teeth were very white and even. His eyes crinkled at the corners when he smiled and those lovely blue eyes danced with merriment. Round one to Viscount Lyndon, she thought as her knees turned to jelly.

But of course she no longer loved him. She despised him.

"This," he said, raising her hand to his lips again, "is going to be a pleasure, ma'am—Caroline. The beach for a walk after luncheon?"

What he should do, Viscount Lyndon thought as he changed after luncheon for a walk on the beach, was summon his carriage and have his coachman drive him directly to London and deposit him at the doors of Bethlehem Hospital. He should have himself fitted into a straitjacket. He was clearly mad.

He had had his ticket to freedom again. The woman had refused him though he had made his offer with no attempt whatsoever to repel her. He had even behaved with strict honor by trying to insist when she had first rejected him. He had tried to make her see that she had no choice but to marry him. Still she had refused.

It should have been like a dream come true. He should have left her at a run and not stopped until there were a few hundred miles between them. He should have shouted with joy as soon as he was out of earshot. He had been free again, free of a leg-shackle and free of obligation, his honor intact.

Instead of which . . . He scowled at his image in the looking glass and decided against wearing a hat. It would probably blow into the sea anyway on such a breezy day. Instead of which he had taken her refusal as a personal affront and had demanded to know the reason why. And as soon as he had discovered the reason—her aversion to marrying a rake—all his old instincts had come into play. His very self-respect had made him incapable of letting her go unconquered.

Poppycock, she had said when he had told her—quite truthfully but with rash stupidity—that he could make her fall hopelessly in love with him in a day. And so he had set about doing just that. It would be easy, of course. He would not even need the full twenty-four hours. But what was his purpose? If she fell in love with him, she would marry him after all.

What he should do was spend the rest of the day making sure she came to dislike him more than she did already. That after all had been his original plan, when he had assumed that she would betroth herself to him without protest. But now, of course, he was facing the challenge of a wager. And he had never in his life been able to resist a wager.

She was in the hallway, talking with some of the other sweet young things, including the horsey one, who favored him with melting glances as he came down the stairs. The general intention among the young people, it seemed, was to walk down to the beach. Lady Plumtree was in the hallway too, tapping one foot on the tiles and looking grim and haughty. He had had no opportunity to explain to her why he had failed to keep their tryst the night before.

Caroline Astor detached herself from her group and turned to him while the others gaped and Lady Plumtree turned sharply away to smile dazzlingly at Willett's father.

"Everyone is ready for the walk, then?" Colin called cheerfully from somewhere close to the front doors. He caught the viscount's eye and winked as he sized up the situation. "Anyone for a bathe?"

The horsey girl shrieked. "But there are waves, Colin," she said. "And it is cold."

"Caroline." The viscount took her hand on his arm and patted it. "Trying to rival the sunshine, are you?" She was dressed in all primrose yellow, a quite inspired color with her auburn hair. She really was remarkably pretty. He was surprised he had not noticed her anywhere during the Season. But then he was not in the habit of noticing any but the beddable females—beddable in fact as well as in looks.

"Oh, and succeeding in outshining it," she said, smiling at him as dazzlingly as Lady Plumtree had just smiled at Colin's father. "You must add that, my lord, and I shall be so delightfully flattered that I will fall headlong in love with you and win your wager for you when our day has scarcely begun."

He was taken aback. He had noticed earlier in the morning, of course, that his first impression of timidity had been wrong. She had shown spirit. Now she had clearly decided to go on the attack. Well, it might be an interesting day after all, though he dreaded to think what would be awaiting him at the end of it.

He grinned at her. "But of course," he said, "you succeed in outshining the sun. My eyes are dazzled."

Her mouth quirked at the corners.

"Women who are about to fall in love with me are permitted to call me by my given name," he said.

"Alistair," she said. "I suppose it cannot be shortened, can it?"

"The first boy at Eton who tried found himself on his back stargazing with a bloody nose," he said.

"I'll not try, then," she said. "Alistair."

They followed along behind everybody else, through the formal gardens and across the long lawn that finally mingled with sand and gave place to the open beach. It was a sunny and warm afternoon, though several clouds were scudding across the blue and there was a steady breeze to prevent the heat from becoming oppressive.

"Tell me about yourself," the viscount said as they walked.

"Beginning at the cradle?" she asked. "Do you have a few hours to spare?"

"I do," he said, "But let me be more specific. How is it that you are twenty-three years old and unmarried?"

"Because I have been waiting for you?" she said, directing a melting look up at him. Her eyes were not quite green, not quite gray. They were a mixture of both. "How old are you, Alistair? Thirty?"

"Right on the nose," he said.

"And why are you thirty and not married?" she asked.

"Because I have been waiting for you, of course," he said, looking directly into her eyes in a way he knew had a powerful effect on women. In reality he wanted to chuckle. She really was a woman of spirit. He rather thought he was going to enjoy himself—if he kept his mind off the consequences.

"Ah," she said, "and amusing yourself with other women while you wait."

"Practicing on them," he said, "so that you might have all the benefit of my expertise, Caroline."

"Ooh," she said. "This is the part at which my knees buckle under me?"

"I would prefer that to happen in a more secluded spot," he said. "Where I could proceed to follow you down to the ground."

"Then you must not talk yet about your expertise," she said.

He chuckled suddenly. "Why *are* you still unmarried?" he asked.

"For a number of reasons," she said. "At first I did not want to leave the country for all the silly formality of a court presentation and an appearance on the marriage market, even though I could not feel any great attachment to any of the eligible gentlemen at home.

Then when I finally decided that perhaps I should make an appearance after all, my grandfather was inconsiderate enough to die. When we were coming out of mourning for him, my father decided to follow in his footsteps. I finally made my curtsy to the queen and got myself fired off this spring at a shockingly advanced age."

"And no one wanted you?" he asked.

"Would I admit as much even if it were true?" she said. "Actually, it is not. I had two offers, both from perfectly eligible and amiable gentlemen. I refused both."

"You make a habit of refusing marriage offers, then," he said. "Why? Were they rakes too? Or do you have your mind set against any marriage."

"Neither," she said. "I just have the silly notion that I would like to marry for love. Mutual love. I would find it equally distressing to marry a man who was indifferent to me when I loved him as to marry a man who sighed over me when I could feel no more than liking or respect for him."

"Which was it with your two suitors?" he asked.

"One of them loved me, I believe," she said. "With the other, as with you, there was a mutual indifference of feelings."

"So," he said, "you are a romantic."

"Yes." She looked at him and regarded his smile of amusement in silence for a few moments. "Most people feel great embarrassment about admitting such a thing. Most people go immediately on the defensive. But it is romance that gives life its color and its warmth and its joy, my lord—Alistair. It is romance that lifts life from being a rather nasty accident into being a thing of beauty and meaning. Yes, I am a romantic. And yes, I will marry only for mutual love."

And so, he thought, he need not worry about the morrow and what it would bring. For even if he won his wager—*when* he won his wager—she would not marry him. Before she would agree to marry him, he would have to be in love with her too. He was safe. Free. He could enjoy the day, knowing that he would be free at the end of it.

Her cheeks were tinged with color and her eyes were glowing. Her lips were parted in a soft smile. It was an attractive idea—*a thing of beauty and meaning*. He almost wished for one moment that he was the sort of man who could believe in love and in commitment to the beloved. Instead of which he believed only in lust and commitment to his own pleasures.

"You will die a spinster," he said, "rather than compromise your dreams?"

Her smile lost its dreamy quality. "Oh, I suppose not," she said. "I would hate to have to impose my presence on Cynthia and Royston for the rest of my life. And I would hate to miss the experience of motherhood. I suppose that sooner or later I will settle for respectability and amiability if love does not come along. But that will have to be sooner rather than later, will it not? I am almost on the shelf already. It is horrid being a woman and expected to marry so very early in life."

"Have you never been in love?" he asked. He found himself hoping that she would not have to settle for less than her dream. She wanted to love her husband and be loved by him. She wanted children. It did not seem a very ambitious dream. But she was three-and-twenty and had not found it yet.

"Yes," she said flushing. "Once."

"But he did not love you?"

"No," she said. "And I fell out of love with him, too, once I got to know him better."

And a good thing too, he thought. The bounder did not deserve her love if he had so carelessly rejected it. She could do better.

"What about you, Alistair?" She was looking up at him again. "Why are you still unmarried?"

"Because I have never felt any inclination to marry," he said. "Because I do not believe in love. Because my life is too full of pleasure to be given up to the chains of marriage."

"Pleasure," she said. "Pleasure without anyone with whom to share it. I cannot imagine such a state."

"Because you and I are very different," he said.

"Which is probably the understatement of the decade," she said. "What you began to do to me last night"—she flushed deeply—"is probably very pleasurable, is it not?"

He could still regret that that experience had not been carried a little further or even to completion. He had rarely felt more aroused by a woman. His eyes strayed down her body and he could remember the soft, warm curves and the unusual eagerness he had felt to cut short the preliminaries in order to sheath himself in her.

"It is the most pleasurable activity in the world, Caroline," he said, watching her mouth, keeping his voice low.

The tip of her tongue moistened her upper lip with what he guessed was unconscious provocation. "And yet," she said, "you feel no closeness to the woman inside the body? There is a whole person there experiencing pleasure too—I have no doubt, you see, that you give pleasure to your women as well as to yourself. I had small evidence of that last night."

"Did you?" Dammit but he was in grave danger of becoming aroused again.

"If those pleasures could be combined and shared," she said. "If it could be two *persons* instead of just two bodies making love, imagine what it might be like. The earth would move."

"They would hear the music of the spheres together," he said, smiling in amusement. And yet he was not altogether amused. What *would* it be like? It would, he supposed, be making love, a term he usually used to describe what he did to women with great enthusiasm and great frequency, whereas in reality all he did was— Yes, the obscene word that leapt to his mind was far more appropriate to the type of pleasure he took from the exertions of the bed.

"Which way shall we go?" he asked as their progress took them first over the sandy grass at the edge of the lawn and then onto the open beach, which stretched for a few miles in either direction in a wide golden band. "With the others toward the bathing huts? Or the other way, toward solitude?"

"The other way by all means," she said, immediately resuming the brightly flirtatious mood she had demonstrated at the start of their walk. "How am I to make you fall in love with me if we are distracted with company? How are you to make me fall in love with you?"

"This direction it is, then," he said, turning them to their right. "I would have accused you of abject cowardice if you had made the other choice, you know."

"Yes, I know," she said. "Are you in love with me yet, Alistair? I am not in love with you though a few hours of our twenty-four have already passed. My impression of you as a successful rake is fast dwindling. You had better reassure me."

He chuckled and tucked her arm more firmly through his.

She was actually enjoying herself, Caroline realized in some surprise as they turned away from the direction the group was taking and struck out along the empty beach. Even the thought that she should not be going off alone with him unchaperoned did not worry her. After all, he was supposed to be her betrothed or her soon-to-be betrothed anyway. She had told Royston evasively just before luncheon that yes, indeed Viscount Lyndon had made her an offer but that they had not settled the matter definitely yet. They were to go walking during the afternoon. The implication had been that they were to settle matters then.

She was enjoying herself. There was something wonderfully freeing about being able to spend time with a man without having to wonder if he was trying to think of some way to get rid of her. And to be able to talk on any subject that came to mind because she was not trying to impress him or make any particularly favorable impression on him. They had talked about things she had hardly dared even to think about before—like the pleasure a man and a woman might derive from being in bed together, for instance. Gracious heaven.

And it was fun to be able to flirt without being accused of being fast. It was all for a wager. She was expected to flirt. He would think her a poor creature if she did not. And definitely it was fun to flirt with him. With Viscount Lyndon. Alistair. It was rather like something from a dream. This time yesterday she had been studiously ignoring him because she had been feeling the power of his attractions so strongly.

"Where did you think you were last night?" she asked.

He looked at her sidelong, his eyelids drooping over his eyes. "In heaven," he said.

"For shame," she said, checking the laughter that was bubbling up inside her. "Such carnal pleasures would not be appropriate in heaven."

"Then perhaps it is as well," he said, "that my behavior thus far in life makes it likely that I am bound for the other place. A heaven without the pleasures of sex would be a dull place."

She should be outraged. She was not, and she was enjoying the freedom of not having to pretend that she was. "Where *did* you think you were?" she asked again.

"Never mind," he said. "That would be telling. Suffice it to say that taking the wrong turnings or opening the wrong doors or climbing into the wrong beds can definitely have their compensations. Though I could wish that this particular compensation had lasted longer."

"No," she said. "That is nonsense. I was asleep most of the time. Besides, I know nothing."

"I believe, Caroline," he said, again with that sideways glance, "that you are fishing for a compliment."

She was. She wanted to know why he had wanted it to last longer. She wanted to know what her attractions had been. But even her newfound boldness would not allow her to ask the questions aloud.

"You were warm and soft and shapely and inviting," he said. "And responsive in a languid, highly alluring sort of way."

"And yet," she said, "you thought I was someone else. Is she like that too?"

"Let me just say," he said, "that I was pleasantly surprised."

She was pleased. Ridiculously so. She wanted to fish further, but there were limits to her immodesty and she had reached them.

"Are you going to her tonight?" she asked.

"Heaven forbid," he said. "I might find myself in bed with the birthday lady herself—your Great-Aunt Sabrina."

Caroline exploded into mirth. The mental picture his words had painted was just too tickling to be resisted.

"Exactly," he said. "It does not bear thinking of, does it?" He chuckled and then threw back his head and roared with laughter.

They looked at each other and were off into peals of mirth again until he released her arm, took her hand in his, and laced his fingers with hers.

"Caroline," he said, "you are a shocking young lady. How could you have found that idea funny?"

She laughed again for answer. Walking hand in hand with a man, especially with their fingers laced, seemed far more intimate than walking arm in arm. His hand felt very large and strong.

"How did you like London and the Season?" he asked.

"Oh, very well," she said, "though all the entertainments can be very tedious, especially the balls. One feels all the necessity of appearing to enjoy oneself when one is without a partner and to be quite bored when one is not. I always felt the perverse urge to do the opposite."

"And shock the *ton*, Caroline?" he said. "I hope you never gave in to temptation."

"Under normal circumstances," she said, "I behave with the utmost decorum. I always do what is expected of me. That is why you have never noticed me." If someone would just present her with a pair of scissors, she thought, she would gladly cut out her tongue. What a foolishly revealing thing to say.

"Yes," he said, "that would have been part of the

reason. The other is that even if you had behaved un-conventionally you would still have been one of the virtuous women, Caroline. I tend not to notice virtuous women."

"Because they are dull?" she said.

"Because I cannot take them to bed without marrying them first," he said.

"Ah, yes, of course," she said. "So I am not to feel slighted that you did not notice me? I am not to feel forever unlovely and unattractive because the notable rake, Viscount Lyndon, never once allowed his eyes to alight on me? How reassuring."

"Actually," he said, "if I had allowed my eyes to do any such thing, Caroline, I might have found myself behaving atypically. I might have found myself in pur-suit of a virtuous woman. You are extremely lovely, as I am sure your glass must tell you every time you glance into it."

"Oh, well done." She turned her head to look up into his face, allowing her eyes to sparkle, though it was not difficult. The compliment really had pleased her. "Are you now making a concerted effort to woo me? To make me fall in love with you? You came perilously close to scoring a hit that time. Perilous for me, that is."

His eyes smiled at her. "And your enthusiasm," he said, "is doing the like for me, Caroline. It is time for each of us to redouble our efforts and our guard, I believe."

He stopped walking in order to look back over his shoulder. She did the same so that their heads almost touched. There must be almost half a mile of beach between them and the others already. They were clus-tered about the bathing huts, probably trying to decide whether any of them was going to be brave enough to test the water.

"You tasted particularly enticing last night," the viscount said, turning his head partway. She did the same so that they were gazing into each other's eyes, only inches apart. "I wonder if you taste the same this afternoon."

She could not believe the words that came from her mouth. They seemed not to have passed through her brain for approval first. "There is an easy way of finding out," she said.

"And so there is." He had taken her free hand in his and laced his fingers with that too. He took the half step that separated them. "Maybe I should take it."

"Yes." She could feel his thighs warm and hard against hers. Her breasts were pressed against his coat. She had to bend her head back in order to look up at him. And she had not been mistaken. There really had been the smell of him on her pillow last night. An elusive smell—soap, cologne, leather, all three, none of the three. A heady masculine smell. She closed her eyes.

His lips were slightly parted when they met hers. They were warm and exploring. She allowed her own to relax beneath them instead of clamping them into a tight line as she had done with the two gentlemen who had been permitted to kiss her on previous occasions. She willed him to touch her with his tongue again and he did, running it lightly along her upper lip and back along the lower until she felt a sharp stabbing of sensation in her breasts. She wanted his tongue in her mouth so that she could discover if she found it disgusting, as she had not the night before when she had been half asleep. But he made no move to put it there.

"Mmm," she heard someone say. It was a feminine voice and could only have been her own.

"Mmm, indeed." His forehead and nose were against hers and he was gazing down at her mouth.

She felt foolish. "Well?" she asked. "*Do* I taste the same?"

"Last night," he said, "you tasted of bed and sleep. This afternoon you taste of sunshine and sea and beach. And both times of woman."

He was so much more experienced at this sort of thing than she was. Even the pitch and tone of his voice—

"Oh, dear," she said, drawing back her head so that she could look into his face without going cross-eyed. And her voice again acted independently of her brain. "I think we should build a sand castle."

He had the most attractive grin of any man she had ever seen, she decided. Of course, with those teeth and those eyes and the all-over beauty, it was not surprising. She wished she had not said anything so stupid. Whatever had possessed her?

"Or something," she added lamely.

"What a delightful idea," he said. "But we have nothing with which to dig except our hands. Are you willing to get sand beneath your fingernails?"

"Yes," she said. "There is no greater fun than being all over sand." Or at least there had not been when she was twelve years old or less. But she was twenty-three and he was thirty. How ridiculous he must think her.

He set an arm about her waist and started walking again. She had little choice but to wrap her dangling arm about his waist. "A little farther along," he said, "where the sand looks softer. But you do not play fair,

Caroline. I am used to a different kind of flirtation. I am not sure that my heart is proof against this."

Which was clearly the most stupid thing either of them had said all day.

He had thought of a digging instrument while they walked and when they stopped, presented her with his quizzing glass with a bow and a flourish. She looked at it dubiously.

"The rim is somewhat blunt," he said, "but it may help."

"It may never be usable as a quizzing glass again, though," she said. "But then perhaps that is just as well. There is nothing more unmannerly, I believe, than quizzing ladies through a glass."

"But it can be marvelously revealing, Caroline," he said. "And marvelously intimidating too. There is nothing better calculated to discourage ambitious mamas than a quizzing glass and a haughty stance."

She set the glass down on the sand while she removed her bonnet. "I would not imagine," she said, "that there are many ambitious mamas for you to repel any longer."

"Hm, nasty," he said. "You would be surprised, Caroline. A title and fortune and prospects cover over a multitude of sins."

He took off his coat and rolled up the sleeves of his shirt. And they set to the task of transforming one particularly flat and featureless area of beach into a formidable castle strong enough to withstand the attack of the tide. They worked together for fifteen minutes in near silence until he sat down to remove his Hessians and his stockings.

"There is no point in ruining them as well as a perfectly serviceable quizzing glass," he said when Caroline paused in her work to watch him. "Besides, I remember from some nameless outing in childhood that there is nothing more delectable than the feel of sand between the toes."

"Oh," she said with a sigh, "I have been trying to ignore similar memories." And off came her shoes and her stockings. Some of the pins had come out of her hair so that it looked like an untidy and glorious auburn halo about her head.

Half an hour later, hot, sticky, and sandy, the viscount sat back on his heels to view their creation. He could not recall an hour he had enjoyed more. Which was a strange and absurd admission to make. Caroline was on her knees, one cheek almost resting on the sand as she worked with a delicate finger at the arch of a gateway. One lock of hair trailed in the sand. Her derrière was nicely and invitingly elevated. He could have reached out and patted it, but did not. She was clearly enjoying herself as much as he had been doing.

They had been telling each other, between bouts of quiet concentration, about their childhood. He had remembered incidents and escapades that he had not thought of for years.

He spread his coat on the sand and lay back on it, one arm behind his head, watching her lazily. He had set himself to win a wager. He had twenty-four hours in which to make the woman admit that she had fallen in love with him. And yet he was wasting at least one of those hours building a sand castle with her and exchanging stories of childhood. He must be losing his touch.

But he liked her. He could not remember liking a woman for years. Not to the extent of seeing her as a person anyway and enjoying merely talking and laughing with her. And building a sand castle with her. He pictured himself suggesting such an afternoon's entertainment to Lady Plumtree and chuckled aloud.

Caroline turned her head and lifted herself onto her hands and knees. "I am glad I afford you some amusement," she said. "Lazy workers will not be tolerated, you know. They will be dismissed without reference."

"Does that mean I will never be allowed to work again?" he asked. "Do say yes."

She sat back on her heels and admired their handiwork. "It is rather splendid, is it not?" she said.

"It is indefensible," he said. "There is no moat."

She sighed. "Should we dig one?"

"Then we would need a drawbridge," he said. "Besides, Caroline, it is built of sand. Sand castles are impregnable only in dreams."

She swished her hands together in a vain attempt to remove all the sand. "But it is a lovely dream castle, is it not?" she said. "Think of all the glorious knights who would ride in and out of my gateway."

"And all the lovely ladies on my battlements," he said stretching out one hand toward her.

She set her own in it and gazed down at him. "Was this a silly idea?" she asked. "Do you think me very foolish? Have you been unutterably bored?"

He considered. "No to all three," he said. "Come here."

" 'Here' being the sand beside you?" she said.

"Yes." He tightened his grip on her hand and smiled up at her. She looked remarkably untidy and sandy. She looked delicious.

"It would be very improper," she said.

"Yes." He grinned.

She withdrew her hand from his, got to her feet, and then very deliberately sat beside him and lay down, her head on his coat. "I always loved lying down outdoors on a warm day," she said. "Especially on a beach. Watching the clouds, feeling the sun, listening to the waves breaking, and smelling the salt air. But it was never allowed a great deal. Ladies just do not appear with sun-reddened faces, it seems."

He raised himself on one elbow and leaned over her. "There," he said. "I'll shade you from the sun and the ignominy of a red face."

He was back in his own area of expertise, of course. It would be the easiest thing in the world now to win his wager. He smiled at her and she looked warily back.

"This is very improper," she said.

"Yes." He lowered his head and rubbed his nose against hers. "You may very well have to marry me after all, Caroline."

"No," she said.

"What if I tell you tomorrow morning that I have fallen in love with you?" he asked. "And what if you tell me the same thing?"

"But neither of us will," she said, "because we are both on our honor to speak the truth."

Gad, but she was damnably pretty. Even when she was disheveled and sandy. He lowered his head and kissed her, preparing himself as he usually did to lose himself in the pleasure of an embrace even if it was one that could not be taken to its logical conclusion. But he lifted his head again after just a few moments and looked down at her.

The earth would move, she had said. They would hear the music of the spheres together, he had said. If two persons made love instead of just two bodies, that was. If the pleasures of a man and a woman were combined and shared. If they were aware of each other as they gave and took pleasure. What would it be like? he had wondered then. What *would* it be like? he wondered now.

He lowered his head again, opening his mouth over hers, licking her lips until they parted, exploring his way slowly inside. And he thought of the child she had been, much adored as the only girl in the family of men, strictly trained and educated by a much-loved governess. He thought of her in mourning for a couple of years as her girlhood slipped past. He thought of her refusing two offers of marriage just recently because she wanted to both love and be loved by the man she would marry. He thought of her wanting children. He thought of her building their sand castle with energy and enthusiasm.

Caroline. He tested the name in his mind. She was Caroline.

She had her arms about his neck. She was sucking tentatively on his tongue and turning to set her breasts against his chest. He lifted his head and looked down at her again. She was gazing back with luminous eyes. *What you began to do to me last night*, she had said, *is probably very pleasurable, is it not?* She had never experienced that pleasure. He could give it to her. All of it. Or enough of it to leave him free when she made her admission the next morning.

He could make her love him. And she would be honest enough to admit it. But he would still be in no danger. She would not marry him unless he could say the same. And so he would leave her hurt. Twenty-three-years old and as far from achieving her dream as ever. And with a bruised heart.

He lay down beside her and stared up at the clouds.

Her hand nudged against his until he clasped it. "I am a dreadful novice, am I not?" she said. "I did not know that people kissed like that."

"You are supposed to be a novice," he said. "That is what innocence is, Caroline."

"Are you concerned for my innocence?" she asked, her voice curious. "Is that why you stopped? How very out of character."

He surged over onto his side and looked into a flushed face. She had sand in one eyebrow. "Hardly," he said. "I have never corrupted innocence, Caroline. If I am a rake, I am not also a rogue. I have never deflowered a virgin. Yes, that is why I stopped."

"How are you to make me fall in love with you, then?" she asked.

He cupped her cheek with one hand and smoothed his thumb over the sandy eyebrow. "By making you want the rest of it—and me—for a lifetime," he said. He watched her swallow. "And how are you to make me fall in love with you, my innocent?"

"By making you want innocence and virginity—and me—for the rest of your life," she said.

His heart did a handstand. And he lost the battle he had been fighting with some success for several minutes. He felt the familiar tightening in his groin.

And then her hand was cupping his cheek with exquisite lightness and her thumb was moving across his lips. "I know you are no rogue," she said, her voice a mere breath of sound. "I know that you want the one thing you have never had in your adult life—innocence."

Lord God. Skilled courtesans had whispered marvelous eroticism into his ears to increase his pleasure. None of it had had one fraction of the power of her words. The witch! His body and his heart responded to them even as his mind knew that she was determinedly going about winning her wager.

And then he was kissing her again—her mouth, her eyelids, her ears, her throat. And spreading a hand over her breast, feeling the peaked nipple against his palm. And lowering his head to it, spreading his mouth wide, taking her nipple between his teeth until she whimpered, then licking it with his tongue through the thin muslin of her dress. Her hands were in his hair and she lifted her head to bury her face against the top of his head.

"Caroline." He rubbed a palm over the wettened peak of her breast and moved his mouth to the other. She was breathing in audible gasps.

He could not wait. He could not take things slowly as he normally liked to do. Even the time it would take to raise her dress and remove undergarments and to release himself from his pantaloons was too long. He wanted to be able to thrust deeply inside her *now*. Inside Caroline. He wanted to touch her at her body's core. He wanted to be with her. Part of her. Joined to her. Once it had happened, of course, neither of them would be left with any choice at all. There would be just the special license and the rush to the altar.

To hell with choice, he thought, sliding his hand down over her flat abdomen, curving his fingers into the increased warmth between her legs. He found her mouth with his again and was not sure which of them it was who moaned.

Innocence. She was an innocent. He was no corrupter of innocence, he had just claimed, no rogue. He sat up hastily and scrambled to his feet, ran one hand through his hair, and turned without thinking to stoop over her and scoop her up into his arms. He began to stride away from their castle.

"Alistair?" She looked and sounded bewildered. She looked tousled and thoroughly well kissed. And altogether as aroused as he. "Where are you taking me?

Our things. We cannot just leave them there. Where are we going?"

"To the only sensible place," he said grimly.

She glanced over her shoulder. "Oh, no," she said, her arms clutching him more tightly about the neck. "No, Alistair, you wouldn't. Put me down. *Put me down.*"

"We are doubly hot," he said, striding purposefully toward the sea, which was considerably closer than it had been when they had first set foot on the beach. "With sun and with desire. It is time to cool off."

"But we have no towels," she said. "No change of clothes."

His feet touched water. Cold water. He almost changed his mind. But he was still throbbing for her and her body was still heated with desire. It was either this or take her back to the dry sand and tumble her. His experiences of the last several years had not taught him a great deal of self-control. And clearly she had lost hers.

She shrieked as she felt water splash against her bare arms and legs. And then laughed. And clung more tightly. And pleaded more desperately. He looked down into her face when he was waist deep in water and saw terror and laughter mingled there. He dropped her.

She came up gasping and spluttering as he dived under.

"Can you swim?" he asked, shaking his head to clear the water from his eyes.

"My dress will be ruined," she yelled at him. "My favorite dress."

"And you wore it just for me," he said, scooping water with both hands and dashing it into her face. "*Can* you swim?"

"Yes, I can swim," she said. "Can you?" And she dived at him, clasped both hands over the top of his head, and pressed him under.

He caught at her legs on the way down and they came up coughing and laughing.

"You idiot," she said. "You imbecile."

"Guilty as charged," he said, catching her about the waist and dragging her beneath the surface of the waves again, setting his lips to hers as he did so. Which was a foolish thing to do when he considered the reason he had brought her there in the first place.

Her hair was dark and sleek over her head and down her back when they came up once more and found the bottom with their feet. Her dress was molded to her so that she might as well have been wearing nothing. She was laughing, with water droplets dripping down her face. She looked healthy and vital and infinitely desirable.

"You are crazy," she said.

"Is that a new charge?" He caught her to him and kissed her again, a hearty smacking kiss followed by a grin. "How well do you swim? I'll wager you cannot keep up to me."

"A new wager?" she said. "I'll accept it like an honorable gentleman. What is to be the prize?"

"A kiss," he said.

"Done," she said and she was off, swimming with all her energy and with considerable skill and grace parallel to the beach. He swam beside her, doing a lazy crawl, making no attempt to overtake her.

She realized something after a few minutes. "Where does the race end?" she called to him, her voice breathless.

He laughed and swam for a few more vigorous strokes until he was a body-length ahead of her. Then he turned and caught her in his arms. "Here," he said and claimed his prize without further delay. "Have you cooled off?"

"Cooled off?" she said, panting. "After that swim?"

"I mean," he said, "has the sexual heat gone?"

"Oh," she said, her eyes sliding from his, "that."

"Now," he said, "how are we to saunter back to the house and inside it as if we have been involved in nothing but the most decorous of walks? It is going to be tricky, Caroline."

"I could have told you that," she said scornfully, "before you did anything as stupid as this. You did not think, did you?"

"It was not stupid," he said. "If I had not done it, Caroline, you would have lost both the innocence and the virginity you spoke of earlier. We both know it."

"Oh," she said again, turning to wade toward shore. "Am I to thank you for showing gallantry and restraint, then, Alistair? A rake showing restraint? It seems rather a contradiction in terms, does it not?"

"Perhaps," he said, striding along beside her, "I am hoping to win your admiration and therefore your love."

"Poppycock," she said. "It is cold."

"You may wrap my coat about you," he said. "The sun will soon warm us. And dry us."

"Oh," she wailed suddenly as they ran up the beach toward their castle and their belongings, "just look at me. No! Don't look. Oh, goodness me."

But he could not be expected to have acquired all the gallantry in the world during the course of one short afternoon. He looked—and laughed and whistled. Her dress was clinging to her like a second skin.

"I have never been so mortified in my life," she said, pulling the muslin away from her in front and making a delicious contour of her derrière. "Stop laughing. And stop looking. I shall die!"

He picked up his coat, swung it about her shoulders, and drew her against him. He wrapped his arms around her and stopped laughing. "I have never seen a more pretty form than yours, Caroline," he said. "But I promise not to tell anyone else that I have seen it with such clarity. This thin fabric will be almost dry by the time we approach the house. And my coat will cover most of you."

"I have never in my life known a day like this," she said against his wet shirt. "I keep expecting to wake up. And all because you opened the wrong door last night."

"I am becoming increasingly glad I did," he said. And listening to his own words and considering them, he was surprised—and not a little alarmed—to find that he meant them.

By some miracle Caroline succeeded in regaining her room without being seen by anyone more threatening than a curious footman. Of course, he might decide to gossip belowstairs, but she would not think of that. And of course Letty saw her lank hair and her limp, damp dress when Caroline rang her bell to ask for bathwater.

"It was such a warm day," she said with a winning smile just as if she owed her maid an explanation, "and the water looked so inviting, Letty."

"Hmm," Letty said with a sniff. "If you was with *him*, mum, then enough said."

Caroline gathered that *he* was not very high in Letty's favor.

Cynthia arrived in her room when she was toweling

her hair dry after her bath. Caroline was very thankful her sister-in-law had not come half an hour earlier.

"Caroline," she said, "is it all now settled, then? Are you betrothed? This is all so very sudden that it is hard to digest. He is very handsome, and I do see how you were tempted. But oh, love, I do hope your rash behavior will not lead you to unhappiness."

Caroline could not bear to have her sister-in-law think badly of her. "The only rash thing I did was lie to Royston," she said. "I thought he was going to challenge Lord Lyndon to a duel, Cynthia, and you know as well as I do who would have won."

"You did not invite him to your room?" Cynthia asked.

"Of course not," Caroline said scornfully. "He mistook my room for someone else's. Lady Plumtree's I would not doubt." The thought hurt.

Cynthia looked dismayed. "You lied to Roy," she said, "when he was sending the man away, Caroline? He had ordered him to leave within the hour."

"Oh, dear," Caroline said.

"And you are now betrothed?" her sister-in-law said.

Caroline set her towel down and picked up a brush. If she said no, she would be unable to spend the evening with Alistair. Or tomorrow morning. She could return to her usual wise, sensible self merely by speaking the word. It would be dangerous not to say no. Very dangerous. But there was an evening and a morning she could have if she lied. Or avoided telling the truth.

"I am to give him my answer tomorrow morning," she said. "He has kindly given me a little time since we did not know each other at all, Cynthia." Oh, it was an outright lie. First Royston and now Cynthia. She never told lies.

"Think wisely," Cynthia said, her hand on the door-knob. "Perhaps you were compromised, Caroline, but no one need know it but us and I cannot see that any useful purpose will be served by forcing you to spend the rest of your life with that man, handsome and charming as he undoubtedly is." She smiled suddenly. "Why are rakes so nearly irresistible?"

"They probably would not be rakes if they were not," Caroline said. "No woman would oblige them and allow them to build the reputation."

Cynthia laughed. "I am sure you are right," she said. "A load has been lifted from my shoulders. May I tell Roy the truth?"

"After tomorrow morning," Caroline said and stared at the closed door after Cynthia had left.

She should have taken the way out that had just been presented to her, she thought. She should not have pro-longed matters. For she knew now that she was going to get hurt. Dreadfully hurt. She had been in love with him for months—in love with his looks and his reputa-tion. And then for a brief spell this morning she had fallen out of love with him, having perceived him as a selfish and conceited man. Now—well, now she loved him. She had seen warmth and gaiety and charm and tenderness and even conscience in him. He was no longer the handsome rake to be sighed over in secret. He was a person now, someone she had talked with and laughed with and built a sand castle with and swum with. Someone with whom she had known the begin-nings of passion.

Someone with whom she would have made love on an open beach without benefit of clergy if he had not exercised unexpected restraint. Someone she still wanted despite the cold ducking in the sea.

What was she going to say tomorrow morning? She

was going to lie, that was what. She was going to behave with the utmost dishonor. But then she was not
a man. Men had a different notion of honor from
women. If she admitted the truth tomorrow morning,
he would probably feel obliged to marry her after all.
She could not bear to be married to him. Every day
would be an agony.

She could have avoided it all if she had told the truth
to Cynthia and then gone and told it to Royston. She
could have avoided the misery of tomorrow morning.
And replaced it with the misery of now. There was to
be no winning this battle. Caroline sighed and brushed
harder in order to dry her wet hair in time for dinner.
He was going to take her in to dinner. He had said so.
She would have him to converse with all through the
meal.

No, she was not sorry she had told a lie. An evening
and a morning were better than nothing.

Eugenia gave her a wounded look as if Caroline had
stolen the viscount away from her. Irene and all the
other cousins looked at her with interest—and some
envy on the part of the girls. Lady Plumtree pointedly
and with haughty disdain did not look at her at all.
Caroline did not care about any of it.

"Did you escape notice after we parted at the top of
the stairs?" she asked the viscount when they were
seated at the dinner table.

"Escape?" he said, raising his eyebrows and looking
at her sidelong with very blue eyes. "You are joking,
of course. After my valet had taken one glance at the
state of my boots and clothes, I believe he would have
bent me beneath his arm and given me a good walloping
as my father used to do, if only he had been a foot
taller and I had been a foot shorter. How about you?"

"Similar treatment from Letty," she said.

"The amazon who attacked me last night?" he said. "My sympathies, Caroline. I would guess she is quite large enough to take you over her knee even now for a thorough spanking. A dreadful breed, personal servants, are they not? One lives in fear and trembling of their wrath."

Caroline laughed and won for herself a puzzled frown from her brother and a sniff from Lady Plumtree.

"There is to be dancing in the drawing room afterward," the viscount said. "Special request of Colin, bless his heart. It is to be in the nature of a practice for the grand ball in two nights' time for the old lady's birthday. Will she dance, by the way?"

"Great-Aunt Sabrina?" Caroline said. "Oh, assuredly. She will expect every male member of the family to lead her out."

"Will she?" he asked. "Every male member of the family? Not every male in the ballroom?"

She laughed again at the expression on his face. "Are you disappointed?" she asked. "Her card will doubtless be too full for such a lowly mortal as you to find a space."

"Well," he said, "what about tonight, Caroline? One is not to be confined to only two dances with the same partner or any such absurdity as that, is one?"

"It is not a formal ball," she said.

"Good," he said. "You will reserve the first and last sets and every one in between for me if you please."

If she pleased? She was absurdly pleased. "This is part of your campaign?" she said. "You are going to waltz me into love with you?"

"Perhaps," he said. "But I was thinking more of taking you out for turns on the terrace or perhaps for strange disappearances into the gardens. What have you told your brother?"

She felt her cheeks grow hot. "That we are using today to get to know each other," she said. "That I am to give you my answer tomorrow morning."

"Ah," he said. "That rather plays into my hands, does it not?"

"Into mine," she said. "There is nothing like darkness and moonlight and music to arouse feelings of romance. I shall have you sleepless with love tonight, Alistair."

"It sounds distinctly promising," he said, using that low seductive voice she was beginning to recognize.

"I did not mean it quite like that," she said hastily, wishing fervently that she could recall the words and reframe them.

"A pity," he said. "A great pity."

Great-Aunt Sabrina was being helped slowly to her feet and the ladies followed her at snail's pace from the dining room, leaving the gentlemen to their port.

Sleepless with love, Caroline thought, her knees feeling quite weak. What an unfortunate thing to say. And what a glorious thing to imagine. Oh dear, she was growing to like him so very much. She had never talked with anyone more amusing. And all she had left was part of an evening and a morning.

"Caro," Irene said, taking her arm and squeezing it, "what is this? You lucky, lucky thing. He is quite smitten with you. Mama had a fit of the vapors when she knew that Lyndon was to be a guest here this week. So did I, but for a different reason."

"We are merely friends," Caroline said.

Irene laughed derisively.

Dancing in a room full of eager, sweet young things and bright sparks and gossiping matrons and older, sober blades had never been Viscount Lyndon's idea of fun. But this evening was different. He was close to winning his wager, he believed, if it was not won already. She had glowed at dinner and had clearly enjoyed his company.

As he had hers, of course. She was delightful and pretty and desirable. He rather wished that they had set the terms of the wager at one week instead of one day. But he had the evening left. He would make the most of it.

"My country dance, I believe, ma'am," he said when one of the matrons finally sat down at the pianoforte and began to play sprightly scales to warm up her fingers. He bowed formally over Caroline's hand and won a dazzling smile from her and inquisitive looks from the young people surrounding her.

"My pleasure, my lord," she said, dipping into a deep curtsy.

"Was that the one you practiced to deliver to the queen on your presentation, Caroline?" he asked as he led her onto the floor, from which the Turkish carpet had been rolled back. "Your forehead was in danger of scraping the floor."

She laughed. "It would have been a shame to practice such a curtsy for two full hours daily for six months and use it only once on the queen," she said.

She danced with energy and grace, smiling at him and at the other partners with whom she sometimes had to execute certain measures of the dance. He watched her the whole while, not even noticing his own temporary partners, and found it difficult to imagine that he could have missed her throughout the Season. Why had his eyes not been drawn to her as to a magnet? She was altogether more lovely than any other lady in the room. More lovely than any other lady he had known.

He frowned at the thought.

"Oh, this is marvelous," she said breathlessly as he twirled her down the set. "You don't expect me to appear bored, do you, Alistair, this not being a formal affair?"

"If you dare to look bored," he said, "I shall twirl you at double speed and then let go of you so that you spin off into space?"

She laughed.

He had always thought of young virtuous women as dull, humorless, timid, unexciting—the list could go on. But then he had not met Caroline Astor until last night.

The country dance was followed by a sedate waltz. He resisted the urge to hold his partner slightly closer than was considered proper. After all, most of the eyes in the room were probably on them—on Caroline, a member of the family, in the clutches of a man they must feel Colin should not have invited.

"Why have I never noticed you?" he asked her.

"Because you never notice virtuous women," she said. "Because you could not take me to bed without marrying me first."

"Could I have this afternoon?" he asked her, his voice low.

Her eyes slipped to his neckcloth. "You dumped me in the water instead," she said.

"But if I had not, Caroline?"

She looked up into his eyes again. "It is pointless to speculate on what might have been," she said. "The past is the one thing we can never change. But I am not sure that I can be described as virtuous any longer. I have never come even close to behaving like that before."

"I will marry you, then, and redeem your reputation," he said. He did not know quite why he kept saying such potentially dangerous things. One of these times she was going to take him at his word.

She smiled fleetingly.

"Come outside with me after this dance," he said. "We will see what the gardens look like in the moonlight. Shall we?"

"But of course," she said. "I have a wager to win." She peeped up at him from beneath her lashes with deliberate provocation and he grinned back at her.

"How are you going to do it?" he asked. "Do you have a plan?"

But she merely smiled.

It was a subtle plan. She strolled quietly along the terrace with him, first with her arm through his, then with her hand in his, her shoulder touching his arm, and finally with her arm about his waist as his came about her shoulders. By that time they had rounded one end of the house and stepped into a type of orchard.

Very subtle. The moonlight and the branches above their heads made changing patterns of light and shade over her face and dress and she lifted her face. Her eyes were closed, he saw when he looked down at her. She broke the silence first.

"Sometimes," she said, "one feels all one's smallness and insignificance in comparison with the vastness of the universe. And yet how wonderful it is to exist amidst such beauty. How privileged we are. Don't you feel it too, Alistair?"

"Yes." He could not talk on such topics. He had not thought a great deal about the miracle of life and the wonder of the fact that he had one to live. It was a new idea to him. He was wasting his one most precious gift, he thought.

"I am glad we were made to need others," she said. "Would it not be frustrating to see and feel beauty and have no one with whom to share it? I think we would feel loneliness and even terror instead of wonder."

"Yes," he said. He was very aware of her arm about his waist, his about her shoulders. Holding each other against loneliness and terror. It was a novel idea. He had never thought of needing other people, only of using them. He had never thought of other people needing him. *Could* anyone ever need him? Was he that important? That privileged?

She rubbed her cheek against his shoulder. "I am glad it has been you with me today, Alistair," she said. "I am glad it is you out here with me tonight. But I am sorry." She lifted her head. "I said it would be romantic, did I not? I promised to make you fall in love with me. But all I can do is feel warm and cozy with you. All I can do is babble on about the universe and our human need for others. I have no experience in arousing romantic feelings. You asked if I had a plan. No, I have none. We had better go inside before our prolonged absence is noted."

The soft wonder had gone from her voice. She sounded sad suddenly, and he knew it was his apparent lack of response that had saddened her. He had made her feel that after all she was alone. But how could he express thoughts that were so new to him that he knew no words in which to frame them?

He tightened his hold on her shoulders and turned her in against him, wrapping his free arm about her waist. She turned her head to rest one cheek against his neckcloth. He held her for a long time, perhaps several minutes, without either talking to her or kissing her. He did not want to kiss her. He did not want to make love to her. There was a nameless and quite unidentifiable yearning in him that took the place of the sexual desire he might have expected to feel.

For some reason that he could in no way fathom he wanted to cry. He swallowed hard several times. She was soft and warm. A buffer against loneliness. A bundle of gaiety and dreaminess, of wisdom and innocence. There was something in her that he wanted, that he yearned for. Something in addition to her woman's body.

"Alistair." She lifted her face to him finally and touched her fingertips to one of his cheeks.

He took her hand in his and kissed the palm. "Why did you say my name?" he asked her.

"Alistair?" she said, laughing softly. "It is your name, is it not?"

"Lyndon," he said. "Last night. You called me Lyndon. Before you woke fully."

She stared up at him, her expression turning quite blank. "I did not," she whispered.

"Yes," he said, "you did. When I first kissed you. Before there was light. Before you could possibly have known who I was. You called me Lyndon."

She shook her head slowly and he was sorry suddenly that he had asked. Sorry that he had not kept that particular memory to himself.

And then she pushed violently away from him, gathered up her skirt, and fled back the way they had come.

"Caroline," he called and took a few steps after her.

But she only increased her pace, if possible. He stopped. For some reason he had embarrassed her dreadfully. She had been dreaming of him? She had thought the kiss part of a dream, and she had identified him as her dream lover? When he was a stranger to her? A stranger she had seen only during the Season even though he had not seen her.

Damnation, he thought, clenching and unclenching his hands at his sides.

As he expected, she was not in the drawing room when he returned there and did not reappear for the rest of the evening.

It was half an hour before noon when she had met him the day before. It was a little earlier than that when she came downstairs now, pale from a night of little sleep, nervous at having to carry through this encounter, wishing that she could be anywhere else on earth. For starters, she could die of mortification. She had spoken his name aloud! If only she could have slept during the night, she would have had nightmares over that fact. But that was not the worst of it, of course. She was going to have to face him this morning and bring their wager to its conclusion. And then what?

The rest of her life looked frighteningly blank. Not that it would be, of course. The remnants of good sense in her told her that this heightened emotion would not last forever or even for very long. Soon, or at least in the not too distant future, life would settle back into its routine and she would think of her marriage prospects again. But oh, that was no consolation now. Now it felt as if her life was to end within the next half hour.

If he had come, that was. If he had not hidden himself away somewhere—in the billiard room with some of the other gentlemen, for example. Or if he had not gone away, afraid that after all she would trap him into marriage.

He was in the hallway when she came down and looked as if he might have been pacing there for some time. Had she been able to look critically, she might have noticed that his own face showed signs of a certain sleeplessness too. He had not slept well, if at all, and he was not looking forward to the coming hour. It frankly terrified him. He was not an adventurous man, he had realized during the night. His life had been predictable for the last number of years. He liked it that way. He resented the fact that change was sometimes inevitable.

"Caroline." He smiled at her, bent over her hand, and kissed it. "Almost exactly on time. Shall we find somewhere private?" His heart was beating in his chest fit to burst through. How many hours had passed since he saw her last? Thirteen? Fourteen? It seemed more like a hundred.

"Yes," she said.

He led her outdoors and stood looking along the terrace, first one way and then the other, before leading her in the direction of the woods at some distance from the house. There appeared to be no walkers there today.

"Well," he said, "did your amazon sleep at the foot of your bed last night?"

"Yes," she said.

He did not attempt more conversation. They walked in silence, her arm through his, until they reached the shelter of the trees and he could release her arm in order to set his back against the trunk of a tree and fold his arms across his chest.

"The moment of truth," he said. "Do you want to go first, Caroline?"

She turned to look at him in some dismay and down to examine the backs of her hands, spread before her.

"Or would you rather that I went first?"

"No," she said quietly. "You have not won, Alistair. I am sorry. I enjoyed yesterday more than I can say. I learned to like you. And I learned that you are an attractive man, though I knew it already, and could make me desire you. I will not deny what must have been all too obvious to you on the beach. But that is all. I can feel no warmth of love. You have not won fifty pounds from me, you see." She looked up fleetingly and smiled briefly. "But then you need feel no obligation either."

He said nothing for a long while. But she had whispered his name. She had dreamed of him. She had noticed him even when he had not noticed her. And she had *dreamed* of him. She had desired him. But in her mind, desire and love were not the same thing. As indeed they were not.

Let us be done, she thought. Let him say something. She wanted to be back at the house. She wanted to be a stranger to him again. He was holding something out to her. A piece of paper. She looked at it.

"What is it?" she asked.

"A draft on my bank for fifty pounds," he said. His voice was very soft, but it did not have the seductive quality with which she was becoming familiar.

She looked up into his eyes. They looked steadily back at her.

"You have won it," he said.

She had won it? Her mind felt sluggish. "How?"

"You have made me love you," he said. "Take it. It is yours."

She raised her hand. He released his hold on the paper as she touched it. But she was not gripping it. It fluttered to the grass between them.

"No," she said, closing her eyes. "No, please. You promised not to lie."

"And so I did," he said. "Yesterday was the happiest day of my life, Caroline. Not only that. It *changed* my life. It made me realize that I have wasted thirty precious years out of a span of perhaps seventy if I am fortunate. It made me realize that I need more than myself and my own pleasure. And it made me realize that I would like more than anything to be needed. By one person. By the same person as I need. You."

"No," she said, looking at her hands again. "You are being gentlemanly. You still think you are obliged to marry me, and you think to persuade me this way. Don't be cruel."

Cruel? He felt a stabbing of hope. *Cruel?* "But there is no question of marriage," he said. "You do not love me, Caroline. And there has to be love on both sides before you will marry, does there not?"

She looked up at him, her eyes luminous with misery and something else. "No one can change in a single day," she said. "I would be a fool."

Hope grew. If so much had not hung on the words they would exchange over the next few minutes, he would have grinned at her and teased her and forced her to tell him that she had lied. But he was too afraid for the fragility of his own heart to believe what his mind told him was the truth.

"No," he said. "It would take us both longer than a day, Caroline. It would take me many days, I daresay, to realize the wonder of the exchange I had made—numberless women in exchange for you. And it would take you many days, perhaps even a lifetime, to come to trust me and believe that it could happen. But we will never know, will we, if those changes would have been possible. Perhaps it is just as well. The familiar is safer and perhaps cozier than the unknown."

He watched her lower her arms to her sides and rub her palms against her dress, as if they were damp. Her eyes were on the ground at her feet. And then she stooped down suddenly, picked up his bank draft, and held it out to him, her eyes on the paper.

"It is yours," he said.

She shook her head and bit her upper lip. "No," she said. "I did not bring fifty pounds to give to you. If we both won or if we both lost, you said, we would be even. We are even."

"Caroline?" he said, taking the paper from her hand, folding it, and putting it away in his pocket. He found himself holding his breath.

"I lied," she said. "I am no gentleman, am I?"

He ran the knuckles of one hand lightly down her cheek and then set the hand beneath her chin to raise her face.

"I lied," she said again more firmly, a note of defiance in her voice, though her eyes were suspiciously bright. "Now tell me that you did too. Alistair." Her eyes grew anxious. "Don't tell me that you lied too. Please?"

"Why did you say my name?" He was looking at her mouth.

"Because I conceived a deep infatuation for you the first time I saw you," she said. "Because I thought I was dreaming. And I dreamed that it was you."

"Infatuation?" he said.

"I called it love," she said, "until yesterday. Now I know that it was not. Only infatuation. I did not love you until yesterday."

He set his hands on her shoulders. "What are we going to do?" he asked.

"I don't know." She patted her hands against his chest.

"I want to build sand castles with you again," he said, "and swim with you and talk and laugh with you. I want to love you. And make love to you. I want to have children with you."

She raised her eyes to his. "Oh," she said.

"I'm glad you agree." He smiled down at her and

touched his forehead briefly to hers. "Will you take a chance on marrying a rake, Caroline?"

"Yes," she said. "Alistair, I am dreadfully inexperienced. I will not know how to—"

He kissed her firmly on the mouth. "We will teach each other," he said. "We will go back to school, both of us, for the rest of our lives."

"Teach each other?" she said.

"I will teach you how to make love," he said, "and you will teach me to love. Agreed?"

She laughed shakily and relaxed her weight forward against him. "Agreed," she said. "But I think your classes are going to prove to be more exciting than mine."

He chuckled. "If you are that eager to start," he said, "we had better open this school of ours as soon as possible. I will talk with your brother. How does a special license and your brother's home next week sound?"

"For a wedding day?" she said, her eyes widening.

"And a wedding night," he said.

"Oh," she said.

"You have a lovely way of pronouncing 'yes,' " he said, lowering his head to kiss her throat. "A week is an awfully long time to wait, my love."

"Mmm," she said, arching her body against his.

"If it were not for the amazon," he said, his hands coming up to cup and caress her breasts, "I might be tempted to try a few more nocturnal excursions."

"Mmm," she said.

"We will have to set her at the foot of someone else's bed next week," he said, sliding his hands over her waist and hips and around to cup her buttocks and draw her more snugly against the core of his own desire.

"Mmm," she said.

He set his mouth to hers again, opened it beneath

his own, and thrust his tongue inside deeply, once, twice, before withdrawing it and drawing back his head an inch.

"Caroline," he said, smoothing one hand over her sun-warmed auburn hair, "it is not just this I want of you, you know. It is *you*. I have wanted bodies before. I have never wanted a person. I want you. I want to join my body to yours so that we will be closer than close, so that we will share everything there is to be shared. I am on fire for you, as you can feel. But for you, not just for the lovely body that houses you."

She smiled slowly at him. "Joining your body to mine," she said. "Do you know how the very thought turns me weak at the knees, Alistair? Don't expect a shy bride. I am afraid I will be shockingly eager. And the rest of what you said too. Oh, that turns me weak all over. That is how love differs from merely being in love, does it not? Wanting the other's body and everything else too, right through to the soul."

"Speaking of bodies." He grinned at her.

"Mmm, yes," she said, wrapping her arms about his neck and smiling eagerly at him. "What was it you were saying, Alistair?"

"This, I believe," he said, opening his mouth over hers again.

Cat's-Paw

by

Maura Seger

1

"Archer, what a nice surprise," the older woman exclaimed. Her white satin skirt rustled as she crossed the entry hall to offer her hand.

The tall, powerfully muscled man in evening clothes took it and inclined his head. "Delphine, looking lovely as always."

She gave him a pleased smile that turned into an approving assessment as her eyes swept over the long, hard length of him. He was an unabashedly virile man, his skin burnished by the sun, his body honed by hard exertion. He had the tensile strength and indomitable will of a heritage that claimed equal parts Cherokee and Spanish. The finely tailored clothes he wore imparted no more than a thin veneer of civilization.

His hostess, who had more than a little experience judging men, was not at all misled. Her smile deepened. "Really, Archer, where have you been keeping yourself? We've missed you."

The corners of his chiseled mouth lifted. "Here and there."

He would say nothing more but Delphine remembered his penchant for wild, open places beyond the frontier and sighed. She tucked her arm through his and proceeded into the parlor.

A piano played, there was laughter and the clink of glass. Perfume drifted lightly on the air. Several young ladies, all beautifully dressed in the height of fashion, sat on horsehair settees, chatting with one another or with the gentlemen who had come to enjoy their company.

Archer glanced around idly. The women were exquisite and unabashedly sensual. In their gowns of silk, velvet, and lace, they looked like a collection of perfectly ripe flowers merely waiting to be plucked. But no particular one of them caught his eye.

"What are you in the mood for tonight?" Delphine asked softly.

Archer hesitated. He wasn't sure himself what had drawn him from the solitude of his Gramercy Park town house to the bright gas lamps and heady ambiance of Delphine's Place.

He'd only been back in the city a handful of days, drawn by a problem that both depressed and angered him. Perhaps it was relief from that he sought, however temporary.

At any rate, he had been a long time without a woman, too long in his opinion, and Delphine's had the best.

"Nothing out of the ordinary," he said, glancing around.

His hostess hid a smile. The women Archer had bedded in her establishment invariably considered him anything but ordinary, but not in the way he meant.

He had the reputation for being an unusually generous, if demanding lover. Also, and rather remarkably in her opinion, he was said to actually respect women, even when he was paying for them.

With a sudden change in direction, she drew him away from the parlor toward the stairs. "Why don't you go up? I'll send along a bottle of champagne, compliments of the house, and a companion I believe you'll find most enjoyable."

Archer raised an eyebrow. Such generosity was out of keeping with the ever-pragmatic Delphine. "What are you about to get me into?" he asked cautiously.

"Nothing you'll regret. Maeve is a delightful young woman."

"Maeve . . .?"

"Just off the boat. A lovely young thing from County Cork, skin dewy as porcelain, strawberry blond hair, and the sweetest nature you'll ever find. She's perfect."

Archer paled. The unknown Maeve sounded altogether too good to be true. A dreadful thought occurred to him. "She isn't . . .?"

"Isn't what?"

"A virgin?"

"Heaven forbid, dear boy. To be blunt, she'd cost you far more if she was. No, Maeve is quite nearly unspoiled but not, alas, entirely."

Archer stopped and cast a hard look at Delphine. He liked her well enough and preferred her establishment to others of its ilk because she was a good deal fairer and kinder to the young women in her employ. Still, he liked to be sure.

"She is here by her own will, isn't she?"

"Oh, absolutely. Maeve's a very sensible sort. Put simply, she's tired of being poor."

Archer nodded. He understood that well enough having been poor himself at one time. Reassured, and beginning to actually look forward to the encounter, he nodded agreement.

The room he retired to was large and well furnished with a bed, nightstand, and armoire. The walls were papered in plush red brocade. Burgundy velvet drapes were drawn across the windows.

He removed his boots and stood, absently loosening his tie. The sound of the piano floated up the stairs. There was a knock at the door.

"Come in."

The door opened and a young woman stepped into the room. She carried a tray with an ice bucket and two champagne flutes. Her smile was demure, but there was a definite flicker of pleased interest in her eyes as they darted over him.

"Good evening, sir. My name is Maeve."

Archer smiled. He moved to put her at ease. "Good evening, Maeve. I'm pleased to meet you."

His courtesy surprised her. She smiled again, more certain this time, and set the tray on the nightstand. For a moment, she hesitated, then swiftly took a breath and walked toward him.

"May I help you with that, sir?" she asked, indicating his frock coat.

He allowed as to how she could. Her hands were deft as she removed the garment and hung it carefully over a nearby chair. Archer felt a spurt of amusement as he saw how earnestly she went about the job, but a small inkling of doubt stirred in the back of his mind.

This Maeve was undoubtedly lovely, and she gave every evidence of having chosen her place exactly as Delphine claimed. Yet he was accustomed to far more experienced women.

Still, under the gentle but persistent touch of her hands as she undid the top buttons of his shirt, he was becoming aroused. Slowly, he put an arm around her waist and drew her to him.

Against the perfume of her soft hair, he asked, "Maeve, are you sure this is your choice?"

She tipped her head back and looked at him, her

eyes wide with dismay. "Certainly it is." Her lower lip trembled slightly. "Don't you want me?"

He would have been lying if he claimed he didn't. Moreover, she would have known, for she could feel the evidence of his desire pressing through the layers of wool and silk that separated them.

Her eyes lightened and she laughed softly. With unmistakable intent, she took his hand and raised it to the curve of her breast.

As far as Archer was concerned, that settled the matter. He had a beautiful, warm, and willing woman in his arms, a bed nearby, and several months worth of celibacy to make up for.

His dark head bent down, his mouth closed on hers. He thrust his tongue deep even as he undid the laces down the back of her dress and began to slide the gown from her. Maeve moaned, her hands splayed out over his powerfully muscled chest. As one, they moved toward the bed and fell across it.

His hand slid beneath the lacy petticoats to stroke her smooth thighs. She was without undergarments, affording him complete access to the silken mound between her legs. Hot, piercing hunger coursed through him. This first coupling would be hastier than he would have liked but they had the entire night together.

He was just undoing the buttons of his trousers when a sudden sound made him pause. No stranger to deadly danger, his instincts were razor sharp. In an instant, he was rising from Maeve's supine body even as he turned in the direction of the sound.

The door opened. A woman stepped into the room. She was tall and slender with fiery red hair, a heart-shaped face and eyes that appeared to hold a vast thunderstorm in their depths. Her gaze swept scathingly over the pair on the bed. Without hesitation, she advanced toward them.

Maeve gave a yelp and dove behind Archer. "Sweet Mary and all the saints," she whimpered, "it's me cousin, Megan."

"Right you are, Maeve Daugherty," the avenging fury said. "And a fine sight you are here in this den of iniquity. As for you," she added, turning on Archer, "you scum-eating piece of jackal slime, I'll have you know there's a special place in hell for the despoilers of young women."

Archer frowned. Scum-eating what? He wasn't following this. Delphine ran a perfectly respectable—as these things went—bawdy house. Disturbances of this sort were most definitely not supposed to happen.

"Don't let her hurt me," Maeve moaned and tried to hold on to him, but to no avail. The fearless Megan wrenched her free, dragged her upright and said, "Make yourself decent this instant. We're leaving!"

"Now wait a minute," Archer began belatedly, but he thought he could be pardoned for his slow response. The situation was unprecedented. It had an element of farce to it, yet it was also undeniably serious.

Heedless of his own dishevelment, he stood and faced the furious young woman. Despite himself, he found her appearance fascinating. She was taller than her cousin and altogether more vivid—her coloring like fire, her eyes flashing, her spirit evident even beneath the drab maid's clothing she wore.

Tall though she was, he was taller. Scowling down at her, he said, "What do you think you're doing?"

The look she gave him would have peeled paint off the wall. "Saving my cousin from the likes of you." With a toss of her bright head and a further icy glare, she seized the hapless Maeve's wrist and dragged her from the room.

From the hallway, Archer heard, "But Megan, you can't do this. You've no right to tell me how to behave."

"Don't be ridiculous," the fury replied. "I've every right so long as I'm head of this family. Make no mistake, Maeve Daugherty, you're going to mind yourself or answer to me."

"But you don't realize . . ." Maeve protested, her voice growing fainter. "He's Archer Davalos, for heaven's sake, one of the richest men in the country. Why he's . . ."

"I don't care if he's the tooth fairy, old St. Nick, and the Archangel Gabriel rolled into one. You will not dishonor—"

Her voice was drowned out by the commotion her arrival caused downstairs. Delphine's protests rose shrilly above the rest but apparently without effect. A moment later, the front door slammed resoundingly.

Archer sighed. He lay back on the bed, arms folded beneath his head and contemplated the nymphs cavorting on the ceiling. His manhood, single-minded as always, still strained against his trousers. But the mood was shattered and all the dark thoughts he had been trying to hold at bay surged to the fore once again.

The fiery-tempered Megan had cost him a night's enjoyment and left him in an undeniably uncomfortable state. That did not make him charitably inclined toward her.

It was unlikely that their paths would ever cross again, but were they to do so, he would not hesitate to exact appropriate retribution. A hard smile curved his mouth. Indeed, he would look forward to it.

2

"Two days," the fat, bald-headed man said. "Then you're out on the street, the lot of you."

"You'll get your rent," Megan snapped. Her stomach churned and her hands were freezing cold but she'd be damned if she'd let this bloodsucking landlord see that.

His small, piggish eyes went over her, seeming to see straight through the worn white blouse buttoned to the throat and the blue serge skirt shiny in places where it had been ironed too often.

"A pretty girl like you shouldn't have to worry about money."

Megan's full mouth twisted in disgust. "I'll have your filthy money, be sure of that, but that doesn't mean I have to listen to your blathering. Get away with you."

His face darkened with fury. "We'll see how brave you are when you've no roof over your head. You'll come begging to me, you will, and I'll—"

Whatever he intended, Megan did not hear. She slammed the door and stood with her back to it, trembling. Brave words indeed, but at the moment they were all she had. Unless she could come up with two dollars and fifty cents by the day after tomorrow, they really would be out on the street.

Not that the apartment was much better. Despairingly, she looked around at the main room of the cold-water flat on the east side of Manhattan.

There was another, smaller room off the far end where her brothers slept. She and Maeve made do with beds unrolled in front of the battered table where they all ate on the rare occasions when they were actually all there. Most of the time, they were out looking for work.

Without any success. The only one of them who had

come even close to employment lately was Maeve and that was better not thought about.

Exhausted by the confrontation, and by the fact that she hadn't eaten in a day and a half, Megan went to the stove. A meager soup was simmering, made mainly of water but with a few carrot ends and a precious sliver of meat bought for pennies from the butcher down the street.

It was food her family wouldn't have looked at even in the hardest times in Ireland, but now it made her mouth water. It was all she could do not to allow herself a taste. Her brothers would be home and soon Maeve would be, too. They would eat together, sharing out the tiny portions and trying to find what pleasure they could in having survived another day.

She shook her head impatiently. Self-pity loomed precariously close but she refused to yield to it. She was a Daugherty, by God, and no one was ever going to feel sorry for her, especially not herself.

Instead, she busied herself with more of the never-ending laundry. Cleanliness was difficult to maintain but also an absolute necessity. Her brothers would have freshly starched and ironed shirts when they went out to look for work or she would know the reason why.

She had just finished the last batch when the apartment door opened. Her eldest brother, Seamus, walked in. At twenty, four years her junior, he was tall and painfully thin but with an engaging smile that never seemed to fail him.

"Evening, lass," he said, coming over to give her cheek a quick kiss. "How're you keeping?"

"Well enough. You?"

The seemingly simple question held a wealth of meaning for them both. Seamus's smile cracked, but to give him credit, it did not disappear. Resolutely, he said, "It'll be better tomorrow. Something'll turn up."

Megan nodded but turned away to hide her disappointment and the fear that was beginning to curl around the edges of her soul. Seamus was the oldest of the boys and the one most likely to find work. Despite his thinness, he had a strong back. Added to a good mind and a willing nature, there was no end to what he could do, provided he only got the chance to show it.

"Did you happen to see Ned?" she asked as she quickly stirred the soup, as if by so doing she might somehow make its contents expand.

"Ran into him down by the Stock Exchange. He wasn't having any more luck than me, I'm sorry to say."

Ned was the second brother, eighteen a month ago, and much like Seamus. There were three others—Padraic, who was sixteen, Desmond, fourteen, and the youngest, Sean, who was twelve. The Daughertys' clockwork precision in producing sons had been a source of much amusement—not to say envy—in the old country.

Had it not been for her close friendship with her younger cousin, Maeve, Megan would have felt rather isolated in a family of boisterous young males. As it was, they had brought out the deeply maternal streak in her nature.

"Do you ever think," she asked softly, "that we made a mistake coming here?"

Seamus looked surprised. It was the first time he had ever heard his indomitable sister suggest such a thing.

"It's early days yet, Megan," he reminded her. "We've only been a few months. Something will turn up."

Silently, she prayed he was right. The meager nest egg they had brought with them had dwindled to almost nothing. If they didn't find work soon, the alternatives were bleak.

"I could try the factory again," she suggested.

Piecework shops at the clothing factories had been a lifeline for many a young immigrant woman. But the economy was in a slump at the moment—something the Daughertys hadn't realized when they left County Cork—and few of the factories were hiring.

"Where?" Ned asked. He had just come in and overheard their conversation. "Only Molloy's putting anyone on and we know all about him."

Megan tried to hide a shudder but couldn't quite manage it. She had innocently gone to Daniel Molloy's factory when they first arrived and had been hired on promptly. But the job had lasted only a day. She'd fled when the hard-fisted, pig-eyed owner slammed her up against a wall, grabbed her breasts, and informed her there was a price for being allowed to work fifteen hours a day stitching in poor light for the munificent sum of eighty cents.

"They're saying he raped another girl," Ned said harshly. "How many do you suppose that makes?"

"Too many," Megan murmured. Her cheeks flushed but she didn't resent her brother's frank speaking. Although it would have been impossible back home, this was a new world with new ways. Some of the ways were terrifying, but the openness was refreshing and, she thought, sensible.

Which reminded her that she had been anything but open with her brothers on the subject of Maeve. The two women had agreed between themselves that nothing would be said either about Maeve's brief and heartbreaking affair with a young man back in Ireland or her abbreviated stay in Madam Delphine's establishment.

The Daugherty sons were good men, intelligent and sensible. But Ned had already indicated his desire to separate Daniel Molloy from this life and he had barely touched Megan. There was no telling what he or any of the other lads would do if they found out what Maeve had been up to.

"The problem," Desmond said a short time later as they all gathered for supper, "is that we don't know anyone here. All the jobs that do exist go to friends of the ward captains. I can't even find someone from our own village who might give us a leg up."

"The only people we've met are others like ourselves," Padraic agreed, "or bloodsuckers like the landlord." He cast a quick glance at Megan where she sat at the head of the table. Since the death of their father a few weeks before their departure for America, Megan had become the de facto head of the family. It was an unusual position for a woman but she was the oldest and, by common consensus, the smartest. What she herself thought of the responsibility, no one asked.

"Did he stop by again?" Padraic asked, his brow furrowed.

Instinctively, Megan reached out a hand to soothe him. "Don't fret about it. We'll manage."

Padraic didn't respond but she could see the doubt in his young eyes. It hurt her deeply even as she couldn't deny that it was just. They were running out of time. If they hoped to keep a roof over their heads and even a meager amount of food in their stomachs, something had to be done quickly.

We don't know anyone, Desmond had said and he was right. That was the heart of the problem. Jobs were scarce and much sought after. The ward captains handed them out like the great favors they were to those who were bound to them by blood or allegiance. Alone as they were, the Daughertys had to find a way to manage on their own.

If only they knew someone—

But we do, a tiny voice whispered in the back of her mind. Instantly, she tried to dismiss the thought. To suggest that she approach Archer Davalos, a man she had met only once and then under the most unpropitious circumstances, was absurd.

And yet, as the evening wore on, and her all-but-empty stomach rumbled, she returned again and again to the thought. The more she examined it, the less preposterous it seemed.

Until finally, toward dawn, she was at last able to convince herself that at the very least she should give it a try.

After all, the worst he could do was say no.

Wasn't it?

3

"There is a young woman to see you, sir," the butler said. His tone and the pinched look around his nostrils made it clear what Bertrand thought of that.

Archer glanced up from the book he had been half-heartedly perusing. "A woman?"

"A young woman, sir. I tried to discourage her but she is most insistent."

Archer ran down a mental catalog, trying to determine if there was any particular young woman who might feel compelled to call upon him. Aside from the fact that he had been uncharacteristically celibate of late, he was also unfailingly careful.

Whoever she was, she was not a lady. That much was clear. A lady would have been admitted to the parlor and directed to wait, not—as Bertrand said—discouraged.

"What does she want?" Archer asked.

"She doesn't say, sir, except of course to indicate that she wishes to speak with you."

Archer sighed. Beyond the walls of his study, rain lashed the almost deserted city streets. It was a dull, depressing day. He had hoped to distract himself from it, and from the problem that seemed to occupy his every waking moment, but he'd had little success.

Perhaps the young woman—the very insistent young woman—would at least prove a diversion.

"Show her in."

Bertrand obeyed, but not without a final sniff. Archer put his book to the side, stood and walked over to the window. He was standing there, looking out, when the butler returned.

"Miss Daugherty, sir."

Archer turned swiftly, and stared at the bright-haired young woman. His eyes swept over her critically. She was drably dressed and the rain had done nothing for her appearance, but he could not deny that she was extraordinarily lovely. The same fire he had glimpsed in her before still burned, but now more fiercely than ever.

"Miss Daugherty," he said, and inclined his head.

She did not smile nor did he expect her to. Instead, she waited, saying nothing, until Bertrand finally remembered himself.

"I shall be below, sir," the butler said pointedly. He cast a final, censorious glance at Megan. "Should you require anything."

The notion that he might need assistance amused Archer. His tone mocking, he said, "Thank you, Bertrand, but I believe I can manage. Would you care to sit, Miss Daugherty?"

Her nod was so slight as to be almost imperceptible. Gingerly, she advanced into the room and lowered her-

self into the large wing chair he indicated. Keeping her
back ramrod straight, she said, "I appreciate your seeing
me."

Archer's black brows rose. "Did I have a choice?"

A faint flush of color stained her cheeks. Her voice
was low and muted. He could not help but notice how
very soft it was, with the pleasing trace of a slight accent. "No, I suppose not."

He frowned, looking at her. She was more slender
than he had remembered. There was an air of frailty
about her entirely out of keeping with the strength of
her spirit.

On impulse, he asked, "Would you care for a glass
of sherry?" It would warm her, if nothing else, and it
might help her to relax and tell him why she had come.

Her eyes widened. She looked surprised and ever so
slightly alarmed, as if any kindness from him was to
be viewed with the utmost caution. "No, thank you."

"Tea then?" He felt an astonishing desire to do something for her, comfort her in some way. It was so out
of keeping with his nature, and with the promise he
had made to himself after their previous meeting, that
he hardly knew how to credit it.

Again, she shook her head. "If you don't mind, I
would prefer to keep this purely a business matter."

Archer stepped away from the window. He sat down
in the wing chair opposite her, his long legs stretched
out in front of him so that the tips of his highly polished
boots almost, but not quite, touched the frayed hem of
her skirt.

"Business?"

She took a deep breath and nodded. "Business. You
have a certain, shall we say, obligation to my cousin,
Maeve."

At his sharp look, she went on, "You did try to dishonor her, after all. Most people would agree that incurs a certain obligation."

"Most people?" Archer queried. His face was taut, his eyes unreadable. Although he appeared completely at ease, his long, hard body exuded a sense of coiled strength and remorseless will.

Cruelly, he stated the obvious. "We appear to move in different circles. In mine, a young woman who chooses to take up employment in a bawdy house can expect to be paid for her services, nothing more."

The color deepened in her cheeks, but she did not flinch. "Maeve was not paid."

Truly, there was no limit to Miss Megan Daugherty's audacity. It was past time to disabuse her of whatever ridiculous notion she was entertaining about his obligation to her cousin.

With deliberate crudeness, he said, "I was not satisfied."

She inhaled sharply. Her hands, neatly clasped in her lap, twisted. Just as he was beginning to think that she had been properly subdued, her head lifted and she met his eyes directly.

"You are insufferably rude, Mr. Davalos."

"And you are barking up the wrong tree, as they say. What possible reason would I have for feeling any sense of obligation to your cousin, or for that matter any member of your benighted family? Answer me that."

He had gone further than he'd intended but she got under his skin in a way he wasn't used to. What right did she have to sit there, almost within reach of his hand, looking so proudly courageous? Clearly, Miss Megan Daugherty did not know her place.

But then neither did he; or if he ever had, he hadn't let it keep him from accomplishing what he had wanted to in life. It had taken a fair measure of audacity to rise from the illegitimate son of a California grandee and a young Cherokee woman to become the terror of Wall Street. A part of him felt a certain kinship to the daring young woman before him, however much he tried to deny it.

"What is it you want?" he asked suddenly. And then, because he presumed he knew the answer, he added, "Money?"

To his surprise, not to say astonishment, she shook her head. "A job for one of my brothers." Quickly, before he could interject, she went on, "They're all good workers, strong and quick to learn. If you employ one of them, you won't be disappointed, I promise you that."

"Your brothers? How many do you have?"

"Five," she answered promptly. "Seamus is the oldest, he's twenty. Then there's Ned, Padraic, Desmond, and Sean. They're all good lads. If times were better, they'd have no lack of work. But as it is—" Her hands twisted again—"As it is, things are rather difficult. I understand that you are a very successful businessman. It occurred to me that you might wish to discharge your obligation to Maeve by employing one of them."

"I haven't admitted any obligation," Archer pointed out. He spoke automatically without thought, his mind taken by the significance of what she was saying.

Clearly, this was no easy effort for her. Her excuse for being there was flimsy at best. If he judged the situation correctly—and he was confident that he did— she was driven by desperation.

"Where are your brothers working now?" he asked.

She hesitated long enough to confirm what he suspected. More gently, he said, "They are not. What about you?"

Megan made a small gesture with her shoulders, not

resignation so much as acceptance of what she could not change. "There are few jobs for women to be found."

"And those that are available amount to what Maeve sought for herself without the same level of payment."

"Precisely," Megan said. She straightened her shoulders again—in truth they had been straight enough—and went on. "My brothers really are good workers, Mr. Davalos. Seamus can get the best from any machine and Ned is a whiz with numbers. All they need is a chance."

"They?" he repeated, his eyebrows rising. "I thought we were discussing one."

The small chink of light he had sensed in the wall between them vanished. She withdrew back into herself. "Yes, only one."

That was all she was asking for, one job to stand between her family and destitution. He was sure now that that was what she was facing. Nothing else could have brought her to him.

Even as he considered how he felt about that, he said, "I suppose I could."

The instant, hopeful look that relaxed her taut features sent a stab of guilt through him. It was wrong to play with her like this.

Or was he playing? He could easily employ one of her brothers, or all of them for that matter. If they were half as capable as she claimed, he would benefit far more than they.

Why then did he hesitate?

The only possible answer was as unflattering as it was true: he liked the notion of having the delectable if infuriating Miss Megan Daugherty in his power. It was an emotion unworthy of him, the sort of thing he detested in other men. Yet here he was, giving in to it all the same.

Even so, he could understand why she made him feel as she did. Besides her obvious beauty, undimmed by the harshness of her circumstances, she possessed an indomitable courage he could not help but admire. Moreover, she appeared quite sensible, as she would have to be to feel so deep a responsibility for her family.

In all this, she was markedly different from any other woman he knew, including his sister. Though he tried to avoid it, he could not help but compare Megan's behavior with that of Elizabeth. Much as he loved his sister—and he did devotedly—he had to admit that beside this proud Irishwoman, she was weak and self-indulgent.

Or she had been. He suspected she had learned her lesson. Unfortunately, it was too late or soon would be unless he could intervene to save her reputation and preserve her future.

For that reason he had returned to New York. But so far he had come no closer to solving the problem. Indeed, there did not appear to be a solution.

Or at least there hadn't until Miss Megan Daugherty walked into his life.

"I think," he said slowly, "that we may be able to come to some arrangement."

4

If asked, Archer honestly could not have said what was in his mind at that moment. He was responding purely by instinct. She was there, he wanted her, they would work something out.

The difficulty was how? Clearly, she was not amenable to the usual blandishments effective with women. Were he to even attempt them, he suspected she would hand him his head.

Nonetheless, he was determined, at the very least, to become better aquainted with her. Much better.

"Have supper with me." It was not a request. To her credit, she did not take it as such.

Looking him straight in the eye, she asked "Why?"

"So that we can discuss the future."

"That is a rather broad topic, Mr. Davalos. The only part of it that interests me is employment for my family."

"Patience," he advised with a sardonic smile. At the same time, he rang for Bertrand. The butler appeared with such speed as to suggest that he had been waiting, if not directly outside the door, very close to it.

"Sir?"

"Supper, Bertrand. For two."

The butler's eyes opened a fraction wider, but he controlled himself admirably. "Very good, sir."

"I do not wish to have supper with you," Megan said when they were alone once again. "Without wishing to appear impolite, it is completely unnecessary. If you would be so kind as to give me your answer—"

"No," Archer said.

The color fled from her face. "No what?"

"No, I will not give you my answer now. However, if you would prefer, we can simply make it no to the job and be done with it. Is that what you wish?"

"You know perfectly well that it isn't."

"Then I suggest you reconcile yourself to sitting down to supper with me," he said firmly but with a note of kindness that surprised him. He was not, by any stretch of the imagination, a kind man.

Numerous people in New York and elsewhere who knew him would have found the notion painfully amusing. Yet apparently he was disposed to treat the fiery Megan gently.

Perhaps it had something to do with the fact that she so obviously needed a meal. Although she did her best to appear unaffected as they sat down at the large mahogany table in the dining room, her gaze widened at the food being laid out before them. There were enough dishes to feed at least eight people generously.

A small, humorless smile lifted the corners of a mouth he could only describe as delectable. "Are you expecting guests?"

A tiny flicker of embarrassment moved through Archer. He could have said that his cook was new and still overly inclined to impress him. Or that his servants had a habit of cooking for themselves as well as for him and that nothing would be wasted.

There was a great deal he could have told her but he chose not to. He was not going to explain himself to Megan Daugherty.

For a scant moment before the food was served, her bright head bowed. She did not make any show of it at all but he realized, with a small shock, that she was giving thanks.

When had he last been with anyone who felt genuinely grateful? Not in the city, that was for certain. But out on the frontier there were such people. Those who lived closer to nature—and to death—took far less for granted.

This unlikely visitor to his Gramercy Park world appeared to be one such. But appearances, as he knew too well, could be deceptive.

Who exactly was she? The avenging fury who had descended upon him at Delphine's Place? The proud but desperate young woman who faced him in the study? Or this creature of earthly beauty and spiritual strength who sat across the damask-covered table from him. Her eyes were discreetly averted, but there was a faint hint of mutiny in the set of her delectable mouth.

And make no mistake, it was delectable. Maeve was a pretty girl; her cousin was beautiful. Even dressed as plainly as she was, Megan would capture any man's attention. Moreover, she had courage and spirit, and also—he suspected—intelligence. All of which eased his conscience regarding what he was about to do.

"Eat," he said, indicating the lobster bisque Bertrand had placed in front of her, and proceeded to do the same himself.

They dined in silence for several minutes. The bisque finished, the plates were whisked away and replaced with servings of fresh trout in a light dill sauce.

Megan took a small bite. Her eyes closed reflexively. When she opened them again, she was smiling slightly. "You have an excellent chef," she said, very politely.

He was struck by the incongruity of it all. She had the manners of a lady-born but dressed as if the wolf was at the door. Her speech was perfect, her voice cultured, her posture erect. She knew exactly which fork to use and held her wine glass as correctly as any etiquette mistress could have wished.

All this from some backwater Irish village where they'd be lucky to see porridge twice a day?

"Tell me about yourself," he invited.

Megan looked surprised—and reluctant. She set her fork down carefully. "There is little to tell."

"Try."

It was a command, yet no more lay behind it than a whim. He was bored, out of sorts, and troubled.

Miss Megan Daugherty had robbed him of his pleasure. The least she could do was provide a more tepid form of entertainment. After all, it wasn't as though he was asking her to sing for her supper.

The slight tensing of her shoulders suggested that she felt otherwise. Still, she accepted the inevitable.

"I was born in the village of Ballycollogh near the city of Cork," she said. Her voice was low and pleasant. He realized with a start that he enjoyed listening to her.

"My mother died when I was very young and I helped my father to raise my brothers. We had a small farm, but the land was good and we managed well enough."

"Why did you leave then?"

She hesitated. Slowly, her eyes scanned his face. Whatever she saw must have reassured her enough to provide a starkly honest answer.

"The British. I had a sixth brother—Finn. They killed him for daring to believe that Ireland should be ruled by the Irish. Then they burned our house and drove our cattle off."

There was more, he sensed, that she wasn't saying but she didn't need to. Like her, he had seen acts of wanton savagery masquerading as the will of a lawful government, had seen the horror they brought down on the young and helpless particularly.

"Were you there when it happened?" he asked.

She nodded curtly. "I hid in a barrow back behind the sheep byre."

"What is a barrow?"

"An ancient mound built by the old ones before St. Patrick brought Christianity to the land."

"Some of the Indian nations built mounds to honor their dead and propitiate the Mother of us all."

Her eyes widened slightly. "So was it with the Celts."

He smiled. "There, you see, we have something in common after all."

She didn't deny it, but she did keep a wary eye on him as they finished the trout and the beef was carried in. He waited until they had both been served and Bertrand had once again absented himself with a censorious glance in his employer's direction, before he said, "Regarding the matter of employment."

"Any of my brothers . . ." Megan began promptly.

"It is not them I am considering."

Her eyes narrowed. "Indeed."

"The position requires a woman."

Color suffused her cheeks—not of embarrassment but of good, wholesome anger. She snatched the linen napkin from her lap, dropped it onto the table, and rose. "I might have known."

"Sit down."

"If you think for one moment that I . . ."

Softly, but with unmistakable authority, he repeated, "Sit down."

She did not, but he could see the hesitation stopping her and moved to take full advantage of it. "If you walk out now, you forfeit all chance for a job that, while admittedly illegal, is not remotely immoral. And which, I might add, pays extremely well."

Megan's finely arched brows drew nearer. "Illegal . . . but not immoral? How can that be?"

"You ask that? A woman whose family suffered under the hand of authority? Do you really imagine everything the law does is right and conversely, everything done outside the law is wrong?"

"I know it isn't always right," she admitted slowly, "but I don't see how anything illegal can help but be wrong."

"If you saw someone beating a child mercilessly, would you intervene?"

"Of course."

"But if the person doing the beating is the parent or guardian, your intervention is illegal. Indeed, you can protect a horse more readily than a child."

"That's terrible," Megan protested.

"I agree. What if you saw some other terrible wrong being committed but with the full protection of the law, wouldn't you feel that you had to do something anyway?"

"It would depend," she said, still careful of him. Clearly, this was no easily biddable female. All the better for what he had in mind.

"Sit down," he said pleasantly, "and we'll discuss it."

Slowly, never taking her eyes from him, she lowered herself back into the chair. "What terrible wrong are we discussing?" she asked, a final bite to her voice as though to suggest that in her estimation he was far more likely to be the wronger rather than the wronged.

"An injury to my family," he informed her.

Megan's face softened. "I am sorry."

Her instant sympathy, so readily given despite her justified suspicion of him, sent a pang through Archer. Not enough of one, however, to change the course he was now bound on.

"Something has been taken from us which, if revealed, could cause significant pain to one I care for a great deal. It must be recovered."

"I see . . . But why don't you simply go to the authorities?"

"Because in the eyes of the law, the one holding this something has the legal right to it."

Megan nodded. She appeared thoughtful and composed, her interest engaged. "I understand Mr. Pinkerton's organization can be more, shall we say, understanding."

He smiled faintly, amused that she should know any

such thing, or think that she did. "Unfortunately, Mr. Pinkerton does not employ females."

"And you are convinced only a woman can take care of this matter?"

"I think it highly likely. The person involved is far less likely to suspect a woman."

"Is this person dangerous?"

There lay the crux of the matter. His conscience stirred him to be as honest as possible. "No more so than an irate customer at Madame Delphine's."

The color returned to her cheeks. It appeared to be a handy barometer with which to read her emotions. She lowered her eyes slightly but continued to regard him through the thick fringe of her lashes.

"You are quite sure of that?" she asked.

"Reasonably."

"Perhaps you should tell me more about the situation so that I may judge the degree of hazard for myself."

It was a sensible request, but one he could not grant, at least not yet.

"The job is sensitive in its nature. First you must agree to accept it, then you will be given the full details."

"Isn't that rather like buying a pig in a poke?"

"You could see it that way," he allowed reluctantly. "But do you have a choice?"

Her small white teeth worried her lower lip. An instant before he could succumb to the impulse to ease that miniscule hurt in a way that no doubt would have quite shocked Miss Megan Daugherty, she said, "All right, but there is another matter that must be settled now: the question of payment."

Archer leaned back in his chair. He was well pleased with the results so far and was prepared to be munificent. "How much do you want?"

"Five hundred dollars."

"What?" Five hundred dollars was a year's wages for a skilled craftsman. It could well support a large family in the style of the burgeoning middle class. She had an extraordinary amount of gall asking for such a sum. "That's absurd."

"As you will," she said calmly. "I bid you goodnight."

"Wait . . ." Archer thought it over in his usual lightning fashion. Large though it was, the amount was actually inconsequential to him. He could spend a hundred times that much and not miss it. It was merely the idea that while he was willing to take advantage of her, she might be doing the same to him that rankled.

Still, the bargain had gone too far to be dismissed now.

"All right," he said, "five hundred dollars it is. Half on account and half when you are successful. Agreed?"

Very slowly, as though she fully suspected she was going to regret her decision, Megan nodded.

5

"Sherry?" Archer asked. They had adjourned to the study after mutually agreeing that supper was over. The door was firmly closed. Bertrand had been sent off to his duties below stairs.

Seated in front of the fire, her hands neatly folded in her lap and her ankles crossed, Megan accepted the small glass he offered. It was fine crystal, catching the firelight in diamond-faceted shards and turning the pale liquid within to the color of the dying sun.

She sipped gingerly. The liquid was velvet fire, sliding over her tongue and down her throat with consummate ease. Warmth followed it, along with a creeping sense of well-being that was patently false.

Swiftly, she set the glass down. Above all, she had

to keep her wits about her. They were far too close to being beguiled as it was.

Archer Davalos was an extraordinary man—extraordinarily dangerous, extraordinarily audacious, extraordinarily attractive.

Not to her, of course. She was immune to the blandishments of men, being completely concentrated on protecting her family. Never mind that his tall, lean body appeared to hold some untoward fascination for her. Or that the midnight black hair, the chiseled purity of his features, the burnished skin, and the overall air of masculine power bid fair to send her senses whirling.

They were absolutely not going to whirl; she was not going to succumb; and he was not going to make a fool of her. She was Megan Maira Katherine Daugherty and she was damn well going to remember it!

And yet, a tiny pang of envy tugged at her soul when she thought of what he had said about one he cared for a great deal. What fortunate person was that?

A wife, most likely, even though that seemed at odds with his visit to the pleasure house. Or perhaps a daughter, although, if such a person existed and was other than a small child, he would have to have fathered her at a very young age. Not that he couldn't have, a small voice whispered. This was a virile man accustomed to taking what he wanted from life.

It was a trait she might do well to adopt for herself. So far the Daugherty clan had been tossed hither and yon by contrary fate. It was time to take control of their destiny, starting with the five-hundred-dollar stake she was determined to wrest from the dark, compelling man standing at the mantel, his eyes regarding her with quiet scrutiny.

"Don't you like it?" he asked, gesturing to the discarded sherry.

"It's fine," she assured him hastily. "I am not accustomed to spirits."

The corners of his mouth lifted. He appeared amused by her propriety. Undoubtedly, he was accustomed to far more sophisticated women who took all such things in stride. Well then, she would show him what an Irish lass could do.

"You were about to tell me what it is you want me to do."

"Indeed, I was. But first, tell me, how did you get into Madame Delphine's?"

Megan hesitated. She would greatly prefer not to discuss that matter further. However, he was now her employer—strictly speaking—and she could not rightly refuse.

"I dressed as a maid and went in through the back door."

"No one tried to stop you?"

She shook her head. "In my experience, if you look as though you belong, people tend to take you at face value. Irish maids are everywhere and therefore completely taken for granted. People don't really notice them at all."

"Perhaps not in a large establishment such as Madame Delphine's. In a private house, it would be harder."

She thought for a moment, her brow furrowed. A private house? Was that where the something taken from him was being kept?

"You want me to enter a private house and recover the object you are missing?"

He nodded. For a moment, he hesitated. The subject was clearly distasteful to him. Anger seethed below the seemingly imperturbable surface of his nature, yet it was a controlled anger channeled into decisive action.

Whatever else he was, Archer Davalos was no slave to his emotions.

"The house is on Long Island in the village of Southampton," he said. "It is occupied by a Chester Daniels. Mr. Daniels is in possession of certain letters written to him by a young lady. She wants them returned; he is refusing."

"Who is the young lady?"

"That is not important for you to know."

"On the contrary, if I am to undertake this task and conclude it successfully, I must have as much information as possible."

Archer shot her a rapier look that would have started many a stalwart man to quaking. Megan bore it unflinchingly. She knew that she was right. He could not possibly expect her to flaunt the law, enter Chester Daniels's home illegally, seize letters which might well have been given to him freely, and emerge successful if she had only half an idea of what she was dealing with.

Moreover, she was not about to be intimidated by him. Not for a single moment.

"The woman is my sister, Elizabeth. She has been very foolish, which she now sincerely regrets."

At Megan's instant, if unspoken, reaction, he laughed humorlessly. "Not because of anything I have done, I assure you. Elizabeth acted impulsively. She knows full well what it may cost her."

"Should I conclude," Megan asked softly, "that these are letters of a compromising nature?"

Archer's nod was curt. "Chester Daniels is threatening to publish them unless his demands are met."

"What are those demands?"

"A large sum of money to begin with, access to certain business information, sponsorship in one or two clubs that would otherwise never consider admitting him—that sort of thing."

"And you are unwilling to comply?"

"To what end? Giving him what he wants this time won't help Elizabeth. Not really. He will still have the letters and still be able to hold them over her head whenever he chooses. She will never be able to get her life back in order."

"You have spoken with him directly?"

"Once," Archer acknowledged. The memory was clearly not pleasing. "He took great pleasure in informing me that should any harm come to himself, the letters would be published at once. Further, if any effort is made to recover them, he will make them public."

"It sounds as though Chester Daniels knows what he's about," Megan said quietly. She was beginning to form a picture of the man—smooth, seductive, with a certain superficial charm not unlike a snake.

They didn't have snakes in Ireland, St. Patrick having seen to that long ago. But she could still recognize one when she saw it.

Just as she could imagine what being thwarted by such a man must mean to Archer Davalos. Only genuine love for his sister could have stayed his hand.

Again, she felt that small pang of envy, but stalwartly ignored it. Elizabeth Davalos had quite enough problems without Megan adding to them. On the contrary, she had been hired—and would be extremely well paid—to help set the young woman's life to rights.

"What happens if I bungle it?" she asked. "Won't he release the letters?"

"Most likely. I presume you are capable of deciding whether or not they can be recovered safely. If they cannot, you will have to withdraw."

"You leave that in my hands?"

He shrugged, his massive shoulders moving beneath the perfectly tailored cloth of his frock coat. "I appear to have little choice. You are clever, resourceful, and courageous. No Pinkerton operative would have as good a chance of succeeding."

Pride warmed her cheeks. Not wishing to consider why she was so affected by his praise, she moved on quickly. "When would you like me to begin?"

"Tomorrow."

Megan rose and smoothed her skirt. "Very well. I will inform my family that I have received employment on Long Island and arrange for transportation there. As soon as I am settled in the village, I will send word to you of my progress."

Archer set his glass down. "No," he said quietly, "you won't."

"I beg your pardon?"

He walked toward the door of the study and opened it. Turning back to her, he said, "You are in possession of delicate information regarding my family. I do not intend to have you share it with anyone."

"I wouldn't dream of—"

"You mean you wouldn't be tempted to drop a hint to your brothers or your dear cousin? You expect them to allow you to go off to Southampton without knowing all the details of who is employing you and why? Come now, Miss Daugherty, you can't be that naive. And you certainly can't expect me to be."

Her hands were suddenly damp against the worn serge of her skirt, but Megan kept her voice steady. "I cannot leave without any word at all to my family."

"You will send them a brief note which I will dictate, assuring them of your well-being. I assume you will also want to enclose at least some portion of your payment, although I don't advise you send the whole thing, as that would arouse concern."

His bronzed hand closed gently but implacably on her arm. "As for the rest, you will remain here tonight. We will travel to Southampton together in the morning."

"I cannot—" she began, suddenly struck with real fear of spending the night under his roof. He was too compelling, too unpredictable, and she was far too susceptible where he was concerned.

A sardonic smile lit his dark brown eyes. It was as if he could see directly into her soul and was amused by what he found there.

His voice was slightly husky. "Be assured, Miss Daugherty, you will be as the chick in the nest, completely safe. If you are sensible, you will get a good night's rest, for you may need it."

Embarrassed by her wayward thoughts, Megan relented. If she went back to the drab, coldwater flat, she would face a barrage of questions from her brothers and Maeve. Despite her best resolve, they might get enough of the truth to prevent her from going.

She did not want that to happen. Not only for the money but, she realized, for Archer Davalos himself. She wanted to help him if she could. She also simply wanted to be with him.

Moon-addled nonsense, she thought, and firmly turned her mind from it. Yet later, lying in the large, four-poster mahogany bed in the guest room she had been given, surrounded by greater luxury than she had ever known, she thought again of the hard-faced man who had parted from her below.

Staring up at the embroidered canopy where lords and ladies rode over emerald dells against an azure sky, she drifted to sleep thinking of an enchanted place in which all things were possible, even dreams.

6

He was insane to be doing this. It was bad enough to involve Megan Daugherty in his family's problems, but to harbor her under his own roof was the next thing to madness.

Archer poured himself another brandy and stood, holding it, beside the fireplace. It was very late. Megan had gone to bed hours ago and he should have done the same.

Separately, of course, most definitely separately. Never mind that his body tightened when he did no more than look at her. If he had even the smallest amount of sense, he would keep his distance.

She was trouble, he could tell. A woman of fire and independence, but also deeply rooted in family and faith. A woman who could never be easily dismissed. A woman for a lifetime.

Exactly the sort of woman he had always avoided and with good reason. He accepted that his sister was his responsibility—although she argued otherwise—but apart from that, he preferred to go through life unencumbered. The last thing he wanted was a woman he couldn't forget.

She would do what he had hired her to do, they would both benefit in the process and she would be gone. In a week's time—at most a month's—he would barely remember her.

A harsh laugh broke from him. Who was he trying to convince, himself or the gleeful imp who perched on his shoulder nattering at his predicament?

She was perfect for the job. If anyone could fool Chester Daniels, it was her. But the job was dangerous. She might be caught or hurt. Either possibility assaulted a conscience which had hitherto been sensibly quiet.

Miss Daugherty had awakened it, along with other things. Meanwhile, she undoubtedly slept sweetly.

His big hand closed around the brandy snifter until the delicate crystal threatened to crack. Reluctantly, he loosened his hold but only fractionally.

The way she had looked at him when he told her she had to stay, that defiant flash of her eyes and the angry toss of her head. Any sensible woman of her standing would be afraid of him, but not his Irish lass. She merely straightened her shoulders and met him head-on.

His lass? Oh, no, he wasn't about to start thinking like that. Do the job, pay the money, and good-bye Miss Daugherty. He'd go west afterward, back to the wild places he preferred. His businesses could look after themselves for a while.

Or he might go in the other direction, to Europe. He'd visited it several times and found much to amuse himself.

Or he might do both. The world was vast and he was free to wander over it. There was no need to tie himself down, no need to prefer one woman above all others, no need—

Why was he going on so? With a grimace, he swallowed the rest of the brandy and put the snifter down on the mantel. As he did, the clock in the marbled entry hall chimed twice.

He intended to get an early start in the morning. A few hours sleep would be well advised. The house was silent as he climbed the curving staircase to the second floor and walked down the hall.

His own quarters were at the back of the house overlooking a small garden. To reach them, he passed the guest room where Megan slept. The door was closed and, he suspected, locked.

He paused for a moment, struggling with the image of her tousled fire-born hair and slender body. Beneath his roof, near to his hand, and despite his stern reprimands to himself, very much in his life—if only temporarily.

He shook his head wryly. Miss Megan Daugherty most likely slept with hair tamed into a stern braid and the covers pulled up to her chin. Yet that image, too, did nothing whatsoever to calm the rampant heat coursing through him.

It would be a restless night.

"How much farther is it?" Megan asked. They were seated in Archer's private train car heading east from the city toward Long Island. Already the buildings had thinned around them, the sky was clearer, and there was a hint of salt air.

Megan sat opposite him on a plush velvet bench. She wore the same sensible black serge skirt and white blouse she had worn the previous day. Her hair was swept up under a sensible black hat with a sensible black feather. Her posture was sensibly erect, her hands sensibly folded. Her entire air was that of a sensible young woman going about her sensible business.

Archer resented it deeply. He had spent not merely a restless but a sleepless night thinking of Miss Megan Daugherty. The more he thought, the less he liked the conclusions to which he came.

She was looking out the window, her attention absorbed by the passing view. He cleared his throat.

"How exactly are you planning to get into Chester Daniels's house?"

"I masqueraded as a maid once and it worked. I thought I would try it again."

Just as he had thought. "I don't advise it. The house is small and requires little staff. I have the impression that Daniels has only one employee, who has been with him for years. He prefers it that way, no doubt, to keep his activities private."

"I see—" Megan worried her lip, a habit of hers apparently. He shifted slightly on the seat. "What would you suggest?" she asked.

"There is another way," he said and began to tell her what he had decided during the interminably long night.

"I can't possibly do this," Megan protested. She stood in front of the full-length mirror in the guest chamber— one of many—on the second floor of the "cottage" by the water.

The cottage was Archer's summer home, where he stayed when the city palled but he still needed to be near it for business. Built by a robber baron in the previous decade, it had passed into Archer's hands, as legend had it, on the turn of a card.

This time the story was actually true but, as usual, incomplete. He had taken the house in settlement of a very large gambling debt owed to him by the ne'er-do-well son of the robber baron. Archer also paid the son's various other debts. In fact, he had given a fair price for the house but no one wanted to believe that.

"I can't," Megan repeated, drawing his attention back to her, though in truth it hadn't wandered far. She stood, still looking into the mirror with an expression on her face somewhere between shock and bemusement.

She could be pardoned for feeling both. The woman looking back at her from the beveled glass surely bore little resemblance to the way Megan was accustomed to seeing herself.

The dressmaker had outdone herself, creating a gown of aquamarine silk and pale lace with a narrow skirt, tiny waist and low-cut bodice that perfectly complemented Miss Megan Daugherty's most unsensible figure.

Firelight danced off her bare arms and shoulders gleaming like honey-touched porcelain. Her luxurious hair was swept up in a cascade of curls that framed her perfectly shaped face. Eyes the same shade as the dress looked out from beneath finely arched brows.

So lovely was she, so exquisitely feminine and ethereally elegant that she might have stepped intact from the pages of the latest ladies' magazine, the epitome of all its readers aspired to be.

Not bad for a poor Irish girl.

"Leave us," Archer said quietly.

The maid who had been fussing over Megan responded at once. She cast a nervous glance at her employer, another at the young woman before the mirror, and darted for the door. A moment later she closed it behind her.

Archer set down the cheroot he had been smoking and crossed the room to stand directly behind Megan. He put his hands on her shoulders lightly.

Her skin was warm velvet, the bones beneath it delicate but strong. A ripple of desire coursed through him so intense that he had to catch his breath before he spoke.

"Of course, you can do it," he said. "You're perfect."

Her eyes met his in the mirror. She looked at him disbelievingly. "This isn't me."

"How do you know that? Have you already been everything you possibly can be?"

"No . . . I don't know . . . perhaps."

She was wearing a light floral perfume that on her seemed more potent than the far more seductive fragrances other women of his acquaintance favored. He had the sudden, searing sense of what it would be like to lie with her in a sun-dappled field of flowers and love away a summer day.

Madness.

"You can't possibly believe that," he insisted. His hands tightened on her shoulders. "Look at yourself," he commanded. When she did reluctantly, he said, "That woman there, that's Megan Daugherty. That's who you are. Not what other people have told you or what circumstances have forced upon you. That beautiful, confident woman is who you were always meant to be."

Her eyes widened. He saw the tenuous belief trying to be born in them and on impulse turned her to him. Her breasts brushed the fine white silk of his evening shirt. She gasped softly and tried to pull away but the gesture was halfhearted.

His arms tightened around her. Behind him, the fire leapt. Outside a summer storm was blowing far out to sea. But within the room overlooking the shore, a man and woman were lost in a world of their own.

Her mouth was soft, warm, beguiling. Gently, his lips parted hers, his tongue caressing with light, careful strokes. He was determined not to go too quickly, not to take advantage of her obvious innocence.

But he hadn't bargained on the effect she had on him. The fire leapt higher. She made a soft sound deep in her throat and stood on tiptoe to twine her arms around his neck.

Archer groaned. His hand clasped the back of her head as he held her still for a kiss that was blatantly possessive, his tongue thrusting deep even as his other hand slid down to cup her buttocks and lift her to him.

His self-control, so long maintained, slid toward the brink of a chasm. He let it go without regret, thinking only of lifting Megan in his arms, carrying her the few steps to the bed and—

There was a knock at the door. Bertrand called out, "Sir, the carriage is here."

Archer raised his head. Megan's eyes were smoky with desire, her cheeks becomingly flushed, her lips trembling softly. Beneath the taut silk bodice, her breasts were full, the nipples hard. He could not remember ever seeing a woman more exquisitely aroused.

"Sir?" Bertrand called again.

Suppressing the urge to throttle the man, Archer took a deep breath. He set Megan from him but held on to her hand. She swayed slightly and looked at him in confusion.

"We must go," he said. Before he could think better of it, he drew her from the room, past the butler who was discreetly looking the other way, and out into the glittering night.

7

Mary and all the saints, what had she landed herself in? The room in which she stood, to which Archer had brought her, might easily have graced any of the finest palaces in Europe. Or at least she supposed it could, having never seen any such place for herself.

Stretching into the far distance, walled in marble and gilt, and filled with the most magnificently dressed men and women, it seemed like a scene from a fairy tale. Yet it was all too real.

She was here, on Archer's arm, her mouth still

slightly swollen from his kiss, her body sheathed in silk and lace, and her entire notion of who she was going up like so much smoke.

"What is this place?" she murmured.

"It belongs to Lucinda Plessis. Heard of her?"

"Who hasn't? A person can't pick up a newspaper without reading about this fabulous party given by the fabulous Mrs. Plessis or that magnificent ball hosted by the same or this soiree or that ensemble. For heaven's sake, does the woman do nothing but entertain?"

Archer laughed, a deep, masculine sound like water running over gravel. It sent a shiver through her. "I doubt it. She is in a major battle with Mrs. Astor for control of the illustrious Four Hundred. As things stand now, Lucinda actually has a chance of winning."

"Do you seriously think that matters?"

"Of course not, but a good many other people do. If nothing else, their antics are amusing."

"You enjoy watching people make fools of themselves?"

"Only when they're so very good at it," he said.

Megan smiled ruefully. She couldn't manage to be angry with him, no matter how hard she tried. Indeed, she could barely manage to do anything at all, so busy was she trying to keep both her feet rooted to the ground.

"Why are we here?" she asked after Archer had taken two champagne flutes from a passing waiter and handed her one.

"Daniels is likely to attend. This is as good a way as any for you to meet him."

"And thereby to get some sense of how I might enter his home without being detected." She swallowed some of the wine and nodded. "It's a good idea."

Archer shot her a skeptical look. "You really think so?"

"Of course," she assured him, surprised that he should ask. "Isn't that why I'm rigged out like this?"

"Rigged out? I'll have you know that was made by one of the most exclusive couturiers this side of the Seine. You make her sound like a sail maker."

"Pretty expensive sail," Megan muttered, fingering the silk. She finished the wine, spotted another waiter and gave him a smile that froze the man in his tracks. Helping herself to a fresh glass, she said, "It's rather warm in here, don't you think?"

Archer took the glass from her hand, set it back down on the tray, and drew her off toward the high French windows. "You need fresh air," he said sternly.

"I'm thirsty," she protested, "and besides, it's got all those bubbles in it. What harm can they do?"

"You'd be surprised," he muttered and led her out onto the stone terrace that gave way by a few steps to a garden. The night air was fragrant with the scents of roses and honeysuckle. Behind them in the great house, music played. But few of the guests had found their way outside yet. They had the long gravel walks and the shadowy paths among the yew trees to themselves.

"Holy Mary," Megan said suddenly, "what's that?" She pointed to a pale form along the path up ahead. As they neared, it resolved itself into the shape of a naked male.

"It's a statue," Archer said and raised his eyes to heaven. It was the only possible source of help in such a situation, enthralled by a woman with no awareness of her own power and shielded by an innocence that would not be denied.

"There's another," she said and, indeed, there was. This one was female but similarly devoid of clothing save for a discreetly placed swatch of veil nestled between her thighs. "Good Lord," Megan said, "they're all over."

"Lucinda collects them," Archer said with a sigh. "She may have the largest collection of truly bad sculpture in the world."

"If you ask me, her problem is she's got too much money."

"I didn't—ask that is—but I suspect you may be right. There are a good many people like that."

Megan laughed. To her astonishment, she was genuinely enjoying herself. It might have had something to do with the champagne, or merely the headiness of a moon-drenched night. Or then again, being so close to Archer might have been at least partly responsible. Every time she thought of that kiss they had shared—

But no, she wasn't going to think about it. She was going to be a good, sensible girl and keep her mind on her work.

"Shouldn't we be getting back?" she asked reluctantly.

"Only if you promise not to drink any more champagne. You need a clear head if you're going to deal with Daniels."

Half-stung by the notion that she would do anything so foolish as to drink more than she should, and embarrassed and disappointed by his readiness to part with her company, Megan said, "Only with Daniels? It seems you're the one who keeps overstepping himself, Mr. Archer Davalos. I'll remind you we have a simple business relationship. You'll be kind enough to keep it in mind."

"Will I?" Archer murmured in that deceptively soft voice she had already come to recognize. He took a step close to her. "And what if I don't?"

It was foolish to challenge such a man, out here alone

in the dark. Delightfully, astoundingly foolish. So unlike her sensible self.

"You'll be making me forget what I'm here for," she answered quietly, the defiance gone from her as suddenly as it had flared. In its place was only regret that it couldn't have somehow been different between them, a different time and place, different lives. For surely it would take nothing less.

A pulse leaped in Archer's square jaw. His hands brushed lightly over her bare arms, the thumbs just grazing her breasts. A tremor ran through her, impossible to hide from him, impossible to deny.

"Megan," he murmured and drew her to him. His mouth touched the corners of hers, sliding down along the slim white line of her throat to nestle in the hollow between her collarbones. She barely felt the rough bark of a tree at her back as he pressed her against it, his hands free to cup her breasts, then fit themselves around her waist, and shape the graceful chalice of her hips.

Thickly, he said her name again in the instant before he took her mouth with devastating thoroughness. For long moments, they clung together, oblivious to any reality save what their desire created.

He was fire and hunger, steely strength and unrelenting masculine need. Whereas she, too, matched the fire with her own and with the yielding grace of her body emboldened by an ancient feminine knowledge old as passion itself.

A footstep on the gravel and the sudden sound of voices dragged them back into the larger world. Archer cursed under his breath—something about damned interruptions—but he set her from him quickly. She had her skirt smoothed and her hair more or less rearranged before their solitude was ended.

"Davalos," the man who approached them said with a fine edge to his seeming pleasure, "I hadn't heard you were here."

Archer's hand tightened on Megan's waist. He drew her to him in a gesture that struck her as oddly protective. A moment later, it seemed odder still.

"Daniels," he said easily as if the name didn't stick in his throat. "Nothing better to do this evening?"

"Like you," the other man said, "I am at loose ends." His eyes skimmed Megan with an intensity that was neither polite nor at all flattering. He was a good six inches shorter than Archer, with a slender build, dark brown hair, and a carefully cultivated mustache. His clothes were elegant but just slightly overdone, his manner falsely gracious.

"Or perhaps not," he added, smiling sardonically. "It seems you are well occupied."

Archer shrugged as though it was of no matter. He made no effort to introduce Megan, but merely walked her past Daniels and back toward the house. "Don't wander too far," he advised. "The woods are dark this time of year."

Daniels frowned, the first genuine expression Megan had seen from him. He suppressed it at once. "You are not a fool," he said and inclined his head to Megan, his eyes once more encompassing her.

"I don't understand," she said to Archer when they had walked some distance back toward the house. "Wasn't the whole point of this for me to meet him?"

"You did meet," he said, his voice curt, his hand firm on her arm.

"But you should have introduced me, should have done something to throw us together, should have—"

"Don't tell me what I should have done," Archer said suddenly. He spoke quietly enough but his words had

the ring of steel. Belatedly, she realized that a fine rage
simmered within him. Had merely seeing Daniels been
enough to provoke that?

"You met," he added, more calmly. "It is enough."

Megan could not see how but she was not about to
say so, not again. Not yet. Instead, she went back with
him into the gilded room and presently, when the or-
chestra struck up a waltz, they danced.

Or rather they flew, for such was her impression of
the evening then and whenever she thought of it in the
days to come.

8

A boat drifted past, borne along by the wind, its white
sails gleaming in the midday sun. Seated where the
long, rolling lawn of Archer's house came down to the
beach, Megan watched the boat pass.

Her knees were drawn up to her chin, her arms
wrapped around them, her eyes pensive. She was
dressed in a white silk dress with an overskirt of sheer
cotton and tiny puff sleeves. Her hair was caught up
at the crown of her head.

No one coming upon her could have sensed the turmoil of her emotions. She looked calm and at ease there
on the great lawn with the house rising behind her and
the sea sparkling in the sun.

In fact, she was anything but. A week had passed
since the dance where she had "met" Chester Daniels.
A week of bewilderment and delight, anticipation, and
dread.

She and Archer had been together almost constantly—riding, walking, fishing, attending more of the
parties that seemed to be scheduled every hour. Yet he

had scarcely touched her. There had been no repetition of the heated kisses they had shared.

She was glad of that, of course. It was most improper to do any such thing. The disappointment and frustration that grew in her with each passing day were best ignored.

Besides, their relationship appeared to have moved onto a higher plane. They had discovered a mutual love of literature and music, a deeply rooted pleasure in horses, and an inclination to spend long stretches of time in companionable silence.

When they did talk, which was frequent, he told her of his upbringing in the west, growing up the son of an Indian woman and a Spanish grandee, the struggle to find a place for himself in a world determined to reject him, and the hard, brutal work that, with a dash of luck, had led him out of poverty to wealth and power.

But he also listened to her quiet stories about Ireland, the layers of pain peeling away to reveal the beauty beneath, about her family and her tenuous hopes for a future in this new world that would justify everything they had suffered on their path to it.

Megan could not remember ever having someone to talk with in such a way. Nor did she fool herself. In its own way, the intimacy they shared at such moments was as potent as the kisses they both avoided.

She sighed and laid her head on her knees. It was all too much for her. She was a simple girl who seemed suddenly to be living in a fairy tale. Yet she would be ill-advised to think of it as such. Although he had neglected to mention it of late, Archer had hired her to do a job for him. She had a responsibility to make sure it got done.

Today was the first opportunity she'd had to really

sit down and think about what was happening to her. Archer had been called back suddenly to the city—something about a company he wanted to buy finally coming up for sale. He had promised to be back that evening, but the long hours of the day still stretched ahead of her, waiting to be filled.

But not idly. She was determined to put them to good use. Rising, she shook her skirt to smooth it and set off decisively in the direction of the house.

Bertrand was below stairs in the butler's pantry, checking what silver needed polishing. He stopped the instant he saw her.

"Madame," he said cautiously, not unlike a wary animal whose den has been invaded.

Megan beamed him a smile. She knew full well that he disapproved of her but he was far too good at his job to ever say so directly. Or perhaps he was merely sensible enough to avoid Archer's anger.

"I'm sorry to interrupt you," she said, "but I would like to go into the village. Is the trap available?"

Bertrand hesitated. He looked as if he wanted to deny it but couldn't think of a good—or safe—reason.

"I'll have it readied for you, madame," he said finally.

"No need," Megan replied. She had no intention of waiting whatever length of time it would take him to see a duty he clearly thought should not be performed. "I'll take care of it myself."

"But, madame . . ."

His protest faded behind her. She left the butler's pantry, climbed the rear stairs back to the first floor and from there took the immense, curving marble staircase to her own room. Without summoning the maid who had been assigned to her—an English girl of all things!—she removed the fragile summer dress and rummaged in the closet for something sturdier.

Archer's insistence of decking her out in a wardrobe he called merely appropriate was embarrassing, but it also had its uses. She donned a dark blue skirt, white starched blouse, and walking shoes. With a final glance at herself in the mirror, she hurried back down the stairs.

The stables were off to the side of the house in an enclosed courtyard. They were meticulously clean and well cared for as were the half dozen horses Archer kept. A groom was already at work harnessing the trap. Megan smiled when she saw him. She was beginning to understand the irascible Bertrand. Disapprove of her though he did, he would not allow the proper order of things to be disrupted. Guests of the master, whoever they might be, did not harness their own carriages. Not while he still had anything to say about it.

"There you are, ma'am," the groom said as he finished. He gave her a quick, respectful smile that was not entirely without a note of frank curiosity. All the servants were like that, cautious around her, but also clearly puzzled by what she was doing there. Archer seemed not to be in the habit of bringing women to his "cottage" retreat, or if he was, they were of a very different stamp from Megan.

She thanked the groom and stepped gracefully into the seat. The slightest touch of the reins was enough to move the horse. With a shake of its glossy mane, it moved off across the cobblestone yard and out the high wooden gates to the drive.

Beyond lay the main road, newly paved to the consternation of the locals who felt it would bring too much congestion. So far it had not. Megan had it entirely to herself almost all the way into the village.

She left the trap at one end of the small main street and proceeded to walk. The shops fascinated her, not the least because they reminded her of those in her village in Ireland—or how they would have been if the people had been more prosperous. New York was a huge, intimidating presence she had to grapple with, but this far smaller, contained place—this reminded her of home.

She walked slowly, peering in each of the windows. The people who passed her were friendly, the men tipping their hats and the women smiling. She saw no one she had met at any of the parties she and Archer had attended, and was glad of that. These were ordinary people, far less inclined to judge her.

In the back of her mind, she knew that she was not there simply to window shop. She wanted to find Chester Daniels's house and try to figure out some way into it.

But before she could begin to do so, Daniels himself appeared. He dismounted in front of the inn across from where Megan was standing, hitched his horse to the post and went inside.

She took a quick breath and followed.

9

Archer threw down the papers he had been trying to read and stared out the window of the train. They would be entering the city soon. His private carriage would meet him at the station. Traffic would be heavy, but he should be at his Wall Street office in little more than an hour.

The opportunity that had suddenly presented itself was one he had long sought. Ordinarily, he would be pleased to take full advantage of it. Instead, all he could think of was Megan.

He had not wanted to leave her. Although she would

be only a few hours away, the separation irked him. He resented anything that took him from her.

The week they had spent together was the happiest of his life despite the immense strain of not touching her. But that strain was now beginning to tell. He slept poorly, if at all, and the physical demands of his body were rapidly taking control.

Something had to give.

He stood up and walked the length of the private railroad car. A steward had set up a silver coffee pot and a selection of breakfast rolls, but Archer let them all be. He didn't want food or drink. He didn't even want the pleasure of concluding a successful business deal and adding to his already immense fortune.

He wanted Megan.

Sweet Lord, how he wanted her. She was a fire in his blood, a yearning in his soul, and an absolutely unparalleled distraction. His fists clenched at his sides. Dark eyes narrowed to slits. Against the fine wool of his trousers, his manhood strained.

A sardonic smile curved his mouth. He simply could not go on like this. Something had to give.

There was a station up ahead where travelers to the city waited to board. Before the train had come to a full stop, Archer stepped off. He strode purposefully toward the public stable.

"Oh, absolutely," Chester Daniels said. "I couldn't agree with you more. Nothing surpasses a fine library. In fact, if I do say so myself, my own collection is not without merit."

Megan was not at all surprised that he thought so. In the short time she had been talking with Chester Daniels, she had revised her opinion of him. He wasn't merely snakelike. Somewhere along the line a peacock had been involved.

It had been the simplest matter to pretend to accidentally encounter him at the inn and engage him in conversation. He remembered her, of course, and made a sarcastic reference to how refreshing it was to see her out of Archer's shadow.

Megan declined to comment on that, instead turning the conversation to Daniels's favorite topic: himself. Whatever his background—and she suspected it was not what he wished everyone to presume—he went to great effort to present himself as a cultured gentleman of independent means, attentive but unthreatening, gracious and soft-spoken. The kind of man a young woman could trust.

Undoubtedly, that had helped him to lure Elizabeth Davalos. Megan wasn't fooled for a moment. She had the advantage of knowing the kind of man he really was, but she would have been wary of him under any circumstances.

"I've just had a thought," he said. "As you are so interested in books, would you care to see mine?"

Megan smiled. It was a ploy the most naive girl from County Cork wouldn't fall for—and she was very far from being that. Upper-class young ladies must be a good deal more gullible.

Smiling with what she hoped would be taken for guileless innocence, she said, "What a marvelous thought, I'd love to."

"I'm sorry, sir," Bertrand said, a shade nervously. It did not do to anger the master, but in this case it was unavoidable. "Miss Daugherty is not here. She took the trap and went into the village."

"When?" The pang of disappointment he felt was bad enough, but beneath it apprehension stirred. He didn't like the idea of her being on her own while Chester Daniels was in the vicinity.

"About an hour ago, sir."

Archer nodded curtly. "Have a groom return the horse," he said and went to get one of his own from the stable. They were faster than the hack he'd hired.

He reached the village a short time later but could see no sign of Megan or the trap. Could she have decided to go on by herself, perhaps taking the scenic shore road? It was a pleasant drive, one she would enjoy, but he could not quite bring himself to believe that was where she had gone.

A small boy was coming out of the back of the inn. Archer tossed him a coin. "Have you seen a young woman with red hair hereabouts?"

The boy caught the silver dollar on the fly, looked at it with gleeful disbelief and nodded. "Yes, sir. She was here a short while ago. Left with Mr. Daniels, she did."

The curse that broke from Archer had such bite as to impress the boy who was something of a connoisseur of such things. But his admiration did not prevent him from jumping back out of the way of flashing hooves. He stood a moment, watching the big horse vanish down the road, before going off whistling with the silver dollar snug in his pocket.

"Marvelous," Megan said, fingering a volume of Byron's poems. It seemed to be Chester Daniels's favorite word, so she thought she should use it liberally.

"What a superb collection," she cooed and even managed to bat her eyes admiringly. "Truly, you are a man of intellect."

Had she been loading it on with a shovel, the praise could not have been more overdone. But Daniels was loving it. He preened, puffing out his chest and nodded in full agreement.

Slyly, he asked, "Does Davalos have anything similar?"

Archer's library was to this as the glory that had been the great library of Alexandria was to a fragment of stone tablet, but Megan suppressed the urge to say so. Instead, she murmured, "Let's not talk about him, all right? You're so much more interesting."

She was going to have to wash her mouth out when she was done here, not to mention say a penance. But it was all in a good cause, she assured herself. Somewhere in this house were the letters Elizabeth Davalos had written. Megan was determined to secure them. But how?

"You must be a terribly clever man to read all these books," she said.

Chester did not deny it. "Clever enough," he said, moving closer to her, "to sense that something troubles you."

What troubled her at the moment was his proximity. It made her skin crawl. As subtly as she could, she moved a few inches away. "It is a matter of some delicacy," she said.

"I am the soul of discretion."

Deliberately widening her eyes, she gazed up at him. "Is it truly possible that I can trust you?"

"Dear lady, I would go to the ends of the earth to deserve your confidence."

Good Lord, this was starting to sound like a bad play she'd once seen performed by a group of traveling actors. Drawing room farce, they called it, and it was dreadful.

Anxious to limit her role, she took a breath and stepped right off the edge. "I am in possession of some rather sensitive information which I admit I don't fully understand myself. It has to do with business. Mr. Davalos is most insistent about seeing it."

Daniels's eyes lit. Understanding dawned. "Is that why he has been keeping you so close?"

Megan lowered her gaze modestly. "I'm afraid so. Since my dear father's death"—please let her real Da' forgive her—"I have been at quite loose ends. It is all so complicated. But Mr. Davalos says . . ."

"Never mind what he says," Daniels interjected quickly. "It is preposterous that he should be allowed anywhere near you. The man is a scalawag of the worst sort. Why I could tell you stories—"

"Oh, dear," Megan interrupted before he could get started, "I just knew that you would understand. When I saw you at the ball, I thought you looked such a fine gentleman, so much more the sort of person I was accustomed to dealing with when dear Da—that is, Father—was alive."

"Which is exactly what I am, dear lady. Be assured, I will not rest until you are out of that villain's hands. But in the meantime—"

"I am dreadfully afraid he will get the documents from me," Megan interrupted. "If only there was somewhere safe I could leave them, someone who could be trusted to look after them."

"Seek no further," Daniels declared. "You may rely on me utterly. I will be only too happy to keep them out of Davalos's reach."

"But can you really?" Megan entreated. Perhaps she should consider a career on the stage. She was far better at this than she had ever imagined she could be. Her mouth trembled softly. "He is such a domineering man."

"Not to me," Daniels said stoutly. "Besides, I have

some experience keeping things from Davalos. You could not have come to a better person."

"If you're sure," Megan said, hinting at surrender but still holding on to a thread of doubt, all the while watching Daniels intently.

His eyes flicked to the wall at the far end of the library. "Have no doubt, I can easily thwart him."

Her hand fluttered at her breast. "I am so relieved. This has all been such a terrible burden. Oh, dear—"

"What's wrong?" Daniels demanded.

"I fear I'm a bit lightheaded. The sudden release of strain and all that. If I might have a cup of tea . . ."

"Of course," he assured her. Quickly, he helped her over to a chair. "My servants are shockingly lazily. I'll have to rouse them myself, but it won't be a minute."

Please God let it be at least a little longer, Megan thought. The instant the library door closed behind him, she jumped to her feet and ran to the wall. Daniels had definitely looked at it when he mentioned keeping things from Davalos. But why?

Her first thought was that there was a hidden safe. In books she had read as a child, sneaking them at night when she was supposed to be asleep, there was always a safe concealed behind an ancestral portrait.

But the wall held no paintings of any kind, nothing behind which anything could be hidden. There was only wood paneling except around the fireplace which was framed by old bricks, probably part of the original residence.

Swiftly, she felt along the panels, trying to find one that might be loose. When that failed, she turned to the bricks. Seconds were speeding by. At any moment, Daniels would return. But she couldn't give up now, not when she was convinced that she was so close.

She had almost reached the end when her hand suddenly touched a brick that wobbled slightly. She pulled on it more firmly. It came away, revealing a small, dark space built into the mantel of the fireplace.

Footsteps sounded in the hall. In the space of a heartbeat, Megan acted. She had just replaced the brick and was straightening up when Daniels entered.

"The tea will only be a—" He broke off, staring at her where she stood beside the mantel. "What are you doing there?"

"I was feeling chilled," she said, and in truth she was. The sudden suspicion stamped on his features sent a ripple of fear through her. Shivering delicately, she made an effort to brazen it out.

But Daniels was not so easily lulled. Stepping farther into the room, he said, "There is no fire."

True enough and rather a crimp in her story. She looked down at the dead ashes as if surprised. "Oh my, how silly of me. I must be even more out of sorts than I thought."

Swiftly, she walked away from the fireplace, anxious to put as much distance between it and herself as she could. Daniels stood between her and the door. He did not appear inclined to move.

"I am feeling much better now, however," she said. "Your kindness has greatly reassured me. I think it would be best for me to secure the documents and bring them immediately, before Mr. Davalos returns."

"Sit down," Daniels ordered.

"Thank you but I really think I should—"

"Damn you, I said to sit."

The sudden shift in his behavior took Megan just enough by surprise to stop her where she was. That hesitation proved her undoing. Daniels reached her in an instant. His hand seized her wrist. "I should have known you weren't what you seemed," he snarled.

"Whatever are you talking about?" Megan protested, trying valiantly to keep calm. The gracious gentleman was gone without a trace. Stripped of his false self, Daniels was an out-and-out bully, vicious in his anger and, she suspected, capable of anything.

"You set me up for this, didn't you?" he demanded. "You and Davalos. I should have known he'd try something clever, but it won't work. By God, I'll make you both rue the day you crossed swords with Chester Daniels."

"If that is your real name," Megan said haughtily. Inside, she quaked but she was damned if she'd let this vicious braggart see it. "I perceive you are not at all what you pretend, sir. Indeed, I wouldn't be at all surprised to learn you are some sort of criminal."

Daniels laughed, a harsh, grating sound. "The outraged miss routine won't work with me, now that I've seen through you." His hand tightened cruelly on her wrist. "I give Davalos credit though: he picked a beauty. He's been having you, I presume. Maybe I should sample what he's enjoyed."

"No," Megan said and lashed out, trying to kick her way free. But Daniels was strong and fueled by a mixture of rage and lust. It was a terrifying combination.

Already, he was pushing her back toward the couch. The door was closed. The servants, even if they did remember to bring the tea, were unlikely to be much help. She was completely alone with no one to help her but herself.

Tears stung her eyes. She blinked them back furiously and renewed her struggles. This was not going to happen to her. She absolutely would not allow it.

But there was only so much that she could do. Daniels had hold of her around the waist. He shoved her onto the couch and came down on top of her.

Megan screamed. She struck out, trying to get to his eyes, but he put a hand around her throat and squeezed hard. Colored lights danced in front of her eyes.

From a great distance, she heard his voice, "Lie still and let me do what I want. If you try to stop me, I'll kill you." As though to emphasize the threat, his hand tightened even further.

She could not breathe. Blood pounded in her ears. A terrible well of despair seemed to open up within her.

She could feel herself falling and tried desperately to stop but there was nothing to grab hold of—no help, no safety, no hope. The well deepened, pulling her down.

10

"Megan, for the love of God, answer me."

The voice low and urgent, filled with pleading, reached Megan as though through a dark, cloying fog. It drew her irresistibly. Slowly, straining against the blackness that tried to hold her, she moved upward toward the light.

Toward Archer. He was bending over her, his eyes dark with what looked astonishingly like fear and his big, hard body sheltering hers. She was lying on the couch, safe within his arms. Beyond, in the library itself, people were moving around.

"Who's here?" she whispered, her voice rasping.

"The police. They're taking Daniels away."

She had a sudden, horrifying thought. In the time she had been unconscious, could he have—

"He didn't?"

Archer's face, already grim, went grimmer still. "Didn't what? Rape and kill you? No, he'd only managed to all but strangle you when I finally got here. Damn it, how could I have let this happen? If he had . . ."

She stared up at him, incredulous. That was not only fear in his dark eyes. Tears, too, glittered there. For her? ·

Slowly, her hand reached up to touch him gently. "Hush," she whispered, "I'm fine. You stopped him."

She had no doubt that was exactly what he had done but she didn't want to know the details of how. In the corner of her vision, she could see that Daniels was being carried out. He lay still and silent on a stretcher. She suspected it would be some time before he could stand again.

"You could have died," Archer said, "and for what? Because I involved you in a situation you should never have had anything to do with. I should have stopped Daniels once and for all when this whole business started."

"You didn't because you care for your sister," Megan said gently. "There's nothing wrong with that."

"I care for you, too, in a very different way." His arms tightened around her. She was drawn hard against his chest. "Damn it, woman, you scared the daylights out of me."

Her breath filled with the scent of him—leather and wool, sunlight, wind, and pure man. His arms held her with fierce tenderness. His body was steel against her own. She was filled with a dizzying sense of utter contentment and fierce, almost unbearable excitement somehow mixed up together.

He cared for her, this indomitably strong, proud man, this man of books and music, quiet walks, and heated lovemaking. This man so many others feared but she herself loved.

Heaven help her.

"Where are we going?" she asked as Archer strode from the room with her in his arms. No one made any attempt to stop them, undoubtedly sensing that it would have been futile.

"Home," he said and swiftly made good the promise.

Bertrand was waiting for them, a sternly disapproving Bertrand as usual but with an unexpected note of genuine concern in his voice when he saw them. "Is there anything I can do, sir?" he asked, trailing them up the stairs to the second floor.

"Hot water for a bath," Archer ordered, "and the medical kit. When that's done, tell the staff we aren't to be disturbed."

His orders were followed with alacrity. Before she was hardly aware of what was happening, a steaming tub was filled in the alcove of her bedroom. The servants vanished as quickly as they had appeared.

"Hold still," Archer ordered. She was seated on the edge of the bed where he had placed her. His hands were gentle but insistent as they undid the top buttons of her blouse, then the middle buttons, then the bottom ones.

"I can do that," she tried to say but it came out as a croak and he ignored it anyway. Without giving her any chance to protest, he stripped the blouse away and began gently to apply a soothing ointment to her throat.

Nude from the waist up except for a lacy camisole that concealed little, Megan thought she might well die from embarrassment. Or something else. Certainly, her senses were whirling and she was having a great deal of difficulty remembering all the rules that had been drummed into her as a child. Surely, she shouldn't be allowing this to happen and yet she could not seem to lift a hand to stop it.

When her throat had been seen to, Archer lifted her

again and stood her on her feet near the tub. She fully expected him to leave then, allowing her to bathe alone, but he had other thoughts.

"Don't say it," he ordered when she tried to speak again. "I'm not letting you out of my sight. You were almost killed because of me. The least I can do is take proper care of you from now on."

"Is that what you're doing?" she asked very faintly. Never mind the injury to her throat, she couldn't have spoken clearly anyway. Not when he was undoing the wide belt around her waist and sliding her skirt down her long legs.

A sound like paper crinkling punctured the heated silence. Archer's eyebrows rose. A small smile danced across Megan's face. She had forgotten.

"The letters," she murmured. "I found them in a hidey-hole beside the fireplace."

He shook his head in amazement but let the skirt drop, the letters untouched. They no longer concerned him.

Kneeling, he removed her walking shoes. When he stood again, his face was flushed and his breathing appeared faster than usual. "You deserve to be cared for, don't you think?"

"Hmmm, I suppose . . ." Whatever this could be called, it felt marvelous. She was even forgetting to be embarrassed standing before him now in only the camisole and matching pantaloons. She could bathe in those. At the convent school she'd briefly attended they had done so. Surely, he didn't intend . . .

He did. Big hands brushed the straps of the camisole down her bare shoulders, lifted it over her breasts, stripped the pantaloons from her, touching her lightly, completely, in ways no one had ever touched her before until her knees buckled and she had to cling to his broad shoulders to keep from falling.

"Into the tub with you," Archer muttered huskily. He placed her gently in the heated water, but his hands still did not leave her. It was as though he could not bring himself to allow her beyond his touch even for an instant.

Slowly, with maddening thoroughness, he laved the scented cloth over her. Megan tried to protest, but whatever objections she had were poor, weak things that couldn't stand up before the onslaught of desire he had unleashed.

By the time he had finished, she was quivering with need, clinging to him, her nipples hard and the secret place of her womanhood hotly moist.

With a groan, he lifted her again and carried her to the bed. There he lay her, still damp from the bath, her hair spread out around her, her skin pale as alabaster against the dark counterpane. Standing before her, he stripped off his clothes hastily.

She could not take her eyes from him, drawn by fascination and unabashed curiosity. What she saw made her gasp. He was magnificently made in all ways.

Swiftly, he came down beside her, soothing her with a gentle caress. "Forgive me," he whispered close against her ear, "we will make this right later but I simply cannot wait. Not after having come so close to losing you."

She made a small sound of agreement and welcome mingled in one. He groaned and kissed her deeply, savoring the taste and feel of her. Big hands cupped her breasts, the thumbs rubbing over her nipples.

She twisted on the bed, trying to get closer to him, trying—

Archer thrust a muscled leg between her thighs and

held her still for him. Slowly, drawing out each exquisite moment, his mouth trailed down her body, across
her flat abdomen to the silken skin of her thighs. He
caressed her with a boldness that robbed her of breath
and turned her blood molten. When she would have
stopped him, he grasped both her hands in his and held
her prisoner to his loving passion until at last she could
bear nothing more.

Only then did he move to part her legs further, his
hand cupping her moist womanhood, assuring himself
that she was truly ready for him. When he entered her,
the small hurt briefly pierced her consciousness but it
was gone in an instant, drowned out by a floodtide of
pleasure.

Never had she felt so complete, so real, so loved.
They moved together as one, her hips rising to meet
him as he thrust deeper and deeper until at last fulfill-
ment seized them both.

EPILOGUE

Megan turned over lazily in Archer's arms. They had
returned to the house a few hours before after a brief
outing and adjourned by mutual accord to the bedroom.
The interlude that followed had been infinitely satisfying to them both.

But now something had intruded into the haze of
contentment that surrounded her. Something . . .

Footsteps downstairs and raised voices.

She sat up and reached for the robe she had left at
the bottom of the bed. "Archer, wake up," she said.

He did so but reluctantly. However, the instant his
eyes opened, the familiar fire leaped in them. He
reached out a hand to her.

Reluctantly, she slipped away and stood, tying the

robe around her waist. "Something's going on downstairs. It sounds as though . . ."

"Sir," Bertrand called through the closed door of the master suite. He sounded genuinely alarmed. "I am most dreadfully sorry but . . ."

"I'm coming," Archer said, standing swiftly. He strode toward the door. Megan ran after him and thrust his own robe into his hands. He shrugged into it and opened the door. "What is it?"

Bertrand looked pale and, incredibly for him, disheveled. "Ruffians, sir," he said, "here in the house. I tried to tell them but . . ."

Archer didn't wait to hear more. He walked quickly down the corridor, his long legs eating up the distance. Megan had to run to keep up with him. They reached the top of the curving stairs.

From below, a voice shouted, "There he is, by God, the filthy blackguard. Let's get him."

Her heart sank even as her stomach did a quick flip. Merciful heaven, it was—

"Seamus," she cried just as her eldest brother launched himself at Archer. Ned followed right behind, as did Padraic, Desmond, and even little Sean. All of them bent on mayhem. Maeve hovered in the distance, wringing her hands and looking from Megan to Archer with blank amazement.

"No," Megan shouted. She jumped between her brothers and the tall, powerful man who regarded them bemusedly. Holding up her hands, she ordered, "Stop this at once, the lot of you. What in heaven's name do you think you're doing?"

"Saving you from your debaucher, girl," Seamus shot back. "Although by the looks of it, we're a bit late." He doubled up his fists and made at Archer again.

"Stop," Megan ordered, but that had no effect. The

Daugherty men were bent on revenge. Desperately, she said, "For the love of God, we're married."

That stopped them right in their tracks. Seamus was the first to speak. "What's that?" he demanded.

Quickly, Megan went to stand beside Archer. He cast her a fond look. By all evidence, the imminent danger of attack from five outraged Irish males had not concerned him. She would have to try to talk a little more sense into her loving husband, but that could wait for later.

"Married," she repeated.

"This morning," Archer added helpfully.

Seamus scowled. He stared at them both. "Who by? Some bloody justice of the peace?"

"By a priest," Archer said. "A very understanding one."

Silence reigned. Megan could hear the ticking of the clock on the stair landing.

Abruptly, Seamus grinned. "Ah, well," he said softly, "that changes things, doesn't it?" Laughing, he gave Archer a swift blow to the back that was undoubtedly meant to be congratulatory. "Welcome to the family, brother."

Megan sagged with relief. They were surrounded in an instant by the bunch of them, all saying as how they'd never believed she'd really do anything so foolish, but when they'd tracked her to Davalos's New York house and finally, wrangled the truth from Maeve, well they could be pardoned, couldn't they, for fearing the worst.

Not now though. Now everything was grand. Megan married, imagine that. And Archer a fine man, obviously, with a great deal of backbone to be sure which truth be told, he'd be needing.

Not that she wasn't a splendid lass, absolutely splendid. He was lucky to have her.

"A toast to it," Seamus said when they had all assembled in the drawing room. Bertrand scurried about, handing out glasses and trying hard not to look appalled.

"To the newest member of the Daugherty clan. As we say in the old country, may your days be sweet and your nights sweeter still, may love fill the hollow places in your heart, and in the fullness of years may you come together to everlasting peace."

"I thank you," Archer said quietly. His arm around Megan, he looked at her boisterous family, filling up his drawing room and he suspected his life as well. A sardonic smile lit his eyes. His days of solitude were apparently at an end. He bid them farewell without regret.

"It's a pleasure to meet all of you," he said and meant it.

"All?" Megan repeated innocently. She met Maeve's laughing eyes. "Heavens, this isn't all. There's a good hundred or more of us still in County Cork."

"A hundred?" Archer repeated.

"At least," Seamus assured him.

Bertrand gasped and seized a champagne flute. He downed its contents in a single swallow.

Archer threw back his head and laughed. The others joined in. The sound of their happiness filled the great house by the sea.

Highway Robbery

by

Anita Mills

Oxfordshire, England: April, 1742

The line was long until the rain began to pour, and then most who were there dispersed, grumbling that they'd be back when there was less danger of a soaking. But Anne Hardinge waited, her knitted reticule held close to keep the few banknotes within reasonably dry. She had ridden nearly fifteen miles over miserable roads to bail out her brother from the small, makeshift jail, and she had no wish to come again later. Indeed, she was mortified to be there at all. Never before in memory or history had any of her known relations been arrested for anything.

Finally, she was allowed into the building and told to wait. Water dripped from her wide black silk skirt, spotting the dirty floor. Behind the counter, a man in a cheap bagwig looked up from a sheaf of papers.

"Tuppence," he said abruptly, nodding to a fellow she took to be a jailer. "One fer 'im, one fer me."

"Two pence? To visit my brother?" she asked incredulously.

She dug into her damp reticule and drew out the money, muttering, " 'Tis robbery," under her breath.

The man in the bagwig looked her up and down, taking in her face and figure so slowly that she wanted to give him a sharp set-down. His closed-mouth smile was somewhere between a grin and a leer.

"His sister, eh?" He turned to the apparent jailer and winked. "We got another 'un, Jem."

"I beg your pardon?" she responded stiffly. "Sir, I assure you—"

"Oh, they all been assurin', mistress." He shrugged, then nodded. "Don't guess hit'll make any difference, eh?"

"Not where he's going."

She felt a knot tighten in her stomach, and she wanted to tell them that it had been but a boy's prank. But her words died before they were spoken. The report of a gun startled her.

"What in the world is that?" she demanded. "It sounded much like a shot."

"The prisoner," the fellow called Jem answered.

"Surely not! He is still armed?" she asked incredulously.

" 'Tis what they pays ter see. He drinks 'em, and he shoots 'em." The man in the shoddy bagwig waved her aside with the back of his hand. "Take 'er down, Jem. She can have"— He turned a small glass over, and the sand began to pour through the narrow hole—" 'Bout five minutes, I'd say. Fer more, it'll cost ye a guinea."

"Five minutes?" she echoed. " 'Tis not nearly enough! And . . . I had hope he could be released!"

He laughed outright at that. "Ain't no bond fer 'im, mistress. Be the devil's own luck if he don't swing on the Nubbin' Cheat."

Her heart sank like a rock in her breast. "Oh no," she managed feebly. "We'll get a solicitor, and—oh, but five minutes is not enough!" she repeated. "I shall need much more time!"

"A guinea then."

"I ought to complain to the magistrate," she told him with feeling. " 'Tis a disgrace, an utter disgrace!" Nonetheless, she handed him the coin. "Now how much time do I get?"

"How long does it take ye?" he countered suggestively.

Another shot was fired, seemingly directly beneath her, unsettling her. "This entire jail is a disgrace," she declared angrily. "I cannot think the Home Secretary is aware of the ramshackle manner of business here."

"He ain't been here in a while." The man grinned broadly, finally revealing cracked, blackened teeth. "Jem, you remember when last we was ter see 'im?"

"Ain't never."

"I should like to see my brother now," she said stiffly.

As Jem led the way down the back stairs into the cellar, either a rat or a very large mouse ran across her foot, disgusting her further.

"You ought to have cats, you know."

"Uh," he grunted noncommittally. He stopped at the bottom and pointed toward an open door. "In there."

Relief washed over her. Surely she'd been hoaxed of her money. Surely Robin could not be in such terrible difficulty if they did not bother to even lock his door. But as she crossed the small hall, she could still smell the acrid odor of gunpowder in the air.

"Robin, whatever do you think you are—?" She stopped to stare. "You are not Robin!"

The black-haired man lounging on the bed cocked his pistol, then fired at empty bottles sitting on a long, narrow trestle table. The report was deafening, and the subsequent billow of smoke nearly choked her. As the echo reverberated off the wall, he twisted his head to look at her, and a decidedly sardonic smile lifted the corners of an utterly sensuous mouth.

"Unfortunately, I am not," he murmured. Laying his pistol aside, he swung long legs over the side of the bed to sit up. "Got three to go," he muttered.

"Three what?"

"Bottles." His brown eyes regarded her lazily for a moment, then his smile deepened. "My gain is decidedly Robin's loss." His tall frame unwound fluidly as he rose, and he walked with the grace of a cat as he crossed the room to her. "Most decidedly," he murmured. "Poor Robin."

"I—uh—have the wrong door," she said lamely, backing away from him. "You are not my brother."

"I'm not repining," he assured her, moving closer.

"There has been a mistake," she protested. "I came to see Robin Hardinge." She took another step backward and found herself pressed against the wall. "It is his first scrape, and—"

"Like all females, you talk far too much."

To her horror, his hands had caught her waist, and before she could protest the familiarity, his face was so close it blurred. She closed her eyes just before he kissed her. Her own hands came up between him and her stomacher, pushing at his very solid chest, but his lips were on hers, first teasing, then demanding, frightening her. She struggled briefly, but he was far too strong. It was not until she ceased fighting him that he released her.

"Obviously, you do not have much experience," he observed. "A Puritan. I must suppose."

Two red spots burned her cheeks as she sputtered, "You, sir, are a disgrace to humanity! You are no gentleman!"

He inclined his head slightly, but the amusement never left his eyes. "Devilish clever of you to note it— particularly given the circumstances of my incarceration."

"Yes, well—" Again, she backed to the door, her hands clasping her reticule as though it were a shield against the fiend. She kept her eyes on him even as she shouted, "Guard! Guard! 'Tis a mistake!"

He moved suddenly then, reaching the door before her, and as the guard's steps could be heard on the stairs, he caught her, this time sliding his arm beneath her chin. She felt the cold steel against her neck, and she stood very still.

"You, my dear, are getting me out of here," he murmured softly behind her ear. "Walk very slowly, and do not say anything. I should very much regret cutting your lovely throat."

Jem rounded the corner, then stopped when he saw the knife. "But Gov'nor, ye promised ye wouldn't!" he protested. "Ye said if we was ter let ye keep yer pistol, ye wouldn't try nothin'," he added plaintively. "Ye said we could charge 'em ter see ye hit the bottles."

"I said I would not use it to escape," Anne's captor reminded him. "Your mistake was allowing me a blade for the joint."

"Ye said the meat was tough!" the fellow fairly howled. "And I trusted ye!"

"Alas, but I was unworthy, wasn't I?" the man who held her acknowledged softly. He nudged her forward with his body. "How much money did I earn you, Jem?"

"I dunno. Gov'nor, they ain't going ter fergive me," he whined desperately. "They was sendin' soldiers ter take ye ter Lunnon fer trial. How'm I ter tell 'em the Black Swann's bolted?"

"You may state I have declined the honor."

"The Black Swann," Anne repeated foolishly. "The highwayman?"

"My wicked, wicked rep," he murmured. "Lead the way, Jem."

Indecision mingled with fear in the jailer's face. "They'll hang me fer letting ye go." For a long moment, he eyed the knife as though he calculated his chances.

"If you think you can take me, you'd best consider that you will have Miss—er—Hardinge, is it? Yes, Miss Hardinge's blood on your hands." For emphasis, he laid the cold blade against Anne's jugular. "A waste of beauty, don't you think?"

"But what's ter tell the magistrate?" Jem wailed.

"I have unfortunately discovered another, more appealing engagement," Swann decided. "Yes, you might say that. Now—you will go up the stairs before us as though naught is amiss, if you please."

"But—"

"Have you ever seen a hog butchered, Jem?" He asked silkily.

"N-no."

"They cut its throat from here to here," he answered himself, moving the knife across Anne's neck. "And then the creature bleeds to death. Not a very pretty sight, I am afraid."

As he spoke, Anne considered her chances of breaking away, of falling to the floor, but then she could see that poor Jem was unarmed. It was as though Swann knew her thoughts. He leaned closer, speaking into her ear.

"I wouldn't," he said so softly she had to wonder if she'd even heard him. "Play the game, and I'll take your Robin with us."

She found her voice then, shrieking, "Please don't kill me—please don't! For love of the Almighty, I beg of you!" She felt the knife prick her neck, and she closed her eyes, swallowing to hide her fear. "Please," she whispered.

"The choice is yours, Jem. Miss Hardinge, tell him who you are," he urged her.

"Who I am?" she echoed feebly. "But what—?" The blade moved slightly in warning, prompting her to try. "Well, my uncle is Baron Hardinge of Crow's Cross, and my great-grandfather was William Hardinge who served as Queen Anne's Master of Horses." She swallowed again, then went on, groping for an illustrious ancestor. "There have been Hardinges at Crow's Cross since Good Queen Bess gave it to them, sir," she declared defiantly.

"Do you want to join me on the Nubbin' Cheat, Jem? I doubt Baron Hardinge will wish to ignore the demise of a favored niece, you know."

The jailer took in her best silk dress and the neatly starched stomacher, then capitulated. "Ye ain't gettin' far, Swann," he predicted sourly. "They took yer devil horse to th' stables, and there ain't nothin' but slugs here."

"Up the stairs."

As the fellow started across the small hall to the stairwell, Anne's captor eased his grip on her slightly while he retrieved his pistol.

"Where's your brother?" he hissed at her.

"I wouldn't make him a fugitive if I could," she retorted. "And I think you have cut me, you miserable miscreant."

"Alas, but I have been called worse," he countered cheerfully. "Much worse." Nonetheless, he turned her head and pushed her hair away with his hand. "A scratch merely," he assured her.

"Once you are outside, you will not need me," she reminded him hopefully.

Without answering, he caught her shoulder again and pushed her up the stairs after the jailer.

"He's escapin', Sims," Jem told the man at the desk. "Took the female fer hostage."

"The devil's arse, Jem!" Sims rose so quickly that his

wig slid over one ear. "Here now, sirrah! No, I say—no!"

For answer, Swann leveled his pistol, and the fellow's face went white. "Just so," Swann murmured, dragging Anne to the desk. "How much did I earn you, by the by?"

"Not nearly enough," Sims muttered. "The earl'll have me head fer this."

"Warrington?" One black eyebrow rose, then the sensuous mouth smiled. "Give him a kiss for me, will you? With my compliments, of course. You must remember to tell him that." To Anne, he said, "Reach over the desk and retrieve the money, my dear. As the freak he exhibited, I think it must surely belong to me."

Afraid she would be accused as his accomplice, she hesitated. "Uh—"

"The money, if you please," he insisted curtly.

She picked up a large box off cash. "Surely not all of this. I mean, well, there must be fifty pounds here."

Instead of being impressed, he turned his pistol on Sims. "Where is the rest of it?"

"Ow, Gov'nor, ye ain't going ter take hit all?" he complained.

"All, Sims." The voice dropped low, menacing the man. "All."

"Jem's got 'is 'alf," Sims said finally.

"Ye lyin' bugger!" the jailer exploded. "I ain't neither!"

This time, the pistol was aimed at Jem's middle. "Do you know what a ball does?" Swann asked softly.

"Ye said ye wouldn't use the pistol ter bolt!" the fellow shouted at him.

"Consider me bolted then." A faint smile played at the corners of Swann's mouth. "This is property retrieval."

Once again the jailer measured him, deciding that

Swann's hand was too steady, the pistol already primed, the distance too close. And again he capitulated, this time gracelessly. Reaching into his vest, he drew out wads of notes as Swann's smile faded and the dark eyes went cold. Regarding his erstwhile prisoner balefully, Jem dug deeper to draw out a fat purse, dropping it at Swann's feet.

It was Anne's chance. As the notorious highwayman bent to pick up the purse with his pistol hand, she half-turned and ducked beneath his other arm. The gun fired, filling the room with black smoke, and Swann cursed as his hand closed over her arm, wrenching it painfully.

"Damn you!" he shouted at her. "What the devil are you trying to do?"

"I don't want to go with you!"

Already Jem was down on his knees trying to recover his money. But when he found the purse, Swann's booted foot found his hand.

"I'll break every bone," he warned.

The fellow eased his hand away gingerly and stood, his face a mask of fury. "Ye can't take the both of us!" he spat out. "Sims! We got ter nab 'im!"

Swann backed toward the door, holding Anne before him. When he was nearly there, they charged him. In an instant, he pushed her into the wigged fellow, sending both of them sprawling; then he caught Jem with an uppercut that seemed to make the jailer's neck stretch before he fell. Sims' wig sailed across the floor to land incongruously atop the spittoon, and as he gingerly felt of his bald pate, Sims was torn between his dignity and a fight. Anne disentangled her wide skirt and panniers from his legs and began scrambling indecorously for the door on her hands and knees, while Sims chose to save his most prized possession.

The highwayman jumped over the counter and came up with a rapier, flexing the thin blade as Jem once again advanced. The faint smile on Swann's lips did not begin to warm his cold, dark eyes.

"Do you really wish to die?" he asked with deceptive softness. "For the likes of Warrington, do you really wish to die?"

"N-no."

"Then we are understood." Waving the rapier, he gestured toward the opposite wall. "Stand over there. And if you give the hue and cry before you have counted to five hundred, I shall come back and take your miserable lives. Are we agreed?"

"Y-yes."

"Five hundred."

"Dunno if I—"

"If you err, I suggest you err on my side." Swann spied a relatively new ramillie cock hat and set it on his head. "Good day, sirs." This time, he actually smiled. "Take heart, Sims—it never showed your wig to advantage."

As he left, the two men regarded each other with a sense of hopelessness. Finally, Jem spoke up. "Well," he said, sighing unhappily. "I expect it ought to look like we was overpowered, ye know. Ye can hit me with th' chair, and I'll crack yer head with the spittoon. Then if we was ter roll on th' floor—"

"You idiot! You silly fool!" Sims railed at him. "If any is ter be hit, 'tis ye—and I'll take the spittoon ter ye!"

Due to the pouring rain, there was no one in the street, but Anne gamely called for help, shouting, "He escapes! The highwayman escapes!" But the rain drowned every word. "Please! Will not someone help?" she cried out, running toward a row of narrow houses.

"Very dramatic, I am sure," Swann said behind her. "Come on." He caught her arm again.

"But you have no need of me!"

His eyes raked over her wet gown, pausing ever so briefly where her stomacher stretched over her breasts. "I might think of one," he decided roguishly. "And Hardinge's influence might keep my head on my shoulders, once 'tis known I have you."

"I assure you he would not care if I perished in this street," she declared bitterly.

"My, what an actress you are, my dear." He pulled her after him toward the stables, and as she stumbled over her wired oilcloth panniers, he muttered under his breath. Finally, he stopped. "Take it off—you cannot ride like that, anyway."

"What?" she fairly shrieked. "I will not!"

"If you don't, it will come up in your face, and the world will be favored with a most indelicate view," he countered.

"I cannot go with you!" she shouted at him. "Do you not understand? If 'tis thought I am your accomplice, I shall never get Robin out of jail! And he is but a foolish boy!"

He couldn't tell if she wept, or if it was the rain that wet her cheeks, but it didn't matter. Unmoved, he shifted the rapier to the crook of his elbow, then reached for her waist.

"I've a fair notion of how to get it off you."

"No!"

"No one is looking."

"Here? Oh, but—" His hands were fumbling at her stomacher, loosening the corded velvet ties at her waist, slipping inside to find the tapes that held the undergarment. Her fingers found his, stalling him. "All right, I will do it."

"I thought you would."

Her face flaming, she looked both ways to determine they were alone, then she reached beneath the wilting stomacher to untie the tapes. Averting her head, she pushed the hooped petticoat down and stepped from it.

"Much better," he decided. "You would have frightened Diablo."

"Is everything about you associated with the devil?" she asked icily.

"The appellation seems to fit me." With rapier in one hand, he grasped her elbow with the other. "Try not to fall, will you? You are getting me muddy enough as it is."

"I cannot help it," she muttered, trying to match the length of his stride and falling short. "Nor can I keep up. You are better advised to leave me."

"In a pig's eye, I will."

"But I am of no value to you, I tell you!"

He halted outside the stable and whistled loudly. The sound of banging, followed by the crack of wood splintering, hung in the rain-soaked air. One of the ostlers opened the door, then ran for cover, shouting, " 'E's gone mad, 'e has! Tried ter put out me lights!" Behind him, a huge black gelding charged, then reared, sending the ostler rolling out of the way in the mud. Tossing his mane, the horse then trotted to Swann.

The highwayman ran his hand over the glossy neck, speaking softly to the animal. "Easy, boy, easy. As lowering as you may find it, we are abducting a female." The horse stood perfectly still.

Swann lifted Anne easily, and the gelding's size frightened her too much to struggle. She knotted her hands in its mane as her captor swung up behind her.

"I-I cannot hold on," she said desperately. "There is no saddle nor bridle."

For answer, he pulled her back against him, encircling her waist with his arm. "He won't throw you," he reassured her curtly.

"My dress is ruined," she muttered, "and I do not have another decent one."

"You can wear one of the countess's."

"Huh?"

"Lady Warrington," he answered succinctly.

"What?"

"My, how monosyllabic you have become," he noted sarcastically. "It is my intent to pay a call to Oakhill."

"*What?*" she gasped.

"Have you no conversation, Miss Hardinge?" he chided.

"But is it not Warrington who charges you?"

"Let us just say I have become a thorn in his miserable hide."

"You *are* determined to hang, aren't you?"

"Not until he and I are even."

"Mr. Swann, if you will have no regard for your own life, I pray you will think of mine. I have not the least wish to hang with you," she declared sourly. "I refuse to be an accomplice to anything."

"Nicholas."

"What?"

"There—you are doing it again. I much prefer Nicholas to Mr. Swann, you know." He pulled her closer. "In fact, my closest acquaintances call me Nicky."

"And they are many, no doubt," she observed acidly.

"More than you would expect."

She was cold and wet, but forebore complaining further, telling herself that Nicholas Swann was merely a madman bent on mayhem, and the first chance she got, she intended to escape. Nonetheless, she allowed herself a sidewise glimpse of the most arresting countenance she'd ever seen.

"Interested?" he inquired lazily.

"No, of course not," she retorted, sitting straighter.

"At Oakhill," he continued conversationally, "I mean merely to acquire dry clothes and a more suitable conveyance for a lady. Then I will take you to your uncle at Crow's End."

"Crow's Cross."

"Crow's Cross, then." Once again, he pulled her closer, this time encompassing her wet body with his shoulders, and she realized with a start that he was trying to keep her warm. "You may acquit me, Miss Hardinge. Never in my life have I molested an unwilling female."

"I don't precisely live in the house at Crow's Cross," she admitted painfully. "My brother and I live in relative penury in one of the crofter cottages. My uncle, you see, refuses to acknowledge us."

For a moment, it seemed as though his arms closed tighter about hers. "Then we are both blessed with miserable relations, aren't we?" was all he said.

Oakhill, seat to two hundred years of Earls of Warrington, rose ahead like the giant Elizabethan palace it was, with perhaps thirty chimneys reaching skyward. It was indeed an awesome sight, and as Anne stared at it, she was nearly speechless.

"Impressive, isn't it?" Nicholas Swann murmured behind her.

"Yes, but—"

"Oh, they are not at home," he assured her. "But it wouldn't matter if they were."

"They'll have you arrested again."

"I don't think so. I told you—he's not here, and the

others will not stop me." He nudged his horse with his knee, then took a back lane onto the estate. Her heart nearly stopped when a fellow stepped into the road before them, but Swann merely called out, "I told you I'd be back, didn't I?"

"Aye, ye did at that, me lad," the man answered, grinning. " 'Tis mad as fire ye'll be making him."

"I need a carriage ride and some dry clothes for the lady."

The grin faded to a frown. "Devil take ye, Nicky. Ye'll be having me hanged with ye."

"I'll send you back trussed like a bird, if you wish," Swann promised him. "It adds to my consequence, anyway. And," he added lightly, "in fact, I'll send everything back—except the dress for the lady."

Despite the rain, the fellow squinted up with her. "Eh, Nick, but she don't look like yer usual doxy."

"She's a hostage and there'll be the devil to pay if she takes her death, I expect." As he spoke, Nicholas Swann swung down, then reached up for Anne. Dragging her down, he set her away from him, then steadied her with his arm. "You are shaking," he observed. "You'll have to get warm."

"I am not going into the house. 'Tis bad enough to trespass," she muttered through teeth clenched against chattering. "Please—I cannot."

"Alas, but I have abducted a Puritan, as you can see, Billy."

"But a fine-lookin' one," the man countered. "Ye never seem ter find the ugly ones now, do ye?"

"No." Taking Anne's elbow, Swann propelled her, not toward the big house, but rather to a small, moss-covered cottage reminiscent of her own at Crow's Cross. "It isn't much," he admitted cheerfully, "but when I choose to make it so, I call it home."

"Here? Beneath Warrington's very nose?"

"Let us just say it amuses me to be here. 'Tis a convenient place for tweaking his nose, so to speak."

"And no one gives you away?"

"No. As far as most of them are concerned, I've as much a right to be here as he." He let her go and leaned past her to unlock the door.

It creaked inward on rusty hinges. The single room, made even more dreary by the weather, was perhaps the most spartan place she'd ever seen. Her own small place at Crow's Cross was much more a home.

"You live here?" she repeated foolishly.

"When I wish." He favored her with a faint smile. "The authorities have never thought to look beneath his very nose, as you so aptly put it. They are forever rousting inns on this rumor or that, you see."

"But you live elsewhere also."

"Miss Hardinge, I live everywhere it suits me." He walked in and sprawled in a rickety chair. "Sit down and rest yourself. While Billy gets the carriage, I shall go up to the house and discover something suitable for you to wear home." His eyes raked over her again, taking the measure of her, making her acutely embarrassed. "You blush well, my dear," he murmured, lifting his empty hand as though he toasted her. "Yes, I think her clothes will fit you, though she is perhaps a trifle heavier in the bosom."

"Have you no manners at all?" she demanded. "Are you so lost—"

He sat up at that, and his face hardened. "Being a highwayman, my dear, I don't have much need of them. It is ever so much more effective to call out, 'Your money or your miserable life,' rather than 'Your purse, please.' "

"If you are so very clever, how is it that you were taken?" she asked tartly.

"The usual reason, I expect. I was fool enough to trust a female more interested in Warrington's reward than my neck."

"Oh."

Smiling wryly, he heaved his tall body from the chair. "Anything more to satisfy your curiosity, Miss Hardinge? I have no illusions about myself, you know. Without doubt, I shall one day grace a hangman's noose. But not yet—not until I am done with Warrington."

She couldn't help asking, "But what did he do to you?"

" 'Tis more a matter of what he did not do," he responded levelly. "All I have ever wanted is justice of him." At that, he crossed the dusty floor and reached the door. "You are welcome to the blanket to warm yourself, but I wouldn't risk a fire." With that, he was gone.

She was so cold that her body shook, and once he left, she didn't care how she looked. Moving to the crude bed, she pulled off the covers and wrapped herself in them. Then she went back to sit in his chair before the empty fireplace. As the rain pelted the roof, she felt almost sorry for him.

Every tale she'd heard told of the Black Swann's exploits had made him seem larger than life, a figure of romance and mystery. Yet for all his words to her, she already knew him for a bitter man bent on some terrible vendetta against the Earl of Warrington. And from all she'd heard, he'd been successful at that. As powerful and rich as Warrington was, the Swann had proven a constant source of vexation to him. Scarce a guest or business acquaintance dared to go to Oakhill for fear of having his purse lifted. Once, the soldiers had escorted

the incredibly wealthy Duke of Sutherland here, only
to have him robbed in broad daylight as he left.

She looked around the tiny, cramped room, wondering what Nicholas Swann did with his wages of sin.
He surely was not Robin Hood, for she'd never heard
it whispered that he shared any of it. But he did not
always live there, she reminded herself. Perhaps he had
it stashed somewhere else. Perhaps he even banked it
under an assumed name.

He returned in a dry, snowy, open-necked cambric
shirt, his long legs covered with well-fitted dark breeches
tucked beneath turned down jack-leather boots. His black
hair was combed and tied back from his face with a
plain grosgrain ribbon, drawing attention to his dark
eyes, making him seem handsomer still, if it were possible. Swinging back a wide, full cloak behind his scab-
bard, he produced an armful of clothes hastily wrapped
in a blanket to keep them dry.

"Here—see what you fancy."

"I cannot steal the countess's clothes," she protested.
"I cannot."

"She won't miss them," he assured her. "Besides, I
left payment and a note for her."

"You told her you were taking her clothes?" She
shook her head in disbelief.

"It amuses me to have her know 'twas I," he said
simply. "Well, do you like any of them or must I go
back?"

She eyed covetously what he produced, then had to
restrain herself. "I—I cannot."

"Miss Hardinge, I have gone to a great deal of trouble
to procure you decent gowns," he said impatiently. "If
I have to put you in one of them myself, I am prepared
to do it."

He'd brought three dresses and an expensive cloak,

as well as a lace-edged lawn chemise. Drawn to them, she allowed herself to touch them gingerly. " 'Tis a fortune to wear," she murmured, more to herself than to him.

"And I have paid a fortune for them. Go on. There is not all day. Billy has the horses put to harness already."

"There is no place to dress," she protested.

"I shall turn my back," he promised.

Uncertain as to whether he would attempt to dress her, she capitulated reluctantly. "All right. As I am in mourning, it should be black, but the green gown will suffice."

"I thought you might like it."

"It will hang without panniers."

"There is no room for them in the coach, I'm afraid."

"But I have none at home." She reddened again. "I'm afraid mine were left muddy in the street."

"I'll buy you the finest to be had—once you are safely back at Crow's Cross." He regarded her soberly for a moment. "In mourning for whom?" he asked quietly.

"My grandfather."

"I'm sorry."

"So am I." She sighed. " 'Tis the reason Robin is in jail, I'm afraid."

That brought a decided lift to his black brows. "He killed your grandfather?"

"Of course not," she retorted. "But we believe my uncle destroyed Grandpapa's will, for there was no provision for Robin or myself in the one that was read, and we cannot think—" She stopped abruptly. "Well, in any event, 'tis not your concern, is it?"

"No." He walked away to stand staring out the tiny, nearly opaque window. "You'd best get dressed."

Keeping her eyes on his back, she shed her wet clothes hastily, then pulled on the countess's dry chemise and the green gown. Adjusting the starched, carefully pleated stomacher over her breasts, she began lacing the gown across it, pulling the satin cords tightly to hide the deficiency he'd already noted. The countess was definitely more endowed there than she was.

"Why would he destroy the will?" he asked suddenly.

"Because Robin should be the heir!" she shouted at him, exasperated.

"I am not deaf, Miss Hardinge," he reminded her.

"I'm sorry. But Robin is Grandpapa's first son's only son, and by rights Crow's Cross is his," she managed more calmly.

He turned around at that. "That should be easy enough to prove, my dear. There is, after all, the parish register."

"No. Papa married Mama in Spain, you see. I think it was a mad, impetuous elopement—quite romantic, actually."

"Still, there had to be marriage lines, if they were wed."

"There were. And after Papa died of a fever, Mama gave them to Grandpapa for safekeeping."

"And?"

"And it appears my uncle has purloined them."

"If your grandfather acknowledged you, there should be witnesses," he argued reasonably.

"We have not lived here. We were with Mama in Cornwall for the milder climate, and we did not know of his death until the money stopped coming."

"I'd say the matter rests with your mother, then. Let her petition the courts."

She looked up at that. "She cannot. She died shortly after Grandpapa."

"How inconvenient."

"Is everything a jest to you?" she demanded hotly.

"Have you no mercy for anyone? Mama was in poor health for years, else we should have lived here. But she did not wish to burden Papa's relations."

"Apparently she took their money," he countered.

"It was an allowance based on her marriage portion!"

"All right, I am sorry."

"Anyway," she spoke more quietly, "once we inquired, we were told it had been stopped because Uncle Joseph no longer wished to support his brother's illegitimate issue. Illegitimate issue, he called us!" she cried. "As though Mama had lived in sin with Papa—when she did not! And—and at Mama's behest, we engaged a solicitor, paying him the princely sum of twenty pounds to have him tell us that without Mama's marriage lines for proof, we had no case," she recalled bitterly. "I think it killed Mama, if you would have my opinion of it. I think it was the final thing for her."

"And you confronted your uncle?"

"Of course we did! He insisted that the allowance Mama had received was but Grandpapa's largesse to Papa's by-blows, and that he felt no incumbency to continue it. But, given the fact that his brother had sired us, however unholy the union was, he would see we had a roof over our heads and forty pounds per year. As though we were nothing! I daresay he pays his valet more than that. And he sits, rich as you please, in Robin's house!"

"Apparently, Miss Hardinge," he said softly, "we have more in common than I first thought."

"What?"

His dark eyes met hers and held. "We are both bastards."

"Robin and I are not bastards! I tell you Papa wed Mama in Spain!"

"The Catholics keep excellent records, I am told."

"I told you—it was a runaway marriage. 'Twas an English divine who married them." She took a deep breath, collecting herself before she went on. "Mama did not want Papa to give up his religion for her. And so she ran away with him. They were wed in Barcelona before they came to England. But without the marriage lines, we have nothing," she said tiredly. "Robin went to Crow's Cross to look for them, and he was taken. My uncle charges him with illegal trespass and attempted robbery. 'Tis rich, isn't it? Robin is in jail for breaking into his own house."

"A devil of a coil," he admitted, "—if 'tis the truth."

"It is the truth! And if something is not done, Robin will go to prison for it! And I shall be alone! There— I have said it!" Her chin quivered and she had to bite her lip to still its trembling. Bright tears threatened to spill from her eyes. "I'm sorry. 'Tis not your affair, is it?" she managed finally.

"I don't know." His expression was odd, almost soft. "I'm going to hang, anyway, I suppose."

"There isn't anything you could do. There isn't anything anyone could do," she said sadly. "Now I can only hope that Robin does not go to prison, for I shall die without him." She caught herself, then looked at him with wet, dark eyes, as her voice dropped to a near whisper. "I'm sorry. I cannot expect you to understand, I think, but without him, I shall have no one."

"Miss Hardinge, there is no need to keep apologizing to me," he assured her. "And I expect I understand quite well," he added gently, "for I have never had anyone care so much as a button for me."

"Your mother—"

"My mother does not precisely count, my dear," he retorted, returning to his earlier manner. "She trod the boards as an actress, and no one gave a damn when she died. I cannot even remember her."

"Then who . . . ?"

"Reared me?" There was a harsh, bitter tone to his voice. "If you could call it that, I'd suppose the honor falls to Peg, who counted herself an actress and supported herself by whoring."

"I'm sorry."

His temper flared. "I don't need your pity, Miss Hardinge!" he all but shouted at her. "I grew up with a surfeit of it for myself!"

"I did not mean—that is—well, what of your father?"

"My father." His lip curved disdainfully. "My father—'tis a rich appellation, signifying nothing."

"I collect he does not claim you," she said softly. " 'Tis a pity, for I think he makes you what you are."

"What I am, Miss Hardinge, is none of your affair."

"No, I suppose not," she admitted, sighing.

He stared unseeing at the thick-paned window for a moment, then swung to face her again. "Do you know what I am, Anne Hardinge?" he demanded finally. "A damned highwayman doomed to swing on the Nubbin' Cheat."

For all the harshness in his face, there was a vulnerability in his eyes. "No, I don't think so. I see a bitter man, sir. And a lonely boy beneath," she answered simply.

"He wants me dead, you know," he went on, ignoring her. "He sees me as an embarrassment to his consequence."

"Then you know who your father is?"

"Yes."

"And you have confronted him?"

"More than once, I assure you." Again, there was the harsh laugh. "If there is any justice to be had, it is that I am his only son. 'Tis rich, isn't it? I am the only son, and I was born on the wrong side of the blanket. His legitimate, whey-faced wife has given him naught but two daughters."

"And he denies you. How very foolish of him."

"He is sworn to see me hang." He sucked in his breath, then let it out slowly before settling his shoulders. "Well, Miss Hardinge, I expect I ought to get you back to this Crow's Cross while there is still light enough for Billy to find his way home after."

She was vaguely disappointed. "Yes, of course."

"A strange name for a place," he observed.

"Crow's Cross? Yes, I suppose it is." She forced a smile. "When Papa was alive, he was used to tell Robin and me that one of his ancestors had set a large stone cross on the hill above his house, saying it was God's beacon in a difficult time—during Cromwell's reign, you see—but when spring came, it was covered with crows. And instead of receiving God's blessing for it, that Baron Hardinge lost his crops."

"An enlightening tale," he murmured. Nevertheless, the corners of his mouth twitched. "I suppose there must be a moral to it, don't you think? Something like not praying in public, I expect."

"Most likely," she agreed.

It was late afternoon ere they reached Crow's Cross, with Billy driving up the lane as boldly as he pleased. Nicholas Swann's Diablo was tied behind the earl's carriage. Inside, the highwayman regarded Anne Hardinge soberly from beneath his purloined hat.

She was in truth a very pretty young woman, and very definitely not the sort of female common to his acquaintance. Her dark eyes were frank, unguarded, in a delicate oval face, and her lips were as kissable as any he'd seen. And yet there was a dignity about her that he rather grudgingly admired; something that told him she was not meant to be his next flirt. Regretfully, he pushed back the ramillie from his forehead.

"Where would he keep your mother's marriage lines, do you think?" he asked suddenly.

"What?" Jarred from her own thoughts, she gave a start. "I'm sorry, I was not attending," she murmured apologetically.

"You know how to wound a man, don't you?"

"Well, it was not my intent, I assure you." She sighed as she looked out the carriage window almost absently. "I was thinking of my brother."

"Did he take anything?"

"No, but what if Uncle Joseph should say he did?"

"They won't hang him."

"You cannot know that," she said slowly. "These are lawless times, and there are always those who wish to punish everything with a hangman's noose."

"Well I know that," he admitted dryly. "But I daresay this uncle of yours is more intent on insuring his silence than in prosecution. I mean, how is it to look if he is accused in turn of depriving your brother of his inheritance?"

"I don't know." She straightened in her seat and looked across at him. "In any event, it does not concern you, for we are at Crow's Cross already."

He stared out into the wet parkland for a moment, seeing the large house on the hill. "Which way?"

"The low road. It runs into the crofters' cottages."

At that, he tapped the roof, then shouted upward, "Keep to the right, Billy!"

" 'Tis the last one," she murmured. " 'Tis as though he cannot bear to see us. Not that I wonder at it," she added bitterly. "I am sure if I stole a man's patrimony, I should not wish to look him in the face either."

His face took on an odd expression for a moment, then he looked away. "A man's patrimony is everything, Miss Hardinge," he said tightly. "Everything."

"And the lack of it makes Robin feel as though he is nothing, as though he has failed," she agreed. " 'Tis a heavy burden for one who has but turned eighteen."

"Eighteen," he repeated. " 'Twas another lifetime, it seems."

"As you are so old?" she chided.

"No. If you must pry, I am but five-and-twenty— and not like to live to see six-and-twenty. But I can scarce remember eighteen, other than that I was in that den of birch, buggery, and bottle they call Oxford."

"Oxford? You went to Oxford?" she asked, disbelieving him.

"Not for long." He favored her with a rueful grin. "All it offered was a place in line for a church living, my dear, and even on our short acquaintance, you must surely agree I am unsuited to the life."

"Yes. But who . . . ?"

"My illustrious father."

"I thought you said he did not—"

"He doesn't. There is a great deal of difference between sending a few pounds to a boy and acknowledging him as a son, Miss Hardinge."

"But if he sent you to Oxford—"

"His solicitor sent me."

"Oh."

It was his turn to straighten his shoulders. "We seem to be arrived, my dear."

"Yes, of course."

Almost before the carriage halted, he'd opened the door and jumped down. Reaching up to her, he caught her waist and lifted her out. For the briefest moment, she met his eyes and the thought crossed her mind that he meant to kiss her again. But instead, he set her down and stepped back. Turning to the small thatch and stone cottage, he frowned.

" 'Tis old."

"Yes."

Something within her did not want to let him go. "Uh, if I had a fire, I should offer you some tea," she ventured shamelessly. Then, fearing he should think her the veriest trollop, she blushed deeply. "That is—"

"I suppose I could set your fire," he said. "But first I'd best send Billy home."

"Yes, of course. I hope you do not think—" she blurted out.

"Miss Hardinge, if you are a hussy," he responded, cutting to the heart of the matter, "then I am an Oxford don. Is there wood inside?"

"Yes."

As she opened the door, she was conscious of the plainness of everything. In truth, it was not much better than the place he'd taken her, only it was cleaner, neater. Acutely aware that she had no business entertaining any man in her brother's absence, she snatched the white mob cap from the crude table and pulled it over her dark curls.

"What the devil is this?" he asked, coming up behind her.

" 'Tis supposed to signify that I am quite on the shelf," she told him severely. "An old maid, to be precise."

"How old?" he asked bluntly.

"Two-and-twenty."

"A veritable old hag," he said, smiling.

"And one utterly without expectation," she added dampeningly.

His gaze moved around the room, taking in the neatness, the perfect order of the place, and he felt an odd pang. It was the sort of place where a man ought to come home. Pushing that traitorous thought from his mind, he went to kneel by the cold fireplace grate. After a time of coaxing flint and tinder, he stood.

"I think I'd favor the tea," he said softly. "Unless you have some rum."

"Only tea, I'm afraid. Robin," she declared flatly, "has not yet acquired many vices. He cannot afford them."

"That never stopped me."

As she bustled about, he watched her, thinking it was a pity she would probably never marry. She was the sort of female a man wanted and ought to have. Idly, he dropped into a chair before the newly made fire and stretched out his feet toward the flames.

Fresh rain hit the oilcloth windows, and the wind came up outside. "Poor Billy," he murmured.

"What did you do with your horse?"

"Billy left him."

"Untied? But—"

"He won't wander." He stared for a moment into the fire, then nodded. "Best horse I have ever owned."

"He's quite an animal," she conceded as she dipped the precious tea into the pot. "I halfway expected you to say you had stolen him."

"I did."

"You are a strange fellow, Nicholas Swann. When you are first met, you seem all puffed up with your own conceit, and then later you are quite kind."

"Your first impression serves you the best, my dear." he looked up at her. "But I suppose in that respect I am not so very different from other men."

"Only you are Nicholas Swann and therefore dangerous to know."

"Guilty as charged."

"Why don't you go away?" she asked suddenly. "Why must you wait to be taken?"

"And do what?" he countered. "I told you I never finished Oxford."

"If you were not Nicholas Swann, who would you wish to be?" she dared to ask him.

"The Earl of Warrington," he answered without hesitation.

"What?" For a moment, she was taken aback. "Surely not."

"Why not? He has everything, Miss Hardinge—everything." His dark eyes betrayed a hint of amusement. "That surprise you, doesn't it? That a bastard should wish to be landed, I mean?"

"Well . . ."

"Land and birth go hand in glove, my dear. A man is but what he owns." As she opened her mouth to dispute it, he lifted his hand. "Think on it: why does it mean so much that your brother has his patrimony?"

"Because it is his right."

"Precisely."

She stood waiting for the tea to steep. "Where will you go?"

"When?"

"Now."

His eyebrow lifted perceptibly. "Why would you care? Unless of course you are offering me shelter."

She could feel the heat rise into her face. "Of course not. It would not be proper, and I—"

"And you are always proper, aren't you?"

"Yes."

She poured the tea and carried a cup to him. Then she sat by the fire across from him, watching as he drank it. And an intense loneliness washed over her. It was such a waste, such a terrible waste for a man like Swann to hang.

For a time, they sat in relative silence, each sipping the hot liquid, each lost in thought. Then he drained his cup and stood abruptly.

"My thanks, Miss Hardinge."

"It was nothing," she said, rising also.

He closed the space between them, and again, she thought he meant to kiss her. But he lifted her chin with his knuckle and looked into her eyes instead.

"Until we are met again, my dear," he murmured.

"I do not think it likely, sir," she managed.

"One never knows."

With that he was gone, disappearing into the rain, leaving naught but an empty cup on a table. For a long time she listened, hearing nothing but the wind and water on the oilcloth windows. It was, she realized listlessly, as though he'd never been.

He cursed the moon as his horse crossed the silent parkland. But already he'd waited three days for another rain, and it had not come. He knew his time was nearly done, that it would be but a short matter of time before he was taken. Already the reward sheets were out, with Warrington offering one thousand pounds for his capture. One thousand pounds. Enough to make all but the best of friends into enemies.

In the distance, close to the house, a hound bayed. He reined in and listened, lest someone come out to silence it. But there was no sound beyond the hound. He turned Diablo from the road to the soft grass and rode straightway for the garden wall. As he dismounted, the moonlight reflected off the horse's eyes eerily. He let the reins drop, leaving the horse to stand within the shadow of the wall. Then, rapier in hand, pistol in his belt, he climbed the rough-hewn stones and paused for a moment, ready to spring to the ground below.

The hound's bark echoed, this time farther away, indicating that the dog chased something. He sucked in his breath, then dropped down into the garden. The thin rapier blade shone like a ribbon of silver against the darkness. He flicked his wrist, testing it, then eased his way along the wall to the house.

He knew he was a fool for attempting such a thing, for robbing a man in his house was a far different thing from lifting his purse on the road. Here he was exposed, vulnerable on a ground not his own, where there was greater risk of not escaping.

For three days he'd waited and wavered, first telling himself that Anne Hardinge was nothing to him, that her predicament did not matter one whit to him. But in the end, it had been the notion that no man ought to have his patrimony stolen that had swayed him. Before he swung, he ought to attempt righting at least one wrong, he supposed.

He moved along the house, testing each door gingerly, until he found one left unlatched. The toe of his boot pushed it inward, opening into a cavern of blackness, and for a moment, he thought he'd merely discovered a cellar. But it was a long, narrow hall. As his hand brushed against the wall, he could feel the grease, and he knew it for the passage between the kitchen and the rest of the house. He moved silently down it to another door.

Opening it, he saw the faint light of a sconce, its blackened chimney nearly obscuring the flame. Now the walls were covered with expensive Venetian paper, the polished floor parqueted beneath the floral woolen carpet. Apparently the crows had not taken everything, for it appeared as though the subsequent Baron Hardinges had definitely prospered.

He lifted the candle from the sconce and moved deliberately now, leaving the room to search for a bookroom or study, some place where a man might hide a document of importance. Not that he really expected to find any marriage lines, for unless Joseph Hardinge were a complete fool, he'd no doubt already disposed of them. But on the chance he had not . . . well, after all, there were fools born every day.

The bookroom was musty, as though it were seldom used for its purpose. But at one end there was a closed desk littered with papers. Fastening the candle into a brass holder, he sat at the desk and riffled through the baron's bills. Nothing of import. Opening a drawer, he discovered a metal box of the sort used for valuables, and he quickly pried off the lid. Then he paused for a moment of reverence, for in it were neatly tied sheaves of banknotes, nearly too many to count. There had to be well over a thousand pounds, perhaps even twice that. But as his fingers deftly sorted through the notes, he found no marriage lines for anyone.

His first impulse was to take the money and flee, to give it to Anne Hardinge in recompense for what her uncle did to her and the boy. But there was no recompense for a stolen patrimony, none at all, he recalled bitterly. Walking to a window, he opened it and carefully set the box on the sill.

He ought to leave now, while he was ahead. But he was a fool, he knew it, for he could still see those dark eyes, the oval face, the flawless skin. It was too late for himself, for he was already doomed, but a woman like Anne Hardinge deserved a chance to live decently.

Now he walked boldly, crossing the room to the hall, traversing the marble-floored foyer to the wide, balust-

-ered stairs, climbing them beneath the distant gazes of Anne Hardinge's ancestors. He was going to beard the baron in his bed.

Joseph Hardinge slept heavily, but he awoke with a start of the cold feel of steel against his ear. As he reached to push it away, it flashed in the darkness, and he cried out.

"What's this, sirrah?" he demanded, struggling to sit. "Dash it, but you have pinked me!"

The blade dug into a fold beneath his chin as Nicholas Swann swung his leg over a chair and sat to face the baron. "One loud word, and you are dead," he said silkily.

The man's mouth gaped open, then closed quickly. "Wh-who the devil are you?" he managed weakly.

"Swann—Nichoals Swann."

Joseph Hardinge's eyes widened. "The highwayman? But I thought—"

You thought I was safely away," Swann finished for him. "But as you can see, I am here."

"Wh-what do you want?"

Nicholas leaned forward, but the rapier did not move. "It is a matter of marriage lines, I believe," he said softly. "Your brother's to the Spanish woman, to be precise."

"What? 'Tis the bloody little bastard as sends you, ain't it? Well, he don't—" He got no further as the blade drew blood, and his words ended in a frightened squeal.

"You sound like a damned pig at a slaughter," Swann told him contemptuously. "And I don't like the word bastard. Now, where are they?"

"Where is what?" Hardinge growled.

"Proof of your brother's marriage."

"There ain't any, I tell you."

"You know, it would appear you have difficulty hear-

ing, wouldn't it?" The blade moved deftly from the
baron's chin to one of his ears. "Shall I perhaps clear a
passage for my words?"

"N-no—no!" The baron was pale against the darkness. "Heh-heh, you was funning, wasn't you?"

"No." Nicholas Swann touched the rapier point to
the delicate center of the ear. "I never jest, Joseph."

"The boy's a filthy little bastard, I tell you! M'brother's by-blow, and—Owwwwwwwwww!"

"I told you, I don't like the word," Swann murmured.

"I am pricked!" the baron fairly howled. "Damn you!"

"Where are the marriage lines?"

"There ain't—" He stopped as the thin point dug
deeper. Beads of perspiration shone on his forehead.
"Look, I got money . . ."

"I know. But money is poor compensation for a man's
name, isn't it?"

"What is it to you? You ain't—" Hardinge laughed
nastily then. "Oh, I collect you've seen the chit, eh?
Well, I can tell you she ain't anything but a—" This
time, his words ended in a high-pitched shriek that reverberated through the house.

As Swann withdrew the blade, a rivulet of blood ran
down the baron's neck. "Now, the truth, I think, or
else your miserable life."

"She cannot prove anything!"

"Her grandfather acknowledged her and the boy."

"He was an old fool!"

"The marriage lines, Hardinge! My patience thins!"
Swann snapped.

"Well, you won't find 'em, 'cause they are gone."

"Did you burn them?"

"What if I did? She cannot prove it, and ain't any as
would believe it."

"Get up." The blade swished through the air, cutting

it, then rested again beneath the baron's chin. "I ought to slit your throat, you know."

"N-no!" But even as he protested, the older man tottered unsteadily from the bed. "She's lying, I tell you!"

"Where are they?" Swann persisted. "For the last time, where are they? And do not deny their existence, if you would live."

"I don't have 'em. Not anymore, anyways!"

"Ah, Joseph, but you offend me." Nicholas flicked his wrist deftly, this time catching the front placket of the baron's nightshirt. A button flew, landing somewhere on the bed. "Shall I mark your heart, do you think?"

"For the love of God, sir!"

"Strange words from a man who would steal an inheritance. As I recall it, the Almighty takes a decidedly bad view of such things." Abruptly, his manner changed, and his expression hardened. "Now for the last time, where are the marriage lines?"

"Gone for ashes," the baron muttered. "Aye, gone for ashes," he admitted more boldly. "Ain't a thing she can do now, is there?"

"Say your prayers, Hardinge. No, 'pon reflection, don't. It might make the Almighty merciful, and you don't deserve that."

"Please, oh, please, no. I got money," the baron blubbered, afraid again. "Please."

"Are you lying?"

"Gone, they are gone," Hardinge choked. "I-I-" This time, as the rapier cut his skin, marking it with an *X*, the older man fainted.

For a moment, Nicholas Swann stared at him in disgust, then he rose. He did not now doubt for an instant that Anne Hardinge had told him the truth. And he was equally certain now that her uncle had destroyed any proof. He withdrew the rapier blade and leaned to wipe it on the embroidered coverlet.

He let himself out again into the darkened hall, stole quickly down the stairs, and out into the night. Passing along the side of the big stone house, he stopped to retrieve the box he'd left on the windowsill. He couldn't prove Anne or Robin Hardinge legitimate, but he could damned well make them rich enough to live somewhere else.

He rode like the devil he felt he was, taking the dark roads back toward Oakhill, planning what he would say to Anne Hardinge on the morrow. He'd have to be careful how he explained everything, else he feared she would not take the money.

"Halt! Who rides there?" a voice called out.

In the moonlight, he could make out the forms of perhaps a dozen mounted men, and he cursed himself for a fool. He'd been carelessly lost in his thoughts, and now he was like to be cornered like a hart in the hunt. Without answering, he wheeled the big black horse around and ran.

" 'Tis Swann!" he heard someone shout. " 'Tis the Black Swann as surely as I breathe. 'Tis he!"

"Halt in the name of the Crown! You are under arrest!"

They were in heated pursuit. He leaned low over his horse's shoulder, his black cape flying, as Diablo's hooves pounded the rock-hard road. Behind him, a soldier rose in his saddle and took careful aim. Even as the report sounded, Nicholas Swann felt the searing path of the bullet through his flesh. For a moment, he had to close his eyes against the pain.

"Did ye get 'im, Tom?" one of them called out.

"Naw. 'Twas too far," came the answer.

If he gave the big horse its head, he knew it would go to Oakhill, and now he suspected there would be a party there ready to greet him. He also knew he bled like a stuck pig, for he could feel the warmth of his own blood beneath his shirt. Abruptly, he kneed his horse to the left, then held on as it jumped the thick hedgerow. Instead of cutting across the field, he reined in, hoping there'd been none to see it, and he was grateful when his pursuers thundered by.

"Devil a bit," he muttered to himself. "Where now?" Wincing as he sat up, he tried to lift his arm. "Got the shoulder. Damn."

Gritting his teeth against the pain, he slowly turned Diablo around and headed back to Crow's Cross, hoping that it would be assumed he'd fled as far as he could get from the scene of his last crime.

At first, Anne Hardinge thought it was the wind, then a branch that tapped at the oilcloth window. Then she thought she heard someone call out to her. Reluctantly, she swung her feet over the side of her bed and rose to pad barefoot to the fireplace. Lighting the wick of a crude cruzie lamp in the coals, she blew until the flame flickered, then took hold.

She went to the door, and without opening it, she called out, "Who's there?"

"Swann."

She threw the latch then, and stared as he slumped against the door jamb. "Mr. Swann! Whatever—?"

"Been shot. Ball in the shoulder."

"Oh, dear."

Shifting the oil lamp into her left hand, she tried to catch him with her right shoulder. "Here, sit you down."

"I am all right. I just need to rest—lost blood, that's all."

Despite his protest, she tried to steady him as he walked to the chair. He dropped gratefully into it.

"But how—?"

"They were waiting for me." He closed his eyes for a moment, then opened them to focus on her. "Damned lucky shot," he muttered. "Damned lucky."

"You are bleeding, sir."

"Clever of you to note it."

"You'll have to have the doctor."

He caught her hand at that and held it. "No, I cannot risk it."

"But . . ."

" 'Tis but a flesh wound." He gingerly touched his wet, sticky shirt. "The ball went in the back and came out the front."

"But you are bleeding!"

"Like a stuck pig," he acknowledged. "But 'twill eventually stop. Just let me rest here for awhile, and I'll come about." But even as he spoke, he felt dizzy. "Got to rest," he repeated.

He'd leaned back, his black hair spilling over the chair back, his face pale and damp. His eyes closed again, frightening her. She started to shake him, then she felt the warm, wet blood beneath her fingers, and she knew she had to try to stop it. But first she had to see.

In a matter of seconds, she assembled nearly every candle stub in the small cottage on the nearest table, then lit them for light. Then she proceeded to build up the fire and put the kettle on it. Finally, she filled the washbasin with cold water and carried it to where he sat.

Very gingerly, she lifted the soaked shirt, trying to see the wound beneath. Taking a cloth, she dabbed at it gently, wiping at the welling blood. Again, he caught her hand.

" 'Tis not meet, Mistress Anne. Leave it be."

"I cannot." She peered at the wound anxiously. " 'Twill not stop," she insisted. " 'Twill have to be staunched ere you swoon from the loss."

"Yes."

" 'Tis terrible."

"You are looking at the worst of it," he said, trying to reassure her. "The hole the ball comes out is always the bigger."

"Oh."

"Need to hold something tightly against it."

"Yes, of course." She was terribly afraid he'd faint, and she knew she could not manage him if he did. Throwing all propriety to the wind, she said baldly, "I think it would be best if we got you to the bed. Do you think you could move again, sir?"

"Nicky," he murmured. " 'Do you think you could move again, Nicky?' " he repeated for her. Holding his shoulder, he rose from the chair awkwardly, nodding. "Yes."

For a horrible moment, he swayed, then he got his balance and walked toward her bed. Sitting on the side, he looked up at her. "I don't think I would have swooned, mistress."

"Well, if you had, I should have to leave you where you fell, sir."

"What a weak fellow you think me." He looked down at the welling blood and shook his head. "You'd best put something beneath me, else 'twill look as though a hog has been slaughtered in your bed."

Agreeing, she knelt to remove a storage box from beneath the bedrail, then drew two old blankets from it. The first she folded and placed over her feather mattress.

"You may lie upon that."

"My thanks."

She moved her candles and the basin closer, then looked once more at his ruined shirt. "I shall have to cut it where 'tis dried," she decided. "And then I will clean the rest."

"No. Just get something heavy to lay over it."

Something heavy. Glancing around the room, she spied her heavy iron skillet. Picking it up, she carried it back to the bed.

"I hope, 'twill do," she murmured.

Taking an old tablecloth, she cut it into strips, then made a heavy pad from one of them. Sitting on the side of the bed, she forced it under him, telling him, "Your weight should be sufficient to hold that."

"Yes."

His eyes were closed, frightening her again. For an awful moment, she wondered how she could ever explain it to anyone if the highwayman should die in her bed.

It was as though he knew her thoughts. "You needn't worry," he reassured her. "I'll live to swing yet."

"I would that you did not say that," she retorted.

"Why?"

"Because it is so very fatal to you. Perhaps if you would throw yourself on the mercy of the court, they would not hang you."

That elicited a hard, short laugh. "If not for Warrington, mayhap, but he is determined to see me gone forever."

"Why?"

"It doesn't signify."

She worked quickly now, soaking his shirt where the blood had dried, lifting it carefully, then cutting the cloth away. But the clot that was forming was not nearly large enough to stop the bleeding. Undeterred, she wiped around it, then dusted it liberally with basilicum for drying and healing, and covered the wound with another pad. Finally, she picked up the skillet and laid it over her handiwork.

"I do hope you can breathe, for it is quite the heaviest thing to be had."

"You are a clever woman, Anne Hardinge," he replied.

He'd lost much blood, she knew that. And she'd heard that one should drink to replace it, but if he sat up, he'd dislodge the skillet. She emptied more water into a bowl, got a clean rag, and sat on the bed again. Dipping the rag into the water, she carefully dribbled water into the corner of his mouth.

"I can drink," he protested.

"But you cannot sit up, and you might strangle," she told him matter-of-factly.

"Ugh—'tis water," he grunted, pushing her hand away.

"There is nothing else." Undeterred, she soaked the cloth again. "Besides, 'tis good for you."

One eye opened to regard her balefully. "How wifely you are, Mistress Hardinge."

Once again, she could feel the hateful heat rising to her face. "You know, perhaps I should leave you to the hangman's noose," she said tartly. "Besides, I'd do this for a dog."

He felt an instant shame. "I don't suppose water can hurt me." His expression lightened as he forced a rueful smile. "Do you realize, Annie Hardinge, that you are the prettiest female when you blush?" he asked softly.

"No."

"Oh, but you are."

"And I would that you did not call me Annie, sir," she managed stiffly.

"Why?"

"Because 'tis what Papa was used to do."

"I'm sorry."

She rose and moved away to tend the small fire, leaving him to stare at the rough-beamed ceiling. When he could stand it no longer, he felt it incumbent to blurt out, "I have never killed anyone, you know."

"What?"

"I only took purses."

"And that made it right?" she asked, her voice rising incredulously. " 'Tis still stealing."

"It sustained me." He sucked in his breath against the pain, then let it out slowly. "But I nearly killed Hardinge for you tonight."

She turned around at that. "You went to see my uncle?" she asked, surprised. "But why?"

"To get your mother's marriage lines for you."

"You were in the house?"

"Yes. And he admitted he burned them."

"I see." She sank to a chair and sat very still for a time. "Well, it was to be expected, wasn't it?"

"Yes."

"But why would he admit such a terrible thing to you?" she asked hollowly. "Surely—"

"I cannot think him overly concerned for my word against his," he reminded her dryly.

"No, of course not."

His shoulder throbbed now, and he would have given a king's ransom for some rum. He swallowed hard and tried to think of the other. "It cost him, Anne, it cost him."

"How could it?" she demanded bitterly. "He has Crow's Cross; he has Robin's inheritance."

"Not all of it."

"I don't—"

"There is a box outside your door. Go on, look in it."

She hesitated, thinking him out of his mind from his wound, then she rose and went to the door, opening it. Lifting the embossed metal box, she carried it inside.

" 'Tis Grandpapa's. I should know it anywhere."

"Yes."

"But how?"

"It only seemed just that you and your brother should have it. Look inside."

"Oh, but I could not." Still, she was drawn to open it, and as she gazed down on the tied banknotes, she gasped. " 'Tis a fortune—a fortune!" Shutting it quickly, she took a deep breath, then shook her head. "I shall have to see it returned. I cannot keep so much."

"Don't you think it small recompense for stealing your brother's name and property?" he countered. "No, 'tis yours, my dear. Any attempt at giving it back must surely cast suspicion your way."

"And any attempt at spending it must do the same."

"Hoard it, then. Use it to let your brother begin anew."

She opened it again and stared at the money. Then she began to count it, her voice reflecting her growing awe. " 'Tis two thousand pounds," she said finally. "Two thousand pounds."

"Go somewhere where you can start over with it," he advised. "The American colonies, perhaps."

"The American colonies?" she echoed. "I don't—"

"There have been times when I have considered it," he admitted. "Times when I tired of this. There you and your brother can go into trade or buy property even. They are not so very concerned with how you are born, I am told."

"Because so many are criminals, no doubt," she muttered.

"Debtors, Annie," he said quietly. "Debtors with a chance to start anew."

"It is not the same with Robin. But for the fact he is cheated, he is Baron Hardinge here."

"Anne—"

She closed the box again. "No, I cannot keep it," she declared resolutely.

"I told you, 'tis yours. Think on it. Surely your grandfather would have wished you and Robin to have something."

"Yes, but—"

"And it is your only redress for what Joseph Hardinge does to you." He tried to turn his head to look at her. "But if you do not want it, I will take it." His dark eyes met hers soberly. "Unlike you, I am possessed of no scruples."

"Except you do not kill a man."

"Only because there was never the need."

She moved away again, this time to stir the fire. Her back to him, she dared to ask, "Why don't you take the money yourself and flee to America with it?"

"Because Warrington would have won."

"He will win anyway if you are hanged."

"But then he will carry my curse to his grave."

"You are a strange man, Nicholas Swann," she decided, sighing. "What is this between you and Warrington?"

"A feud of blood and pride."

"And foolishness."

"And foolishness," he conceded.

"Then why—?" She caught herself. "I'm sorry, I should not have asked."

"No."

She came back to lift the frying pan and look at his shoulder. "I think the bleeding stops."

She was so close he could smell the lavender water she used in her hair. As she leaned over him, her breast brushed his arm, and her long, dark hair fell like silk over him. He felt again the acute loneliness. He looked up into her lovely face, for once wishing he'd been as other men. Had he been born of the gentry, had he prospered lawfully, she would have been precisely the woman he wanted.

"It grows late," he heard himself say, his voice oddly strained. "You'd best get the rest of your night's sleep." He tried to rise. "I can take the chair."

"No. I shall merely move to Robin's bed. And you should not try to do anything lest the clot pull away." She watched him lie back. "I sleep lightly, sir, so if you have need of me, you have but to call out."

"All right."

Without thinking, she smoothed the black hair that fell against his temple, much as she would have done a child's, then she started to draw away. But he caught her hand, holding it, pressing her wrist to his lips, sending a shiver of excitement down her spine. Embarrassed, she retrieved her fingers from his.

"Goodnight, sir."

" 'Tis Nick," he reminded her again.

She awoke late, for the sun already brightened the cloth window, and she sat up with a start. As her gaze traveled around Robin's tiny room, she remembered Nicholas Swann, and she wondered if he'd called out and she'd not heard. Rising hastily, she pulled on her brother's dressing gown and went to the doorway.

The outer room was too still, too empty. She stood

there listening, her heart pounding in her ears. It was the only sound.

"Mr. Swann? Nicholas?"

There was no answer. Frightened, she crossed the room quickly to the bed, and she was stunned to see it had been neatly made. She cast about wildly, wondering where he could have gone, then she saw the note by the guttered candles on the table. She picked it up with nerveless fingers and read:

My dear Anne,

My thanks for all you have done this night—may the Almighty return your kindness one hundredfold in this life. Should I not see you again, I pray you will wed and prosper, making some worthy gentleman utterly happy. Take the money. It is more yours than Baron Hardinge's, I assure you. Mayhap we will meet again one day—in this life or the next.

He had signed it merely with an *S* distorted into a swan. He was gone. Her eyes swept the room, seeing no sign that he'd even been there until they rested on her grandfather's money box. She turned around, this time to the fireplace, where small bits of bloody blanket still smouldered.

She felt an aching loneliness within her breast, an unreasoning aching loneliness that made no sense. He was naught but a thief, a fellow who rode the high toby, taking other people's money, but there had been something about him that made her care. She sank into a chair, recalling his handsome face, his fine, dark eyes, his twisted smile. And she felt an intense sympathy for the man who'd once had none but a whore named Peg to mother him.

In the distance, she heard the sound of horses, many

of them, their hooves pounding on the road, and she said a quick prayer for his safety. Then she realized they were coming toward her small cottage. She rose hastily to kick the last of the blanket bits into the live coals, then she picked up her grandfather's box, wondering where she could hide it. Moving quickly, she opened her worn traveling chest and was about to put it in when she realized that someone might search there for it. And Swann had been right: it was hers and Robin's as much as Uncle Joseph's.

She lifted the lid on her stewpot and emptied the banknotes into it. Surely there'd be none to look in a cooking pot, after all. That done, she carried the box around the room, trying to decide what to do with it. It wasn't so very big, after all. On impulse, she stuck it into the empty chamberpot, then left the pot in plain view.

It was then that she looked down at her nightgown and saw Nicholas Swann's blood on it. As the horsemen drew closer, she quickly tore a piece of cloth and wrapped her hand, tying the bandage with her teeth. When she sat back down to wait, she reflected grimly that she was no better than Swann, that she had a soul bent toward larceny.

"Mistress Hardinge!" Someone pounded loudly on the door. "Open in the name of the Crown!" Another called out also, shouting, "Open in the name of King George!"

Running her unbandaged hand through her tangled hair, she pulled her brother's dressing gown closer and threw open the door. Her eyes widened as she saw the redcoated soldiers.

"Yes?"

"You are Anne Hardinge?"

"Yes. Uh, would you care to come in, sirs?" she

asked politely. "I am cooking a stew, but I daresay I can move the pot to make some tea for you."

An officer looked her up and down, obviously liking what he saw. "No time for tea, I'm afraid," he said as he swung from his saddle to the ground. "But I will come in."

"Yes, of course." She smiled pleasantly and stepped back from the door. "You must pardon the disorder, but last night I cut my hand."

"Oh?"

"My brother is in jail awaiting the setting of bail, I'm afraid, and I am no hand at all at cutting the bark for tinder."

His eyes narrowed briefly. "Robert Hardinge is your brother?"

"Yes. Why, officer? Is something wrong?"

"No, no. I understand he is still being held." He studied her face briefly, then asked, "You are acquainted with Nicholas Swann, are you not?"

"Well, I should not call it acquainted, precisely," she answered quickly. "I had the misfortune to be his hostage when he escaped." Her hand crept to her neck, then pushed back her thick, dark hair. "He threatened to slit my throat, and I thought he meant to do it."

"He cut you there?" He moved closer to look at the small, thin scab. "The bastard." Collecting himself, he recalled his purpose. "How did you get home, Miss Hardinge?"

"It was quite odd, sir. He purloined a carriage for the purpose, then left me here."

"And you have not seen him since?"

"No. Officer, is something the matter? Surely you do not think he would linger in the area with everyone looking for him, do you?" she asked, feigning anxiety.

"As to that, I am uncertain. He has been reported at Crow's Cross last night."

"Last night! Surely not!"

"You heard nothing?"

"Well, I am not close to my uncle's house, of course, but I cannot say I heard anything unusual. There is a rather nasty owl who calls at night. Come to think of it, I must have slept rather deeply, for I did not even hear it."

"I see." He cleared his throat nervously, then said, "Your uncle is of the opinion that you have employed him."

"Employed my uncle, sir?" she asked incredulously. "We do not even speak!"

"Not Sir Joseph, mistress, Swann. It seems that Swann stole a considerable amount of money from Crow's Cross last night, though it was not discovered until this morning."

"So that was why he asked about my uncle," she murmured, her voice low.

"What?"

"Nothing. But when he brought me home, Mr. Swann did inquire as to why Robin and I lived here rather than in the house. I told him, and then he inquired as to whether Uncle Joseph was wealthy."

"And?"

"Well, I told him I did not know, but that I supposed so."

"I see. well, no doubt he went there last night to discover for himself," the officer mused. "And knowing of the quarrel between your uncle and your brother, he used it to intimidate the baron. Does that sound probable to you?"

"I could only speculate, sir."

He looked again to the bloody front of her nightrail. "You must have taken a terrible cut, mistress."

"The hatchet slipped." She smiled hopefully up at him. "I do not suppose one of your men could be persuaded to cut a bit of tinder for me, could he?"

"Happy to." He went to the door and called someone inside, then turned back to her. "It must be terribly difficult for you now, Miss Hardinge."

"Terribly. I miss Robin so very much, and I must wait for enough money to pay his bail. Hopefully, I shall have it within the week, for there will be egg money."

"You keep chickens?"

"One has to do something, sir."

"Yes, but—"

"And I am a decent female."

"Never thought otherwise," he assured her. "Come to think of it, don't mind if I do take tea, mistress."

Her stomach knotting, she nodded. Going to the fireplace, she removed the stewpot of money, then set the tea kettle closer to the coals. "It is not quite as hot as I like it," she told him. "Hotter water seems to save the tea, which is quite precious."

He followed her, coming up behind her. "A woman like you ought not to be alone."

"Then release Robin!" she cried, whirling to face him.

"Now that I have not the power to do." For a moment, she feared he meant to touch her, then he stepped back. "But I would call on you, mistress. To see how you fare, I mean." He raised his hand awkwardly, then dropped it. "You are not betrothed, are you?"

"I have no expectations, sir."

"Well, I am a younger son, and—"

"Captain, it looks like someone's burnt a blanket," the soldier spoke up."

"Yes," Anne explained. "It was old and ragged. I did not have enough tinder, and I was afraid to attempt cutting any more."

"Oh."

Somehow she managed to get through a cup of tea with the captain, then she walked him to the door, where he caught her unbandaged hand and lifted it gallantly to his lips, promising he would call again as soon as possible. As he swung again into his saddle, she heard him tell the others that he expected Hardinge had been mistaken; that once Swann had escaped, every cutpurse in Oxfordshire claimed to be the highwayman. Personally, he declared, he was more inclined to look at Oakhill, for Swann was known to have an odd affection for the place.

He'd been a fool to leave Crow's Cross, and he knew it, but he could not risk endangering Anne Hardinge. And he knew also that her uncle would lodge a complaint immediately, laying her open to search. He only hoped she had discovered the means to keep the money.

He no longer tried to guide Diablo, but gave the horse its head. He was tired and weak, and he no longer cared if he were caught or not. From time to time, he touched his shoulder to see if it had begun to bleed again. It had not, and for that he had to be thankful, he supposed.

He thought of Anne Hardinge's iron skillet and smiled wryly. It must surely have been the first such application ever, but it had worked. She was a resourceful female, he had to give her that. And he admired her loyalty to her brother, for he'd seen deuced little female loyalty to anyone. No, she was different. But it stood to reason, he reminded himself. She wasn't like Peg or any of the others. She wasn't a whore.

He was dizzy. He had to focus his thoughts on something, so he allowed himself to wonder how it would have been if he'd met her under other circumstances. If he'd been landed. He could almost envision paying proper court to a woman like that.

Instead, he was going to die. One way or another, he was going to die—and soon. He felt that in his bones. He slumped forward, resting his arms on the big horse's shoulders, wondering how it would feel when they hanged him. Warrington would be there to watch, he did not doubt that. And when the time came, he was going to spit in that cold, aristocratic face. For that alone, it would be worth the hanging.

No, he was deluding himself. He didn't really want to die. He wanted to live, to court Anne Hardinge, to rear sons no one dared call bastards. For a moment, he considered going back to ask her to run with him, but he couldn't do that to her. Not even if she would.

He leaned farther forward, laying his head against Diablo's mane. He was too weak for anything. Too weak to ride. Too weak to care now.

He closed his eyes, then slid from the saddle, his jack boot still in the stirrup, and the great horse stood guard over him. His last thought was that perhaps justice was being done, that he was going to die on the very road he had used to such advantage.

He felt nothing, not even the soft rain, until someone turned him over with a booted foot. Too tired to open his eyes, he only dimly heard the hated voice say, "Aye, 'tis he. Take him to the constable." Then the man leaned closer to him, murmuring, "You are a fool, boy—a bloody fool."

*   *   *

Anne collected her egg money as thought it was all she had, and was about to put it into her knitted reticule when Mrs. Baxter remarked that the roads would be safer again, "Now that the monster Swann has been taken."

"What?" Anne asked, her heart thudding against her ribs.

"They ain't going ter wait this time," the woman declared smugly. " 'Tis ter Lunnon he goes fer trial."

"There must be some mistake."

"Humph! Only mistake is his, I'd say." Then Mrs. Baxter brightened. "Ought ter go ter see him ere they take him. Got ter put up the bond fer poor Mr. Robert, anyways, don't ye?"

"Yes."

"Not as ye can see 'im do anything, mind ye, fer he's more'n half-dead, Mr. Baxter says. Serves 'im right, I say."

Nicholas Swann had been taken. It was as though a cold chill had washed over Anne. Nicholas Swann had been taken. She closed her eyes briefly, seeing him as he'd been in her house. No, it was too much of a waste. She felt as though she could not bear it.

"They'll hang 'im, ye know," the Baxter woman rattled on. "Wish 'twas here, so's I could go, but they say the earl wants 'im in Lunnon." When Anne said nothing, Mrs. Baxter peered more closely at her. "Look queerlike, mistress. Is summat the matter wi' ye?"

"I cannot wish anyone to be hanged," Anne managed finally.

"Oh, they ain't going ter hang yer brother, I'll be bound. All ye got ter do is pay the bond, don't ye know?"

"Yes." Moving as though she were in a trance, Anne began to untie her apron. "The bond."

"If ye was ter do it terday, ye might get a glimpse o' him," Mrs. Baxter added cheerfully. "If he ain't dead. He was shot, they say. Took the ball in his chest."

"Shoulder," Anne murmured without thinking.

"Eh?"

"Nothing. And you are quite right, Mrs. Baxter— Robin has been in jail quite long enough."

"Ye got the blunt fer it? Mr. Baxter—"

"Just enough, thank you."

But once she was back inside her small cottage, Anne sat before her cold fireplace and contemplated what she could do. And the reality of it all sank in, answering that she could do very little. For a moment, she considered taking the money he'd brought her and using it to bribe his guards. But if he were worse, he might not be able to ride. And where could she take him, anyway? Not to Crow's Cross. Not to Oakhill. In truth, she had nowhere to go herself.

But she had to see him. And she had to pay Robin's bail. The only thing that had kept her from the latter had been a reluctance to let anyone know she had any money, lest they suspect the rest. Just now, she was willing to spend her half of it, every last shilling of her share, to free Nicholas Swann.

Somehow she managed to complete her toilette, to dress in the countess's green gown, pulling it over her old, poor panniers, and then to walk nearly a mile to engage a neighbor's conveyance. The man was reluctant until she allowed as how she could actually afford five pence for his service.

All the way into the town, she could think of nothing beyond Nicholas Swann, alternating between hope and despair for him. Poor Robin, how miserable he would be to discover that his sister was head over heels for a notorious highwayman. But she was. She did not doubt that in the least.

She composed what she would say to Swann, hoping she would not cry when she said it. But she wanted a man who'd had none but a whore for mother to know she cared.

"Ye ain't well, mistress?" Mr. Parkborn asked finally.

"I am merely tired."

"Ye look like 'twas yer brother they was a-hanging instead o' Swann."

"I should not wish anyone to hang," she said again.

"Eh? If 'twas here, I'd be a-taking me boys," he admitted. "Tell 'em not ter rob the gentry."

"Or anyone," she added dryly.

"Aye."

"It isn't as though he's killed anyone, you know."

"Don't matter ter the gentry. Them as got don't want ter share the purse," he declared succinctly.

" 'Tis Warrington's fault."

"Aye."

"But why—?"

"Ye ain't never seen 'im, have ye?"

"No."

"If ye was, ye'd not ask."

"But he has so much! Not that I favor robbing anyone, of course," she added hastily, "for I do not. But one would think they could transport Swann—or something." Even as she said it, she seized on the notion. "Yes, 'tis the very thing," she told herself.

There was a sign displayed before the makeshift jail, announcing that no tickets were to be sold for the viewing of the "Notorious Nicholas Swann." And inside, Mr. Sims sat behind his counter, his soiled bagwig crammed onto his head. He looked up when he saw her.

"Oh, 'tis ye, is it?"

"I have come to post bond for my brother. The magistrate has set it, hasn't he?"

He nodded. "Twenty pounds. Jem!" he barked.

"Twenty pounds seems rather high."

"Humph. That's what it is, anyways."

"All right."

He looked up, then looked away. "Ye don't look like ye took any harm from Swann."

"No."

"Sorry fer the thing, though. Thought ye was come ter see 'im, don't ye know?"

"It was an understandable mistake." She counted out the money, then added another pound. "This time, I should like to see Mr. Swann."

"No visitors. Warrington's orders, mistress."

She added another pound, then watched him waver greedily. "Why would ye want ter?" he asked suspiciously.

"To satisfy myself that he is incarcerated."

"Oh. Well, he ain't got no pistol, nor no knife neither," he assured her. "Got ter eat with 'is hands."

"How wise of you."

"Ain't me. 'Tis that captain as takes his lead from the earl." He leaned forward to confide in a near whisper. "Warrington don't want him out—ever."

"Two full pounds, Mr. Sims," she reminded him.

"Well . . . Don't guess ye can do any harm. He ain't goin' ter bolt now, I can tell ye."

"And while I am speaking with Mr. Swann, I should like the papers prepared to release my brother."

"Aye. Going ter miss the boy, though," Jem told her.

"Ye'd best be grateful fer it—boy's a Captain Sharp at the cards," Sims remarked. "How much do ye owe 'im?"

"Too much," the jailer snapped.

This time, Nicholas Swann had far different quarters. Instead of an open door, he was locked in the cellar. As she followed the jailer into the musty, dank depths, she nearly lost her nerve. He stopped at the bottom of the stairs and unlocked a solid wood door. When she hesitated, he mistook the reason.

"Oh, he ain't any threat ter ye this time, mistress."

"No, of course not."

"But the wound don't fester, so I 'spect he'll hang," he added. "I'll stay if ye want."

"No."

He eyed her oddly then. "Ye ain't going ter try anything, are ye?"

"How could I? I am but one poor female," she reminded him.

"Aye. Don't think ye could carry 'im up the stairs," he admitted to himself. "Well, go on wi' ye—the man's inside."

He was seated, his back toward her, his shoulders slumped forward. "Why did you come?" Swann asked, his voice cold.

Her resolve nearly deserted her, and she had to force herself to walk around to face him. "I had to see how you fared," she answered softly.

" 'Tis not meet, mistress. You'll be cream for the gossiping tabbies. Go on."

"No." She dared to move closer. "I have decided to keep the money, you see."

"Wise of you."

"Well, I do not know how wise I am, but Uncle Joseph does not deserve it. I thought," she ventured almost casually, "that perhaps you were right—that Robin and I should begin again in America. If he will go, of course."

"He's a fool if he does not. There is not much room for a bastard to succeed here," he replied bitterly.

"No, there is not." He was not giving her much encouragement, but she had to know, to put it to the touch. "I only wish you were going with us," she said quietly.

"Me? 'Tis too late for me, mistress."

She closed her eyes and held her hands tightly at her sides. Swallowing her pride, she managed to whisper, "For what 'tis worth to you, you are loved by more than Peg." When he said nothing, she gambled desperately. "I think I am more than half in love with you, Nicholas Swann."

She heard the chair scrape the floor as he managed to stand, and then his arms were around her, holding her, and she could not control the flood of tears. "I don't want you to die, Nicky. I don't want you to die! I cannot bear it if you are to hang!" she cried against his bandaged shoulder.

His hand smoothed her hair and held her head against him. "Don't, Annie. For God's sake, don't. I am not worth it."

" 'Tis foolish of me, and I know it, but—"

"There is no hope for me, Annie."

"You could throw yourself on Warrington's mercy!"

He stiffened momentarily. "He has none. For twenty-five years, he has had none."

"But—"

"Believe me, I want to live, Anne Hardinge," he whispered against her hair. "And there is nothing on this earth I should rather do than go away with you."

"Then?"

"But I won't beg Warrington for my life."

"You must!"

"I cannot." His arms tightened around her for a moment, then he released her and turned away. "But for what it is worth to say it, Anne Hardinge, if my life had been different, if I'd been worthy of you, I should have offered for you the first time we were met."

"Then why don't you?" she asked softly.

"Because I am naught but a bastard and a criminal," he answered harshly. He swung around to face her, his own eyes wet. "You deserve the best man you can get, Annie. You ought to be a rich man's wife, but . . ." His voice broke for a moment, then he went on, telling her, "But God aid me, for I love you also."

"Then you have no right to let them hang you without a fight!"

"He would not listen to me. Believe me, he would not listen to me."

"Are all men fools?" she nearly shouted at him. "Is it pride that makes one wish to die rather than admit a wrong?"

"I told you—even if I could ask, he'd not listen."

He was telling her there was no hope, that there was no hope for this fledgling love between them. "I see," she said finally. "Well, then perhaps I should just go."

"Yes."

"But do not expect me to be in the crowd that watches when you are hanged."

"I would hope you are not."

Feeling very much the fool herself, she walked to the door without looking back. And it was as though everything ached inside her. Tears blinded her eyes until she could scarce see the stairs.

"Anne!"

She stumbled on the first step, and then he was behind her, pulling her back, holding her. She turned into his good shoulder and began to weep.

"Don't, Annie. Please," he whispered, lifting her chin

with one hand. "All I ask is a memory to take with me."

He kissed her gently as she clung to him, her panniers flaring behind her. Then as her lips parted eagerly, he groaned and pulled away. "Ah, Annie, what you do to me," he said, smiling at her. "I'd give eternity to hold you."

"I'll engage a solicitor. I'll come to London," she babbled almost incoherently. "But you must not die!"

"Ye've got ter go, mistress," Jem announced from the stairs. "Yer brother's a-waiting, and Warrington is come."

"Yes, of course." She untied her reticule and pulled out a handkerchief to wipe her wet face. Looking back at Nicholas Swann, she forced a smile. "Until we are met again, in this life or the next," she whispered.

As her footsteps receded on the stairs, he sank back down into his chair. He was the greater fool, and he knew it, for he'd had no right to embroil her in his life at all. For an instant, he actually considered throwing himself at Warrington's feet to plead for his life. But he knew the man would deny him. There was too much between them.

Anne was numb as her brother handed her up into the old coach. She leaned back against the squabs and closed her eyes that Robin would not see her cry.

"Fancy that," he said, whistling low. " 'Tis Warrington himself."

She looked then, and what she saw made her heart nearly stop. "*That* is Warrington?" she asked with disbelief. "It cannot be!"

"Well, it is. Saw him last year at the races," Robin declared smugly. "He don't come 'round much, but Biggersley pointed him out to me."

"Are you quite certain?"

"Dash it, Anne—the man's important! Got German George's ear, they say! Don't you think I would have marked him?"

Suddenly she understood.

Her brother sat back and pushed his hat forward. " 'Twill be good to get home," he said. "But I'd begun to think you could not make bail for me."

" 'Twas twenty pounds."

He whistled again. "Well, no wonder. 'Tis a lot of egg money, Annie."

"I didn't use the egg money." She leaned forward and took his hat, forcing him to look at her. "Robin, I pray you will do nothing foolish again, for there is no use to it."

"I still intend to find Mama's marriage lines," he declared defiantly.

"They are not there. Uncle Joseph burned them."

"You went to him? Annie, how could you?"

"Of course not, stupid. 'Twas Nicholas Swann. I collect he coerced Uncle Joseph into admitting he had destroyed them."

"Then to all the world I am a bastard," he muttered. "No, I'll not believe it! If I have to wring his bloody neck for him, I'll make my uncle pay for this, Annie— I swear it!"

"You cannot, and Swann already has." As his face clouded ominously, she hesitated to explain. "He went there and confronted Uncle Joseph, Robin."

"Coming it too strong," he protested. "Why would the Black Swann care?"

"I told him the tale," she answered simply. "But he evened the scales a bit for you. We now have two thousand pounds in compensation."

"Two thou—two thousand?"

She nodded. "I was going to give the money back, but—"

"Don't you dare! With two thousand pounds, we can go anywhere. We can do something."

" 'Tis what Swann said. He suggested we go to America, where none will care how it is believed we are born."

"Not me," he declared flatly. "I got other plans."

"You are not going to gamble it away."

"No, of course not, but it ain't for you to say if I do," he retorted. "You take your half, and I'll take mine. Thing to do, ain't it? I mean, I cannot be on your leading strings forever now, can I?"

"Robin Hardinge—"

"Dower yourself with it. Me, I'm going to London."

"And do what?"

"I don't know. Sow a few oats. Read law, mayhap. Don't look at me like that, Annie," he said defensively. "Ain't anything as says we got to live in each other's pockets, is there?"

"No. No, I suppose not," she answered slowly. "But I thought—"

"You thought I'd be your little brother forever," he finished for her. "Well, I ain't, and 'tis time you were living for yourself."

She glanced back down the street, but Warrington was nowhere to be seen. She straightened her back against the worn squabs. "You are precisely right, Robin," she said finally. "I should have known it."

"Good. Then we are understood. One thousand to you, one thousand to me."

"Yes."

She'd taken the news of his independence surprisingly well. He watched her suspiciously for several minutes then blurted out, "Well, what are you going to do with yours?"

"I am going to call on the Earl of Warrington," she decided.

Her hands were like ice, so much so that she had to rub them together in her lap while she waited. It had seemed so easy when she'd first conceived the notion, but now she was not so sure. The earl was a cold man, everyone said so, and after her glimpse of him, she could believe anything of him.

"Miss Hardinge?"

She jumped at the sound of his voice, then collected herself. Extending her hand, she murmured, "I am come on a matter of extreme import, my lord."

His gaze raked over the green dress, making her flush guiltily. Then he smiled faintly. "You appear to have a gown very much like one of my wife's, Miss Hardinge."

It was going to go badly, and she knew it. She drew a long breath, then exhaled while he waited expectantly. "You must wonder at my audacity, sir, but I have come to beg for your son's life."

He gave a start. "You are mistaken," he declared, recovering, "Lady Warrington and I have no son."

"I am speaking of Nicholas Swann, sir."

He started to deny it, then changed his mind. "I see. Am I to collect he told you, my dear?"

"No. He is rather under the impression that you hate him, I'm afraid."

"Hatred is not the word for it," he muttered tersely.

"No matter what he has done, he is still your son," she argued reasonably.

"I have never claimed him."

"And that is the problem between you, is it not?"

"Miss Hardinge—" He stopped himself and walked

away to stand at a tall, multipaned window. "What he has done is utterly reprehensible," he said.

"But somewhat understandable, nonetheless. How could you expect him to be anything more, sir, when you denied him? When you let some . . . some trollop named Peg rear him?"

"I sent money for a tutor!"

She stared at his back incredulously. "In a brothel, sir? What he needed was not money, but you!"

"And I saw he went to Oxford, Miss Hardinge. But the fool managed to get himself sent down after one term."

"Why didn't you acknowledge him?" she asked suddenly. "He is in your image, isn't he? How could you deny him?"

He didn't answer for a time, and when he did, he spoke low. "When I inherited, there was naught but a title and this pile of rock that you see, Miss Hardinge. Being desperate, I wed for money." He paused, then turned to face her as his mouth twisted. "I have earned every penny she brought to me."

"That does not—"

"Ah, but it does. When she discovered I had been less than faithful to my vows, my wife threatened to leave me, saying that she would have her father ruin me. As I was young and ambitious, I dared not risk the scandal. Queen Anne was on her last legs, and not overgiven to forgiveness. Indeed, but she died shortly after Nicholas was born." His dark eyes met hers and held. "I was a coward, Miss Hardinge. I chose a court career over my son."

" 'Twas twenty-five years ago," she reminded him brutally. "What of later? Why did you never right the wrong?"

"It was too late. For all that you would sympathize with him, my dear, he is but a common criminal."

"No. There is nothing common about Nicholas Swann at all."

"I warned him. I told him I should not stand by while he robbed and terrorized the countryside. Miss Hardinge, the only reason he has not hanged before now is that I was not hard enough to let it happen."

"But you are making a dreadful mistake! You have seen he has no identity—no birthright! What was he supposed to do? Work in the fields? Shoe horses?"

"He could have read law."

"Mayhap he was too bitter by then, my lord."

"He is a thorn in my side, Miss Hardinge, and will be so until he is gone."

"Precisely."

He blinked at her agreement. "I thought you came to beg for his life."

"I have." Once again, she drew a deep breath before putting her proposal to the touch. "You could use your influence to have him transported, my lord—to America."

"How should I know he will not return to vex me?"

"I would promise you." Her chin came up and her own dark eyes fixed on his. "We should never return here, sir."

"*We*, Miss Hardinge?"

"Yes."

"You are not his usual doxy, my dear," he murmured sardonically.

"Oh, I quite expect to marry him," she admitted shamelessly.

"And if he does not change?"

"He does not have to do so for me. All he has ever wanted is to be landed, sir. 'Land and birth go hand in glove,' he told me, so I expect we shall become planters."

He studied her soberly, then sighed. "I can almost believe you could do it."

"Then you will help him?"

"It is beyond my powers to do anything more for him, I'm afraid."

"But he is your son! Let him redeem himself in America!"

"Your belief in Nicholas Swann is most admirable, my dear. I can only hope it is not misplaced."

"But—"

"Miss Hardinge, I suggest you go home. What little I can do for him has already been done."

She took that to mean he'd not intervene further. She'd lost. Retrieving what little dignity she had left, she squared her shoulders. "Very well, my lord. But I shall still make every effort in my poor power to see that he does not hang."

"And I wish you well," he said noncommittally.

"I have a thousand pounds, and I am prepared to spend every penny of it in his defense."

"I pray it will not come to that, my dear." Before she knew what he meant to do, he reached for her hand and lifted it to his lips. "You have my admiration, you know."

"I should very much rather have your aid," she retorted.

"Good day, Miss Hardinge. Perhaps one day we shall meet again."

She sincerely hoped not. If Nicholas Swann died on the gallows, she would never forgive Warrington.

When Mr. Parkborn let her down outside her cottage, she felt utterly, completely dejected. She did not even know how she could face the irrepressible Robin, not while her heart was breaking for her highwayman. But there was no sign of her brother.

She opened the door and stepped inside. "Robin?"

There was no answer. She removed her shawl and deposited her reticule on the table, then turned to survey the cold fireplace tiredly. If there was to be supper, she was going to have to lay the fire. How very like Robin to leave such a thing to her.

The room was dim, the sun barely diffusing through the oilcloth windows. Telling herself she could afford such things, she resolutely lit a candle, then turned her attention again to the hearth. It was then that she saw the booted feet, the long legs extending from the chair. And she knew it was not Robin. Her breath caught.

"You have escaped again?" she asked foolishly.

"No." He stood and opened his arms to her. As she went to his embrace, he held her close, savoring the sweet smell of lavender, the very warmth of her. "If you will have me, Annie, we are going to America."

"What?" Her voice rose in disbelief. "But they'll watch the ports, won't they?" she asked foolishly.

"I have but two weeks to prepare, then I am being transported."

"I don't understand—"

He smiled fondly at her. "I decided my pride was not worth a hanging, Annie. That I'd rather have you than anything. I'm afraid I have thrown myself on my father's mercy, you see, and in return for my promise not to return to England, Warrington is having me transported to Georgia."

"When did this happen? And what of your wound?"

"Right after you left. And the wound will heal on the way. My greatest complaint with it was the loss of blood."

"Then he already knew. Oh, of all the wicked things to do!"

"I asked him to tell none but the magistrate until I had the chance to see you, to tell you myself."

"But I went to see Warrington, and he let me think you were going to hang," she recalled with feeling. "Nicky, I have been half out of my mind! I shall never forgive him!"

He kissed her then, blotting all else from her mind. As his mouth possessed hers, she thought she would die from the ecstasy of being held by him. Finally, he released her and stepped back.

"Well, Annie?"

"Yes, oh, yes!" Smiling through tears of happiness, she told him, "You can have my thousand pounds to buy land, Nicky."

"It won't be necessary," he assured her, grinning. Reaching into his shirt, he drew out a thick leather folder. "I'm afraid when I passed by Oakhill, I could not quite help myself," he added apologetically. "I took a thousand pounds from my father's money box. Somehow it did not seem quite right for me to bring nothing to the marriage."

"Nicholas! What if he should change his mind over it?" she cried. "How could you risk it?"

"One last act of larceny, but he will not count the loss—'tis enough that I have agreed to leave," he murmured, reaching for her again. "I'd wed you today, Annie. I'd not wait," he whispered against her ear. "Otherwise, I am not at all certain I can remain respectable."